PRAISE FOR

SWEPT AWAY

"*Swept Away* is that rare story that feels like a brand-new version of romance with unlikely lovers in a confined space in a way you've never quite seen before. Suffice to say I drowned happily in this book."

—#1 *New York Times* bestselling author Jodi Picoult

"An epic romance expertly woven into an adventure thriller, *Swept Away* had me swooning and gasping at the turn of every page. Truly, no one writes falling in love like Beth O'Leary, and this one completely stole my heart."

—Annabel Monaghan, *New York Times* bestselling author of *It's a Love Story*

"*Swept Away* is a one-of-a-kind story and an absolute treat. Completely original, so romantic, funny, fresh, and deeply heartfelt; this is Beth O'Leary at her very best. . . . *Swept Away* has my whole heart."

—Lindsey Kelk, *Sunday Times* bestselling author of *Love Story*

"My new favorite Beth O'Leary! This story completely captivated me."

—Paige Toon, international bestselling author of *What If I Never Get Over You*

PRAISE FOR

THE WAKE-UP CALL

"Beth O'Leary can do no wrong! I've loved each and every one of her books, and *The Wake-Up Call* is yet another gorgeous, evocative romance. Beth has a gift for creating complicated, tenderhearted characters and dreamy, whimsical settings that you never want to leave behind. Put this on your TBR immediately."

—Carley Fortune, #1 *New York Times* bestselling author of *Meet Me at the Lake*

"This delicious rom-com will please even the most jaded readers."

—*Good Morning America*

PRAISE FOR

THE NO-SHOW

"Beth O'Leary is that rare, one-in-a-million talent who can make you laugh, swoon, cry, and ache all in the same book, and *The No-Show* is her most moving yet. O'Leary's wit, charm, and heart are on full, fantastic display in this cozy, surprising, and deeply satisfying novel. I couldn't possibly love it more."

—Emily Henry, #1 *New York Times* bestselling author of *Book Lovers*

"Achingly clever."

—Sophie Cousens, *New York Times* bestselling author of *Before I Do*

"There are few authors who are able to capture the realities of romance and the deep impacts of trauma, let alone in the same book. . . . As O'Leary's layered and enthralling story unfolds over the course of the book, she reveals her characters to be so unavoidably human it's hard not to relate to them, even if you've never climbed a tree."

—*USA Today*

PRAISE FOR

THE ROAD TRIP

"*The Road Trip* is a humorous yet deeply moving journey toward confronting the past, forgiveness, and reconciliation, with a poignant detour to a summer of young love in Provence. I loved the vivid cast and the depth and intimacy in O'Leary's writing."

—Helen Hoang, *New York Times* bestselling author of *The Heart Principle*

"Read this! Absolutely loved it!"

—Christina Lauren, *New York Times* bestselling author of *The Soulmate Equation*

TITLES BY BETH O'LEARY

The Flatshare
The Switch
The Road Trip
The No-Show
The Wake-Up Call
Swept Away
The Name Game

The NAME GAME

BETH O'LEARY

BERKLEY ROMANCE
NEW YORK

BERKLEY ROMANCE
Published by Berkley
An imprint of Penguin Random House LLC
1745 Broadway, New York, NY 10019
penguinrandomhouse.com

Book design by Jenni Surasky

Library of Congress Cataloging-in-Publication Data

Names: O'Leary, Beth author
Title: The name game / Beth O'Leary.
Description: First edition. | New York: Berkley Romance, 2026.
Identifiers: LCCN 2025041223 (print) | LCCN 2025041224 (ebook) |
ISBN 9798217190676 trade paperback | ISBN 9798217190683 ebook
Subjects: LCGFT: Fiction | Romance fiction | Novels
Classification: LCC PR6115.L424 N36 2026 (print) | LCC PR6115.L424 (ebook)
LC record available at https://lccn.loc.gov/2025041223
LC ebook record available at https://lccn.loc.gov/2025041224

First Edition: April 2026

Printed in the United States of America
1st Printing

The authorized representative in the EU for product safety and compliance is Penguin Random House Ireland, Morrison Chambers, 32 Nassau Street, Dublin D02 YH68, Ireland, https:// eu-contact.penguin.ie.

For Lilsa-Lou

The NAME GAME

Friday August 8th 2025
First day of new life.

What a sentence. Isn't it beautiful? Have wanted to write that for so long, and now here it is on page one of a brand-new diary. Life. Starts. Here.

New me is:

* Peppy. Maybe not peppy, actually—that sounds annoying. But positive. Upbeat. Inclined to wear hair in bouncy ponytail and look on the bright side, but does not require everyone else to do so (see: don't want to be annoying).
* Independent. New me relies on nobody else for validation. She makes her own decisions. She can do it alone.
* Bold. I mean, look at me. I'm on a boat, sailing toward a secluded island to start picture-perfect new life running island farm shop! Am going to be like one of those women on Instagram who live on photogenic homestead and bake their own bread with stunning vista in background. Except without all the Reddit content dedicated to whether or not I'm in a cult.

Am wondering where the line is between manifestation and

kidding yourself. Want to fill diary with positivity but don't want to, you know, lie.

Truth is, I'm sitting here on a chugging old ferryboat, feeling a bit freaked out. Remembering former life of good job, nice coffee, steady boyfriend, and now considering future life of seclusion on relatively small rock in the English Channel. Don't want to seem spoiled, but argh, will there be a coffee machine on the farm?

Once again unsure if this is wild adventure or mad pre-midlife crisis. Horrible suspicion that you can't actually know until end of story, i.e., glorious happily-ever-after vs. perishing sad and alone in farmyard.

Spirits lifting again as island approaches. It's beautiful! Rugged, shadowy crags jutting from the sea, tangles of wildflowers painting the rocks in greens and pinks . . . Looks too pretty to be real, like Sabrina Carpenter. Am buoyed by new confidence that my future is here on the Isle of Ormer, population 500. Soon to be 501.

Here's what I know about the Isle of Ormer:

1. There are no motorized vehicles on the island except tractors. Everyone gets around on horses and bikes, like medieval people. Feel positive about this, particularly given the six points on my license.
2. The island is three miles by one mile. Tiny! With a real sense of community, according to Google. The perfect place to build a new family. (Getting ahead of myself, as per.)
3. Most of the land is farmed, and Bramblebay Farm has a shop, aka my new place of employment. Popular with visiting tourists, but a lifeline to the locals, too. Am envisioning crates filled with earthy potatoes, fresh milk in glass

bottles and me swanning around with wicker basket under arm.

4. No streetlights on the island. Great: fits perfectly with new resolution to go to bed at nightfall and rise with the dawn like the lark. Or the blackbird. Whichever bird gets the first worm, that's going to be me.
5. Ormer is a Crown Dependency, so kind of part of UK but not? It was feudal until 2006, which is the year Justin Timberlake released "SexyBack," i.e., about five minutes ago. So: slightly odd. But they've got a democratically elected government now, so that's all sorted, and I have decided to consider this whole business quirky and cute.

That's enough fact-based content for now—we've reached the harbor!

Arrived in harbor looking significantly more disheveled than I did in Guernsey (sea air very bracing) but quickly realized Ormer is not a place where anyone gives a shit about how your hair looks. The harbor—a concrete walkway between the rocks, poking out into the sea—was awash with people in work boots and worn jeans. Above me, the cliffs were dark and imposing, all shadows and sharp edges in the sunshine. A cargo ship had just cleared off in time for the ferry to dock, and the harbor workers were busy shifting the cargo into battered, ancient-looking tractors to be carted up the hill.

It was immediately apparent that health-and-safety rules are pretty chill here on the Isle of Ormer.

"Watch your head!" someone shouted at me.

I looked up. A rusted shipping container was swooping above me, dangling precariously from a crane-type structure on the harbor. I ducked—maybe screamed—and stumbled back.

"Watch your feet!" someone yelled.

I looked down to find myself mere inches from a precipitous drop into the sea. No railings, no big yellow warning signs, not even a casual traffic cone.

I stared around, slightly breathless. A few middle-aged tourists traipsed off the ferry behind me, dressed in white canvas hats, looking about as wary of the harbor activities as I was. A burly guy in his thirties barged through the middle of them, head down, a blue cap backward on his head. His sports bag whacked me in the hip as he powered by, knocking me off-balance.

"Hey!" I yelped.

He turned. The first thing I noticed was his deep scowl, then the gray eyes that met mine for a sharp half second, narrowed against the sun.

"You dropped something," he said, nodding to the ground. His lip twitched slightly, as though he was trying to hold back a smirk.

"Excuse me?" I pressed a hand to my thundering heart as I scuttled further inland. This was not a comfortable place to lose footing.

The man pointed wordlessly, already walking backward away from me.

Argh. It was this diary, precariously close to the edge—must have slipped out of the top of my bag when he knocked into me. Which meant he could now see the cover, complete with the message Brianna had doodled there while helping me pack yesterday:

Secrets of my tender heart enclosed within

I swore and went to snatch it up. The other side reads:

I'M CHARLIE JONES, MOTHERFUCKER,
BOW BEFORE ME

Would it be better if it had fallen that way up? Probably not, there were kids around.

"Thanks," I said. "Though I wouldn't have dropped anything if you'd not . . ."

He didn't care enough to hang around for the end of this sentence.

"Arsehole," I muttered.

I watched him go. His neck was a bit sunburned, and his cap said "CJ" on it—my initials (how weird! I thought). Shame he was clearly a bit of a dickhead, because he was hot, actually. The rugged scowliness, the earthy-blond scruff of hair beneath the cap, the long-sleeved tee clinging to defined pecs and biceps. It was giving "I'm a hot mess—try to fix me, why don't you?"

Not a shame, actually, shouldn't have written that. Sexy rugged men are firmly off new life agenda, even unproblematic ones, and he had "problem" written all over him. I focused on restoring the diary to the safety of my handbag and looked around the harbor again. A young woman in baggy skater-style shorts and an "Explore Ormer" T-shirt was waving to the tourists beside me, bouncing on the spot as if she couldn't wait to get started. Her black, curly hair was streaked with blue dye, and she had at least six piercings—nose, eyebrows, a few in her lips. She caught my eye and smiled. It lit her up—she had an earnest golden-retriever energy to her.

"Visiting for the day?" she said.

Probably not reasonable to be miffed by her mistaking me for a tourist, but nonetheless, felt disappointed.

"Actually, I'm moving here," I said, adjusting my straw hat, and then wondering if the hat was what made me look like a tourist, and promptly removing it. But—hat hair, plus boat hair . . . I put it back on again. "I'm the new farm shop manager."

A tractor reversed by me at speed, the man in the driving seat twisted almost 180 degrees to look out of the dirty back window.

"Oh, no way!" the Explore Ormer woman said, beaming at me. "You're Charlie! I'm Red. Tour guide, as of six weeks ago—I'm pretty new around here, too, but it already feels like home. I've been helping out at the shop as well, since Rosie and Marly are so busy on the farm for harvest season—everyone's been desperate for you to arrive. I saw Rog bringing your luggage up from this morning's boat, I wondered when you'd get here! Didn't pack light, did you!"

Actually tried to pack as little as possible—donated bags and bags of stuff before leaving the mainland. Briefly wished I was a "oh, my whole life is in this bag" sort of woman, but some things you just can't change.

Red pointed through an archway cut into the rock, with the words "Welcome to the Isle of Ormer" in chipped paint above it.

"Head through there to get the rattle up to the Rue, if you don't fancy walking in the heat."

I understood very little of this, particularly the rattle part, but was painfully aware of already seeming clueless, so just nodded and hoped all would become clear once through the archway.

This was not the case. Ahead of me was a steep, dusty road, a random collection of seemingly abandoned tractors and a trailer that read "Rog's Carting and Gardening and Waste Disposal! Call this number! I do all sorts!!"

Hovered for a while, listening to the waves, the seagulls, the chu-chu-chug of the old tractor engines. There were a few people about, all looking busy, all ignoring me. No sign of rude CJ cap guy. Was more disappointed about that than I should have been. Eventually Red and the plodding gang of tourists appeared behind me.

"Oh, still here!" she said cheerfully. "Rog!"

Rog popped out of one of the abandoned-looking tractors like a cartoon character appearing from inside a flowerpot. He was wiry and sun beaten, and when he smiled, he flashed several gold teeth.

He wasn't a big man, but I felt quite sure that Rog would beat almost anyone in a fight, like a scrawny alley cat.

"Fifty pence each for the rattle," he said, stretching out a palm.

The tourists dutifully unzipped their bum bags and produced fifty-pence pieces. Had they been forewarned about this? I wasn't getting an Apple Pay vibe from Rog and was starting to sweat. Would I be kicked off the island because I didn't have a fifty-pence coin? What was a rattle, and was it going to be as unpleasant as it sounded?

"Don't worry, this is Charlie, the new shop manager," Red said, clocking my stricken expression. "She's good for it."

Rog eyed me with interest.

"Ooh. Welcome to Ormer," he said. "Hope you like cows."

I blinked. Why did that sound vaguely threatening?

"Hop on, then, here we go," he said.

Red began to usher the obedient tourists onto the trailer. I saw now that it was in fact some sort of transportation system—Rog was fixing it up to one of the ancient tractors, and the tourists were settling themselves into the rudimentary seats along the trailer's sides.

I joined them, and after a moment we started making our way up the wide rocky track cut into the hill. The trailer did indeed rattle. A <u>lot</u>. Clinging to the side, I was struck once again by a wave of panic. Was this life now? Dirt roads, decrepit tractors, ominous-sounding cows?

I gripped my seat, then lunged to catch my handbag as it went sliding out of my lap. Rog was driving the tractor as though it was a sports car, one palm flat on the steering wheel as he dragged us around a bend. A large cart horse plodded by, pulling a carriage containing two of the workers from the harbor. They barely blinked as they passed through the cloud of dust kicked up by Rog's tractor.

Had to shade my eyes with my hand when we reached the top of the hill. The track opened out to reveal a stunning sea view. The water of the Channel was dreamily blue, and the island's greenery tumbled away from us toward the cliffs, a scramble of wildflowers and bracken.

The panic quieted. Who wouldn't want to start life over in this place? It was magical.

Ahead of us were some single-story shops, flat fronted and painted magnolia yellow. I recognized it instantly: it was the Rue, the dusty track that serves as Ormer's high street. The carriage pulled away ahead of us, the cart horse swishing its tail to bat the summer flies away. There was a Wild Westness about it all, as though any second now a ball of tumbleweed would go rolling by.

Rog hopped off the tractor as Red helped the slightly shaken tourists out of the trailer.

"For Bramblebay Farm, you want to go thataway until you see the dairy," Rog said to me, producing a bottle of water from one of the pockets in his cargo pants and taking a swig. "Then turn right. If you hit the sea, you've gone too far."

"Right," I said. "Thank you. I think I'm supposed to be staying at the old stables—is that near the farm itself?"

"Everything's near everything, love," Rog said with a grin.

Felt horribly aware that I sounded like the archetypal city girl turning up in the one-horse town in stilettos. (Metaphorically—obviously wore trainers, I'm not that clueless.) Drew myself up a bit.

"Of course. I'll figure it out."

Twenty minutes later, standing in the middle of a field surrounded by cows, was not quite so confident.

There was the dairy. There was the little footpath cut into the undergrowth, heading right. Hadn't hit the sea yet, but could see it hazily in the distance between two trees. And between the cows.

When they first came sauntering over to me, I'll admit I panicked a bit. Cows are a lot bigger and more . . . muscular than they look from a train window, and I don't think I've seen one in person (in cow?) since I took that hungover hike after Bri's wedding.

But the new me is a countryside person. She loves the great outdoors. She's going to work on a farm, for God's sake. So I pulled myself together and held my ground, plotting a reasonable escape route if the cows' slow amble developed into a sudden urge to stampede. As it happened, they just hung around, a bit like men who dance over in a club but don't know what to do next. Fine: I know how to handle hoverers. I stared at my phone, resolutely ignoring the cows, perplexed to find that Google Maps was convinced I was standing in the middle of a supermarket.

Looked around, then back down at the map. Everything else was right—it had me loaded in the right spot. But . . . Can Google Maps be wrong, I typed into Google. No, apparently. And yet, this was definitely not a Carrefour.

A brief foray down an Ormer-specific rabbit hole on Reddit and I discovered the problem: this tiny island is so random and remote the maps haven't been updated for years. No street view option either as there are no cars allowed. Once upon a time, presumably, a Carrefour had stood here, but now it was just grassland, and Rog's directions were all I had to go on.

Trudged on, trailing cows. The path had long since disappeared, and I was just starting to lose hope when I spotted a barn behind a hedge. Perking up, I set off toward it, but I'd obviously gone wrong somewhere, because there was no break in the hedge, and no way through.

Hadn't seen the farm shop at this point—no picture with the job ad—but it was described as a converted barn on the edge of the farm, and this looked promising. A bunch of old crates lying by the back door, a bike rack to the side . . . I figured I was just approaching it from the back.

I weighed it up. Return the way I had come and try to find the main entrance? Or hop the hedge?

It looked sturdy. Obviously had no idea what sort of bush it was made of, but there were branches in there that I could use as footholds, and I was hot and sticky from walking in the sun and did not fancy running the cow gauntlet again.

The less I write about this bit the better. I don't fancy dwelling on it. The shredded Oliver Bonas dress, scratched-up thighs and entirely lost dignity are enough of a reminder.

I had bits of shrub in my hair. I was sweaty and disheveled. I had a strong suspicion I smelled of cow. This wasn't the first impression I'd hoped to make on my new employer, but by this point I was just desperate to get out of the sun, so headed around for the front entrance.

There was no front entrance. I walked all the way around the gray stone barn and ended up back where I started: the back entrance. The only entrance.

Now that I was right in front of the door, I could see that a piece of A4 paper had been stuck beside it with the words "Bramblebay Farm Shop" scrawled in pen. "Farm shop hours vary. If you're after one of the Nicoles, try the farmhouse," it said underneath, with a helpful arrow pointing north, or possibly up to the sky. Then, in smaller, different handwriting, "Don't forget Rog does all sorts! Call this number!!" And at the very bottom, in different pen altogether: "If you're Charlie Jones, head on in, will be with you in a mo, just dealing with a goat thing!"

I was, apparently, in the right place.

To say that spirits had dipped at this point would be an understatement. The barn was almost as disheveled as I was: corrugated-iron roof clumsily patched up, windows filthy, wood peeling on the wide barn doors.

And, stepping inside, things only got worse.

Not the shop itself. That was surprisingly bright and clean, given the outside of the barn. There were fridges full of—yes, milk bottles, and sacks of potatoes on the flagstones, and shelves of chutneys and pickles in charming jewel tones.

The problem was the familiar-looking man standing directly in my way.

"Excuse me," I said, trying to step around him.

There wasn't much room—the shop was set up with crates of vegetables narrowing the space between the door and the till.

Man didn't move. He had his back to me and was looking around the shop. It was cap guy. He'd lost the cap, but clearly not the attitude.

"Excuse me," I said again, louder, in that particular British way that can mean a great number of things, all offensive.

"We're not open," he said, barely looking at me—he seemed to be examining the stock.

"That's fine," I said. "I work here."

He turned at last. Arms folded, he stared at me. His eyes weren't quite gray, as I'd thought earlier—they were actually a washed-out shade of denim blue, shadowed under a broody frown that was way too engrained to be only on my account. He had the sort of fair skin that can end up looking tanned because of the sheer number of freckles—there were darker ones around his eyes and across his nose, too. I generally think of freckles as cutesy, but there was nothing cute about this man. Even his stubble looked pricklier than average.

"Who are you?" he asked.

"Charlie Jones."

Wondered about shaking his hand, but his arms were resolutely folded, so aborted this plan and just stood there. It took powerful strength to resist the urge to check my hair for shrubbery.

"The new farm shop manager," I added.

"That's right," he said. "And who are you?"

"What?"

"Yes, correct, I'm Charlie Jones, the new farm shop manager," he said impatiently. "And who are you?"

"No, sorry . . . I'm Charlie Jones, the new farm shop manager, is what I meant."

The deep furrow between his eyebrows became—impossibly—deeper.

"No," he insisted. "You're not Charlie Jones. I'm Charlie Jones. And I'm the new farm shop manager."

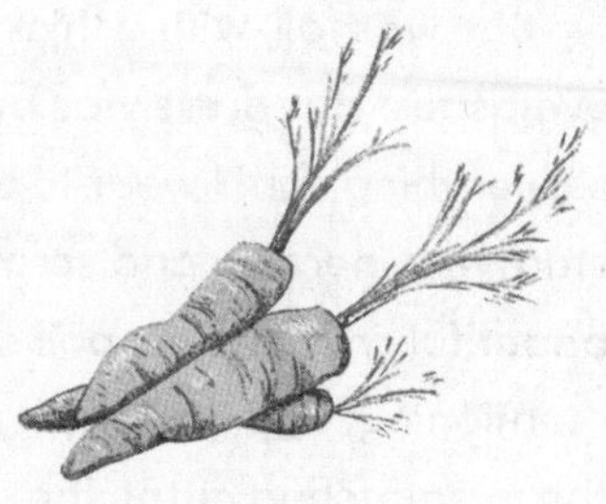

FROM: Charlie Jones
TO: Charlie Jones
SUBJECT: Day one sober

Hi. Hey. Here I am, holding myself accountable.

. . . This already feels incredibly strange. What do I do, just write down everything that happens? How do I know which things to pick? Do I write about the weather, or the walk up from the harbor, or the fact that the sadness is still clinging to me, as though it refuses to be left behind?

I feel incredibly self-conscious right now, but I suppose that'll wear off. A deal's a deal, so here goes.

I'm on the Isle of Ormer, starting my new life, but there's a woman here, too, and she's trying to nick it.

My new life, I mean. She wants it. She just stood there in the middle of my farm shop looking like she might have been literally dragged through a hedge backward, and told me *she's* the new farm shop manager. She's Charlie Jones, she said.

I told her she's not. Obviously.

"No, *you're* not Charlie Jones," she snapped back. "Or, well, I suppose you could be Charlie Jones. But you're not *the* Charlie Jones. You're not the person who got offered this job. Because that's me."

She was tall, with a thick, dark fringe that almost touched her eyelashes. Her dress was bright blue and tied with a ribbon, the sort of thing you'd wear to a wedding or something, but she had sturdy trainers on and scratches all over her legs. She was also beautiful, in a classic, poised, regal sort of way. Probably worth mentioning, as it somehow made the whole look even stranger—the mismatched outfit, the disheveled hair. I couldn't really get a sense of who she was.

But anyway, whoever she was, she was *not* the new farm shop manager.

We did a bit more "you're not Charlie Jones," "no, *you're* not Charlie Jones," and then Rosie Nicole showed up, which is probably a good thing, because me and Other Charlie could've been at it for a while, otherwise.

Rosie stopped in her tracks as soon as she saw us both. Her hair was pulled back with a flower-patterned scarf, and she was in long drapey tie-dye clothes, but in a music-festival way rather than an art-teacher way, if you know what I mean. She was younger than I'd expected—twenties. Her boots were sturdy and caked in mud.

She stared between me and Other Charlie with total bafflement.

"You must be Rosie!" Other Charlie trilled into the bemused silence, heading toward her with arms out for a hug. "I'm Charlie Jones."

"Oh my God! Hi! Welcome!" Rosie said, hugging her right back.

Hang on, I thought.

"Sorry, no."

I stepped forward. They both looked up at me, a little alarmed, maybe. I tried to look less ogreish than usual.

"*I'm* actually Charlie Jones," I said. "And this is *my* job."

Rosie's mouth fell open.

"You're Charlie Jones?" she asked.

"Yes."

"But I thought . . ."

"I'm Charlie Jones," said Other Charlie. "That guy just . . . is as well." She spread her hands. "I'm as confused as you are, Rosie."

"You're both called Charlie Jones?" Rosie looked back and forth between us.

"Yes," we said in unison.

"And you both think you got offered this job?"

We confirmed this, once again in unison. I glared at Charlie—she kept taking all my lines.

Rosie looked totally stunned by this. "I'm sorry, I don't understand. I only offered the job to one person—we only have the funds for one shop manager. I sent a letter . . . Does one of you have the job offer letter?"

We both reached for our phones in our back pockets, like two cowboys reaching for their guns.

I showed Rosie my photo of the letter. Other Charlie did the same.

I examined her screen. This is where things got very weird. It was the letter—the *exact* same one. There was the same crossing-out on line two. I have *no idea* how she got hold of it.

Rosie reached for one of the maps for sale by the till and began to fan herself. "But neither of you has the original?" she asked.

It hadn't occurred to me that I would need to show the original. Who cares about originals these days?

"Did you send out two by accident?" Charlie suggested. "I guess we both applied with the same name, which maybe confused the system?"

"What system? The post?" I said. "That's the exact letter I had. It looked exactly the same."

"That's not possible," Charlie said. "Rosie? That's not possible, right?"

"Could we have . . . sent two, somehow?" Rosie said faintly. "I handed the letter to my wife, Marly, to sort, I didn't put it in the envelope myself . . . I can't believe . . . You're *both* called Charlie Jones?"

Now we were getting somewhere. Human error—or interference—seemed plausible.

"Could your wife have made a copy of the letter, and sent it to two of us?" Other Charlie asked.

"Well, we do have a scanner . . ."

Of course they have a scanner here. The technological equivalent of a horse and carriage.

"But why *would* she?" Other Charlie asked, looking at me. "Why would she send the job offer to two people with the same name?"

The genuine bafflement on her face gave me pause. She looked as confused as I felt.

"She might have forgotten she posted the first one?" Rosie hazarded. "And then did it again, but picked up the other Charlie Jones's application, and used their address . . ."

We all stood around for a minute, wearing similarly dubious expressions.

"What do I do now?" Rosie asked, wide-eyed.

"Don't you remember if the person you wanted for the job was a man or a woman?" Other Charlie asked.

"I didn't know," Rosie said. She was beginning to look slightly tearful. "I just know they were called Charlie Jones."

"Well, which Charlie do you want to employ?" I asked.

"The one who . . . I don't know!" Rosie said, her voice rising a pitch. "You *both* applied? You both want to work here? Which of you wrote that lovely handwritten letter about how special Ormer seems?"

"Me," I said immediately.

"That was me," said Other Charlie.

No way. I was not buying this.

"Do you have the winning application on hand?" I suggested. "We could just check which of ours it is?"

Rosie went still. Then she started fanning herself more rigorously.

"Just let me think for a moment," she said. She pressed a hand to her forehead.

"OK. OK. Two Charlie Joneses. Both want to come and live here. Both offered the job, apparently . . ."

I reiterated that finding the successful job application would almost certainly clear this whole thing up.

"Right," Rosie said, and then, "well, no, I can't do that. I . . . binned them all. Sorry. Burned them, actually—Marly does this thing where she stuffs spare paper into old loo rolls and it makes great firelighters. No. That won't work. Now that you're both here, and we've offered both of you the job, I think the only thing for it is to get to know you both. Yes. What do you think?" She looked between us. "A trial period! It seems so unfair to send one of you home now. Why don't we just give you each a couple of months . . ."

"You want to . . . employ us both?" I asked slowly.

"Yes! Yes, what a great solution," Rosie said breathily. There was something quaint about her—a bit otherworldly. "We're always run off our feet during harvest season—I'm sure two managers would be a huge help."

"And you'll pay us both?" I asked.

Rosie's eyes widened again. "Oh. I forgot about the money part."

I shared a brief side-eye with Other Charlie.

"Both of you really want to be here?" Rosie asked rather desperately.

"Very badly," I said.

"More than anything," Other Charlie said. "I can't even tell you, Rosie. I've been so excited about this incredible opportunity—starting life over here in this beautiful place, with this amazing project, reviving the farm shop at the heart of the community . . . It's my dream."

Her voice wobbled. I looked away from her. It's going to be a lot easier to keep hold of this job if I don't feel sorry for Other Charlie, but I've never been great at keeping other people's feelings out. All the more reason to start life over on a remote, secluded island, I say.

"It's my job," I said. "I'm sorry. But I'm not walking away from this."

I can't go back home. Home isn't even there anymore. This is me now, all there is of me: a name, a job, a totally new life. The minute I stepped off that ferry and breathed it all in, I knew it was the right decision. I can be sober in this place. I can be better—I can be brand-new.

"I guess you could interview us both," Other Charlie said. "See who you would rather give the job to?"

For the first time, at that, I felt nervous. I'm confident I'm right for this role, but this poised, attractive, well-spoken woman with her posh dress was definitely the kind of person who looked like she should be running a farm shop, not a scarred, bitter ex-bartender like me. If this actually was a misunderstanding, there's a chance she *was* the person who'd been offered the job.

This opportunity was a lifeline for me. The thought of losing it now . . .

"The trial period idea," I said. "It could work."

Other Charlie's eyes were so sharp.

"But I can't pay you both," Rosie said sadly.

"Well, I'd take half wages for the next two months," I said, then belatedly ran the calculation, and winced. It'll be just about doable if I dip into savings.

"You'd do that?" Other Charlie asked.

"Would you? For this opportunity? You'd have to take the salary cut, too."

Her gaze was steady on mine. She was trying to figure me out. I imagine I was about as confusing to her as she was to me.

"This place has so much potential," she said slowly. "I wouldn't be surprised if we could justify two manager salaries at a place like this, once we've made some changes. If we work together, maybe we could both have a future at the farm shop."

I met her gaze. What was this? A compromise—a peace offering? Why? It looked like an admission that the job wasn't hers, but then, perhaps by offering to take half pay, I looked like I was conceding something, too. Should I just go back to the interview idea, I wondered, and take the risk?

Charlie was right: there were so many easy, obvious ways to fix the shop up. Visitors come to the island all through the summer, but there's nothing directing them here from the harbor. A bunch of tourists arrived on the ferry with me this morning, and they were just *gagging* to overpay for some island-made honey or something.

"You'll both work here for two months? But we only have to pay one person's salary?" Rosie asked.

We both said yes, avoiding each other's eyes now. I couldn't decide if I was being incredibly stupid or had just secured the safest way to keep my precious new life. The key thing was that Charlie and I evidently thought this job was the absolute dream and were not willing to give it up, and Rosie seemed to think it was not very important, didn't really mind who did it, and mostly just didn't want to upset anyone.

I guess if you live on a beautiful farm on a stunning remote island, and you always have, then you maybe don't realize how incredible that is.

"And you'll just . . . sort the farm shop out? But for half pay?"

"For two months, yes," I said. "At which point, hopefully, we'll have each proven ourselves and you can pay us both."

Or one of us will have given up and bowed out. Not me, obviously.

"That's *great*," Rosie said, sagging back against the counter. "Thank God. I'm so relieved I don't have to send one of you home."

It wasn't ideal. It wasn't what I'd signed up for. But it was a hell of a lot better than losing this chance altogether.

"But what shall we call you both?" Rosie asked, brightening. "We can't have two Charlies."

I explained that I'd like to go by Jones anyway.

"Perfect! Meant to be!" Rosie said.

"I know you need to get on with things," Charlie said smoothly. "Are our bags . . ."

"They'll be at the stables, which is all set up for you." Rosie's eyes widened. "Oh. All set up for one of you."

I closed my eyes for a moment. "I'll stay somewhere else tonight," I said, picking up my rucksack from the floor and yanking on my cap. By this point, I just wanted to get out of there. I was hot, I was stressed, I wanted a drink.

"The farmhouse is a B&B, right?" Other Charlie said. "Perhaps Jones could have a room there?"

I know I'd just offered to give up the stables for the night, but still, she really ran with that, didn't she?

Rosie's face fell. "Sorry, we're full. There are no spare rooms."

Other Charlie turned to me with a sympathetic smile. "Let me know if you need any help finding somewhere else."

Hot, stressed, thirsty and irritated now.

"I should ask for references," Rosie said suddenly. "Can you give me someone to call, each of you?"

We both said that was fine. (Thank God she only asked for one person.)

"We'll take it from there in the morning, and give you a tour of the farm! Give me your numbers." She pulled out a surprisingly up-to-date iPhone. I had her down as the sort of person with an ancient flip phone. "I can't wait to get to know the two of you . . . Oh, I get such a good aura from you both."

This made me seriously question Rosie's ability to read auras, but fine.

"Ormer is a really special place. And we love to take in strays here. Not to call you strays! But I just sense . . . a tender quality, bruised souls . . ." She waved a hand in front of our faces. "Broken hearts, complicated pasts . . . I'm convinced the spirit of the island led you both here for a reason!"

"Fate, maybe," Other Charlie said, with a smile.

Fate? No. An administrative mix-up, *maybe*. A meddling postal worker, at a push. But by far the most likely truth, as far as I'm concerned, is that Charlie Jones is a liar, so while I've agreed to work alongside her, I certainly don't plan on trusting her.

Well. There we go. Day one done—I'm off to find somewhere

to crash tonight. Presumably there are other B&Bs on this island, although, now I think about it, there can't be *many*, given the size of the place. Hmm.

I'm not quite sure how to sign off this email. *With love* feels . . . well, yeah, not that. But *all the best* is pretty weird, too. Maybe I'll just say,

Bye for now,
Charlie Jones

Saturday August 9th 2025

Just woke up in beautiful converted stables to sound of birdsong. Everything had warm, dreamy quality. Sunbeams through enormous windows, fluffy duvet tucked beneath my chin, promise of bright fresh start ahead of me.

Last night, walking to the stables in the dusk, it felt as though I'd met the real Ormer. The moment the last tourist ferry left, it was as if the island breathed out. The horse-drawn carts disappeared, replaced by the occasional local on a rusted bike with a sleepy dog trotting at their back wheel. Birds hopped out of hedgerows, as though they knew it was safe now. Everything was slower and softer. The dust kicked up by the tractors in the daytime was settling like glitter as the sun set, and the whole island shimmered.

As I woke in the stables, I allowed myself a minute to manifest my beautiful new life here. Me, slipping out of bed and into a cute dress and Birkenstocks ahead of a day at the farm shop. Overnight oats, freshly squeezed orange juice and a quality coffee machine waiting for me in the kitchen. The generous walk-in wardrobe transformed into a nursery—soft cream on the walls, a textured rug, a moon-and-stars mobile above the cot—all ready for me to take that next step I've been longing for.

Then I returned to reality.

"Just so you know," said Jones, emerging from said walk-in wardrobe, "that is *not* big enough to be a bedroom."

. . . There had been nowhere else available to stay on the island. Not a single room, apparently—there isn't much accommodation anyway, as people generally come here on day trips from Jersey or Guernsey, and the island is (as discussed) tiny.

Thought there would be <u>somewhere</u>, though. But Jones rocked up at ten p.m. with a thunderous expression, chucked his bag on my sofa and announced that unless I wanted him to sleep in a cow barn, we were going to need to find a way to share.

And here we were. <u>Both</u> of us. Even though I was fine with the Jones-in-a-cow-barn plan, actually.

He stomped past the end of my bed—the only way out of his "room," in fairness, is through mine. He was dressed in gray jogging bottoms and a sagging white T-shirt. Why are gray jogging bottoms such a good look on a man? It's not fair—when I wear them, I look like someone just broke up with me. I pulled the duvet up higher, though I needn't have bothered—he didn't look at me once.

"Is there coffee?" he said as he marched through the bedroom door, leaving it swinging open.

The stables are gorgeous, but it's definitely compact in here. There's this bedroom with its walk-in wardrobe, a bathroom with a surprisingly roomy shower and a freestanding bath that looks over the fields, and then the rest of the long building is a kitchen leading into a living space with a wood burner and cozy sofa. An idyllic place to live alone, or with a little one.

<u>Not</u> an idyllic place to live with a stranger who claims that your lovely new life belongs to him.

"I don't know," I said, "did you make coffee?"

"I've only just got up."

"And I'm still in bed, in case you hadn't noticed."

"I noticed."

"OK, so, no, there is no coffee waiting for you in the kitchen, since I haven't even— Oh, all right then," I finished. I'd just heard the shower door slam shut. "I guess you're not part of this conversation anymore."

The shower turned on. I lay back on the pillow. Manifest, manifest, manifest. Maybe if I get really good at it, I can manifest him right back to the mainland.

Ten missed calls from Brianna. A string of irate WhatsApps:

* Hello? I know you're starting a new life but you can't get rid of ME, YOUR BARNACLE, YOUR LIMPET, YOUR ADDITIONAL LIMB
* What do you mean there's another Charlie Jones?! Surely not. How many bloody Charlie Joneses can there actually be in the world?
* I've googled, there are over a million Charlie Joneses in the world, who would have thought it! CALL ME BACK.

Yanked a cardigan on over my pajamas and went outside to call her. She launched straight in.

"As if another person with <u>that exact name</u> has just <u>by coincidence</u> decided to take a job in a shop on a tiny arse-end-of-nowhere French island—"

"British island," I interrupted. "It's British."

"Really? I looked on a map and it's right by France."

"You want to talk Anglo-French history right now?"

"No, I really don't," said Bri. "You know I don't respond well to being educated. I want to talk about you. You backed down! You <u>know</u> they didn't offer the job to two people accidentally, but you didn't want to challenge this guy for lying about getting the job, so—"

Moved the phone away from my ear and winced. Brianna has always had a slightly Janice-from-Friends quality to her voice when particularly animated. On the few occasions I've visited her on the Eastside Close set, have noticed the cast get jumpy when she adopts this voice, and that several of them refer to her as "Ms. Director, ma'am." Sometimes wonder whether I'm the only person in her life who isn't scared of her.

"Bri, look, it's a man's world," I said, in my most sensible tone, when she paused for breath. "The odds were in his favor, not mine. And maybe they did give him the job, too! It's a reasonable explanation for how this happened, isn't it?"

"No! You're just letting him stay because you're scared. Why are you assuming he deserves this more than you?"

"Oh, I don't know, because he probably does?"

"What have we said about low self-esteem?"

"Men find it a real turn-on?"

"Eww, disgusting. But true. How old is he, by the way, the imposter—is he old?"

Thought about it. "Midthirties, I reckon? But he's kind of"—lowered voice—"rugged. Sort of ageless. You know, like . . . Daniel Craig."

Glanced around nervously. Was standing on the little patio outside the kitchen, looking out at a hard-mown patch of hedged grass that would've been called a "stunning south-facing garden" by a London estate agent, but that Rosie had called "the wee patch if you'd come with a dog." Last I heard, Jones was still in the shower, but I would not like him to hear me comparing him to a former James Bond.

"Ooh, OK, I get it: if he looked like Daniel Craig I'd let him sleep in my bedroom, too. Tabbie! Have you washed your hands?"

Tabbie yelled an indignant yes in the background. Felt a pang of nostalgia for Bri's house, with Tabbie's crayon artwork in frames on the walls and her sticky jam fingerprints on the sofa arms.

"He's not in my bedroom, he's in an adjoining room."

"Is there a door?"

"There's a doorway."

"Uh-huh."

"Look, it's not like that. You know where I'm at—I'm done, Bri. Romantically finito."

"Sworn to celibacy?"

"Well, maybe not celibacy for life. But I want to be a mum someday soon, on my terms, and that means no men."

"I do think that's wise," Brianna said.

"And definitely not this man."

"On account of how he's a job-stealing liar?"

"Well, that, possibly, and the fact that he seems to be in a perpetual bad mood. And now he's my colleague and housemate. Anyway"—I adopted my brightest Cheerful Charlie voice—"I don't mind having a comanager."

"You don't mind working with the imposter?"

I mind. This was definitely not on the script of my picture-perfect new life, nor was the massive salary cut. But . . .

"Running a remote farm shop is a super cute Hallmark movie job, but it's also a job and I don't have a ton of relevant experience, so . . . I don't mind sharing the load with someone else."

"Don't say that experience thing to anyone else," Bri said sternly. "You've got to—"

"Fake it till I make it, yep, I know."

"Do I need to come out there, however a person does that, and check you're really all right?"

"No!"

The idea of BMW-driving Bri getting pulled up the hill from Ormer's harbor in a tractor trailer made me feel very stressed.

"Fine, but don't trust this guy, OK? He could be a real con artist or something. And don't do anything mental," Bri said. "Don't join any weird island cults or sleep with anyone I wouldn't sleep with. Sensible me, that is, not the old me, she slept with that guy from Casualty, you don't want to be like her. I'll call you again later, Mabes needs me. Stay strong, remember you are going to be great at this job and keep your eye on the prize."

I had a chat with Tabbie before she lost interest in me and left Bri's phone on the sofa, and now I'm just sitting out on the sturdy little bench in the garden, listening to the island. You can't hear the sea from the stables, but it's misty this morning, and every so often a foghorn sounds through the white glow behind the hedges, reminding me that I'm never more than a short walk from the world's edge. I'm just taking it all in, one breath at a time. Maybe the grief and the sadness really have stayed on the mainland. Maybe I can find happiness here.

I'm not going to deny Jones his chance at this beautiful life—I'm not willing to risk the possibility that he might take mine. But if he does try to muscle me out or suggest to Rosie that she should just keep one of us on, then I'll come back at him with claws.

This new me might be positive and peppy and ponytaily, but she still knows how to fight her corner.

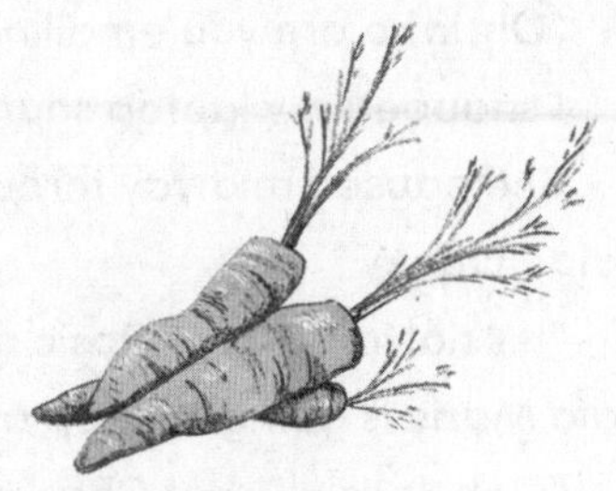

FROM: **Charlie Jones**
TO: **Charlie Jones**
SUBJECT: **Day two sober**

Two days since I left, two days since I last had a drink. I have what must surely be the world's worst hangover, and last night—honestly—I might have had a beer if there had been one in the stables. Or an open shop where I could buy one. I guess a perk of living on a remote rock with a woman who seems to only drink chamomile tea is that I'm unlikely to really put that urge to the test.

Because, yes, I live with someone now. Me, aspiring hermit, the man who chose to come and live on a secluded island where nobody knows him. I now live with a woman *also* named Charlie Jones, who sings a medley of every track from *Reputation* in the shower, and leaves potfuls of gloopy, seed-speckled oats hardening on the kitchen sideboard, and shares not only my name and my house, but also my job.

She just barged into the kitchen, fresh out of the shower. It felt way too intimate. I could smell her shampoo. I could see a distracting amount of her legs. I shouldn't know that this random stranger has fluffy rabbit slippers, but I do.

This situation is too messed up. I need *some* part of my life that this female doppelgänger does not inhabit.

"Oh, who are you emailing?" she asked.

I snapped my laptop shut. "Myself," I said.

She paused midway through opening the fridge. "Hmm!" she said. "Quirky."

"It's not important. Rosie rang while you were showering. She said Marly is going to drop by."

"Ooh, lovely!" said Charlie, with a smile. "See you soon!"

I watched her take her tea into the bedroom. That smile of hers. The airy positivity, the way she talks to me like we're friends even though she *must* want me gone. I don't know. It feels all wrong.

I have a very strong suspicion that Charlie Jones is full of shit.

More soon,
Charlie Jones

FROM: **Charlie Jones**
TO: **Charlie Jones**
SUBJECT: **Day two sober (cont.)**

This Marly is an interesting character. An Australian, a fair bit older than Rosie—early forties, maybe. Gray pixie cut, square face, unimpressed eyes. She marched into the stables out of the rain and stood in front of the wood burner, dripping rainwater from her waterproof jacket. An adoring spaniel stood by her heel, spinning in the occasional excited circle. Charlie and I ended up sitting on the sofa side by side, looking up at Marly like schoolkids waiting for a telling off.

"I did not post two bloody letters," she said, not bothering with a hello. "I put Rosie's note in an envelope and handed it to . . ."

She squinted for a moment. "Someone. Galoshes? Kim? Anyway, whoever it was, they did the address and they'll have given it to Rog to post. And none of those people have any reason to engineer this bizarre situation, so who the fuck knows what's gone on."

We stayed silent. I glanced at Charlie. She looked a bit wide-eyed. Finally unable to contain herself any longer, the spaniel made a dash over to the sofa to give us an excited sniff, until Marly called her back with a sharp "Ginger, here."

"But as weird as this overabundance of Charlies is," Marly went on, as Ginger returned to her heel, "it's got me two shop managers for the price of one, and I'm not the sort of woman who looks a gift horse in the mouth, even if she suspects the gift horse is playing funny buggers, do you know what I'm saying?"

We confirmed that yes, we got the idea.

"Fact is, either the island postal service is being more crap than usual, or someone is messing with us all, or one of you is lying about getting Rosie's letter. But honestly, she wants you both here, I'm run off my feet, and until you arrived, Galoshes was in charge of the farm shop, and she can't tell a profit margin from a turnip, so unless you're going to rob me, which I wouldn't recommend, by the way—"

Who would dare?

"—then I'm going to make the most of the free labor and let you both stay on until harvest festival—October 6th. All right? That's about two months. Then we look at the state of things and hope you've both earned your keep."

Charlie and I nodded.

She glared at us. "I don't trust either of you right now. But I'm not saying I won't one day. We're open-minded people here on Ormer. We believe in second chances. But cross us and you'll realize that this place isn't always as sweet as it looks to the tourists.

We've got our own rules, and we make sure people keep to them, that's all I'm saying."

Drip, drip, drip, went Marly's waterproofs.

"Now," she said abruptly, marching back toward the door. Ginger scrabbled to catch up. "Weather's clearing up. Time for a nice picnic lunch."

So that's what we did. I'll be back to write again soon—Charlie wants to discuss something about kitchen rotas. I already know I'm going to hate this conversation.

Bye for now,
Charlie Jones

FROM: **Charlie Jones**
TO: **Charlie Jones**
SUBJECT: **Day two sober (cont.)**

Let me have a go at describing Bramblebay Farm.

Think . . . tumbledown stone walls, rolling golden fields, gnarly hedgerows, ripening blackberries, rich chocolate clumps of soil, knobble-kneed sheep, great swaths of wildflowers . . . and behind it all, the occasional glimpse of a flawless blue sea.

My endless hangover eased a little along with the rain as we headed out for the tour and picnic. I felt better just being outside, though traveling across the farm in Marly's rattling, rusty tractor did ramp up the nausea a bit. The farm is two hundred acres, mostly arable, but a few animals, too, and several fields of apple and pear trees. We covered what felt like most of this before the promised picnic actually occurred.

Rosie met us there with a large basket on her arm. She was more practically dressed today—less flowy tie-dye—but there was still an oversized moon pendant sticking out of the zipper of her waterproof jacket.

We set up for lunch in the orchard, Ginger lying between us all. The grass was long and wet, peppered with flowers, and we had to dodge the wasps that were already circling some of the fallen apples. It smelled amazing—that post-rain scent, with the hint of sweetness from the fruit. It felt as if we were somewhere wilder than an orchard. Everything is a little wilder than average here—extra lush, extra verdant.

Marly bombarded us both with information about the running of the farm during the journey to the orchard, so I'd not heard much from Charlie. But now that we were eating sandwiches (cheese and pickle, but *good* cheese, island cheese, and locally produced pickle, too—I need to check this out for the shop), it was conspicuous how quiet she was being.

As we ate, Marly asked us why we both wanted the job. Charlie and I glanced at each other; she looked slightly tense, I thought. I was, too—was this going to be an interview after all?

"I'll go first," Charlie said.

She was in a knee-length floral dress, her hair pinned back, and was wearing wellies, the kind with a buckle on the side. Pure class, that's what my dad would have said, but I wasn't sure—there was something about it that looked like a game of dress-up.

"I want a new start," she said. "I want to strip things back to the basics, and I think your amazing farm shop is such a perfect place to do that. I love that you sell local people local produce, like, we grow things, we pick them, we cook them, we eat them, it's so much more . . . *connected* than the way we live in a city."

"You felt disconnected?" Rosie said softly. "A little lost?"

"God, yes," Charlie said. "I felt like I needed to go back to the starting line, you know?"

Rosie was gazing at Charlie with a total fascination that I'm not sure this conversation deserved. Was nobody aware that this was the vaguest possible answer to this question? Connectedness, fresh starts, a load of fluff about local produce that she presumably thought would chime with the two farmers sitting across from us?

"And what is it you want to do here?" Marly asked her.

She wasn't regarding Charlie with quite the same fascination.

"I want to start over and build the life that's right for *me*," Charlie said, tucking a strand of hair behind her ear.

"What do you mean by that?" Marly asked.

"Gosh, I'm not quite sure yet," Charlie said.

"Do you want to settle here? Long-term?"

"I absolutely see a future on the island," Charlie said, but Marly was already interrupting.

"What does that future look like, though?"

Charlie was flustered now. She stammered a bit about following dreams or something. Her eyes flicked to me, and then back to Rosie and Marly. She'd trailed right off, and for the first time since meeting her, I had a sense that we'd reached something real. This wasn't a topic she wanted to discuss.

"Marly, they're just settling in," Rosie said gently, squeezing her wife's knee again. "Please, don't feel you ever have to share anything with us that you're not ready to share. That's really important to us. We want to know you, of course, but we want you to show yourselves as and when you're ready."

She pressed a hand to her heart. It was all quite intense from an employer—we're just the new shop managers, after all—and maybe Marly thought the same, because she broke the moment by shifting the conversation on to crisp flavors (I went salt and vinegar, obviously; Charlie chose ready salted, which has got to be a red flag).

"How about you, Jones?" Marly said, watching me insert crisps inside my sandwich with a nod of approval. "What is it that you're seeking here?"

The plan is to keep myself to myself. No more friends to lose, no more relationships to screw up—just some time quietly getting sober and starting afresh. I wasn't intending to open up to anybody, least of all my new employers. But having watched Charlie bullshit her way through answering that question, I suddenly felt like telling the truth.

"I quit drinking the day I left the mainland," I said.

Charlie went still, watching me, a crisp held neatly between her forefinger and thumb. She looked a little shocked.

I told them that I wasn't a proper alcoholic, even as my head pounded. Even as that wolfish little voice in my head said, *In fact, why are you stopping drinking at all? Wouldn't it be lovely to have a lager with this picnic? And what would be the harm?*

"The rural way of life appealed to me as well," I said, "and the island life—I think it'll—"

"So, you're two days sober right now," Marly interrupted. "How's the withdrawal?"

"I'm fine," I said, jamming my shaking hands between my knees. "I assure you, it won't affect how well I can do my job."

It probably was a bad idea to tell them about the drinking. But I think I'd needed to say it out loud. The way I need to write *Day two sober* as the subject line on this email. Now I have no choice but to stick to it.

"Well, good for you, mate," Marly said, rummaging in the bag and pulling out a large fruit tart wrapped in brown paper. "I'm coming up to nine years."

"Sober?" I asked, surprised.

She handed me a slice of the tart. Ginger's eyes tracked it. It was spiced apple, buttery and flaky, totally delicious.

"Yep. Stumbled on some seasonal work here while traveling the world, met Rosie, did the same as you—used moving here as a chance to start over. Rosie had just inherited the farm, and there was so much to be done. I wanted to be the best I could be, for her." Marly gave me a quick smile. "It's good you told us. I appreciate that."

When I made the decision not to go down the route of joining an alcoholic support group, it was because I was confident I could do this by myself, and I still feel that way. But today has been a fucking hard day. And it's actually quite good to know that if it gets *too* hard, someone on this island knows what that feels like.

Charlie asked Rosie about the story of the farm and how she inherited it. She was still flustered, I think. Maybe she didn't like that I'd found something to connect with Marly over—or maybe I'm being unfair. Thinking the worst of people, of situations, of anything—another bad habit I'd like to shake.

"When my parents died," Rosie said. "Ten years ago now."

"Oh, I'm so sorry—of course, you don't inherit something without losing someone," Charlie said, wincing slightly.

Rosie reached for her hand. "It's OK," she said. "I can talk about them. I'd love to talk about them, actually."

"It helps, doesn't it?" Charlie said. "With grief? I find the more I talk . . ." Her cheeks pinked again—embarrassed at the admission, I think. "Anyway, tell me about them—they must have been such special people to have created this incredible farm."

Rosie explained that Bramblebay had actually been in the Nicole family for generations. Her parents had only run the farm for a few short years before their deaths in a car crash on the mainland.

Charlie said something generic—"I'm so sorry," maybe, or "Sorry for your loss"—but the way she said it had real weight. The sorry of a person who knew that sorry would never mean enough. Whatever else Charlie is, she's someone who's lost people.

"Inheriting the farm when I was still a teenager was a *lot*," Rosie said. "I was so out of my depth. Sometimes I think I still am, even since meeting Marly and having her here with me to run the place. It's partly why we decided to recruit someone to manage the farm shop—it's so much more than just a place to sell our produce, but we weren't able to give it anywhere near the time and attention it needs. Imported goods cost a fortune here; locals really rely on us to sell food and products that are made on the island. The producers rely on us, too."

"No pressure," Marly added dryly.

We were going to meet the committee of local producers on Thursday night, apparently—Rosie said they were excited to get to know us, and Charlie chirped about how great it would be to get their input on potential changes to the shop.

"Ah, it's not so much about . . . input," Rosie said delicately.

"The local producer committee has a veto on any major changes to the shop," Marly said. "You'll need their approval to make any significant alterations. And any major spends need their sign-off. That's how things work here. It's a community shop, after all."

Charlie and I exchanged a glance. Not to sound like I want to be farm shop king, but wasn't this island feudal until about five minutes ago? I'm already having to share decision-making with my female counterpart. I could do without a democratic committee with veto power.

"Wonderful!" Charlie said. I'd never heard her sound so insincere, and that was really saying something.

When the time came to leave, Marly put a hand on my arm to stop me as Rosie and Charlie headed for the tractor.

"Look, I know Rosie's got this whole thing about how you and Charlie were called here for a reason—her usual kooky stuff," she said, with unmistakable affection. "But this island *does* call to a certain kind of person. The fact it's got its own ways and its own government, fewer rules and restrictions . . . the fact it's pretty much a little rock in the middle of nowhere and nobody gives a damn about it . . . It appeals to a particular type, that's all I'm saying. There're a lot of people here who'll know what it feels like to want to get away and start over somewhere where life's a bit different."

I thanked her, but she wasn't finished.

"There're a lot of people here who know what it feels like to hit rock bottom, too," Marly said. "Me included. OK? You need something—anything—you ask."

Maybe it was the hangover, but my throat felt tight. She doesn't even know me. She didn't have to say that.

We began to follow Charlie and Rosie back toward the tractor through the orchard, Ginger dashing ahead of us, ears wet from the grass.

"Holds her cards close to her chest, that one," Marly said, nodding to Charlie. "I wonder why."

Charlie looked like some sort of advert for Ormer right now, fingers trailing through the branches above her as she walked in her pretty flowery dress with the picnic basket tucked under her other arm. It was hard to imagine she could be up to anything genuinely nefarious. She looked too . . . bucolic.

"She's miserable, anyway," Marly said. "I can tell you that much."

"Charlie? Miserable?"

I stared at the woman walking ahead of us. She looked like she might be about to break into a skip. Even her hair was perky.

"I know a wounded woman when I see one," Marly said. "And that girl has history. Whatever it is she's dealing with . . . it's broken her heart."

I don't know what to make of that. It's easier to manage this woman's presence in *every* part of my new life when I can tell myself I don't need to feel bad for her. But I don't like the thought that Charlie might be miserable. And I don't like that I want to know why. Her past is none of my business, just like mine is none of hers. Right?

So long,
Charlie Jones

Peak District, one year earlier

It's funny how life turns out, Charlie thought. She was not at all interested in cycling, for instance, and yet here she was at the crack of dawn (eight thirty a.m.) in a bike café in the Peak District, queueing behind two elderly men in skintight Lycra holding forth about wind speeds. She glanced back at her table, where Oliver and Fearne sat, both sweaty and energized from riding, and her heart warmed. She would follow those two anywhere, even if it meant a disgustingly early start and coffee that smelled faintly of bike oil.

Oliver looked particularly gorgeous—his cycling gear clung to the tight muscles of his shoulders and upper arms, and his hair was all mussed from his helmet, giving him a surferish bed-headed look. He caught her eye and gave her one of his trademark tiny smiles. Oliver could smile without really moving his face at all. He just *projected* a smile, capturing the essence in his eyes and the very slightest rise to the corners of his mouth.

It was easy to read his general expressionlessness as placidity—she had when Fearne had first introduced them—but he was actually very funny and warm. Just understated. Subtle. Charlie, who had never been described as understated, had found his calmness almost intoxicating: spending time with Oliver was like taking a warm bath or going to a yoga class. They'd been dating for three months now, and Charlie felt her brain chemistry was forever changed as a result. It was still chaos in there, but spending so much time with Oliver had made her realize how overstimulated she often was, and how much it benefited her to occasionally sit with someone in companionable silence.

"Make it a hazelnut latte!" Fearne yelled at Charlie across the café. "No, sorry, back to gingerbread! A gingerbread mocha!"

Charlie grinned. Fearne was perhaps the reason why Charlie had never experienced much companionable silence before. She was the closest thing Charlie had to a sister—something Charlie would never have said in front of Brianna, who would definitely have taken offense. But her relationship with Bri was so complicated. And Fearne had come first: Brianna was a friend from secondary school, but Fearne had befriended Charlie when she was an odd, lonely six-year-old on the playground bench, the one everyone whispered about, even the parents. *She's adopted, you know. Did you see her crying at parents' evening? Miss Braddery says she's got "issues."*

Fearne was effervescent, exuberant, high on life. She swept Charlie up and loved her unconditionally, something Charlie had never experienced before and found frankly life-changing. Fearne's mind seemed to match Charlie's, too—they both thought at 1.5 speed, with too many programs running at once.

As the two men in front of her in the queue spoke—just a *touch* too loudly—about carbon-fiber wheels, Charlie pulled out her phone and scrolled idly through her favorite bookmarked websites. The Isle of Ormer community page, the Isle of Ormer estate agency site, her Ormer Google Alerts . . .

"What can I get you?" the barista asked.

Charlie had become engrossed reading about plans to set up a Christmas tractor run on the island. God, how adorable.

"Two flat whites, please, and one—" She looked over her shoulder again.

"White chocolate hazelnut latte with cream on top!"

"—of those," she said. Fearne had been loud enough for the barista to catch every word.

As she returned to the table, Charlie almost collided with a young woman in padded leggings clutching a large takeaway cup.

"Oh my goodness," she said, stepping in front of Charlie to speak to Oliver. "You're Oliver Brennon, right?"

Charlie watched Oliver's face cloud with embarrassment, just as Fearne's lit up with total delight.

"He *is*," Fearne said, rocking her chair onto its back two legs and clapping her hands gleefully. "Are you a fan?"

"I've seen you race—you're amazing," the girl said to Oliver.

Oh my fucking God, Charlie mouthed at Fearne behind the girl's back, then she had to go back to biting her bottom lip to keep from laughing. As far as she was aware, this had never happened to Oliver before. He was a semipro downhill mountain biker, as Fearne was—that's how they'd become friends, and it was Fearne who'd introduced Oliver and Charlie—but it was not a profession that made one famous. Except in a bike café, maybe.

"Will you be competing at Downhill Dash next weekend?"

"Yeah, yeah, I'll be there," Oliver said, rubbing his jawline awkwardly. His eyes flicked to Charlie and warmed with amusement as he clocked her jumping on the spot slightly, back to mouthing *oh my fucking God* again.

"I'll be cheering you on!" the girl said, heading off to the door with a smile.

"Maybe she'll bring pom-poms!" Charlie said as she slid into her chair.

Oliver put his face in his hands as Fearne laughed uproariously.

"You're *famous*," Fearne said. "Oh my God—Charlie Jones, girlfriend of a celebrity!"

"Please. Is Taylor Swift a celebrity's girlfriend?" Charlie said.

But she was slightly thrilled by it all, actually. She knew Oliver was a total catch—of course—but sometimes she found herself comparing him to her ex more than she should have. She'd loved Berty so much, that was the trouble. They'd gotten together as teenagers, when she'd hardly believed that anyone, let alone the aloof, handsome Berty, wanted to take *her* out to a movie. Even after almost two decades together, Berty had never stopped being her dream guy—she'd always felt so blessed to have found him.

And then he'd left her. Walked out of their flat with a random assortment of their shared possessions shoved in the suitcase they'd taken to Barbados the summer before.

But now she was with lovely, gorgeous Oliver, so none of that mattered anyway. And if she didn't quite idolize him as she had Berty, that was probably a good thing—perhaps it wasn't healthy to love a person so much. It certainly hadn't felt healthy when Berty had left. Nobody should cry as much as she had cried; nobody should feel so agonizingly undone. Oliver was sexy and enigmatic, but less assertive and dominant than Berty had been. Berty-lite. Just what she needed.

Still, meeting one of Oliver's fans did give him an air of mystique that he might have otherwise been lacking, a little.

The barista brought their coffees to the table, smiling at Fearne's effusive thanks—nobody did gratitude more earnestly than Fearne. The three of them sipped their drinks. Oliver still looked amusingly uncomfortable. He was such a nice guy; Charlie felt bad for even thinking of him as in any way *less* than Berty. She gave him an extra warm smile over her coffee cup; his eyes crinkled back at her.

"We should get these for the shop," Fearne said, pointing at the set of vintage cycling jerseys hanging beside the TV currently playing old highlights from the Tour de France.

"This is why I'm on decor," Charlie said, examining the garishly colored T-shirts. "And also why there is a Pinterest board. Neon does not say *Vintage, Please*, Fearne."

"Does it not?" Fearne pouted, unoffended.

She was not *always* the perfect business partner—absent much of the time for training and racing, uninterested in details, questionable taste—but the two of them had dreamed of opening a vintage clothing shop together since they were at school, and Charlie felt lucky every time she unlocked the door of Vintage, Please. She felt lucky all the time, really. Except occasionally at three a.m. when the insomnia was bad and the worst thoughts crept in, and she'd find herself thinking, *You're still not good enough, are you, Charlie? Will you ever be?*

"Oh, you're obsessing over your island again!" Fearne said—she'd just shamelessly unlocked Charlie's phone, seemingly in order to check the weather forecast. "A tractor run. Adorbs. Shall we go see it this Christmas?"

"No!" Charlie said, a little too loudly. "No," she repeated, in a more measured sort of way. She focused on Oliver—Fearne was not difficult to distract, thankfully, and this ought to do it. "You look *so* uncomfortable with your life of fame," she said to him, leaning over to press a kiss to his cheek. He reached for her, pulling her onto his lap and burying his face in her neck.

"You delight in my embarrassment," he said, voice muffled.

Fearne grinned, instantly sidetracked. "Don't worry, Oliver, one bouncy blonde does not a fan club make."

"It's a good thing!" Charlie said, giggling as she extricated herself and returned to her seat. "It means your profile is rising."

"I don't want my profile to rise," Oliver said, hands still linked with hers. He twisted several of her rings between his fingers, sobering a little. "I just want to ride bikes. Really fast. And win races."

"What for?" Charlie asked.

Fearne and Oliver seemed surprised by the question. She gave a small shrug. She'd always assumed Oliver's competitiveness was at least in part a desire for fame and glory—why else did winning matter?

"Because it's *fun*," Fearne said, just as Oliver said, "Because it makes me feel alive."

There was another silence. Charlie could have guessed Fearne's response to her question—Fearne's brain was an easy read for Charlie, like curling up with a comfort book. Oliver's was a surprise, though. He clocked their expressions and gave a rueful laugh.

"Sorry," he said. "Was that melodramatic?"

"A *bit*," said Fearne.

"Were you waiting for 'The Wind Beneath My Wings' to kick in?" he said, returning to his usual poker face.

"Kind of," Charlie said, relaxing slightly as they settled back into their normal rhythm. "If you're going to say things like 'It makes me feel alive,' then you need to work on your delivery."

"Yeah, it was nowhere near grand enough—'alive' needed caps lock, a distant stare, some gesticulating at the very *least*," Fearne said, twisting in her seat. "Did we not order cakes?"

"You didn't say you wanted cake," Charlie pointed out, already knowing this was not going to matter.

"Millionaire shortbread!" Fearne yelled as she headed to the till.

Oliver and Charlie watched her go.

"She's going to come back with something else," Charlie said.

"Oh, I know." Oliver gave Charlie a little secret smile. "Hi," he said. "Thanks for coming today."

"Of course!"

They kept smiling at each other for a while, Charlie's wide and goofy, Oliver's small and smoldering. He really was gorgeous. And *hers*.

"You look cute in the mornings," Oliver said.

"No, I don't," she said. "I look headachy and cross. It's not my fault, it's just how my face wakes up. I've tried a silk pillow, but there's nothing doing."

"Muffins!" Fearne said, plopping back into her chair and plonking a large tray of baked goods in the middle of the table. "I got every kind. Even the oaty one. Though I don't want that one. Looks bird foody. Oh my God, Oliver, what's that you're wearing?"

Oliver blinked at her with the patience of a man who had been friends with Fearne long enough to expect this sort of treatment.

"Oh, it's an air of celebrity!" Fearne said, with a cackle.

Charlie grinned into her coffee cup, good mood blooming. Screw three a.m. Charlie—these two glorious humans were surely all she would ever need. Who was she to long for more?

The next weekend, Charlie was hauling spare bike wheels into the boot of her car and examining her face idly in the window of her downstairs neighbor's flat. Mornings definitely didn't suit her.

"Best girlfriend ever," Oliver said, kissing her on the cheek as he passed her his bag. "First prize. Every time."

Charlie glowed. Oliver had never learned to drive, and since they'd gotten together, she had taken charge of ferrying him to competitions across the country. Oliver competed at a higher level than Fearne—he had a sponsorship deal now with an energy drink company, and talked about giving up temping in pubs and going full-time—so there were quite a few of these races, but Charlie didn't mind. She tended to stay in the car, watching the setup through the window. She would bring a thermos of her special coffee from home and a library book, with its fingerprinted, laminated cover, the serrated edges digging into her palms.

"Did you get any sleep last night?" Oliver asked as they settled into the car.

She shook her head, starting the engine. "Some," she said. "It was all right."

Charlie's sleeping patterns had been a major point of conflict with Berty. During her spells of insomnia, she would feel almost stiflingly claustrophobic, lying there still as a corpse with her eyes wide open. But if she allowed herself to roam, she'd wake him, and he'd huff about it. Oliver was so chilled out, in contrast—he'd just head back to his place if she was struggling to sleep. He made everything easy.

"You binge-watch *Grey's Anatomy* again?" he asked, with one of his tiny smiles.

"Absolutely," Charlie said, though actually she couldn't even remember what she had watched—sleepless nights tended to turn blurry the next day. "I'm basically a doctor now."

She reached for her thermos, then glanced down, fumbling fingers unable to find it in the drink holder.

"Charlie!"

Her head whipped back to the road just in time to catch a white car in the lane beside her with its signal on—she was in their blind spot. She braked hard, eyes flying to the rearview mirror. The white car switched lanes, the driver holding up a hand in apology.

"Oh my God," Charlie breathed, pressing a hand to her chest. Her heart had already been thundering—now she could feel its beat right down to her toes on the pedal.

Oliver let out a trembling breath. "Are you OK?"

"Yeah, I'm fine, no biggie."

He said nothing. She glanced at him.

"What?" she said.

"That was quite a close shave," he said carefully, after a moment.

"Not my fault, though."

"No, but I just . . . I've been wanting to talk to you for a little while about . . . You're not always that careful? With yourself, I mean."

"Careful with myself? What does that even mean?"

"Like yesterday, on the stairs at my place . . ."

Charlie frowned, bewildered. Oh, yes, she'd tripped—but she'd always been clumsy. They joked about it: she was the classic rom-com heroine, destined to stumble into some charming man's lap or spill her drink down the back of his shirt.

"And you trapped your finger in the door, too? Last week. The tiredness doesn't help, but I do wonder if we need to talk about it," Oliver said. "The—the accidents. Your concentration always seems to be—"

"Interrupted by my boyfriend? This is our junction, please just let me get in the lane."

Oliver went quiet, startled into silence, perhaps. She'd snapped more than she'd meant to, but Oliver had never talked to her like this before, and it was making her hot and panicked. She could feel an argument brewing—they never argued, and it felt even nastier for being new.

Charlie drove with aggressive care, indicating loudly and early, checking her mirrors as though she was taking her driving test. Then she stopped doing that, because it felt odd, and actually made it a lot harder to drive. What did her trapping her finger have to do with someone pulling into her lane unexpectedly? She simmered resentfully as the satnav's voice filled the car.

"I'm sorry," Oliver said, a little wretchedly. He didn't like conflict, either. "I really didn't want to upset you, just to say that you seem quite distractible at the moment, and—"

"I am not distractible!"

In fact, when Charlie set her sights on something, *nothing* distracted her. She'd been this way with the shop. For months, all she had talked about was retail costs, rent prices, Pinterest boards of decor inspiration. She'd driven everyone mad with it, even Fearne. The trouble was, her fixations didn't usually quite reach completion, which then made the whole business seem less like focused productivity and more like whimsy. She loved to plan, but actual *execution* was so much harder.

"I mean distractible like . . . struggling to concentrate," Oliver said. "I'm not trying to be critical, honestly, Charlie, you know I think you're amazing. I'm just trying to say I'm a bit worried about you." He took a deep breath, turning to look at her properly. "I wonder if you should go to the doctor."

"The *doctor*? What would I say, my boyfriend thinks I'm pathologically scatty?"

"I'd say you're sleeping worse than when we first got together, and you're forgetful, less coordinated . . ."

"I'm just tired! And I've always had patches of bad sleep when things are stressful, you know this."

"What if it's a brain thing?"

"What brain thing?" Charlie said, eyes wide. "Being a busy woman, that brain thing?"

"No, like . . . a tumor."

"What?" Charlie said, with an incredulous laugh. "Where is this coming from? I'm *fine*. If there was something wrong with me, don't you think I'd want to fix it?"

"I don't know. You're not really a thinking-about-the-future kind of girl," he said, voice soft, as though the sentence already held the apology he knew would need to follow it.

Charlie blinked in shock. Is that how he saw her? Nobody, surely, could live in the moment less than Charlie Jones. She thought constantly of the family she wanted; she built and rebuilt her future a thousand times a day. Why did he think she had those Google Alerts set about the Isle of Ormer? Why did he think she talked so much about her childhood, how unloved she had felt, the cruelty in how her adoptive parents had handled the death of her birth parents? Her eyes pricked with tears. She had not had to explain these things to Berty. He had known her for so long, and so deeply. It was exhausting trying to start a life over with someone new—like finding yourself logged out of everything, with no clue to your passwords.

"Believe me, Oliver," she said, voice sharp now, "if anything threatened the future I want for myself, I wouldn't hesitate to deal with it."

Monday August 11th 2025

My brain is a great big squished-up mess of information about yields, ciders, grains, cow poo (very important, apparently). Am <u>full</u> of hope and excitement.

Not because of the cow poo. (Did I need to write that?) It's because now that I'm here, in this wonderful wild place, actually starting a family <u>my</u> way seems possible. Sure, it's not exactly the way I used to dream it would happen, and, yes, being here on the island will probably make the fertility treatment appointments (they're in Guernsey) a little bit more of a faff . . . but Brianna was right: the opportunity was so perfect, and it just had to be here. It had to be different. After denying what I want for so long, this feels so right.

And oh, I want it. But the feeling's different now that I've made the decision to do it alone. The panic has gone. I always said I wouldn't let anything get in the way of the life I want, but I wasn't being honest with myself about what that life was, that was the problem—and now I am. No more secretly, quietly longing for something I don't have. I'm going out and getting it. By myself, for myself.

Won't take any steps now until the job's confirmed—probably sensible. Don't fancy managing the fertility drug injections while squashed into a one-bed with someone else, for starters. Plus I want a support network in place before my baby comes along, and right now my new life involves—kind of by definition—absolutely zero people I know. But it's obvious everyone looks out for each other here, just like I hoped. Saw someone fixing up a neighbor's cart this morning, and Rog has already offered to help us brighten up the garden at the stables ("This looks shit," he said, when he dropped a few imported groceries around for us, "you want some bedding plants?"). There's even a sign Sellotaped to the wall in the farm shop that reads, "We help each other out here on the Isle of Ormer. If you need a hand, but you're not sure who to ask, call the Ormer Neighborhood Deputy, who will put you in touch with a friendly face."

A friendly face! Back home you'd have to really look like you were going to buy something if you wanted to get one of those from anyone.

Life's simpler here, and it's <u>beautiful</u>—so much better than it looks online. The towering cliffs, the little moon-shaped sandy bays, the island tracks dappled with tortoiseshell light under the trees . . . It feels as though there's more light and shade here—more color. It would be the most magical place to raise a child.

However. Raising a child on my own will mean I <u>really</u> need a steady income and somewhere to live, ideally minus large grumpy coworker in walk-in wardrobe. Which means working with Jones to a) turn Bramblebay Farm Shop into sufficiently profitable business to sustain two managers and b) figure out how to get the stables to myself ASAP. Having accommodation as part of the job—with space for a nursery—was a huge part of the appeal, and cannot raise baby with alternative, burlier Charlie Jones occupying (considerably more than) half the space. (He's a <u>natural</u> manspreader. Even his towels manspread across the bathroom floor.)

Back soon—off to meet our staff!

<u>The permanent* staff.</u>

*Apparently "loads of other people help out now and then." Presumably we pay these people, but nobody has mentioned how this works, or if any records are kept. Note: legalities of this??

Rog: Yes, Rog the tractor driver, postal worker, island gardener. Seems that on the Isle of Ormer, one does not simply do one job. One either does half a job (see: Charlie Joneses) or all the jobs (see: Rog, and everyone else). Apparently he helps out with cleaning and DIY at the shop.

Caloshes: Think her name is actually Sally, but nobody would confirm this. Pink hair, pink glasses, lots of pink. Aged about sixty-five. Works as full-time shop assistant, very morose, said "But that's not how we do things" three times in initial meeting. Am flagging as potential pain in the arse.

Red: Friendly tour guide from the harbor. Early twenties, at a guess? Part-time shop assistant—helps out at "busy times," which nobody could define and apparently cannot be planned for. Strikes me as someone who has been through tough times but nonetheless remains resolute in her opinion that humans are great. Current fave.

Toby: Nineteen years old. Full-time shop assistant, sweet, mumbly, with prawn-like posture. Almost invisible behind hair carefully gelled to cover most of his face. It's a lovely face and I felt an immediate maternal desire to tell him so, but repressed it—inappropriate. Need to have a baby soon or am at risk of aggressively mothering anyone under the age of twenty.

Not a bad bunch. But vibes were weird. Toby not looking at anybody, Caloshes glaring at me a lot, Rog spending half the meeting taking calls about gardening jobs, Jones and I tussling to take charge of the conversation ... It did not scream "well-honed team." Am putting staff issues top of the farm shop to-do list. Well, maybe not top. Top is probably "Create sign for farm shop so people actually know it's there." But then it's figuring out the issues between all the team members.

Now that I'm thinking about it, there is a lot to put on the farm shop to-do list. Had hoped this job would be idyllic escape, but am starting to feel a bit stressed. What if I can't do it? What if I get it all wrong, and make the place even worse, and then I lose my job and, worse, everyone here thinks I'm the dickhead who turned up and ruined everything?

I won't get a second fresh start. Really can't screw this up.

Just a reminder to self: no sad thoughts, no sad thoughts, no sad thoughts. Blank slate! New life! Starting over, la la la! I shall expand and grow like the apples in the orchard. Have started a Pinterest board for the farm shop and it's filled with gorgeous autumnal delight. This will cheer me up.

All right, had a little cry. That's fine, that's allowed. Can't just repress feelings through sheer force of will—that way lies traumatizing your future children with your emotional inadequacy. Very boomer. Must avoid.

Oh, God, this is all quite hard, isn't it? Jones is back now—went to speak to the owners of a boujee rental in Little Ormer (other end of the island) who were away over the weekend, but even they don't have any availability until October, so it seems the accommodation problem remains. We're about to sit down at the kitchen table for summit on this topic. Would very much like this place to myself, but imagine he feels the same way. Whatever the reason for this bizarre mix-up, there's only one new dream life available, and we're both trying to fit into it. Things are getting bloody cramped.

Both played it very "I'm a mature, sensible adult" for the summit. Cordially sat down at table with cups of chamomile tea. (New me is a chamomile tea person. Jones grimaced with every single sip, so not sure he's on board. It was a bit dusty. Maybe more local honey next time, though not sure how much more would actually dissolve in there.)

Discussed the fact that sleeping arrangements from last few nights are not ideal. We have agreed to work together, but I do not want to live with this man, and he does not want to live with me.

"Yeah, no, absolutely not," he said.

There was a real tone to it.

"Though obviously I'm an excellent housemate," I said.

He snorted.

"At least I don't leave towels on the bathroom floor," I said.

"No, you just don't turn on the exhaust fan, or put anything in the dishwasher."

Confrontational, unfriendly silence.

Tried again.

"Look, I don't want a housemate. I want to settle down."

Felt him looking at me curiously over his mug at that, so I got up to put things in the dishwasher (loudly and pointedly).

"On your own?"

"Sorry?" I said, without turning.

"It's just, normally when people say they want to settle down, they want to settle down together. With someone."

"Yes, well, there is no someone anymore. I'll be settling down on my own."

"Ah," he said, his voice a little softer now. "Yeah. I think that's what I'll end up doing, too."

Bristled slightly at this—wasn't saying I have "ended up" alone. This is what I've chosen. Also, no way this man will end up alone. He's a bit messed up and complicated, undoubtedly, but what's a murky past and a bit of alcoholism when you're an attractive man in your thirties? He'd clean up on the apps.

Anyway. His relationship status is not my business. Whatever his deal is, he needs to be dealing with it out of my walk-in wardrobe.

"But the job had accommodation included," he said. "Ultimately, the stables . . . This place is part of the deal. For me."

"Or me."

Unmistakable rise in tension.

"Not you. But yeah."

"It could be me."

"It's not you. You know it's not you."

"I am actually <u>very</u> confident the job wasn't offered to you," I countered, slamming a bowl into the top rack of the dishwasher, "but let's not get into this, shall we? We've agreed to share."

"Yeah," he said, a little darkly for my liking.

On my glare, he added, "You can't be <u>that</u> confident the job isn't mine, or you'd have made a play to have it all to yourself. But you didn't. You agreed to share."

"I'm not a risk-taker," I said. Is that strictly true? Not sure, actually. "And there was a lot at stake. So I compromised. Besides, you did the same."

"Like you say," he said steadily, "there was a lot at stake. It's a prepackaged ready-made new life, isn't it? And somewhere so epic." He waved a hand out at the island glimmering beyond the kitchen windows.

Felt a little unsettled by how much he got it. Am often unsettled by Jones. He's just . . . distracting. Find myself feeling jittery around him.

"Well then. We both want the same thing. We just need to sort the sleeping situation," I said.

"We do."

"There's nowhere else available."

"No."

Silence. Stalemate.

"This is getting us nowhere. I'm going to go shower," he said.

Felt like I should say, *You can't, it's my shower*, but didn't. And now he's in there, using up all the hot water. Am even more hyper-aware of him than normal, knowing he's showering just on the other side of that door.

Things are prickly. Worryingly so. Our alliance is precarious. Without it, there's the risk he'll try to oust me and keep the stables and the job for himself, and I'm not in a strong position here. I don't *know* that he didn't get the job fair and square. If he starts kicking up trouble with Rosie and Marly, it might be curtains for me, and the very thought of having to head back to the mainland . . .

Not an option. Ugh, I'm crying again! Am doing so much better, am genuinely happier than I have been in *so* long, but I'm *feeling* so much *stuff*. Sad! Guilty! Ashamed! Joyful! Maybe now that I've finally started being honest with myself about how I feel, I can't bloody stop? It's so annoying—how can I leave the past behind when it keeps sneaking up on me like this? Just want to be *Charlie*, the Charlie I'm finding here, and mustn't let this business with Jones get in the way.

But also have nowhere else to stay.

We're stuck. Am going to ring Rosie. Marly is quite straight-talking, no bullshit—Jones's sort of person. Think I'll click better with Rosie, who believes things happen for a reason, an idea that basically got me here.

Very positive conversation with Rosie. She was quite sympathetic to our plight—think she considers the Charlies mix-up to be her fault, which it might be, to be honest. She is lovely but absolutely radiates benevolent incompetence, and I have no other workable theories for how the hell this has happened, aside from Jones being some sort of scheming liar, but if he is one, he does a very good job of pretending not to be.

Anyway, we're getting a door put on the walk-in wardrobe.

"A door," Jones said, when we reconvened at the farm shop later.

The plan was for us to give the place a deep clean after closing. I'd turned up in dungarees and rubber gloves; felt irrationally irritated to find him in the same clothes he'd been in for the staff meeting earlier. Jeans, plaid shirt. Just made me feel like he wasn't taking any of this stuff seriously.

He stared at me across the shop floor with those shadowy gray-blue eyes. This man does not mind a bit of eye contact.

"And as soon as there's a spare room at the B&B, one of us will get first dibs," I continued, setting to work on the shop windowsills. Outside the darkening sky was flecked with silver drizzle. "Do you want to scrub the front door?"

"I thought I'd fix up the roof first. Is anyone moving on from the B&B soon?"

"Well, no," I admitted. It was immensely satisfying to discover a lovely Cotswold green color under the grubbiness covering the paintwork. "Rosie said nobody plans to leave anytime soon. But she said it's all very casual, and people do come and go a bit . . ."

"Right. Great. So for now, we're getting a door."

"Look, I don't want to share with you, either. I'm trying to be positive."

"Yes," Jones said, and there was that tone again. "I can tell."

He headed out of the shop door, leaving it open behind him. His tendency to walk out midconversation was also extremely irritating.

"Are we done, then, or . . ."

"No?" he said, from outside. "I'm just getting the ladder."

I scrubbed harder and raised my voice so he could still hear me. "You know, if the living situation bothers you and you want to leave, you're really welcome to."

"Am I?" he drawled. "Thanks."

Heard him clanking around outside with the ladder. I peered out of the window I was cleaning. He was carrying a fresh sheet of corrugated iron. Where the hell did he get that from? And when? He's barely left my sight for the last three days.

"If the walk-in wardrobe doesn't suit you, I mean," I pushed, "you don't have to stay."

He paused at the window, looking in at me through the rain-stained glass.

"Who says I'm getting the wardrobe? Why do you get the bedroom?"

This was just how we'd done things so far. When he'd turned up at ten p.m. I'd already set up in the bedroom, and we'd made him a bed from sofa cushions in the wardrobe, then he'd stayed there again on nights two and three . . .

"I'd like the bedroom," he said. "We should flip for it."

Met his steady eyes through the glass. He has crow's-feet that suggest he liked to laugh once, though I've barely seen him crack a smile since we got here.

We <u>could</u> flip for the bedroom. But then, I thought, I might lose. There had to be a better way.

"Here we are again, with the risk avoidance, hmm," he said, moving away again. "Would you rather alternate?"

I mulled it over.

"Each of us gets one week in the bedroom, one week in the wardrobe, on and off," he continued. "We could make the wardrobe more habitable, I imagine. A single bed, take out the shelving to create more floor space . . ."

He was up the ladder now. I heard a soft grunt as he shifted the corrugated iron. After a moment, I leaned forward to get a look through the window, my cheek almost pressed to the glass.

"Are you wearing a tool belt?" I asked, slightly shocked.

"Uh-huh."

"Where and when did you get that?"

"It's Rog's."

"Right, but . . ." I trailed off. It was good that he was fixing the roof. I do not know how to fix a roof. But as annoying as it had been when he'd rocked up seemingly unprepared for a deep clean, it was actually more annoying that he was now doing something extremely useful involving tools and . . . <u>skills</u>.

Skills I very much do not have.

Also, the jeans and plaid shirt were <u>so</u> much hotter with the tool belt addition.

"I'm open to alternating," I said in a raised voice, trying to get back on topic as he banged around on the roof above me. "We could add some plants, some soft lighting . . . It could work in the short term."

"Good. We're getting somewhere."

He climbed down the ladder again and wandered off, presumably to pick up some more accessories from whatever Mary Poppins bag he was getting all this shit from. By the time he returned—with a box of nails, of course—I'd done the front two windows and the barn door.

"Nice work," he said, raising his eyebrows slightly as he stepped into the shop again. He lifted his gaze from the doorframe to me. Bam, eye contact.

Felt flustered. Everything Jones says and does is kind of <u>intense</u>, I think that's what I've been trying to put my finger on. And with him around <u>all</u> the time, it gets a bit stressful. Even the way he talks has an intensity to it—his voice is low and soft, like someone who might read you a bedtime audiobook. The sort of voice that makes you do a lovely little shiver.

We kept working for the next hour or two, mopping the floor three times over and clearing the rubbish around the barn. We didn't talk much, but I always knew exactly where he was. We'd had our first argument, reached our first agreement, and now we were officially working together. There was an air of "keep your friends close, keep your enemies closer" about the whole thing.

As the sky turned navy outside the windows, I thought about what I wanted from my life here: this unique place, this supportive community, this prepackaged fresh start, as Jones called it. I didn't have to lose any of it because of this man. He didn't <u>have</u> to be the enemy.

Turned to look at him after a good twenty minutes of mopping in total silence. "Shall we just go to the pub for a drink?"

He stared at me, full bin bag in one hand, brush in the other. Realization dawned.

"Oh, God, sorry, not the pub," I said, cheeks going hot. "Sorry!"

"You can say 'pub' in front of me," Jones said, with slight amusement. "I'm not operating under the illusion that pubs don't exist."

"No, but . . . Sorry. Why don't we go for a walk or something?"

"You want to go for a walk with me?" He held my gaze, his own unreadable.

"I want to have a conversation with you where we're not all . . . snippy. I want to chat."

"Chat."

"Yes! Like you did with Rosie and Marly. Why not? We need to work together now, don't we? Shouldn't we try to get along?"

At last, he looked away from me. Felt my shoulders drop slightly, as though he'd physically let me go.

"I'm not here to make friends," he said, hefting the bin bag over his shoulder.

"Oh, I'm sorry, are we on The Bachelor?" I pretended to peer out at the empty fields.

"It's nothing personal. But I don't want to chat. Or walk. Or pub. I just want to keep myself to myself."

"But . . . we're managing the farm shop together. We live together. We don't even have a door between our bedrooms, currently," I said, baffled. "I'm really not sure how you're going to do that."

"Me neither," he said, slipping a hammer into his tool belt and heading back inside. "But for now, I think we should just try to pretend we each have the stables and the shop to ourselves."

So . . . that's what we did. We kept cleaning—separately—until it got too dark to work, and then I announced I was going home, and he headed back, too, walking along the track behind me. We weren't close enough to be walking together, but we definitely weren't far enough apart to be not together, either. And neither of us said a word.

Every time I glanced over my shoulder, he'd look away, fixing his gaze on the skyline. I tried to do the same, and act like there wasn't a bigger, maler, grumpier Charlie Jones on my tail, but even when I picked up the pace to drop him, he kept sneaking into my brain anyway. I'd alternate between rageful made-up conversations with him ("If you think freezing me out will make me go back to the mainland, you've got another think coming, mister!") and accidentally dwelling on the sight of him with the tool belt strapped around his hips. Isn't it annoying when someone is hotter than they deserve to be?

There was a moment when we got back to the stables, though—hardly avoidable, really, unless I'd slammed the door in his face on my way in. He murmured a low "thank you" as he moved on through to get himself a glass of water. First time he'd spoken to me in hours.

I stayed in the entrance as he braced himself at the kitchen sink, knocking back a whole glassful, back muscles bunched beneath that plaid shirt. He met my eyes as he turned to place the glass above the dishwasher. Clink.

He swiped the pad of his thumb across his bottom lip, and a tiny shiver moved through me.

Jones takes up more space than he has a right to. More air, more attention, more of everything. When he's a few steps away, it feels like he's closer, and when he's close, he might as well be in my head. This island is tiny and this house is tiny and he seems to fill every corner of it.

Anyway, now I'm writing in the kitchen while he's in the walk-in wardrobe. Am trying to act as though I'm here on my own, like he said. But I can hear him moving around. Can hear the low swish of him pulling his jumper off over his head, the slight sigh as he settles back on the bed, the quiet tap of his keys on his laptop keyboard.

How the hell am I meant to pretend this man isn't here when it feels like he's bloody everywhere?

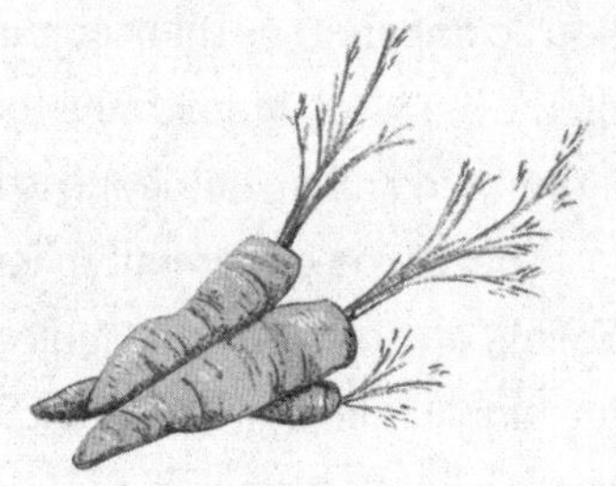

FROM: **Charlie Jones**
TO: **Charlie Jones**
SUBJECT: **Day seven sober**

We now have a door on the walk-in wardrobe. It's astonishing how little difference it makes to my awareness of Charlie's presence on the other side of it.

Anyway, this isn't what I sat down to write about. Tonight, we met the committee. Local producers with a mandate to "help steer and inform" the running of the Bramblebay Farm Shop. And, I discovered later, *also* the running of the post office, the ferry service and the island itself. If there is a committee, these twenty people are on it. In fact, they even make up Ormer's government. All democratically elected, but since there are twenty-two roles and only twenty people stood for election, I'm not sure how relevant that is.

I'll try to paint a picture of the meeting.

"My chocolate boxes need to be at the till," was how Karyn introduced herself to me.

"Oh, hi, you're the chocolatier?" Charlie said. "I tried your truffles, they're incredible!"

Karyn ignored her. "And don't think we don't know that Toby's mum's bread gets front-of-store placement because her son works at the shop. It's favoritism. Nepotism."

"Fascism, I'd go so far as to say," Doc Laurry said solemnly, with an almost imperceptible twinkle in his eye. The island GP, he was there because the rare and obscure herbs he grows in the cottage garden outside Ormer's medical center are sold at the shop, but also, I suspect, because he enjoys the entertainment.

He'd brought biscuits—shortbreads studded with homegrown lilac blossom and basil. I expected people to give them a wide berth, as the flavor was a bit experimental, but it seemed the committee was familiar with Doc Laurry's baking. They were all gone before I had a chance to try one.

Everyone was also drinking Gamede cider, pressed and bottled at the pub from Bramblebay apples. This was more troubling than the lack of biscuits. I don't even like cider, but the condensation beading on the bottles was enough to make my mouth water. That wolfish voice said, *Come on, it's basically juice, and you're so tense—you'll be much more relaxed for this meeting if you just have a drink.*

It's surprised me how hard this week has been. I didn't expect to want a drink *this* much, or maybe I'd not expected the desire to be quite so . . . devious. The voice sounds just like my rational voice, and always has such good reasons why one drink would be fine. I thought after seven days sober I'd feel more confident that I can do this, but I'd say I actually just feel humbled, and a little scared.

Charlie shot the doctor an amused look before returning her attention to the rest of the committee. We'd cleared a space in the middle of the shop, piling the vegetable crates around us to create enough room for a central trestle table and a chair for everyone, though of course we'd miscounted, which had caused some drama eventually resulting in Charlie and me roaming around chairless between the cabbages and leeks, trying to give the impression we were running the meeting while Galoshes used a parsnip as an impromptu gavel.

Charlie raised her voice over a dispute about the ratio of milk bottles to homemade pies in the fridges, trying to gather everyone's attention. She suggested going around and introducing ourselves.

"We all know each other," Galoshes said. "And we know who you two are, too. Now, on to the bike parking. We need more of it. Lots more of it."

"Hear hear," said a man who I suspect runs the island bike rental shop.

"But *we* don't know who *you* are," Charlie said, a little louder.

"You'll figure it out," Galoshes said. "There aren't many people on this island. I think we can all agree we should drop the mustard from the condiments."

"Just because Bill's not here—" someone began, but Charlie was talking again.

"I have an agenda," she said. "I'd really appreciate if we could stick to it. And I'd like you each to introduce yourselves."

"No offense," Galoshes began. She struck me as a "no offense" type of woman. A "someone has to say it" sort of woman. "But we do things the Ormer way at these meetings and we're not about to change that just because you're here for a bit."

"Here for a bit?" Charlie said.

She looked at me. I shrugged. I'd vote for letting this play out. It would be interesting to know how these meetings usually operated anyway, and, if I'm totally honest, concentrating on not wanting a cider was taking quite a lot of my bandwidth. Charlie rolled her eyes at me, and I felt a twinge of guilt for not chipping in, but my fresh start is meant to be about focusing on me. I'm not here to help Charlie out.

In the end, it was Doc Laurry who stepped in.

"Let's show the Charlies an Ormer welcome, now," he said, with warm but unmistakable authority.

"What, get 'em to walk behind Baptiste's horse when he's let her have apples?" someone said, to a chorus of titters.

"Not *that* kind of Ormer welcome. Let's all introduce ourselves and remember that the island needs new blood, and the Nicoles need help. Rosie's parents asked me to look out for that girl and look out for her I shall. So, hello. I'm Doc Laurry. Island GP, Deputy for Health and Emergency Services, herbalist, experimental baker."

He looked pointedly at the woman beside him, who was short, apple-cheeked and wearing a large suede cowboy hat.

"Kim," she said gruffly. "Sheep farmer over on Patchwork Farm, Little Ormer, over the ridge. Deputy for Education, Environment, Agriculture and Sea Fisheries. I supply sheep's cheese, at the moment, and the wool for Galoshes's knitwear."

Karyn the chocolatier came next, with a nervous glance at Galoshes. Then Gintaras the basket-weaver introduced himself, then Jerry the milkman—the island's sole constable, and Deputy for Law Enforcement—and then *another* Karen, this one possibly more hostile than the first, and around it went, every government role more impressive sounding than the last. I belatedly realized I should really have written these down.

Charlie began handing out agendas as the last few committee members introduced themselves. Galoshes wouldn't even take hers. Charlie blinked down at her in astonishment, and then eventually placed the sheet of paper very deliberately beside Galoshes's parsnip gavel.

"Ooh, deliveries to islanders!" someone said, reading from the agenda. "I like that idea."

"That's ridiculous," Galoshes snapped. "Rog is run off his feet as it is, delivering the imported stuff."

Charlie suggested that someone other than Rog could do our deliveries. The room fell silent. Everyone regarded Charlie with horror. Galoshes slowly removed her pink-framed glasses and placed them on top of Charlie's agenda.

"Look. Don't take this the wrong way, but you're still an outsider here—you don't know how things work. Trust is earned on Ormer. We don't just hand it out to strangers, *particularly* ones who don't *necessarily* deserve to be here."

A glance was exchanged with Karyn. (Or maybe Karen.) Then they all looked at me.

"Sorry?" I said, feeling I might have missed something.

"We're on your side," Galoshes said, at a volume that might possibly have been intended as a whisper, if I was being really generous.

Charlie was turning red. I tried very hard not to feel sorry for her, I really did. Walls up, don't look directly at her, think about something else.

Deciding not to care about other people is not as easy as I thought it would be.

"It isn't a competition. We're hoping to get the shop to a point where both of us will be able to stay on," I said.

"Only one of you deserves the job, though, really. Rosie only meant to offer it to one person," Galoshes said.

"What makes you so sure that person was Jones, and not me?" Charlie said, in her cheeriest tone. She was breathing a bit too fast; the papers in her hands were trembling.

"Well." Galoshes pursed her lips. "Only one of you turned up looking like you'd been through the wringer, with half a bush in your hair. Not very professional, was it?"

I winced. "Hang on, Galoshes, that's—"

"How do you know about that?" Charlie interrupted, now beet red.

Galoshes looked at her with genuine pity. "You've never lived somewhere like this before, have you?"

Thankfully, at this point, before Galoshes could make Charlie cry, a pig walked in.

"Oh my God," Charlie said. "Is that a pig?"

Everyone looked quite interested. They peered over their glasses, shifted their chairs to get a good vantage point, made remarks like "Oh, it's one of Baptiste's, I think!" Only Charlie and I seemed to find this situation shocking—even the pig was pretty nonchalant about it.

It was . . . big. We had a dog growing up, a German shepherd. A big dog. This pig was bigger, and a dirty off-pink color with brown spots; it had wiry hair all over its body and looked like a barrel of pure muscle.

This was an absolute bruiser of a pig.

"I'm not sure it *is* one of Baptiste's, you know," observed the woman who supplied mushrooms. "I'd say that's one of Rosie's new ones."

Everyone agreed that a fence must be down at Pipit Spinney, whatever that meant. Having surveyed us all for a few moments, the pig was heading for the hessian potato sacks pushed to the edge of the shop to make room for the committee meet-up. It snuffled and grunted, its trotters click-clacking on the flagstones.

To my shame, Charlie moved fastest.

"Hey!" she said, waving her hands at the pig. "Not that way!"

The pig must have weighed a good three times as much as Charlie. She looked tiny in the face of it, despite her height. I started to feel a bit uneasy. Pigs can be dangerous, can't they?

"This way," I tried. "Come this way, pig."

I was not in the headspace for this.

"Here, pig! Here, pig!"

Some of the committee members were openly laughing at us now. The pig was ignoring us and snuffling at a sack of potatoes. I felt a rising tide of panic. Rosie and Marly were not going to trust us with their shop if a roaming pig ate all their stock, were they? And Charlie was getting so close to it. I didn't like it.

She was typing away on her phone. I wanted to tell her to either move away or at least *look* at the massive animal she was trying to coax out of a tight corner, but instead settled for asking her what she was doing.

"Googling," she said.

The committee members were now roaring with laughter.

"We need to stay calm and quiet," Charlie read, and then shot the committee a surprisingly venomous look. The pig had obviously flustered some of the pretense out of her.

"Then we need to— Hey! No!"

She hauled up a sack of potatoes and dragged it away from the pig, who just followed the bag—and Charlie. It was starting to huff, and its feet were getting skittery on the flagstones.

"You're stressing it out," called Gintaras the basket-weaver. "That's not good for pigs."

"*It's* stressing *me* out!" Charlie said. "Comanager, would you like to comanage this situation with me, perhaps?"

I asked Charlie what Google said, grabbing some vulnerable cabbages from a crate and shifting them to a higher shelf. I also suggested she might want to step back a bit more, which she ignored.

"I'm on the Pork Information Gateway," she said, glancing back and forth between her phone and the pig currently following her around the farm shop as she walked backward, now dragging the potato sack. "It says we need witch's capes. Or . . . sorting boards. What are these things?"

"You've not got 'em," said Kim the sheep farmer. "Which is all that matters right now, I reckon."

The farm shop was starting to feel very small, with the pig advancing on Charlie, the vegetables, and the gaggle of motley local producers. I was sweating and unfocused. I want to believe this was because of the stressful pig situation, but honestly, I was still feeling rough. I was a lot better than I had been at the start of the week, but with all those bottles of cider sitting open on the table . . .

"Maybe just . . . lure it back to the field that way?" I said to Charlie. "But from further away? Maybe? Step back a bit?"

"You want me to walk backward with a bag of potatoes and a pig coming at me, all the way to a random field?" Charlie said, wide-eyed, and then, before I could answer, "That's quite a good idea."

The pig began to toss its head, losing its focus on the sack of potatoes and careening into a tower of crates. Apples cascaded everywhere. The pig really didn't like that. The mood shifted; even the committee members started to look a little perturbed.

I offered to take the potato sack and switch places with Charlie, but she insisted—quite irritably, I thought—that she could handle it.

And then the pig ran at her.

I moved before I was even aware I was moving. It wasn't smooth or heroic—I stumbled over chairs, tripped between legs and root vegetables. But I got to her just in time and threw her flat against the barn wall.

I wrapped myself around her, putting my back to the pig, bracing myself for impact. Charlie shrieked. She was trembling in my arms, her thick, dark hair in my face, her elbow rammed into my stomach.

But impact never came. I was not impaled from behind by a stressed pig. I was just pressing a beautiful woman against a wall, my arm braced above her head, for no reason at all.

This is weird to write about. But I said I'd write about everything. And this was definitely something.

Charlie looked up at me, breathless, her hair a mess, and her expression wasn't a carefully contrived smile or a bright blank look, it was bare and open. Her eyes said, *I can't believe you helped me.*

Or something like that. I don't know. But there was a complexity of emotion beneath the panic in her expression that I related to so deeply, I felt it somewhere in my gut. I looked into her eyes and saw someone who knew that bad things happen and had gone a very long time without anybody standing in her corner.

Charlie looks beautiful when she's faking a smile, but she looks even more beautiful when she's not faking anything. And she was pressed against me, each breath of hers moving me, too—that's how close we were. Body to body, hot skin beneath rumpled clothes.

Up until this point, I'd ignored the fact of Charlie's body altogether. Even when she was wandering through the kitchen in a towel or painting her toenails bare-legged on the sofa. Even when she was getting changed into her pajamas on the other side of a door and I could hear the slow swish of silk moving over her skin.

Or, OK, I'd *mostly* ignored it.

But with the adrenaline, and her hot breath on my collarbone, and the bare, almost curious look on her face, that suddenly became completely impossible.

Anyway, someone shouted *bravo* around about then, and everyone started clapping, which snapped me right out of it. I turned to look over my shoulder. The pig, inexplicably, was gone.

"Went out that way," Kim said, pointing helpfully to the only door.

Charlie shifted a little underneath me and I pulled back instantly, embarrassed that I hadn't moved sooner. She was still breathing heavily, and her pupils were dilated. She touched the back of her head—I had done my best to soften the blow, but it had definitely hit the wall as I had shoved her out of harm's way.

She asked me if I was OK.

"Me? What? I'm fine. Are *you* OK?"

She lifted a hand to my forehead and frowned. "You're hot."

I stepped back. "I'm fine."

It came out too gruffly. She started a bit, like I'd jolted her. Someone—Karyn, maybe—said I was a hero, and everyone agreed, and lots of people patted me on the back. I watched as Charlie rearranged her expression into a perfectly calm smile.

"So sorry for the disturbance to our first committee night—but at least we made it memorable!" Charlie said to everyone. "I think we'd better call it a night. I'll shoot over to the farmhouse and let Marly and Rosie know about the roaming pig, and Jones the local hero will head off in pursuit of it, see if he can make sure the poor thing doesn't get lost."

I snorted with laughter, though I couldn't tell quite how barbed the *local hero* comment was—was she teasing, or pissed off?

"Feel free to help yourself to more ciders if you want to stay awhile and keep chatting. They're on the—"

"Shelf over there," I said, before she could say *on the house*. "You all know where the till is."

Our eyes met. Her lips curved in a slow smile, and I had a feeling that was a real one. A thank-you for being on her team. Teasing, then.

I need to be careful. It'll help if she keeps the act up—the fake smiles, the cheeriness. I've never gone for fakery. I just need to forget the emotion I saw in her eyes as I pressed her to the wall. I need to forget the brief grin on her face when she said *That's quite a good idea*, like deep down she's a woman who thrives under pressure. Like there's a lot more to her than it seems.

I can just about handle a beautiful woman intruding on my new life. But a beautiful, *interesting* woman would be very, very bad news.

CJ

London, eleven months earlier

Jones was uncomfortable, which meant he was at the bar. Stuart had gone home, despite it being *his* birthday party—work emergency—but had urged Jones to stay and "mingle," and, with no excuse to leave, he felt obliged to do as he was told. Without a glass in his hand, he kept finding himself running his thumb across the bare skin at the base of his ring finger. Each time he felt the absence of his wedding band, something seemed to trip in his chest.

"Oh my God, am I invisible?" said the woman beside him.

He looked at her. Her hair was an extraordinary shade of luminous ginger; she was wearing the scrubs the characters on actual *Scrubs* wore, pale blue and ill fitting. She looked vaguely familiar, but he couldn't quite place her—perhaps he'd met her at one of Stuart's things before. Either way, she definitely was not invisible.

"I've been here for twenty minutes. Five eighteen-year-olds in crop tops have come and gone with their drinks. Is this the universe giving official notice that I'm past it?" she asked.

She wasn't actually looking at Jones, and he wasn't sure if he was supposed to respond. Surely the answer was obvious, anyway—she didn't look much older than thirty.

"Hey, what can I get you?" one of the bartenders asked Jones.

"Please don't do this to me," the woman said to the bartender, who looked understandably confused.

"I think she was first," Jones said, tilting his head her way.

For the first time, she turned her gaze on him. His stomach bottomed out. She was the classy, grown-up sort of beautiful that belonged in teacher-student fantasies. Arched brows, quick eyes, a long, elegant neck.

It was the strangest feeling to look at her and *notice*. He had been a married man for so long. It was just habit now to *not* notice a beautiful woman, or rather to notice in the way one might notice an interestingly shaped cloud or a trailer for a new program on one of the few remaining streaming services you'd not caved and signed up for. *Huh, that's nice*, was his default reaction to a woman like this.

But he was single now. Wasn't that why he was at this party? Single, alone, and—according to his friends—far too mopey about it. He was supposed to put himself out there. That was the *idea*.

"Or I could buy your drink," Jones said, inadvertently cutting across whatever she was beginning to say. "Sorry. Go on."

She tilted her head to the side, smiling slowly. "He's a gentleman *and* he apologizes." She turned to the bartender. "Please can I have a large glass of house white and whatever this polite, observant man would like?"

"Oh, no," Jones said, slightly horrified. He was pretty hazy on how dating went these days, but he was definitely meant to buy *her* a drink. "I should pay."

"Don't disappoint me now," the woman said. "Chivalry's dead, didn't you know?"

"I didn't," Jones said. "Do I still pull back your chair when we head over to a table?"

She looked surprised, and then faintly delighted. He was quite surprised himself. Who knew he still had a bit of flirtation left in him?

"You do not," the woman said. "Nor do you walk on the road side, open my car door or carry my bag up the stairs to your flat. You *do*, however, make the first move once we're inside."

She flashed him a grin that made him hot all over.

"I'm Aspen," she said. "And I don't like wasting my time. Do you want to take me home?"

She was the perfect rebound. Sexy, bold, hilarious—every day he spent with her left him faintly breathless.

She was a midwife, working with the community team, so was called out to home births at all hours of the day and night. This only added to the whirlwind of life with her—if she was on call, she might spend twenty-four hours stretched across his bed like a lazy ginger cat, or she might answer her phone while he was still inside her, and hop off with a quick *Sorry!*, already reaching for her car keys. It was completely discombobulating. Jones loved it.

The relationship crept up on him, though. He felt instinctively that it was just a casual thing—he never took her out on dates or introduced her to his parents or close friends. They just spent their days and nights together sometimes, doing whatever they did, and having sex in between. It was only when he received a text from Aspen saying *Don't forget toilet roll!* that he wondered if this easy, companionable way of life was actually a committed relationship. When he thought about it, he did spend at least four or five nights a week with Aspen. They ran errands together, had toothbrushes at each other's flats, ate together often—he was pretty much a vegetarian now, thanks to her influence. He knew a lot about her job; she knew all the various dramas at the bar where he worked, too.

He brought it up one night over takeaway ramen, once he'd had enough beer to make himself brave. They were chatting about Aspen's friend having a baby at her birthing center—she showed him a picture of the happy couple with their daughter, recounting the numerous inconvenient places the father had fainted during the labor.

"I can't imagine being a dad right now," Jones said. "I'd probably faint, too. Listen, can I ask you something?"

"Of course." She put down her phone.

"Am I your boyfriend?" he said, a little more abruptly than he'd intended.

Aspen looked up at him through her eyelashes. "Do you like the idea of me sleeping with other guys?"

"No," he said, quite honestly.

"Do you want to sleep with other women?"

"Where would I get the energy from?"

She grinned. "Then it looks like you're in a relationship with me, yes." She twisted her noodles around her fork. "How does that make you feel?"

There was a slight tension to the question. She knew, of course, about his ex-wife, and though he had shared hardly any details, he suspected Aspen was also aware of how quite utterly the breakup had overturned his life. It was hard to spend any time with Jones and *not* notice this. He had *formerly married* written all over him, from the clothes he wore to the tragically small collection of plates in his bachelor pad's cupboards.

"Good," he said, after some thought.

She laughed. "Your straightforwardness is extremely sexy, do you know that?"

"I've definitely not been told that before," he said, and then winced at himself—it was a thoughtless reference to his ex. Why did he *do* that? He knew Aspen didn't like it, and he wouldn't, either, in her shoes.

Her smile did drop a little. "I really appreciate it," she said, after a moment. "The straightforwardness." She glanced at her phone, which had flashed up with a new message. Not work, though, not someone going into labor—she put it back down again, but her expression remained distracted.

"All OK?" Jones asked.

"Yes! Yes, sorry—you have my undivided attention," she said, refocusing on him.

He felt it, too—Aspen could really bathe you in her spotlight when she wanted to, one of those people who made you feel like you *mattered*. But the beam faltered, and her eyes weren't quite as warm as usual.

"Sorry," she said, picking the phone up again. "It's my sister. The baby's still so little, and she's having a bit of a hard time, do you mind if I . . ."

"Of course," he said.

She squeezed his shoulder and let her hand linger there as she moved away from the table. The contact made his skin tingle. He'd gotten so lucky with her—she was caring and thoughtful as well as fun and sexy. "What genie lamp did you rub to land that one?" his mate from the bar had asked the week before, and he'd laughed, but she *did* seem almost too good to be true.

A month or so later, Jones noticed to his surprise that life with Aspen was still rolling along very smoothly. In fact, he was feeling quite—dare he say it—*happy*.

He was meeting Aspen at an auction event for a perinatal mental health charity she was involved with, hosted at a community space down the road from the hospital. He was late—held up at the bar, some drunk arsehole had smashed up a toilet tank—and walked into the event expecting to find it packed with minglers. But it was sparse, and too bright; lots of polished pine on show and zero ambience. His eyes found Aspen within seconds in the thin crowd, her red hair glowing, her elegant neck holding a rather stubbornly raised chin.

He headed to the bar for a beer before going over to her—she was talking to someone gray haired and important-looking anyway. As he waited for his drink, there it was: a quiet bumblebee hum of contentment in his belly. Strange. It hadn't even been a particularly good day. Why was he feeling so cheerful?

"Hey," he said to Aspen, when she'd made her polite excuses and he could steal her away for a kiss. "This is great."

"Don't lie," she said, with spirit. "It's shit."

He barked a laugh. "It's not shit. It's just too big a space and the lighting's not right."

"No amount of ambient lighting is going to make anyone give a crap about women's healthcare," Aspen said, knocking back her drink and stalking toward the bar. "Nobody *cares.* Women are half of people! More than half! I was just chatting to someone whose research is on endometriosis and it was so depressing—she's going to have to change tack because she just can't get funding."

Jones gestured to the bartender to get Aspen another drink, wondering whether he should confess that he didn't know what endometriosis was. He rarely engaged with this sort of charitable thing, not because he didn't care, but because he found it near-excruciating to expose himself to the raw inadequacy of humanity when he could do so little about it. He'd flail, make huge donations he couldn't afford, feel uselessly miserable. As it was, he was already planning to bid much more than he should on a cruise holiday this evening, having read a traumatic birth story pinned up by the bar. Why was the world so bitterly cruel?

"I'm sorry," he said instead. "I'd be furious all the time if I was a woman."

Aspen looked at him in surprise, and then laughed.

"I kind of am, actually," she said, looping her arm through his.

"Are you?" he said, grabbing their drinks with a thank-you to the bartender. "You're always so positive."

"I suppose I just repress it. Don't worry, society taught me how from a very young age."

"Oh, good?"

She laughed again as they made their way beneath a sign that read *If it takes a village . . . why do we expect women to do so much of it alone?*

It had taken Jones a while to get used to how little looking after Aspen required. He was a nurturer at heart—or had been told so—and was actually slightly thrown at how often Aspen just got on and sorted things herself, whether it was managing her leaking fridge or her family dramas. Walking in here, seeing the empty hall and that set to her jaw, he'd thought, *She needs me.* He'd gotten himself a cold beer and headed over in full confidence he could turn this evening around for her, already tasting what that would feel like. But she seemed to have lifted her own spirits.

"You're something special, you know that?" he told her, pressing a kiss to the fiery crown of her head, but the happy hum in his belly was quieter now, and he couldn't help wishing that he'd had the chance to *do* something for her. He'd liked feeling purposeful for a minute. Much of the time, honestly, he wondered why Aspen bothered keeping him around.

Jones was not the sort of person who wanted to explore his own psyche; he wasn't at all comfortable with spiritual thinking, or philosophical questions like *Who am I?* and *What am I feeling?* He felt a little afraid of such things, actually—deep down he suspected that if he began to dig, he might uncover more than he'd bargained for. Hardly surprising, then, that what he thought he wanted from Aspen wasn't what he needed at all.

When her father died, quite suddenly, she went from needing him very little to needing him an awful lot. They had been together for four months and were still spending most nights together—Jones's flat was closer to the birthing center, so it often made sense for Aspen to crash there. Jones had, by this point, got to know Aspen's argumentative, tight-knit family, but her father, Alisdair, lived in America, so they'd never met.

Her mother came to her flat to impart the news in person; Bridget was already racked with sobs when Aspen answered the door, despite the fact that she had divorced Aspen's father almost two decades ago and had described him at the last family dinner as "too up his own arse to find his feet," a phrase that Jones had puzzled over for much of dessert. Alisdair's primary crime, it seemed, was earning no money while married to Bridget, and then earning a lot once he left her. He was an artist, "discovered" by a music producer in the late 2010s and propelled from pennilessness into the LA creative scene.

"What a loss!" Bridget was wailing, doubled over on the sofa, the sleeves of her fluorescent pink dress draping to the carpet. "Oh, what a great loss!"

"Mum, please, I can't . . ." Aspen paced back and forth, white with shock.

"We've lost such a great man!" Bridget cried. "How will I cope?"

Jones watched Aspen's shoulders stiffen. There was a look on her face he'd only ever glimpsed before—not sadness, he'd seen her saddened plenty of times, but something sharper and rawer. She caught him looking at her across the living room and her expression shifted; she began to cry. He went to her and held her. But he thought of that initial expression again, later. He had a sense, sometimes, that Aspen wore a mask with him—with everyone, perhaps. He didn't know what to make of that except that it was disconcerting.

Alisdair had died of a heart attack, brought on by "hard living," Bridget said, from which Jones had inferred that the LA creative scene had had something to do with it. Aspen seemed to have had no sense of her dad living "hard" at all; to her, he was the sweet, artistic father who had steered her through a childhood with the exhausting Bridget, and could do no wrong, despite walking out on them. "He waited until I was at university," she'd said to Jones when the divorce had come up. "He always thought of us first."

Aspen coached her mother through the early throes of grief, despite her own devastation. Jones had noticed that Aspen's mother seemed to lean on her more than he thought normal, though he had a stilted, stereotypically British relationship with his own parents, so this whole situation was quite odd to him. His mother would *never* have shown up on his doorstep in tears, not even if his dad had died.

Jones found those days after Alisdair's death hard—he didn't know quite how to behave. Things still felt so new with Aspen; *I'll see how it goes*, he'd say to himself whenever he thought about a future for them, but this all seemed so serious, and suddenly he was The Boyfriend, the person who would need to hold her up while she held up her mother. And he *wanted* to be—of course he wanted to help her. But he was ashamed to find himself missing those easy, sexy, early days. He thought he'd wanted Aspen to need him, to lean on him, but now that she *was* relying on him, he found himself feeling a little . . . panicked.

She was behaving differently, too. She was snappy, and much less predictable; sometimes she'd suddenly jump down his throat about something, then the next moment she'd be in his arms again, telling him she loved him. Jones had the sense that life was speeding ahead no matter how often he jabbed at the "stop" button. He was stressed at work—the bar was performing badly, its owners getting antsy and talking of closing—and his flat seemed to have become an entirely shared space. He'd hardly noticed it when Aspen had been cool and self-sufficient, but now he saw that they were pretty much living together. This was definitely not the moment to discuss that, though, so he held her every night and nodded as she'd say *Thank God I've got you* or *I'm so glad we met*, ignoring the uneasy sensation worming through him.

She was so vulnerable now; she loved him, relied on him. Jones couldn't walk away from someone who needed him—it had been agony the first time, and he felt sure that doing it again would break him.

Friday August 15th 2025

The pig thing. If I could draw the facepalm emoji, I would.

Not ideal, was it? The committee sipping their drinks and watching me dash about. The shame of it all. How desperately I longed for them to like me, how incredibly <u>vital</u> that felt.

Ugh. Thought writing this down would help but it's giving me flashbacks. I'm having . . . the nasty feeling. The stifling sickening get-me-out-of-this-body feeling. If I could peel myself away and escape from my own brain I'd do it. I want to disappear.

I hate this. And I hate it more because I was never like this before, was I? Definitely got panicky occasionally, but it used to make me better—it pushed me to work harder, take extra precautions. Anything to avoid feeling this way.

But now when the feeling comes, it takes over. I'm not me, I'm just this. A twitching, whining, frightened animal running scared.

How am I ever going to be a mother when I'm such a child?

Monday August 18th 2025

Been a few days. I'm doing better.

It always passes, that's the thing to remember.

Hope Jones didn't notice me falling apart.

Just reflecting back on The Night of the Pig.

Went straight from the shop to Marly and Rosie's farmhouse to fill them in. It's one of those beautiful rambly houses, all nooks and extra bits, nothing quite matching. The higgledy slate roof is dotted with dormers and Velux windows. Rosie was just letting Ginger out of the ornate old wooden door as I reached the front garden.

"Hey, Charlie, are you OK?"

She stretched a concerned hand out to cup my cheek as Ginger greeted me, tail a blur. Rosie's a toucher, and I love it—I miss being touched. She seems wise beyond her years, or at least considerably wiser than me.

Told her about the pig, and she listened patiently, nodding along.

"OK. We can sort the pig," Rosie said calmly. "What else is wrong?"

"What? Oh, nothing else," I said, as the panic beat through me. "I'm fine!"

She tilted her head. Ginger sat down firmly on my foot, as if to say, "You're going nowhere."

"Really, I'm fine!"

"OK." She smiled. "Well, when you're ready to talk about whatever it is—about anything—I'm here. Just in case you needed to hear that."

Had to look down at Ginger because my eyes were suddenly full of tears. It's hard, isn't it, when someone is nice to you in a moment when it would be totally impossible to be nice to yourself?

"Why don't you come in?" Rosie said after a moment. "Here, Ginger—come, give the woman some space. I was just about to head out to get movie-night snacks for Red and a couple of the other B&Bers, but they can wait, if you want a cup of tea."

I hesitated as Ginger dashed back inside. Would love to get to know Rosie a little better. And the B&B looked so inviting behind her, with a cozy rug on the hall floor and a dark-blue Aga cast-iron stove just visible in the kitchen beyond. But when I have this want-to-disappear feeling, doing something like sitting trapped in someone's kitchen for the duration of a cup of tea, trying to act like I'm not absolutely steeped in fear and self-loathing, is kind of impossible. Particularly if the person is perceptive. I'm good at pretending to be fine, but Rosie has already proven herself to be dangerously skilled at reading me.

"I'd absolutely love to, but can we rain check?" I said. "I think I just need to get home and shower. I'm kind of . . . piggy."

"Well, if you're sure . . . Before you go, can I borrow your phone?" Rosie asked. "Marly's out, but she'll round up the pig if I can get hold of her. Mine's inside somewhere."

This was said with characteristically dreamy vagueness. Rosie does give the impression of being a person who misplaces things. Passed her mine, and she fumbled around with it for so long that I laughed.

"You want me to show you how to call someone? Wow, you've ended up in the real depths of my apps there, shall I . . ."

"Sorry! I'm useless."

"You're lovely," I told her, and she smiled at me.

"Please do come around for that tea sometime, Charlie."

Her expression was almost wistful. Assured her we'd have tea soon and headed back to the stables, trying to figure out whether that exchange had made me feel more or less miserable. Rosie and Marly are so inquisitive. I want a friendly island community, but ideally the kind of friendly that isn't especially interested in the life I had before I got here. Incurious friendly.

The sort of friendly that still allows me to keep my secrets.

Just came home after a slow shift at the farm shop and found Jones making coffee and a bacon sandwich. He didn't offer me one—not that I'd have said yes, but still. Our wary truce felt more fragile than ever. Since the pig event, I've been squirreling myself away in the small bedroom, barely meeting his eyes when we've crossed paths, and definitely haven't done my fair share of the cleaning and cooking. Have been telling myself I'm only doing what he wanted—he said keep to ourselves, didn't he?

"Have you managed to explore the island much yet?" he asked as he rifled through the cupboards for the ketchup. He looks good from behind. Something about the muscular shoulders and narrow waist combo. From the front you notice the scowl and the biceps, and maybe overlook the fact that his build's actually quite athletic.

"You've not been getting out and about much," he continued.

I stopped checking him out.

"I went for a run this morning," I said, irritated.

"That's where you went first thing?"

"Oh, so you did know I'd gone out."

"It's hard not to notice you. Here, I mean—with the two of us practically on top of each other."

My brain, immediately: remember what it felt like when Jones was looking down at you, arm braced above your head, hips against yours, pinning you to the wall?

. . . Because, yes, there may be a secondary reason I've been avoiding Jones. It's hard enough to act normal with another person when I'm having one of these phases, but add in the fact that said person has seen me swoon in their arms as they save me from a rampaging pig? It would be too much for anybody, no?

"You stuck to the main tracks on the island, right?" Jones asked, turning to face me. He seemed to have no issues looking at me post-pig incident. He was still doing his intense eye contact thing, trying to hook me in whenever I risked a glance his way. "As in, the paths where the horses and carts go?"

Implication being that I've only explored about as far as the visiting tourists. This rankled, maybe because it's true—I haven't ventured as far into the wildness of the island as I might have. Want to say it's because I'm so busy with the farm shop, which I am, but if I'm honest, it's also because I'm nervous of going further afield.

I do love it here. But all the things I love are also the parts that scare me a bit. The wildness, the lack of, you know, health-and-safety stuff. Take Windward Ridge, for example.

It's this absolutely stunning isthmus (just googled this word, what an absurd collection of consonants) that connects Little Ormer and Great Ormer, with a narrow path running all the way along the ridge. The land drops off on either side, falling away from you into two sandy beaches far below. Like a walkway through the sky. Stunning—genuinely breathtaking. And there's a set of steps cut into the rock, all the way from the top of the ridge down to the sea. It looks like an incredible place to swim—the water's almost turquoise where it touches the sand.

But the steps are literally just . . . steps. No handrail. No sign saying, maybe, watch your footing a bit because you're miles above the ground on a very steep downhill staircase. And it makes me feel nervous.

Which is very much not the attitude I was shooting for when I turned up here, determined to start life over. To find my brave again. To be the woman I want the mother of my future child to be.

"I'm planning to go hiking soon," I said. This was true, in the sense that right then I had just made this plan. My week is ridiculously busy, though, packed with cleaning, stocktaking and restructuring the shop layout—I panicked slightly. Really don't have time to start hiking. "Next Monday, maybe. When the shop's next closed."

"Great idea," Jones said, taking a bite of his sandwich. "Tackling Pook Rock, perhaps?"

I had no idea where that was. How did he suddenly know the island better than me? We've only been here for ten days.

Was alarmed to notice that even though Jones was irritating me, I was no longer able to use this to help me overlook his attractiveness. Even eating a bacon sandwich looked good on him. Found myself gazing at his forearms, his hands, his mouth. Has the barn-wall moment addled my brain?

"Absolutely," I said. "That's top of my list. How's your . . ." I couldn't think of the right word for it. "Recovery? Going?"

"I'm fine," he said. Bit short—embarrassed, maybe. "And you?"

"Yep! I'm fine, too."

"Great."

We clattered about the kitchen in silence.

"Good that we're both fine," Jones said.

"Yep."

He sighed. He looked as though he was deliberating.

"Are you OK?" he asked eventually, putting his sandwich down on the plate.

"I just said—"

"Charlie, I don't want to get involved in your life, at all, but your hands are shaking so much you're spilling water down your arm."

Put down the glass of water I just poured and knotted my hands behind my back. Didn't think he'd notice the shaking. It's just a stress thing that plays up when my sleep is bad.

"You seem a bit . . . anxious," he said. "Are you? Anxious? In general, I mean?"

"What? Like, do I have <u>anxiety</u>? Oh, no, I'm a bit highly strung, that's all. Probably haven't eaten enough."

Actually do find it super hard to eat when I'm in one of these phases—generally just exist on juice and tea for a while.

"You know, it's OK if you found that whole situation with the committee tough. They were kind of . . . arseholes to you."

The corner of his mouth lifted in a small, sympathetic smile. I could feel tears coming on again, and then I started to go red, because crying in front of this man would be intolerably humiliating, so my face decided to blush, because that was better, and then I just had to leave, because of all the stuff going on in the face department, and then said something like, "Oh, I'm fine, thanks, though, nothing I can't handle!"

Even though it would have been obvious to absolutely anybody, let alone my unsettlingly intuitive life-double, that I am not handling this well at all.

Fled to the bedroom. And now here I am, googling Pouque Rock (not Pook Rock, apparently), just to bloody spite him. Which is me all over, isn't it? What was it Brianna said when we first talked about the idea of me coming here? "Have you ever in your life done something because you wanted to, and not because you thought it would impress someone else?"

Wednesday August 20th 2025

Dramatic morning at the shop. Had a biscuit-related showdown. More soon.

Got there early this morning to finish repainting external window frames. Found Jones already doing it—had wondered where he'd headed off to so early, after scattering his coffee grounds across our kitchen counter. Could've had a lie-in if he'd told me he was doing the windows today. Swallowed back a grumpy comment to this effect when I spotted that Red was also here, sitting on the counter inside, eating a pot of chocolate ice cream.

"I paid for it!" she told me when I came in, hastily swallowing her mouthful. Her blue-streaked curls were scraped back, and she was fresh-faced and dewy, with a blob of chocolate ice cream melting on her nose. Of course Red had paid for her ice cream. She strikes me as the sort of person incapable of deviousness.

"You know you don't need to be here for another"—I checked the time on my phone—"two hours, right?"

"Rosie's getting a mural painted on the wall at the farmhouse," she said, wiping her nose. "Something that commemorates the Nicole family history. Toby's painting it."

"Oh, he's an artist?"

She nodded, eyes briefly lighting up. "He's really good."

"Wow, who knew! And you're therefore here avoiding Toby because . . ."

She froze, caught out. "No, I didn't mean that! I was just hungry. For ice cream."

As predicted, she was an abysmal liar. She wiped her hands on her board shorts.

"Let's get started! I can help you with stuff, since I'm here," she said. "My dad's a builder, I'm great at DIY if you want to redo the shelves like you said the other day?"

She might be bad at lying, but she was good at distracting me. Have used this trick a few times myself over the years, but nonetheless, it worked.

"Ooh, really? I want to rearrange that whole wall." I pointed. "Fewer shelves, and wider ones, so that we can really showcase the— What? You hate it?"

Red was pulling a face.

"Sorry! Sorry. I don't hate it, but Caloshes will," Red said, dropping her voice slightly. "She said the other day that she'll see stock reduced 'over her dead body.'"

"I did not know anyone could care so much about dried goods."

Red laughed, and then immediately looked repentant.

"Caloshes is kind of scary, isn't she?" Red said, dropping her voice even further.

"No," I said, even though I literally lay awake last night thinking exactly this. "All right, we'll leave the shelves for now—I want to create a little cake stand area by the till, start selling coffee and some of Doc Laurry's amazing biscuits."

"Absolutely not," came Caloshes's voice from behind me. "We are <u>not</u> a café."

Red's face froze as she stared at Caloshes over my shoulder. I turned slowly. Caloshes was dressed all in black, bar her pink glasses, and was wearing a truly formidable expression.

She <u>is</u> scary.

"Lots of farm shops double up as—"

"It's a no," Caloshes said. "And that's that."

"You can't actually decide that." Was trying to sound confident but was already starting to sweat.

"You think the committee will vote for what you want? Nothing happens on this island without my say-so, Miss Charlie Jones, and the sooner you learn that, the better."

She turned on her heel and walked out. Don't even know why she walked in. It was still almost two hours until anyone's shift started.

"I think she's probably right about that," Jones said through one of the barn windows.

Had almost forgotten he was here, still painting the woodwork outside. Could've piped up when it would actually have been useful, couldn't he? Felt hot and embarrassed. Wished he'd not seen all that.

"I didn't realize managing the shop was a spectator sport," I said to him.

He raised his eyebrows inquiringly.

"You could've helped instead of just watching me."

"Oh, because you would have loved me to barge in and manage that situation for you."

He was leaning his forearms on the window, infuriatingly nonchalant, a smear of paint on his neck.

Having a comanager was a lot less useful than I'd expected. He just distracted me, did the things I wanted to do before I did, or did things I didn't want done at all. I'd shown him my updated profit-and-loss calculations yesterday and he'd said, "Yeah, these match mine," though he'd not even told me he was going over the accounts. And it had taken me <u>ages</u>.

Folded my arms and looked at him through the window, taking a deep breath and reminding myself to play nice.

"I'll go tidy the space where you guys wanted to put those new picnic benches," Red said, scuttling toward the barn door as the tension thickened.

"You're right, actually," I said to Jones once she'd left. "I <u>do</u> prefer you just spectating. You can stay out there and keep your thoughts on how I manage Caloshes to yourself."

OK, so, not my <u>best</u> playing nice. But nobody else was around to see, so felt safe to let a little snark out.

"I didn't say anything about how you manage Caloshes."

Grabbed the broom and started sweeping the floor—just needed to <u>do</u> something, really. Jones stayed where he was, leaning on the windowsill.

"Not walking off midconversation this time?" I shot at him.

"I thought you told me to stay out here and spectate."

Glanced at him as I attacked the shop floor with my broom. There was amusement on his face now. He leaned his chin on one hand, waiting for a comeback I didn't have.

Fine, I thought. You want to watch? Then watch.

I leaned the broom against the potato sacks and shrugged out of my jumper. Underneath I was in a tight cami and low-rise jeans, the ones that cling to my hips. My skin prickled as I turned my back on him again. I wasn't cold. It was the brazenness of it, I think. Ostensibly there was nothing wrong with what I'd done—nothing indecent about what I was wearing, and it wasn't exactly seductive, was it, sweeping the floor?

But it didn't feel like that. It felt like I was saying, "I know you're watching me, waiting for me to put a foot wrong. So look at me, then. Look at me on my terms. Look at me the way I keep finding myself looking at you."

Jones said nothing, but he didn't move away, either. My skin seemed to fizz. Suddenly every move I made felt deliciously deliberate. I've played to the male gaze plenty of times in my life—sucked myself in, hitched myself up, been the beautiful thing a guy wants to see. This wasn't that. It was about where the power lay, I think, and my intention.

There's something in the way Jones looks at me. That intensity I've been trying to find a name for. It's as if he really sees me, instead of just looking—and he's calling bullshit every time he meets my eyes.

It's unnerving. It puts me on edge. But it's kind of thrilling, too.

So I was playing, I think, when I shrugged out of my jumper. This time I wasn't going to duck away or dodge his gaze, I was going to make it mine.

There was no sound but the sweeping of the broom. Heard him breathe in, just once, when I bent to shift a couple of crates. An unsteady two-part inhale that went right to the core of me. My heart thumped, but still I didn't give him my attention. I just held his.

He didn't move off until Red came back in, chattering about the plans for the picnic benches, and the spell seemed to break. She didn't react at all to the sight of me, which reminded me how ordinary it was to be sweeping the floor in old jeans and a strappy top.

Crazy, really, because for a moment there, I felt the sexiest I've felt in a very long time.

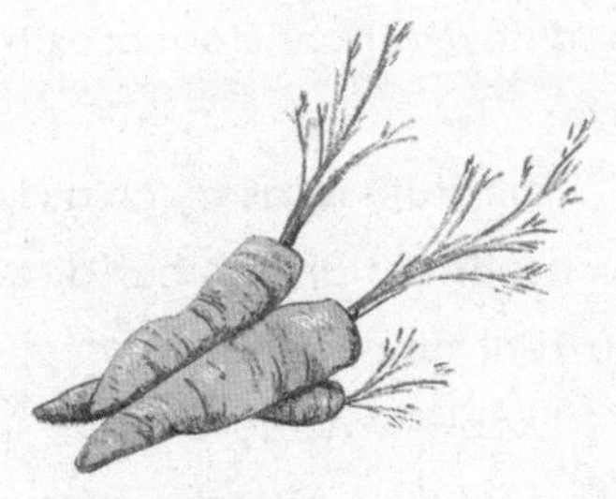

FROM: **Charlie Jones**
TO: **Charlie Jones**
SUBJECT: **Day thirteen sober**

I don't know if I'm strong enough to do this.

I'm inside the Isle of Ormer pub, the Pirate's Den. I've got a lime and soda and my laptop.

I underestimated how challenging this would be. It's the *sound*, that warm pub hubbub. And the smell . . . lager sourness, the hint of old woodsmoke . . . fuck, it's genuinely agonizing resisting the urge to buy a drink. When did I get this bad? How did it happen? I thought these emails were a weird idea to start with, but right now typing this out is pretty much the only reason I'm not at the bar.

The pub door just swung open. The fresh air was a relief. The breeze here smells different from the breeze on the mainland—a hint of the sea, maybe, a kind of sharp, bright cleanness. Writing stuff down all the time is changing how I see the world—I'm always looking for words for things these days.

I should leave. But where would I go? I came to the pub because I didn't want to be at the stables. Charlie's there, and we had this strange intense . . . moment, I guess, at the shop earlier, and now our constant proximity feels more unmanageable than ever.

The truth is, as much as I try to give her space, if she's there I just seem to drift in her direction, as though there's a constant current running her way.

I know way more than I should, too. I know she's been struggling lately. I'm pretty sure she had a panic attack the night of the pig. Yes, we have a door between our bedrooms now, but it's not a very good one. They're still essentially interconnecting rooms, and when somebody is struggling to breathe, you can definitely hear it. I'd stood by the door, hand raised to knock, for an embarrassingly long time.

She's made it so clear she doesn't want my help. I really understand that feeling. But . . . sometimes a person *does* need a bit of help, even if they don't want it.

Should I be doing more for her? Pushing harder, asking more questions? Was I right to walk out of there tonight and leave her on her own even when I knew she was having a hard time?

I guess I'm having difficulty figuring out where the line is between being a hermit and just being a dick, you know?

CJ

FROM: **Charlie Jones**
TO: **Charlie Jones**
SUBJECT: **Day thirteen sober (cont.)**

Home now. I didn't have a drink. I did have a slightly surprising evening, though.

Part of the reason I wanted this job so badly was the remoteness. The isolation. *Five hundred people*, I thought. That's hardly any. A farm on a place like that, it'll be beautiful—and there'll be no shortage of solitude.

But I got that bit wrong. It turns out I'm actually *never* alone here. Someone is always about, whether it's Rog in his cart, or Marly half-visible behind whatever she's carrying—a huge stack of crates, a tower of loaves and, once, an actual sheep—or one of the committee members advising me on how to do my job, expertise unknown.

Tonight, at the pub, it was Red, wearing a Pirate's Den T-shirt and carrying a tray of beers.

"You need to get out of this pub," she said cheerfully, distributing the drinks among the tourists at the next table.

I questioned this, obviously—was she kicking me out? Then her eyes flicked to the pub door, held open by a guy waiting for his friend. I followed Red's gaze just as Charlie turned her head away, too late to hide the fact she'd been looking at me through the door.

I got up and moved past Red. It was more of a relief than I'd like to admit when I stepped outside. Charlie was in running gear and jogging away down the Rue, her heels kicking up dust.

"So you've told everyone, then?" I called down the track.

She slowed, then swiveled to look at me.

"Excuse me?"

"That I'm an alcoholic."

I think that was the first time I've said that phrase out loud. It tasted wrong in my mouth. I wanted to take it back immediately.

She smoothed her ponytail, walking back to me. "Actually, I've told nobody, though you did tell Rosie and Marly, and this is the sort of place where news *really* travels, so I doubt it's still a secret."

"And what did you think getting me kicked out of the one pub on this island would achieve, exactly?"

Her cheeks were pink. "You think I got you kicked out of the pub? You think that's why I'm here?"

"What, it's a coincidence I spot you outside the pub just when Red tells me I have to leave?"

"Yes, I think on this tiny island with about five walkable roads it *is* a coincidence that you spotted me outside the pub."

"You were looking at me," I said. "When I looked out."

She blustered for a moment, then said, "OK, yeah, I was looking at you. I spotted you as I ran by and I thought, 'Oh no, Jones is in the pub. I wonder if he's having a drink.'"

"I really don't need you to look out for me."

"I wasn't looking out for you. I was looking *at* you."

She flushed the instant she realized what she'd said. I thought of the moment this morning, in the shop. I keep going over and over it. I don't even know how to write what happened, because it was nothing—we were having a bit of an argument, she turned away from me, ignored me and got on with cleaning. That was it.

But it wasn't it. Something in the *way* she turned, the way she shrugged off her jumper, the way she moved her body . . . She'd known I was staring. She'd liked it.

I'd liked it.

If Charlie and I are so determined to ignore each other, then why do we keep catching each other looking?

"I wasn't interfering, I wasn't trying to get you kicked out of the pub, I'm just slightly invested, I guess, in you staying sober," she said.

Even now I'm still not sure I believe her. Red looks up to Charlie. I wouldn't be surprised if she'd been able to persuade Red to kick me out.

"If we're done here, I'd like to get on with my run," she said. "As someone mentioned, I could do with getting out more."

The sun had already set. I didn't love the idea of Charlie jogging after dark, given there are no streetlights here. There's only one constable on the island, and it's Jerry from the dairy, who looks like a child's drawing of a constable—smiley and rosy cheeked. He doesn't give the impression that he has much experience fighting crime.

This place does feel incredibly safe in the daytime, but there is a lawlessness to the Isle of Ormer, too. It feels like anything is possible here, and that goes both ways. A nasty drunk might see it as a different kind of opportunity.

"Did I say that you don't get out enough?" I asked. I was pretty sure I hadn't, or at least, not like *that*. "You're very quick to read everything I say in the worst possible way."

"Says the man who decided I'd conspired to have him removed from the pub because I happened to be passing by."

Red poked her head around the door of the pub.

"This looks a little tense!" she said. "Can I make a suggestion?"

She waved a napkin at us both. Charlie reached for it first. There was a map drawn on it in wobbly pen.

"If you want a place to be that isn't the pub"—Red pointed at the napkin—"try here."

She handed me my laptop and satchel—I'd left everything at the table. As the door swung shut again behind Red, Charlie and I stood in silence, looking down at the scrawled lines on the napkin.

"Well," Charlie said, "this is perfect. I was looking for somewhere new to explore."

She pocketed the napkin and started moving away. Like she was going there right *now*, in the darkness. I thought of that table of drunk tourists in the pub.

"I'll come," I said.

"What, now? With me? On my run?"

"You said the other day we should chat. And walk. Would you be up for making it a walk? I'm not really in the right footwear."

"I thought you said you weren't here to make friends."

Yeah, that hadn't been my finest hour.

"I'm not. I'm not trying to be your friend."

"What *are* you trying to do, then?"

I sensed that if I told her I didn't like her running around the island in the dark on her own, she'd send me straight back to the stables. She clearly felt safe enough to be out and about at night, and it definitely wasn't my place to query whether she was right. I should be getting *away* from this woman. Not staring at her. Not spending time with her. Not thinking about her in the rare moments she wasn't there.

But . . . I looked down the dim track ahead of us.

"Red says this place is a good alternative to the pub," I said. "And I shouldn't go back in there."

I can't believe I played the alcoholic card, or, indeed, that the alcoholic card could ever be useful.

Charlie's expression softened. She reached into the pocket on the side of her leggings, pulled out a headlamp, and told me to keep up.

Red's map sent us down a track into a wood, dense with ferns. It was dark enough between the trees that I kept stumbling and grazed a palm, not helped by the fact that only Charlie had a light, and every time she looked around she'd send the beam shooting off in random directions, e.g., directly in my eyes.

We crossed a stream—I heard it rather than saw it, the undergrowth was that thick—and then the path seemed to hug its way around the curve of a cliff. The only hint I had that we were near the sea was the sound of waves, and the fact that the ground to my left dropped away so sharply I'd only need to take one wrong step to go tumbling. Then, suddenly, the woods opened out to reveal a beach below us.

It was a tiny cove, with the stream that had run through the woods dissecting the sand in a dark line, reaching for the sea. There were a few groups gathered on blankets or camping chairs with lanterns, and plenty of people on their own, too, everyone looking out to the water.

Charlie and I headed down the steep steps in the rock. We hadn't said a word to each other since leaving the Rue. By the end it was a scramble, but then we were on the sand, and it was sinking beneath my heels. Someone was playing a guitar, just riffing quietly. A few people raised their heads as we went by, but nobody spoke to us.

"This is . . ." Charlie began, then trailed off.

I didn't know what to call it, either. It reminded me, oddly, of walking into a church.

Charlie asked if we should sit. I hadn't planned to spend the evening with her, but what else was there to do, now that we were both here?

She loosed her hair from its ponytail, looking out at the sea as we sat down together. I wished I had a bottle of something—a crisp, cold lager; a hoppy IPA. I don't think I really know how to do moments like that without a drink.

"I assume you're keeping everyone at a distance because Rosie's right," Charlie said eventually. "That you're heartbroken. Grieving, maybe. She said we both have 'bruised souls,' but I sense you're not into the woo-woo stuff, so I'm paraphrasing."

"I'm not into the woo-woo stuff, you're right."

"Much too manly for that."

I frowned and protested, then stopped—Charlie was biting back a smile. She brushed the sand from her palms and reached to tug off her trainers and socks so she could sink her toes in. I copied her. The sand was cold. The need for a drink became a little quieter, so I buried my feet deeper. Beside me, Charlie did the same.

"You should know," Charlie went on, "you don't get the monopoly on miserable."

I looked sideways at her. She was drawing Xs in the sand with her finger. Whenever I look at Charlie, I think it'll make the need go away—the urge to take her in, see a little more of her. But it doesn't. Looking away is even harder than not looking at all.

"Heartbroken and grieving, too?" I said.

"Rosie's a great reader of people."

"And you're telling me this because . . ."

"Oh, I don't know," Charlie said. "Because you could really screw up my life, and I'd rather you didn't?"

"You want me to like you."

She flinched.

"I want you to remember I'm a person," she said. "Maybe you do deserve this beautiful opportunity, after whatever it is you've been through. But maybe I do, too."

I thought of the moment I'd had her quivering in my arms, up against the wall. Not just how good it had felt—though that came to my mind, too—but the way she'd suddenly seemed *real*.

It's a problem that comes with sadness, I think—you lose the ability to see someone else's pain through the haze of your own. She's right: I've not let myself believe that she really might need this opportunity in the same way I do.

"What happened to you?" I asked.

She looked at me in surprise.

"Before," I clarified. "What brought you here? What's got you so bruised, as Rosie would say?"

"That's a very personal question from a man determined not to get to know anybody. What are you asking for—want to compare traumas? See who needs this fresh start the most?"

I guess I deserved that. The guitar player had shifted to a song I recognized—it took me a minute to realize it was Noah Kahan's "Call Your Mom." The music caught the bittersweet feeling in my chest and seemed to make it bigger, the way a great song can.

"I actually just thought you might want to talk," I said.

She'd been leading me there, hadn't she? That *maybe I do, too* was surely an invitation to ask, even if she didn't know it. And for all my resolutions, I couldn't resist. I used to live for moments like these. Proper deep chats, genuine connections . . .

She swiped a hand through the Xs she'd been drawing in the sand. "I lost someone. But I think I lost myself long before that, really. I've spent a great deal of my life waiting for people to give me the life I want, but I realize now that I need to be the one to *take* it, actually. By myself, for myself."

"You've not given me many specifics there," I said, though actually what she'd said had hit me in the chest the same way the guitar music had—I understood the desire to look after yourself more than I'd like her to know.

"You think you deserve them?"

There was a sharpness to that sentence that felt more honest than anything Charlie had said to me so far.

"I guess I've not given you much reason to trust me."

"No."

"Well. All right. What would you like to know?"

I figured there was no reason I couldn't give her a few specifics.

"What was your last job, before you came here?" she asked after a moment.

I told her about the pub and gave her a sense of how miserable I'd been there.

"The only upside was my dad was proud," I said. "My parents drank too much, too. I never saw so much of him as when I could get him a free beer."

Her expression was serious. She has such an expressive face, all nuance.

"I'm sorry."

"That's all right. My parents aren't bad people or anything, they're just . . . complicated. We aren't close anymore. I'm not sure my mum even knows I'm here."

"Mine doesn't, either." She tilted her head as she looked at me. "So we have that in common."

"And I lost someone," I said softly. "So, yeah. Rosie got the grieving part right. There's that, too."

"That and the bruised soul," she said.

It *was* all a bit woo-woo for me. But actually, it was a pretty perfect phrase for how I felt. Bruised right down to the core.

Anyway, I'm home now, and tired tonight. I can hear Charlie's asleep on the other side of the door. I relaxed once I felt her breathing settle. She's so often awake. I don't know how she survives the days.

I keep thinking of her saying, *By myself, for myself.* I told her a little about my past to help her trust me, but it's made me see her in a new way, too. Between that and the strange moment in the shop this morning, she's thrown me completely off-balance.

I should be focused on my future—who is this new Charlie Jones, this *me* I'm building here?—but I can't be. I'm too busy wondering who the *other* Charlie Jones is.

Good night,
Charlie Jones

Monday August 25th 2025

Shop's closed, and I told Jones I would be hiking today, and hike I shall!

Hurray!

Feeling a teeny bit nervous, actually.

My plan is to explore the west coast, hitting the apparently famous Pouque Rock for a little solo picnic and then heading home. Only thing is, today has sort of got away from me—have been sorting the "pharmacy corner" at the shop, which contains several drugs I'm not sure we can legally sell—and now it's a bit late.

Can't back out, though. Have been wearing hiking gear conspicuously all morning and announcing that I'm "off in a minute" since about eleven a.m.

Plus it's a totally gorgeous day. We're tipping toward September now, and I think I like the island even better than I did in that scorching week when I first arrived. Summer is lovely, but it's all a bit obvious, isn't it? Autumn is so much more interesting, and it's officially on its way.

Right, have wasted another fifteen minutes writing about hiking, messaging Red for advice about hiking, and reminding Jones I'm about to go hiking. He was in the kitchen, snacking—have been leaving out sugary treats for him lately, as the internet says they help with alcohol cravings, and may have created a monster. Lately Jones gets through about eight of Doc Laurry's cardamom custard creams per day.

Ooh, Rosie just dropped off some hiking boots—apparently my trail-running shoes won't cut it, and Red texted her asking if she had spares for me on the off chance. Isn't that so nice? Ended up having massive chat out on the track, and then Red cycled by and joined in, and even Kim the sheep farmer (typically Team Galoshes) stopped her tractor for a while to talk. She's actually *fabulous*. Has an anecdote for everything. And always wears *such* good hats.

Stood in the sunshine with a bunch of fascinating, openhearted women and could have burst with the loveliness of it. Also got loads of great Ormer gossip. Found out when Kim divorced her husband, he tried to get her farm on the grounds that she wouldn't be able to manage it herself. After she took him to court over it, she stood for Deputy for Agriculture just to piss him off. And Red actually left home on the mainland because her dad *kicked her out* for being bisexual, and Rosie heard her story and immediately took her in at the B&B and gave her a job, and now Red wants to live here forever.

Women! We're so great. Am buoyed up by sisterhood, feminism, girl power et cetera—genuinely feel much less nervous about the walk now. Though I really should get going. Never mind, it's good I'm leaving late—I'll time my Pouque Rock picnic with the sunset!

Pausing midhike to jot down some gorgeousness. Am so glad I've ventured off the main tracks at last. It's just stunning view after stunning view. There's a tumbledown stone mansion I'd never have seen if I wasn't on the narrow coastal path—it's on the craggy rocks above Fortitude Bay, which was completely deserted today, like a secret paradise. Also found a tiny abandoned bird's nest in a patch of wildflowers. Very hokey, I know, but I just sat for a while with it in my palms and stared at it. It was like . . . the perfect home in miniature. And then there's the sea, disappearing and reappearing every time the track takes me to a peak in the rocks.

It's about an hour and a half until sundown, but that'll be fine—Google Maps directions aren't loading, as per, but doesn't look like far to go.

This rock Jones was on about.

It's actually kind of an island. An islet? It's a humped, grassy-topped dot to the west of Ormer, connected to the coast by a short, rocky track, wet with seawater. Right now, I'm sitting on it.

A few months ago, I would never have crossed those slippery stones. I'd have left the adventuring to everyone else. This wasn't my kind of fun.

Now, though, I think I get why people make so much fuss about the Great Outdoors. It's the freedom. If I'd slipped on those stones and made a fool of myself, there would've been nobody here to see me.

I'm sweating. My arm muscles are shaking from scrambling up to the plateau at the top of the rock. It's grassy up here, and the greenery is scattered with star-shaped yellow flowers. There's a single rock in the center, a natural pyramid shape, and it's the perfect place to rest with my diary and a squished-up custard cream.

Food is somehow better when you've been hiking. I feel . . . looser, softer, more here. Kind of peaceful, actually. I'm not trying to prove anything to anyone right now. There aren't any members of the committee around to win over (rare on Ormer, I've learned). This beautiful place even softens the memory of them laughing at me during The Night of the Pig. It just . . . doesn't matter what they think of me, does it?

It's something I've said to myself a million times—who cares what anyone else thinks!—but out here alone in the wilderness it actually hits home. Who? Cares? You know? Who cares!

And it's so tiring. Trying to be what I think other people think I should be. It's even tiring to write that sentence down—look at it, what a mess it is, all the thinking in there.

I wanted to be someone new, coming here, and I've been trying so hard to pull that off, but maybe I've been approaching this all wrong. If I really want to start a new life, I've got an opportunity, haven't I?

If I can be anyone I like . . . wouldn't it be nice to actually be me?

What. The fuck.

The walkway has disappeared??

It was just there. I just walked across it.

I've only been . . . what, half an hour?

And now it's as if it never was. Between here and the rocky beach opposite there's nothing but water.

This isn't an almost-islet. This is an islet.

I'm trapped on this rock!?!

I've called Rosie, Red, Marly, Rog, Toby, Toby's mum and even Caloshes. Not a single person is answering their phone. This bloody low-tech island. I'm not even surprised. Rosie left her phone balanced on top of a fence post for three days last week.

I'm alone. There's nobody who can help me.

I'm actually really scared.

Don't want to call him. Don't want to call him.

I'm not going to. Turns out I would actually rather die alone on a rock than let Jones know that I'm dying alone on a rock, so that's . . . healthy.

Feel so embarrassed. Half the island will already know I'm stuck here, too. I've sent most of them panicky messages to that effect. Am sitting leaning against the pyramid-shaped rock, staring out at the darkening hulk of the island, quite possibly about to sink into the sea, and all I can think is . . . everyone's going to think I'm such a fool.

I so desperately want them all to think well of me. And now they all know I can't even go for a hike without humiliating myself.

Trying to hold on to that new feeling I had, the knowledge that it doesn't matter what everyone thinks. But the wanting-to-disappear feeling is rising through me again and I can't help it—I'm crying. Keep thinking about Galoshes and Jones laughing about me at the shop tomorrow, everyone talking about me at the Pirate's Den. Feel desperate to get out of here, to get out of my own fucking head.

I'm so afraid.

The awful, crawling, fearful sensation seems so huge out here. Nothing else to do, nowhere to look but out into the darkness.

I feel like this more often than I would like to admit. And lately . . . more than ever, and worse than ever, too.

Is this . . . normal?

Jones's voice keeps going around in my head. Are you anxious?

I've said that I'm "feeling anxious" before. It's just a word you use, isn't it, like worried or obsessing? But I've never really approached the thought that it could be, you know, official. Pathological. Proper anxiety.

But what if it could be?

What am I feeling? Usually I hate this sensation so much I just shove it down, try not to think about it. But what is actually going on right now?

I'd say . . . the feeling starts in the center of me and spreads outward like a firework. It sizzles down my limbs. My heart pounds. I get clammy with horror. Hot and cold all at once. And within seconds it's taken me over, occupying the entirety of my mind, edge to edge, giving me no space for a single rational thought. Honestly, it is a sensation so unpleasant that I think I would rather die than feel it, which is bizarre, completely bizarre, because surely what I'm afraid of is death—why else would I care that I'm stranded alone on a darkening rock in the middle of the sea, if not for the danger?

You know, I don't think it is the danger I'm scared of, if I'm truly honest. The bad feeling isn't about that part, not for me. The awful, clawing, self-loathing terror is about . . . what everyone else will think.

This is horrible. It is horrible to see all this written down.

I just googled Am I anxious?

Do non-anxious people ask Google whether they're anxious?

There's a test for anxiety disorder. You can do it online if you want. GAD-7, it's called, which sounds more like a military plane, or maybe something you can do instead of A levels? But anyway, it gives you a nice score to tell you how mad you are.

And apparently I'm A* mad. A total anxious wreck.

Definitely shouldn't talk like that. Mental health awareness is so important! And I have friends back on the mainland with this sort of stuff—would never tell them they're mad. Wouldn't even think it.

Me, though . . .

That's a different story. Because I am not <u>allowed</u> to have anxiety. People with anxiety have a real problem, like a proper life-affecting mental-health issue, whereas me? I'm just . . . well. I'm just not brave enough, not together enough. Not <u>good</u> enough.

Though that GAD-7 score was pretty conclusive.

I don't know what to do with it. Keep flicking my phone on and staring at the questionnaire again.

* Over the last two weeks, how often have you been bothered by not being able to stop or control worrying?
* Been so restless that it is hard to sit still?
* Felt afraid as if something awful might happen?

And on it went. I mean, are they serious? This is me almost all the time these days. But isn't this the natural way to behave when you've learned that the worst possible thing <u>can</u> happen?

Aren't I just . . . right?

Brecon Beacons, four months earlier

Charlie was parked up with a Gillian McAllister novel and an excellent view of the extremely steep hill that Oliver and Fearne planned to cycle down today. She squinted through the drizzle that sequined her windscreen. It turned the scenery around her into an abstract painting: streaks of burnt-orange bracken, the heavy gray of the rock face, and the smudgy shapes of her two favorite people at the very top, barely distinguishable from their bikes.

On the drive, Fearne had asked—as she did periodically—whether she could tempt Charlie to have a go.

"You can borrow my bike!" she'd enthused (she always said this, too).

"Would I really be the Charlie you know and love if I opted to spend my free time on a wet rock?"

"It's so fun, though, Charlie!" Fearne had said, leaning forward into her seat belt to pop between Charlie and Oliver in the front seats. "And is it *really* more fun to spend your time in a stationary car?"

Charlie's explanation—the coziness, the reading time, the fact that she was still part of things without having to throw herself down a cliff face—hadn't satisfied Fearne, but Oliver hadn't seemed bothered. He always took Charlie as she was. That was nice. It didn't mean he was apathetic, just that he didn't want to change her.

Charlie's phone buzzed. She put her book down, using her car keys as a bookmark.

Hey, you doing ok?

It was from Berty.

It was the oddest sensation to see his name on her phone again. She and Oliver had been together almost ten months, and things were going dreamily. If they ever argued, it was because Oliver worried about Charlie, a trait that she found difficult because it reminded her of Berty, who had often been overbearing. But she'd recently met Oliver's parents, who both struggled with depression, and had learned a little about the effect that had had on Oliver's childhood. It was hardly surprising that he worried about her—it was what he'd grown up doing, as his mother and father dipped in and out of periods where they were almost unable to care for him. These days, when he fussed over Charlie, she felt much more comfortable reassuring him that she was just fine.

Oliver was the new life she had chosen, and she was committed to making it work.

The trouble was, she had spent twenty years with Berty. She had been so sure he was her future. When she had imagined building her family—when she'd started her very first mood board of the life she wanted, on the Isle of Ormer, with the wild cliffs and the checkered farmland—it had been Berty sitting beside her. *I can't wait for us to start our life there together*, he'd said.

Oliver never said things like that.

She clicked the phone screen off and stared resolutely toward the hill ahead of her. It was heavily wooded, and those tiny smudgy people had set off into the paths between the trees, so she could no longer see Fearne or Oliver, but she imagined their hunched figures zooming between the trunks. She was here with her wonderful best friend and her gorgeous boyfriend. Screw Berty. He'd left her, left that dream, left her absolutely heartbroken. She didn't even need to reply.

What did he want, though? Why was he getting in touch?

The phone buzzed again.

> I know Brianna will have told you I'm seeing someone, too—I'm happy for you and this Oliver guy and obviously not trying to interfere. I just worry about you sometimes. It would be nice to know you're ok. X

Charlie breathed in sharply. Brianna had *not* told her Berty was seeing someone. They'd not spoken much lately—Bri could be so judgmental, and last time they'd hung out she'd launched into a great tirade about the "state" of Charlie's life. Charlie had also noticed herself feeling a little afraid to speak to her about Oliver because she sensed Bri didn't approve of him. Charlie kept up contact nonetheless, which Oliver found baffling. *Why are you even still friends?* he asked her once. *She doesn't seem to make you happy.*

What a strange thing to say, Charlie had thought. *That's not how friendship works at all.*

So yes, Charlie would have expected Brianna to tell her that Berty was dating someone. Why hadn't she?

Charlie was so absorbed she didn't notice the hum of helicopter blades above until it was loud enough to shiver through the car's bodywork. The helicopter was a red one. It was flying low—very low, actually. Everything else was quiet. Aside from the helicopter's ominous, loudening roar, Charlie heard nothing but the wind and the odd bleat from a sheep grazing between tussocks of grass. She stared out of the windscreen and thought, *Does he love this new person the way he loved me, with every fiber of his being?*

The helicopter was close enough now that she could read the letters on its side, though it took her another moment to register their meaning. It didn't help that the first line was in Welsh. *Wales Air Ambulance Charity. Funded by the people of Wales.*

She sat up straighter. The helicopter seemed to be heading toward a clearing on the hillside. It was landing, its blades loud as thunder now. Everything else was so still and quiet, moorland stretching out on either side of her car, but the space around the helicopter was a whirlwind. Trees bent and buffeted, grasses lay flat.

Her phone buzzed for a third time. This time, it didn't stop.

She looked over at the driver's seat, where she'd set her phone down. *Fearne calling.* It spun, slowly, in little lurching movements, like a child's toy.

Charlie looked back at the helicopter lowering itself to the ground. There was nobody else on that hillside. Only Fearne, and Oliver.

As she stared back at the phone—she couldn't answer, she couldn't—another message appeared at the top of the screen from Berty. The full message didn't show, just the first line.

Also, I can't help wondering if you're still looking for—

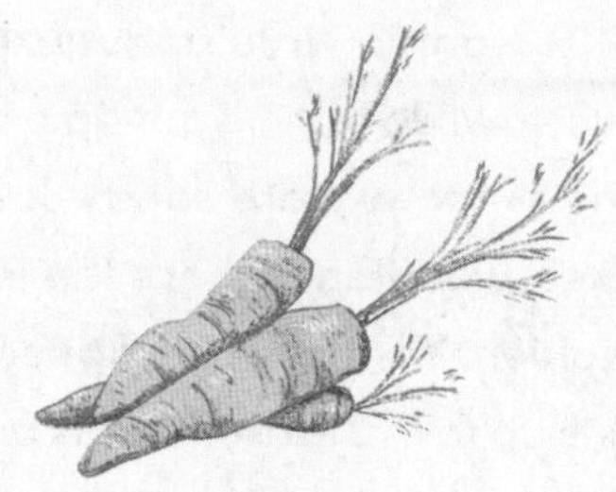

FROM: Charlie Jones
TO: Charlie Jones
SUBJECT: Day eighteen sober

You know what we didn't think about when we decided Charlie and I could cohabit? The laundry.

There's just . . . lingerie. Everywhere. I've only ever lived with women who I've *seen* in the lingerie before it's hanging from the washing line in the garden or draped over the radiator in the bathroom. It's totally different when you see the lingerie *first*. Your brain starts trying to fill in the gaps.

What a ridiculous email this is. It's one a.m., relatedly. I'm going to sleep.

Night,
Charlie Jones

FROM: Charlie Jones
TO: Charlie Jones
SUBJECT: Day eighteen sober (cont.)

The less said about last night's email the better. Who knew I could be that embarrassing when stone-cold sober?

I want to write about exploring Ormer. That's a much more worthwhile topic. I got up early on Saturday and Sunday, heading out to explore sandy coves and caves dripping with stalactites, woodland where the leaves are already beginning to turn golden. Yesterday I grabbed Red as she brought a herd of tourists up to the farm shop as part of her new tour route, and grilled her for a location to visit today, while the shop's closed.

She started coming up with ideas, but Galoshes shushed her—she shouldn't be telling me too much when I'm not a "local," apparently. After a brief pause for me to assure a tourist that he *was* allowed to look at the cabbages (Galoshes has a real thing about people touching the stock), I asked what one needs to do to become a local. After all, Red has only been here for a couple of months and is still staying up at Rosie and Marly's B&B.

"You just have to stick around," Toby piped up from the till. "That's literally it."

Red flinched. She has developed a strange aversion to Toby lately. Charlie and I have discussed it, and apparently Charlie's broached the topic with Red in case there's something worrying there, but Red insists that she has no problem with Toby. She just . . . never looks directly at him anymore. Toby, on the other hand, spends an enormous amount of his time gazing at Red. It's on our list of staff issues to resolve—we've started amending the shift pattern because if you leave the two of them alone together the shop becomes deathly silent and very uncomfortable.

Red was saved from interacting with Toby by the arrival of Doc Laurry with a tray of cacao and chestnut macarons. This time I wasn't about to miss out—I was reaching for one before he even started speaking. Galoshes, meanwhile, was examining the tray with horror.

"Don't tell me," she said. "Tree bark and something or other, I'll bet."

"Charlie asked me to bring in some samples?" Doc said, with an unconcerned smile.

"Did she now!" Galoshes said.

The biscuit was ridiculously delicious. The sort of thing you'd get in an expensive restaurant with a teaspoonful of salted-something ice cream on top. (Charlie's right, we have to sell these.)

"Galoshes has never been a fan of my concoctions. I believe she considers them"—Doc consulted Galoshes—"uppity?"

"Look, no offense, Doc, but we're a farm shop," Galoshes said. "We're here to sell good food to local people. Not pretentious biscuits to nobby tourists."

A passing tourist with a basket full of pickles looked a little startled at this. I pulled Galoshes aside, away from the main shop floor.

"Please, Galoshes, trust us on this one. The changes Charlie and I have made so far, even just the layout, the way stock is labeled, the decor—we're making considerably more money for the shop this week than last. Red bringing tourists up here on the tour has helped a lot, too. We're *up*. Don't you want to be up?"

"Charlie is so obsessed with the tourists," Galoshes snapped. "She keeps changing everything around without telling me, and I can never find anything anymore for real customers."

I could relate to this—Charlie and I aren't exactly communicating about plans, and I often feel on the back foot when I walk into the shop in the morning. It isn't helping.

"Shall I come back another time, with the samples?" Doc said tactfully.

His tray was almost empty anyway. Toby was at the till, looking panicked at the volume of tourists forming a queue.

"That might be best," I said. I took the last of the biscuits, though. For research.

After the rush of sales, Red shepherded her tourists back out of the shop again, all clutching their new local produce. As she walked out, she pointed to a spot on the map of Ormer that Charlie had fixed up next to the door.

"Try there," she whispered to me with a quick thumbs-up. She had holes in the cuffs of her long-sleeved top, as if for this very purpose. "Great views—people often hang out up there." Then, on the glare she was getting from Galoshes: "What? Look at his face. He just wants to be part of things!"

I explained to Galoshes that I was *not* trying to be part of things.

"Don't tell me, love, I don't give a shit," she said.

Galoshes's attitude is also, incidentally, on the list of staff issues to resolve.

Bye for now,
Charlie Jones

FROM: **Charlie Jones**
TO: **Charlie Jones**
SUBJECT: **Day eighteen sober (cont.)**

Tonight I think I saw the real Charlie for the first time.

I headed for the spot Red had tapped on the map. I could only reach it by scrambling up a steep narrow track in dense undergrowth, and for a long time it felt as though I was just getting deeper and deeper into a giant blackberry bush, but eventually I emerged onto a peak with a view that stretched all the way across to Little Ormer. The whole island lay below me—I could even see the winding trail on Windward Ridge joining the two halves of Ormer, like a rope holding the island together. I traced the fields of Bramblebay Farm, realizing I recognized almost all of them—the wheat fields Marly and Rog harvested yesterday, the gem-green clover field, the orchards with their higgledy lines of trees.

There were wine and beer bottles on many of the picnic blankets around me, and I almost turned back around and headed home, but then I heard someone shout "Jones." It was Marly. She waved me over to introduce me to a couple of farmers from the east side of the island. She handed me a lemonade without asking if I wanted anything stronger, but nobody commented or seemed surprised. Nothing staying private on this island has its pluses: it saves you having to explain yourself to anyone.

"We're talking exes," Marly told me, after insisting I sit down with them. "You got any really nasty ones?"

"A really good one, actually," I said, then winced. What was my second rule, after not drinking? Leave the past in the past.

"Oh! A good ex!" one of the farmers said, knocking back his beer. "Do I smell heartbreak?"

I shook my head. "I owe her a lot. More than I could ever repay."

"Money?" Marly asked.

Something in her voice made me glance at her. There was a sharpness to it. She was looking at me keenly—it was a good reminder to keep things vague.

"Not that kind of owing," I said. "She helped me turn my life around. I wouldn't be here without her."

We talked a little bit about the drinking, too, and I ended up saying the word *depression*—I don't even know why. I came here to *stop* burdening people with my shit, but Marly's too easy to talk to, and it felt so good to be out there in the fresh air chatting about stuff that actually matters.

"Ah," Marly said, when I mentioned depression. "I'd been wondering."

"Whether I'm depressed?"

"Where the empathy comes from. Real empathy is one of the few upsides of bad shit happening, in my experience. Some people just turn mean, but the good ones get wiser, connect better . . . Oh, I know you're shooting for a lone wolf thing, but I don't buy it—you're a connector through and through."

I made it clear that this was not correct, and I am in fact an aspiring hermit.

"Give you one tiny nudge and all your feelings come spilling out," Marly said, grinning at me. "It's a good thing, especially in a man—take the compliment."

After that, the conversation quickly descended into a lot of complaining about farming—which, to be fair, did seem like a profession with a lot to complain about. I settled back to listen as the sun set pink over the island. There was rain forecast for the night ahead, and you could feel it in the air. The sadness was still there—it's so fucking dogged—but it was a nice way to spend an evening. The nicest I've had in a really long while.

"Where's Charlie tonight?" Marly asked me.

I explained that she'd gone off hiking, planning to watch the sunset at Pouque Rock.

Marly's face went blank and she checked her watch. "That'll have been high tide."

Everyone exchanged glances.

"What?" I said. "What's the problem with that?"

"It means the rock will be cut off from land." Marly pulled a face. "Do you think she was prepared to get marooned with bad weather on the way?"

I checked my phone. "She's not called or anything."

"Shit," Marly said. "I've got three missed calls from her."

I was already moving. It was me who suggested Pouque Rock, me who encouraged her to get out of the stables more. The viewpoint is only about fifteen minutes from the rock, and—I figured—a lot less if I ran. I had no idea what I was going to do when I got there—it's not like I had any means of crossing the water and reaching her—but I did know that I hated the thought of Charlie there all alone.

I also hated the fact that she'd called Marly, and not me.

The rain began as I scrabbled down through the brambles to the main island tracks. I yanked my hood up and ran faster, heading straight for the coast. The light was low as I wound my way along the narrow tracks of the coastline. I squinted toward the horizon. There was an erratic, blinking light in the direction of Pouque Rock.

It got larger very quickly. I breathed out in relief as I realized a very wet, very angry Charlie Jones was approaching me at speed across the rocks.

She was soaking and still wearing the overpacked rucksack she'd put on that morning for the hiking trip she'd been going on about for days.

"You! You!" she said, the minute she saw me. "Just the person I wanted to see!"

In her sports leggings, with her hair dripping wet and her eyes flashing, she looked like a totally different person.

"Are you all right?" I asked, swiping the rain out of my eyes and scanning her over. "Did you actually *swim* off the rock and back to land?"

I thought of her on the night of the pig, eyes bright as she speed-read information about pig management while walking backward around the shop. There was so much more grit to Charlie than anybody realized. Maybe even her.

"Don't play innocent with me. I know you sent me out here to scare me. Try Pouque Rock, you said! I told you when I left that I planned to watch the sunset here."

I tried to interrupt, but she kept going.

"And not once did you mention any tides! Not once did you bring up the fact that I'd be cut off from land as the heavens opened . . ."

She turned her face up to the sky. Even in the grainy evening light I could see the flush of anger on her chest and neck.

"Do you really think I wanted you stuck there in the dark on your own?" I asked, slightly appalled. I know I've been keeping Charlie at a distance since we met, maybe being a little terse . . . but have I really given her reason to think *that* badly of me?

"I think you're a standard entitled man who is used to getting what you want, and this new life of yours hasn't gone quite how you hoped it would, and—"

This time I didn't let her keep going. I don't often get angry, but I did then. "You think I always get what I want? You think I wanted to be a sad old lonely drunk? Is that what you think?"

The rain was getting thicker and harder. I was already drenched through.

"I think you don't want me here, and you found an opportunity to scare me back to the mainland."

"That's just bullshit. If I wanted to get rid of you, I wouldn't do it by recommending a hiking route. Come on, we need to get out of the rain," I said, striding off in the vague direction of home.

I was a little lost, to be honest. I hadn't ever walked those trails in low light before, and everything looked a bit different. But I couldn't go that far wrong, could I? There was the sea, so that ruled that direction out, and any other route would get me back to the farm eventually.

"Oh, so you had something else planned?" Charlie called from behind me. "What were you going to do, poison my morning coffee? Set another pig on me?"

"I *saved* you from the pig, remember?"

"I did not need saving! And the farm is the other way!" she yelled.

She was jogging to keep up with me, the rain falling hard enough that it blurred my vision and I could taste it on my tongue.

"I'm not trying to go back to the farm!" I lied.

I spotted the island lighthouse perched on the cliff edge ahead of us—defunct right now, its light out of service, but still, somewhere dry to wait out the rain.

"Oh, sure, because why would we want to go—"

"There, the lighthouse!" I said, pointing. "We need somewhere to shelter."

The lighthouse's whitewashed walls looked gray and ghostly. Charlie was holding her hood over her hair now, other arm shielding her eyes as the rain came down in torrents. I started to run, and she did, too, jostling past me to overtake. I sped up alongside her, and then we were squeezing between sodden bushes and scrambling up wet rocks shoulder to shoulder, and at some point, one of us started to laugh.

Was it me who started it, or Charlie? I honestly can't remember, but it all seemed so ridiculous—the two of us, grown adults, soaked to the skin, racing to reach the lighthouse, yelling at each other about pigs and sunsets. I was *so* wet. And I *really* wanted to get to the lighthouse before her. I personally think I've been very mature about sharing my job, lodgings, name and life with this woman, but at that particular moment, I didn't feel mature at all.

I wanted to *win*.

We both broke into a sprint as the ground leveled out. When we reached the concrete platform around the lighthouse, neither of us slowed, racing for the shelter under the lighthouse balcony. I touched the wall first, and then Charlie collided with me just as I turned to lean against the stone. She came at me with enough impact to knock me back into the wall.

The next few moments happened so quickly I still can't untangle it all. Soaked cold skin, hot breath, both of us still half laughing—and my body pressed to the wall, Charlie trying to find her balance . . .

Her face tipped up. My hand found her waist, to steady her, I guess, or maybe not, because once I had a grip on her I didn't want to steady her at all. My hand slid around her waist, fingers splayed across her lower back. Her eyes were on my lips. She breathed out once, sharply, and I recognized the sound from when I'd had her underneath me against the farm shop wall. It had been sexy then, but now it was unbearable.

I pulled her against me.

And fuck. I don't know. My other hand was on the back of her neck, snagging in the wetness of her hair, and then it was happening, I was kissing her, she was kissing me, both of us so drenched our lips were slick and messy and then—

She pulled back with a gasp.

"Oh my God," she said, chest heaving. "What?"

Maybe it was the adrenaline. Maybe it was just the fact it'd been a while. Or maybe it was Charlie, this new real one, rain washed and impossibly tempting with her clothes slicked to her skin. But I wasn't thinking, *What the hell did I do that for?* I was thinking, *Why am I not still kissing you?*

"I don't . . . know," I said.

I was breathless, too. I still had one hand on her, on her waist. It hadn't felt right just to let her go.

She took another step away, out of my grasp, far enough that the rain hit her. She shrieked and ducked back under the shelter of the balcony again.

"OK," she said, pressing her back to the wall beside me. "Right. OK. That was . . . I don't quite . . ."

"No. Me neither," I said, then cleared my throat. "Sorry. I think we lost our heads for a second there."

"Right. Rain madness. Shall we just pretend that didn't happen?"

"That sounds"—*completely impossible,* I thought—"like a good idea," I said.

I was coming back to the real world again. The world where it's incredibly weird for me to grab Charlie by the waist and kiss her in the pouring rain.

Funny, because it didn't *feel* weird at all.

Charlie tipped her head back and closed her eyes. With her hair sodden, she had pushed that heavy fringe back off her face, and it totally changed her—I could see the arch of her eyebrows, and the little worried frown between them. She still looked beautiful, but in a different way. Less guarded, more human. I found that I very badly wanted to touch her again. I took a steadying breath.

"I really wasn't trying to murder you, you know," I said. "With the rock. And the hike."

"Well, that was maybe a little dramatic. But you don't trust me."

The rain was a sheet of solid gray, heavy enough that it splashed our feet as it hit the concrete. I was still so shaken. I've *never* had a kiss like that. Not just the intensity of it, but the way it genuinely seemed to come from nowhere. I didn't think it through even slightly. I was doing it before any thinking had even started. That's just not . . . me.

"Look," I said. "This. Us. As in, the job mix-up. It's *hard* to trust you—don't you feel the same about me? I can't work out why you're here, ultimately, and without that, I—" I pushed my wet hair back. "It's just a *very* weird coincidence."

She looked down at her hands, twisting her fingers together. They were white with cold. I wanted to pull her into me again and warm her up. It was such an odd impulse, right there in the middle of a conversation about how hard it is to trust her. I've never wanted to hold someone I've known so little—not like that, anyway, not the way I wanted to hold Charlie.

"So what's your explanation for it all?" she said eventually. Her voice was trembling, too—we might have moved on from the kiss, technically speaking, but we were both still vibrating with it.

I thought about her question. I've thought about this a lot.

"I can't figure it out. But I can't shake the thought that the job was mine and you tried to take it for yourself. You got a copy of the acceptance letter somehow, saw an opportunity . . ."

"I've thought the same about you, obviously. That you're pretending you got the letter."

She hadn't looked at me since the kiss. She stared out at the steady, endless rain.

"I was surprised when you arrived. If I was stealing the job from you, I would have expected you," I said.

"Same goes for me."

She *had* looked surprised when we met. Shocked, actually, with her scratched-up legs and her sweet blue dress, staring at me open-mouthed.

"I've been choosing to believe it was a mix-up between Rosie and Marly," she said. "I find it makes me less annoyed about having you around."

It was refreshing to talk this way, with a stripped-back version of Charlie, who was honest about wanting me gone.

"Whenever you're with Rosie and Marly, you act like you're happy to share this job and everything else with me. But I know you're not. Why has it taken this"—I meant the rain, the rock, not the kiss, but as I said it, the meaning shifted—"for us to finally have a proper honest conversation about it? Why are you always being so"—I couldn't think of a kinder word for what I wanted to say—"fake?"

"I *am* happy to share," she said, as if catching herself. "I am. It's fine. I can handle you."

Her eyes flicked to mine for the tiniest moment, a glance through her eyelashes. I swallowed, caught off-balance—she's gorgeous, she just kissed me, I *always* love her eyes on me—but I kept pushing. I was getting close to something real.

"I think you're nice to me in the hope I'll be nice back," I said. "Because otherwise, I might try to work out how you got this job. I might want to know what game you're really playing."

"You make me sound like some kind of evil mastermind. I'm almost flattered."

"I don't know who you are."

"Me neither," she said quietly.

She turned her head and looked at me properly at last. The eye contact sent a lightning bolt through me, the same way the kiss had. What is it about this woman? When she's not with me, I think about her; when she is, I can't look away. And yet she's still such a mystery to me. No matter how much I stare, I never get more than a glimpse.

"For what it's worth, I'm not putting on some fake persona because I'm a job-stealing con artist. If I'm being fake, it's"—she huffed a laugh—"wishful thinking, I guess. I wanted to be someone new when I came here. Someone better. Broderie dress, high ponytail, competent, independent." She went still, as though something had struck her. "The sort of woman who could do it on her own." She laughed suddenly. "God, I'm such a joke."

"Do what on her own?"

"Never mind." She squinted out into the darkness. "Come on. I think the rain is getting a little lighter out there."

"It's definitely not. Don't stop talking now. I like you like this."

"What, angry?"

"Open. Candid."

"You're very emotionally aware for a man."

"You know, that's the second time someone has told me that today."

I really thought I'd been doing quite well at the gruff and unapproachable thing. I guess not.

Charlie was quiet for a while, but she made no further movement to step out into the rain.

"I take it back, what I said about you being someone who always gets what you want," she said. "I don't think I was really talking about you, there, to be honest. I know being an addict is impossibly hard. Losing control of your own life like that. And getting sober . . . I appreciate you're going through something tough. So I'm sorry."

I wondered whether I should say I was sorry, too, for the kiss. But I found I wasn't at all. So after a few minutes of silence, I said, "I'm sorry you got stranded on a very small rock in the Channel because of me."

"Well, thanks. It wasn't really your fault. And it was character building. I think you might've been right about the anxiety."

Her neck was bared, her hair all pulled over the other shoulder. I wanted to press my lips against it. Get closer to her, get *more* of her. I wonder if you can become addicted to a person. I think maybe I could.

"There's nothing wrong with having anxiety," I told her, forcing my gaze away.

"That really does not feel true."

"Right. No. I guess it's not nice."

"But then, according to you, neither am I."

That made me laugh—her voice was so sardonic. It was pure, true Charlie, I think.

"Do you think, between the two of us, with all our baggage, we add up to about one competent farm shop manager?" Charlie asked.

The rain was actually getting a little lighter now. I could see the moon, a pale sliver above the cliffs.

"Yeah, I reckon so," I said.

"Not if we carry on like this, though. At the moment, we redo almost everything the other person does. Yesterday you stayed thirty minutes to cash up when I'd already done it. What did you think I'd done, stolen a tenner?" she asked.

"I don't know. Maybe. Nobody can ever get the till to balance, and I don't know what your game is."

"There is no game, Jones," Charlie said. All at once she sounded exhausted. "There's just me, trying to live my own life, and a bunch of people who can't add up trying to count the till. I don't want to steal from the shop. I want it to do well. You want it to do well. We've got an advantage, with two of us, and we're wasting it because we can't trust each other to do anything right."

"What do you suggest?"

"We should split our duties, for starters. And we should start communicating properly. We should have comanager meetings."

I pointed out that we live together (a fact that she might be able to ignore but I absolutely cannot) and are together a *lot* of the time, so meetings surely aren't necessary.

"But we don't talk," she said. "Not like this. Not properly."

I thought, *If we talked like this every night, I wouldn't stand a fucking chance.*

She squeezed the sleeve of her hoodie, sending a little stream of water onto the concrete between us. I looked down at my sodden trainers. The walk home was going to be wet and cold even if the rain eased off.

"I really don't know how we both ended up with this job, Jones. I can promise you that," she said.

And I believed her. For the first time, I really did.

"Maybe it was . . . Rosie, then, and Marly?" I said, shaking my head even as I said it. "Could they have orchestrated the whole thing? Maybe they saw that there were two applicants with the same name and figured they could have two employees for the price of one?"

"That's crazy," Charlie said. "For starters, only two nutters would actually stay for the job for half pay."

"Fair point."

"There is something about them, though," Charlie said. "Don't you think they ask very personal questions for employers?"

My stomach bottomed out as I thought about what I'd shared with Marly that afternoon.

"Why would they want to know personal stuff about us?" I said.

"I really don't know. But they did totally roll with it when we both turned up. They've not pushed to work out which of us they actually offered the job to, not even once."

"Why would they, when they could have two of us?"

"True. I hope it's nothing more than friendliness. I like Rosie. Plus she said I have a lovely aura. I've really been clinging to that."

I laughed, then stretched a hand out. A fat raindrop hit my palm, and then another, but it was definitely slowing. One of us said it was time to go—me, I think.

"We need to do things differently," Charlie said quietly. "The farm shop is doing well, despite the Committee for Not Changing a Single Thing Ever—"

I snorted with laughter. Another flash of Charlie.

"—but it would be doing better still if we worked together properly."

She was right. I'd been so focused on shutting her out that I'd refused to acknowledge it, but the best way to give myself a future here was to trust the woman beside me. You can trust someone and still keep them at a distance, right?

"How about we say that the first farm shop comanager meeting is tomorrow, in the kitchen, at seven thirty," she said. "Nobody shall question the other person's 'game,' nobody shall insinuate anybody doesn't deserve to be here. There will be no, you know, no rain madness, no losing our heads . . ."

"I'm not going to kiss you in the kitchen at half past seven in the morning, Charlie," I said, though the moment I'd said it I imagined doing it, and it didn't actually seem ridiculous at all.

"Right, obviously. We'll just have a sensible, adult discussion about what's best for the shop."

"Do you think you can trust me?" I asked her.

"I find trust a little tricky, these days," Charlie said. "But I'll try."

I'm in bed now—the main room today—and we've lit the fire, which has warmed the whole of the stables. My skin is still tingling from the cold rain. I've thought a lot about everything Charlie said about the job mix-up, but I've thought even more about the kiss.

It's so completely unlike me to get carried away like that. It was such a dangerous thing to do. Now I'm tense and on edge. I should be keeping my life as simple as possible right now, not kissing the woman whose life is inexplicably, inexorably tangled up with mine.

Rain madness, she called it. But if it was nothing more than a wild, unthinking moment, then why am I lying here longing for it to happen again?

Good night,
Charlie Jones

Thursday September 4th 2025

Spoke to Doc Laurry about anxiety. Grabbed him after the committee meeting (abject disaster, as per—nobody would agree to stocking Doc's biscuits, even though they all demolished the ones he brought for the meeting, because they're too scared to cross Galoshes. But at least nobody told me I didn't deserve to be here this time. Well, not out loud. A fair few of them were saying it with their eyes).

"So you know anxiety," I said. "You know, anxiety disorder?"

"Do you want to call the medical center and book an appointment with me?" Doc Laurry said, not unpleasantly.

"No, no, I just want to ask . . . theoretically . . . about getting a diagnosis? Of anxiety? How do you get one of those? Do you need one?"

Doc reminds me a bit of Santa. If you crossed him with the Dalai Lama. He has a white beard and a patient, twinkly sort of smile.

"I like you, Charlie. I think you're livening this place up, and goodness knows it needs that. I wish we had somebody like you on the medical board—if you think the produce committee are a bunch of sticks-in-the-mud, you should meet my lot. But I don't give medical advice except during appointments, when I have sight of my patient's medical notes and can make an informed judgment."

Obviously do not want to make an appointment. Said something hedgy about checking my availability. Doc removed his glasses and sighed.

"If a patient felt they had an anxiety disorder and wanted to discuss medication—"

"Not medication," I said. "Not that there's anything wrong with it, I just hate pills."

"Well, all right, if that was how the patient felt, then I would direct them toward some online resources, and discuss CBT, and talking therapy . . ."

"That's it?" I said. "There's no more stuff you'd do? To make it official?"

"Official for whom?" Doc asked, with a twinkly smile.

Didn't really know what to say to that. But it felt like quite an important question. Why do I feel like I can't have anxiety? Like I'm not allowed to? Like I want a doctor's note that I can . . . what, wave at people who think I'm just making excuses?

Which people?

Galoshes pops into my head. And my mother. Jesus. Let's not look at that parallel too closely.

"If we can let go of the judgment of others, Charlie, then we can know true freedom," Doc said, and with that, and a pat on the arm, he ambled away.

"I'm so sorry," came a breathy voice behind me, "but I heard all of that, and I feel like I need to fess up immediately or I will stew over this for days feeling awful."

It was Rosie. She stepped out from behind Marly's tractor, which was parked outside the farm shop where the committee meeting had taken place. It was late enough that we could only see each other by the light of the shop—Jones was tidying up in there with Red. Would usually have helped them, but since the insane rain kiss (all I am writing on this subject—it must be forgotten) I'm trying to cut down on my Jones time where possible.

"Before you say anything else," Rosie said, "I just want to tell you . . . I'm such an anxious person. Well, better than I used to be, but . . ." She ticked off on her fingers. "I'm petrified of dentists. I can't go in cars—I'll never drive one. And I get this abstract terror about the end of the world that kicks in whenever I'm stressed or tired, or sometimes just hungry, to be honest. I'll say to Marly, but what if there's another Covid and this time we don't find a vaccine and we're all wiped out, even us, even here on the island? And she's like, shall I toast you a bagel, sweetheart?"

That made me laugh. "Oh, I'm sorry, that sounds horrible, but—"

"Funny, right? Laughing at the anxiety is one of my top tricks."

She looped her arm through mine and began walking me away from the shop, toward the track that would lead us to the Rue.

"May I show you another?" she asked.

Looked at her, with her erratic, frizzy curls and her warm smile, and thought to myself, did you really plot to get two Charlies at your farm shop? Why would you do it? Fetish for Charlie Joneses? Fondness for mischief-making? The very idea seemed totally ridiculous now that I was with her. But then, when I'm with Jones, it seems just as ridiculous to think he's lying about getting the job offer, too. And we both ended up here somehow.

"I'd love that," I said after a moment. "Thank you."

When we reached the track, she didn't turn toward the Rue—she led me to a stile into one of the Bramblebay fields left fallow this season, sown with wildflowers instead. Even at that time it was abuzz with insects. The footpath took a petal-strewn route through the center of the field, and there was a flattened patch of grass at the other side, the sort that might be created by a deer looking for somewhere cozy to sleep.

Rosie lay on the ground and looked up at the sky. She patted the grass, so I lay down beside her. Was struck afresh by how incredible it is to see the sky unpolluted by endless city traffic. Thousands of those stars had been hidden from me before coming here, but they'd been shining up there all along.

"Do you know how big the universe is?" Rosie asked.

"Umm," I said, "does anyone?"

"It's infinite," Rosie said dreamily. "It stretches out forever. And do you know how small you seem to the universe?"

"I'd guess . . . pretty small?"

"Yeah." Rosie sighed. "Isn't that nice? Feeling so insignificant?"

"I don't generally like feeling insignificant," I said cautiously.

"Really?" Rosie turned her head to look at me. "You should. It's lovely. Who cares about the dentist when there are countless stars? I am but a speck in this great universe, and the dentist is a speck, too, and when I blink out of existence, will anyone care that I had to get a filling? No, they will not."

"And you find this . . . helpful?"

"It helps me let go," she said. "When the fear feels big"—she pointed up into the dark sky—"I remember what big actually is." She smiled as she turned to look at me. "Does the committee make you anxious?"

"Yeah," I said, swallowing the sudden lump in my throat. This felt surprisingly exposing to talk about. "Yeah. Caloshes especially."

"I get that. But they're just people, just like you, and they're all a bit scared as well—they struggle with change. Remember we still don't have streetlights here, let alone all the cool things you Charlies are introducing up at the shop."

"It's not like we're putting in touchscreens for ordering," I said, looking back up at the stars. "We've not removed a single item of local produce or cut anyone's pay."

Was shocked to feel myself close to tearing up. I just really want to do a good job here. I need to, to justify everything, and I want to, because I care about this place. Even more than I imagined I would.

"It's OK, Charlie," Rosie said softly. "You're doing really well. And you don't have to make the shop brilliant overnight, OK? It's not all about the shop—we want you here, and we want you to feel welcome. I promise you the committee will come around. They're giving you a hard time the way a class of teenagers would give a new teacher a hard time—it's almost traditional. If you can let it wash over you, it'll pass."

It was odd, that comment. It's not all about the shop. Because . . . it is all about the shop, isn't it? What did she want me here for, if not to turn the shop around? Isn't that why they hired me? Or rather, why they hired both of us?

Friday September 5th 2025

Keep meaning to write about the comanager meetings. We've had loads now, without arguing~~—or kissing~~.

Vibe is completely different at the stables since the lighthouse convo. Jones and I are extremely polite to each other these days. Almost too polite, actually. Yesterday he thanked me four times for putting enough water in the kettle for him to have tea, too. But it's good. Definitely better than trying to pretend the other person doesn't exist. And we've divided management roles at the shop, we're splitting shifts so we both have more time instead of getting on top of each other every day . . . It's all working very well.

Things are a bit . . . heightened, though. Do my absolute best to avoid getting too near to him, but can only do so much when we're literally living the same life. He's everywhere I am, by definition. At work, at home . . . Like, he'll come into the kitchen while I'm washing up, and it's a very *small* kitchen, so when I turn he's barely a step away, in a rumpled shirt that shows the freckles across his collarbones. Gray eyes full of messages I can't interpret, hair ruffled like I've had my fingers through it. And if our hands touch, or our arms brush . . . it never feels like nothing, the way it should. It feels like a shortcut back to that night. Rain, laughter, a momentary loss of sanity.

You'd think all the exposure would help, but I'm more jittery with him than ever. Funny, really, as he's actually a very calm person, very measured and deliberate in everything he does. The assured type—the sort of man who would look you right in the eyes in bed, one steady hand on your jaw, then touch you *just* where you wanted him to, staying totally composed while you begged and whined and writhed.

. . . Maybe at this point worth mentioning that my little crush on Jones has grown somewhat since the lighthouse incident. Am not going to write about the kiss, *obviously*. Just mean that I'm no longer thinking of him as an imposter trying to steal my job, and that's changed matters. It was pretty much the only turnoff he had going for him, and now it's gone, and he's just a really good-looking man living in my house, showering in my shower, naked, every day, *right* there.

~~And now I know he's a good kisser.~~

Sometimes find myself daydreaming about doing something I shouldn't. Like leaving the bedroom door open while I'm getting changed and he's in the kitchen. Or kicking the covers off when I go to bed first, in the big bedroom, and I know he'll have to tiptoe through to the small room, but if the curtains are open and the moonlight's coming in, he might see me lying there in my little pajama set . . .

Getting him to look at me, basically. I get a bit giddy when Jones looks at me. He holds eye contact like it's something physical. And I think... I've always been someone a bit different depending on who's looking, but I can't do that with Jones, because he just looks. At me.

By the time he turns away, I'm usually a little flushed.

But obviously all of this is just fantasy, and when we're actually together, we are just very, very polite.

I have my rule. No men. Not now. I'm searching for a different sort of love of my life, and if I let myself fall for another guy, I know what I'm like—I'll lose my conviction. I'll start thinking about what he wants, whether he would be interested in me if he knew I'm pursuing motherhood on my own, so maybe I shouldn't be, and so on and so on.

So no men. No sexy eye-contacty men who make me feel fluttery and safe all at the same time.

And no more thinking about the kiss.

Friday September 12th 2025

Found myself sitting at the kitchen table this morning, drinking coffee and wondering, Who am I?

I blame Rosie. She got me thinking all . . . existentially with her giant universe chat the other week.

Who am I, though? You know? Like, who actually am I? If I do have anxiety, how much of what I think I am is actually . . . that?

I guess giving the anxiety a name separates it from me. And that means I can hate it—the feeling, the thoughts—without hating myself. Before that night on Pouque Rock, whenever I considered my, like, personality, I was so busy either despising or trying to ignore this part of myself I rarely got much further than that.

But now I'm thinking . . . OK, I'm anxious. What else am I?

Oh, bollocks. Briefly pausing existential crisis as forgot to tell Marly we don't need any more wheat to decorate the shop—can see her through the window carrying a whole sheaf over her shoulder like she's stepped out of a tapestry. Shop is already festooned in autumnal decorations thanks to paid-for "natural crafting" session with Karen from the committee, who runs them for tourists (desperate attempt to get her on my side. Medium success. She chats to me now when she drops off her flowers, especially since I started ordering larger bouquets and displaying them in buckets outside the front door. If Galoshes is around, though, I get the cold shoulder).

BRB.

Marly quite irritated—wheat was heavy, apparently. I ended up saying we did need additional sheaf after all. Will just decorate the toilets with it. No reason we can't have seasonal loos.

Saturday September 13th 2025

New day. Am looking in wardrobe. All dresses are very mumsy. Jones was so right about me faking it when I got here. Shouldn't have splurged on new outfits before leaving the mainland—was a costly mistake. Did I really think wearing a knee-length skirt would help me transform into a competent single mum? My self-belief was at rock bottom, wasn't it?

May not quite know who I am, but am suddenly confident it's not a puff-sleeved dress person.

"Umm, hel-lo," was how Red greeted me when I got to the shop today. "Slay, Charlie!"

Could've sworn it was Caloshes and Toby on today, but Caloshes is nowhere to be seen. After close inspection of the shop, finally spot Toby hiding behind the display of Doc Laurry's obscure dried herbs.

Poor Doc Laurry—he's still on standby to bake us daily biscuits for the shop. He's rearranged his whole schedule at the medical center and everything, but each time we try to move forward, it gets to the weekly committee meeting and stalls. This time it was blocked on "environmental grounds" (something about Doc's use of manure when growing certain ingredients), thanks to Kim, who did at least have the decency to apologize to Doc about it afterward. Caloshes has made this her vendetta, and it's clear that until we can talk her around, Doc's outrageously delicious biscuits will remain an Ormer secret, and all those equally delicious profits from hungry tourists will elude us.

"Wow, is 'slay' still in?" I asked Red as I chucked my handbag into the back room.

"I'm an Ormerer now. We travel by horse and cart here. I think I can get away with slaying for another century or two."

"Noted. You like it? I'm trying to wear what I actually want to wear."

She didn't seem to think this at all odd. Red strikes me as someone who wakes up in the morning and chooses what she wants to wear based on what will bring her joy, without thinking about whom she'll be seeing and what they might think. How thrilling. Maybe I'll get there one day?

Meanwhile Toby was sorting packets of dried herbs and looking more-than-usually uncomfortable about the direction this conversation had taken.

"What does this outfit say to you?" I asked Red, twirling.

I'm wearing a long skirt patterned in red and gold—something from my old life that I've always loved, but have styled differently now that I'm an island woman. I'm in a pair of battered brown leather boots that Rosie gave me (the woman is a font of good shoes) and a cozy cream jumper, which I've tucked into the skirt, because I'm too millennial to do otherwise.

"It says . . . earthy goddess," Red said after a minute of gratifyingly close examination. "Earthy goddess who gets shit done."

Delighted with this. Think it might be my true identity? Going to try it out for the rest of the day.

Tuesday September 16th 2025

Oh my God.

Think I know why the till doesn't bloody balance.

Just nipped back to the shop at the end of the day to grab a jar of honey for my chamomile tea (which really needs the honey. Sometimes wonder if I should just not bother with the tea bag at all).

Paused at the door—light was on behind our new Bramblebay Farm Shop sign. The shop's flagstones were freshly mopped, which meant Rog had finished up. Maybe he left the light on by accident, I thought.

Then there was a noise. A thud.

Someone was in there.

A thief! I thought. What do I do?!

Habit told me to ring 999, but immediately realized it would probably be quicker to message Jerry direct. He's the constable, and he also supplies our milk—we speak most days. Suddenly found myself thinking of lovely Jerry the milkman in different light. He's one of my favorite committee members, but he's also <u>deeply</u> unintimidating. And he was the person who was going to see off this thief?

Maybe I should ring . . . someone else? First thought was Jones—he can really loom and has a good glower when he's pretending to be a dickhead. But felt a righteous feminist indignation at having to call my male counterpart to sort this situation. What a pain in the arse it is, being a woman. Maybe I should learn martial arts, then shit like this wouldn't scare me so much.

Tiptoed around to the next window to peek in. Was aiming to get a good look at the thief, decide whether I could sort the situation without martial arts skills or men.

It was Rog. With his hand in the till.

He was humming, and shoving a couple of twenties in his back pocket.

Rog! Stealing! From the shop! Am floored, to be honest. I like Rog. He's sweet—he was one of the first people I ever spoke to on this island. He helped me plant the flowers in our garden, and he never complains about doing four hundred jobs at once.

Belatedly realized he was heading for the door. Looked around frantically. There was the bush I climbed over on my first day here—can't actually believe I did that, it does not look mountable right now—and the bike racks, and the new picnic benches we finally got the committee to allow us . . . Nowhere to hide. At last moment I regained my wits and dove around the side of the barn, flattening myself to the wall as Rog ambled off down the track, spinning the farm shop keys on his finger.

A thief in our midst! Feel crappy about it. Our motley team at the farm shop is completely dysfunctional—nobody gets along, nobody can agree on what the shop needs, but . . . it's our team.

Am a bit gutted. But I guess Rog is going to have to manage with one fewer job.

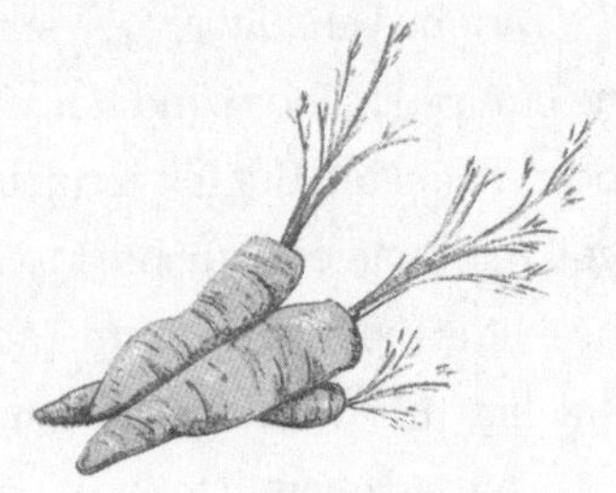

FROM: **Charlie Jones**
TO: **Charlie Jones**
SUBJECT: **Day forty-one sober**

Charlie left me a steaming hot coffee on the kitchen table this morning, with a note.

> *Sorry to skip comanager meeting, but really had to go for a run and clear my head. We need to talk when I'm back. Also, Red will need a hand at the harbor when the morning deliveries come in—all our dried fruit has been dispatched and they've sent us way too many prunes! Rosie has suggested we do a campaign around Keeping Ormer Regular, i.e., she is way too nice and doesn't want to complain / return them. Don't worry, I'm on it. Feel confident you'd agree that bowel-related promotions are not on-brand. Make sure they're turned away, please! Xx*

When I first met Charlie, she seemed acutely unfunny—the sort of person who can't take a joke. Now that she's being herself, she makes me laugh more than I've laughed in . . . longer than I can remember.

I said something like this to her the other day, and she told me not to judge a woman by her "sensible dresses," and that many of the funniest women she knew spent a great deal of their time pretending not to be. The more I thought about that, the sadder it seemed. I'm ashamed to think of all the people I overlooked, in my old life. You have so much less to give when you're drunk and unhappy and pretending not to be.

At least things are different now. I really do think I've changed. Maybe I'm uncovering the person I used to be, or maybe I'm becoming a new version of myself, but either way, I'm getting somewhere.

The coffee is just how I like it—gold-top milk from Jerry's dairy and a splash of Ormer honey. I'm just here, in the quiet of the kitchen, drinking it.

This probably doesn't seem noteworthy enough for an email. But it is, actually. Because I'm sitting here with a good coffee that someone cared enough to make me, thinking about the ways I want to be better, and I'm feeling glad to be alive.

And with that, I'll say,

Bye for now,
Charlie Jones

FROM: **Charlie Jones**
TO: **Charlie Jones**
SUBJECT: **Day forty-one sober (cont.)**

"You look different," Charlie said, when I arrived in the shop.

"So does this." I pointed to the ceiling.

Charlie has hung swathes of orange velvet from the barn

roof, between all of her handmade autumnal decorations. It looks great—the tourists will love it, but it's not so much that it'll alienate the locals, though Galoshes did spend some time muttering about what a pain the drapes were when she was trying to dust away the spiderwebs. But muttering is Galoshes's side gig—I'd be alarmed if she didn't.

Charlie was examining me, undeterred by my chat about the drapes. I immediately went hot. Charlie rarely looks at me for long—she's always the first to drop eye contact or turn away. When she does meet my gaze, it's electric.

"Is it the shirt?" she asked.

It wasn't the shirt. I'd worn it before. I'd just tidied myself up a bit. I'd styled my hair instead of leaving it however it was when I got out of bed, given myself a proper close shave, put on some aftershave and had that coffee.

It was just a coffee, obviously. But also, it was the first time in a very long time that I actually felt one hundred percent pleased to be here, on this planet, existing. So, in that sense, not just a coffee.

"Yep, shirt's new," I said. "You said in your note we need to talk?"

"Yeah, I . . ." Charlie glanced over at Toby, who was explaining to a tourist why Ormer soil produces the best potatoes. She looked back at me. "You look *happy*," she said, as though the thought had just dawned. "Properly happy. That's what's different."

"Don't ruin my image now, Charlie. You know the guys down at the harbor refer to me as Charlie Jones the Frowner? To differentiate me from you, I guess."

She didn't laugh. "Let's talk about my stuff later," she said after a moment. "Now doesn't feel like the time."

"You sure?"

"I'm sure. It can wait."

I hesitated.

"I did have something I wanted to mention to you, actually, if that's OK?" I said.

Ever since the night at the lighthouse, Charlie is very careful around me. It grates on me, to be honest—that urge for more of her is there all the time—but I understand why she's doing it. I want to keep my distance, too—that's been my agenda ever since I got here. So I'm being extra polite as well.

"We need to move forward with the coffee machine and biscuits." I lowered my voice when I said *coffee machine*, and lowered it even more for *biscuits*. Galoshes wasn't in today, but no doubt this conversation would make it back to her somehow. "We've got less than three weeks until our deadline, and profits are up, but not . . ."

"Not two salaries' worth," Charlie said. She sighed. "I know. I know. But Galoshes was right—nobody on that committee will cross her. We're stuck until she comes around to the idea."

"Could I talk to her about it?"

Charlie paused. A few weeks ago, she'd have said a point-blank no—the biscuits were her idea. But we are working together now. We are an actual team. And I didn't want to say it, but we both knew Galoshes has much more of a problem with Charlie than she does with me.

Charlie's shoulders slumped. "Ugh. That would actually be great. Thank you."

She smiled at me—a quick, tantalizing flash—then headed off to meet with Rosie about harvest festival events, which was next on our list of activities to bring tourists to the shop. On rolled the day, same old new life. Except . . . that coffee feeling hung around.

When you're sad, you think sadness is what you need. You

want to sink into it, let it cover you—the sadness is bad, but it's familiar, and it disguises itself as something right, as though feeling anything else would be a lie.

For a long time, I've thought that the only thing that can help me surface from the misery is a drink. When I'm drunk, I'm not exactly happy, but I'm free from the awful grip of that sadness, and that's such a fucking relief.

But the coffee this morning reminded me what actual contentment feels like. And it was better than drunk has *ever* felt.

So yeah. Same old new life. But . . . different.

So long,
Charlie Jones

FROM: **Charlie Jones**
TO: **Charlie Jones**
SUBJECT: **Day forty-two sober**

I've not written about this yet—what does that say, I wonder—but Marly and I have started going for bike rides.

If Marly had said to me when I arrived here, "Let's go for a bike ride before work every Thursday," I would have shut that idea down immediately for several reasons. 1) Planned bonding activities make me want to jump off cliffs. 2) I didn't want to make friends. 3) I don't ride bikes.

But she didn't suggest it. One day I was walking up to the farm shop from the post office, and Marly was out on the tandem bike she shares with Rosie.

She asked me if I wanted a lift. "Just dropped Rosie up at Pipit Spinney," she said. "Got a spare seat."

I told her no, thanks.

"You sure? It's at least a twenty-minute walk from here, if you're heading to the farm shop."

"Anywhere else on this planet, that would be considered close."

Marly laughed. She was doing her best to cycle beside me at walking pace—not easy on a tandem. She tilted, and I lurched to catch her.

"Jeez, savior complex much? I can handle my bike, Jones."

I apologized, obviously, and kept my hands fisted by my sides after that.

"Come on. Hop on. I'll do all the legwork, if that's what you're worried about. I'm used to it with Rosie—she always gets distracted by the scenery and forgets to pedal."

"You don't want me on there. I'm a terrible backseat driver."

"I can really see that. But go on. I won't take no for an answer. Rain's on the way, and I don't want you serving in my shop looking like a wet rat. No, not a rat. That's not right. A"— she examined my face as she wobbled along on the tandem—"badger. A wet blond badger."

I climbed on. I told myself it was mostly to end this particular line of conversation, but as soon as my feet were on the pedals, I knew it was more than that.

I've taken everything so slowly since I quit drinking. Walking pace, literally. But feeling the wind in my hair, even on a tandem, was *so* good. I've not been exercising, apart from walks; I forgot the absolute rush that comes when your heart beats in your chest and the air catches in your throat. There are so many things I've not trusted myself to do since realizing I was an alcoholic. But it was time to get myself moving again.

I rented a bike, a battered, rattled old thing that I immediately fell in love with. And next time I saw Marly on my way to the shop, she was on her mountain bike instead of the tandem, and I ended up joining her for a bit of a loop—I was early, we were chatting anyway. Then it happened the following Thursday, too, and the one after that. Before I knew it, I was waking at half past five on a Thursday specifically to meet Marly by the signpost on the corner of the Rue.

This morning's ride was a particularly good one. Marly and I paused midway, spread-eagling ourselves in the ferns on the side of the track, our bikes propped up against two giant pine trees. The woods are one of my favorite spots on Ormer—less obvious than the beaches and cliff tops, but they get better the more you get to know them. Like most things.

Marly was querying the idea that I came to start a new life here with no plans to make friends, fall in love or really interact with anybody. I explained that, yeah, I wanted to be alone, which is why I loved the sound of a farm job on a remote island in the middle of the Channel.

"You chose to work in a *shop* in a small, tight-knit rural community. Maybe you thought you wanted to be alone, but I'd argue your subconscious wanted different. Do you have family? Any abandoned loved ones back on the mainland?"

"I've not abandoned anybody. Anyone I left behind was quite happy to see me go."

"I can't imagine that," Marly said.

I thought she was being sarcastic, but she wasn't, apparently.

"You think you're such a piece of shit, don't you?" she said. "Well, you're not. I don't hang out with shitty men. And I like hanging out with you."

"I don't exactly think I'm a piece of shit"—anymore—"but I do think I have a tendency to drag people down." I couldn't look at her as I spoke. "I like hanging out with you, too, but . . . you might not like me so much when you get to know me better, that's all. When I'm depressed, for instance, I'm pretty hard work."

"Oh, so you're trying to keep us all at a distance for our own good!" She pointed at me as we both stood, reaching for our bikes again. "Very thoughtful. Very silly. I'm a grown-up girl, Jones, I can look after my own emotions, thank you. So can Charlie, by the way, in case you've been wondering. And for what it's worth, you're absolutely terrible at shutting people out, so stop trying to be something you're not."

She had to raise her voice for that last part—I was riding again, and she was chasing me down. I thought of how hard I'd been on Charlie for being fake when she got here and winced, because Marly was probably right. I've been pretending to be something I'm not, too. Maybe it's time to accept that I'm a really bad hermit.

I like people. I like connecting with people. And if they're willing to hang out with me and let me into their lives, well, maybe I should let them decide that for themselves.

We headed for Windward Ridge. The sky was gray, and the bracken on the cliffs around us was turning rusty orange. I could *feel* the season shifting. As I reached the ridge path, I spotted a group of figures walking slowly across the bay to our left and slowed to take a closer look. I could see Galoshes's pink hair, and Kim the sheep farmer's habitual cowboy hat.

Marly came up beside me, dropping one foot to the ground. "Huh," she said. "That's the whole shop committee down there."

She was already leaning her bike against the railings and heading for the steps to the beach below. I followed her down the narrow steps cut in the side of the rock. We made it safely to the bottom and picked our way across the sand toward the committee members. Kim spotted us first, and nudged Galoshes.

"How are you going, you lot?" Marly called as we approached.

There was a definite response to our presence, but it was hard to say exactly what that was. Awkwardness? Alarm? Galoshes greeted us first, and then Karyn said, "Look, it's not a coup, or anything."

"Karyn!" Galoshes said.

"What! You know they were thinking it."

"I wasn't thinking it," Marly said. "But I'm glad to hear it all the same."

"Told you we should have met in the old pirate cave," Kim muttered.

"I'm not hiding out in a cave," Galoshes snapped. "We've nothing to be ashamed of. Just a group of locals getting together, doesn't have to be official, we're just 'hanging out.'"

The heavy air quotes around *hanging out* did not reduce my suspicions.

"If you guys have concerns," I said, "Charlie and I would love to hear them."

"That's balderdash and you know it," Galoshes said. "You don't want to hear from us. You'd plow on with everything without committee sign-off if you were allowed. I'm just updating the committee, as is my right."

"Nobody is trying to impinge on your rights, Galoshes," Marly said, sounding slightly weary.

This all needed dialing down a notch. I did my best to project calm.

"Galoshes," I said, "can I speak with you privately, please?"

She narrowed her eyes, and then, after a moment, turned on her fellow committee members.

"Well, off you go," she said, swatting them away with both hands.

They scattered. Marly went with Jerry, murmuring something about needing to discuss a calf, so it was just me and Galoshes on the beach. We began pacing slowly across the sand, following the committee's footsteps. It's always easier to talk while walking.

"What do you need from us, Galoshes?" I asked.

Her expression was full of suspicion. "I don't need anything from you," she said.

"To make you feel comfortable with the changes at the shop, I mean."

"It's not about feeling *comfortable*. It's about what this place is, and what people like you want to make it."

There was a lot to unpack there.

"What do you think I want to make it?" I settled on after a moment.

"Posh. Expensive. A café that sells a few local bits. Not a proper shop for the community. A gimmick for the tourists instead."

"You're right—we are trying to draw in more tourists. So are most of the business owners on this island, Galoshes—tourism is the key industry here."

"You think I'm stupid? Of course I know that. But there are some places that are *ours* here. You'd get it if you'd grown up on the island. There's the Ormer the day visitors see—Windward Ridge, the bathing pools on Little Ormer, Karyn's chocolate shop. Then there's the real Ormer. The Ormer that's still here out of season. The cliff paths without signposts, the ones whose names are in old Ormerese and not written down nowhere. The bays no tourist'll ever find. The old Ormer families, like the Nicoles—good people, island people, community people. The shop was part of that world. And you're turning it into the other thing."

For the first time, I considered the possibility that Galoshes wasn't just being obstructive because she didn't like change. I allowed myself to wonder whether on some level, she might be being obstructive because she wanted to protect something important. We *were* turning the shop into "the other thing"—at least a little. And maybe that would make us easy profit and ensure we could both stay on as comanagers, but was it right?

"I hear you," I said. "Let me think on that."

Marly wandered back over in time to catch Galoshes's surprised expression.

"All friends over here?" she said.

"I've always been friends with Jones," Galoshes said.

I laughed.

"What! I have. I've always been nice to you."

"You've been civil to me. I'll give you that. But not to Charlie."

"I'm nice to Charlie."

"You're not nice to Charlie."

"Fine, I'm not. But she's . . ." Galoshes pulled a disapproving face. "There's something about her—she's not telling us something, I'd bet my cat on it. And she's too *much*. With all her pumpkin decorations and her trendy clothes and her airs and graces."

"When people say women are too much," Marly said, "it usually means they're intimidated."

"They mean that if they say it about you, because you are bloody intimidating," Galoshes told her.

"Charlie's got lots of ideas, and she's driven. People like her, too. The committee might all vote with you out of loyalty, Galoshes, but I'll tell you now, she's won at least half of their hearts already. She's good at this job," I said.

"You're being very nice about your competition."

"She's my teammate. Not my competition."

"We'll see," Galoshes said. "I'd watch your back, Jones. Say what you like—I don't trust her."

I do trust her, actually. And I really don't want to be watching my back. I *want* to trust Charlie. I'm choosing to. I'd rather be a hopeful dupe than the bitter, lonely man I became back home.

Bye for now,
Charlie Jones

London, five months earlier

Jones knew that you could not stay in a relationship out of pity. That was an *awful* thing to do. But he also knew that Aspen was struggling, and had been every day since her father's death. She'd recently fallen out with Bridget, too, which was hitting her hard considering all the issues she had with her mother. And it wasn't that Jones didn't care for Aspen or enjoy his time with her. In fact, it had been very easy to slide into her life. Her friends were becoming his friends, which was handy, since he'd lost many of his own in the breakup of his marriage. Her belongings now peppered his sparse bachelor pad, giving it her signature style—classy, candle-heavy, lots of velvet cushions in earth tones.

He was almost shocked to discover how easy it was to stay in a relationship that he knew, deep in his gut, was not quite right.

It did not occur to him that it might have an impact on him that he could not yet see. That faking contentment came at a cost, and waiting to leave her meant putting both their lives on hold.

On a crisp day in early April, Aspen suggested a trip to the theater with a couple of new friends. Jones wasn't a theater person—he found theater people either intimidatingly cool (floaty, posh, lots of jewelry) or enthusiastically uncool (loud, overfriendly, constantly changing hair color) and neither variety ever seemed to take to him. But lately Aspen was picking up new friends all the time and wanted to do different things, really *make the most of London*, and he saw this as a good sign. In the early stages of her grief, she'd not wanted to go anywhere at all.

It was a matinee, as they would both be working in the evening, something he was already dreading—work, like all elements of his life, had become increasingly stressful and unenjoyable.

The roads were thick with traffic on their walk from the tube, and the air smelled distinctively like London: warm car fumes, petrichor. Jones found himself longing for fresh air and a little space—London was losing its charm of late.

"So they won't talk in the Shakespeare kind of way?" he said to Aspen.

Her red hair was piled on top of her head, exposing the sweeping line of her neck above her collarless jacket. She looked breathtakingly beautiful. Why did he not *feel* it the way he should? It was as if she were a work of art he didn't understand—the fault lay in him, he knew, but how could he correct it?

"They will," Aspen said distractedly, searching through her handbag. "But they'll be dressed in modern clothes."

"Oh," Jones said. That wasn't going to help much.

"If you don't want to come, I can just go with Marc and Stefano," Aspen said.

"No, no," Jones said hastily. "I'm looking forward to it."

He'd just get himself a drink and zone out. In these sorts of situations Jones had an ability to think about absolutely nothing if he had to—a kind of meditative state, but without any of the resulting zen. More like . . . an off switch. He had been relying on it a lot lately.

They made their way through the crowds on the pavement with the ease of consummate Londoners—parting midconversation for two influencers with selfie sticks, turning sideways to make room for the vendor selling caramelized nuts from a cart. But one particular car horn cut through the usual hubbub: an Uber driver was hooting repeatedly.

"What's . . . oh," Aspen said, standing on tiptoes.

A crowd was gathering around a gray sedan in the bus lane, stuck behind a string of number 26 buses. Aspen slipped into the bustle so fast she lost Jones for a moment, and by the time he'd pushed through, she was on her knees beside the car's open door, and there was blood all over her cream collarless jacket.

His heart stopped. A woman was screaming from inside the car, a guttural roar.

"She can't have a baby here," someone in the crowd said. "She'll *die.*"

"Don't be ridiculous," Aspen snapped, shrugging off her jacket, always keeping her grip on the woman's leg, just switching hands. "I'm a midwife. She's perfectly safe. She's doing brilliantly. If you don't have anything helpful to say, give me your coat."

"My coat?" the man said, dumbfounded. "What for?"

"To catch the baby in," Aspen said, with satisfaction.

The man backed out of the crowd. Aspen glanced around, searching for Jones. The woman was kneeling on all fours on the back seat, her long skirt covering her from the onlookers, her face invisible inside the vehicle.

"I'm here," Jones said, pushing through to stand at Aspen's side. "What can I do?"

He'd already taken off his coat and handed it to her.

"Can you go around and talk to her? Tell me if she seems woozy? She's in transition. Her pulse is good, but I've not had time to check more than that." She cursed. "I wish I had my bag with me. Gloria, you said, right? Gloria, you're doing *great*. I'm just sending a colleague around to talk to you through the other door, OK? She's got nobody with her but the Uber driver, who's on the phone to the ambulance," Aspen added in a mutter to Jones. "Try to act midwifely."

Jones looked up toward the driver's seat, where he saw the blank, panicked face of a young man in driving gloves with a phone pressed to his cheek. This man had gone through fearing for his upholstery and was now visibly concerned that someone might perish in his back seat.

"On it," Jones said, already moving around the car.

The woman didn't lift her head when he opened the other passenger door. She was half-hidden behind a tangle of sweat-soaked hair, and her shoulders shook with sobs.

"This is not how it was supposed to happen," she said, voice hoarse. "There's a birth plan in my bag. My sister's meeting me at the hospital."

Jones covered her hand with his on the car seat.

"Please," she said. "I can't do this."

Aspen talked about work a lot, so Jones knew losing faith like this wasn't just common in transition—the very last stage before the baby came—but a symptom of it. If Gloria wanted to give up, that meant she was almost there.

"You can. You can do it," Jones said, trying to channel Aspen's confidence, though he actually couldn't imagine how Gloria would be able to do this at all.

Gloria roared her way through another contraction. Jones gripped her hand. Aspen always made birth sound so beautiful—she was passionate about giving women a voice in their own labor, about rewriting the cultural narrative around birth. But this just seemed . . . terrifying. His ex-wife had known she didn't want children, so the idea of childbirth wasn't something he'd ever dedicated much time to thinking about, and though they'd talked in the abstract about labor when Aspen discussed her job, he'd had no idea it would be like *this*. It was absolutely wild. How on *earth* had mankind kidded themselves that men were the strong ones?

Gloria let out another deep, guttural sound. Jones remembered something Aspen had once told him and tried suggesting Gloria should relax her jaw; she swore at him so colorfully he found himself genuinely slightly offended for a moment.

"That's amazing," Aspen was telling Gloria, who had begun to growl. "You're doing it! Listen to your body. Your baby's coming, Gloria, this is it."

"Not here," Gloria panted.

"Here," Aspen said firmly. "Definitely here. I've got you, Gloria. I'm really good at this, OK? And I'm telling you, you're almost there."

The next few minutes were a primal blur, and some of the strangest moments of Jones's life. Soon, Aspen was calling his name—perfectly calm, with a streak of blood on her cheek like war paint—and handing him his coat, now soaked and stained. Gloria's baby was pressed to her mother's chest, screaming and pink beneath the blood, and Gloria's face was beatific. Jones himself felt fundamentally changed. As though he'd just seen some sort of religious miracle, perhaps, or a supernatural occurrence.

The ambulance was five minutes away, much to the Uber driver's profound relief. Aspen had climbed in beside Gloria now and smoothed the woman's hair back from her face as Gloria shifted her top, bringing the baby beneath it to keep her warm. Her little eyes were scrunched closed, her tiny hands balled in fists. Jones leaned on the car door, looking down at them all. It seemed almost impossible that this miniature creature would eventually grow into a person, with opinions and habits all her own.

"Isn't she beautiful?" Aspen whispered.

Jones nodded, awed. "That was amazing."

"Right?" Aspen said, beaming at him.

He couldn't remember the last time he'd seen her smile that way. Something fluttered inside him. He did love Aspen, he *did*. Perhaps he simply couldn't fall in love the way he had once—perhaps when your heart had been broken that badly, it was never quite the same again.

"*You* were amazing," he told her. "We're sacking off Shakespeare, right? Shall we go to the pub instead? You deserve a drink after that."

Aspen's smile dropped to something questioning. "It's half past one. And I'm on shift later."

"Right, right," he said hurriedly. "Of course."

His brain was like cotton wool. Gloria's roars still seemed to be ringing in his ears, and his broken heart felt sorer than ever, for reasons he couldn't quite name, but felt sure were to do with the baby. He looked down at the child's tiny, bloodstained feet. She was the smallest person Jones had ever seen.

Jones pressed his hand to his chest. What was it he was feeling? Whatever it was, it was big, and he didn't understand it at all.

Friday September 19th 2025

Guess what was in the pile of post Rog just brought me?

Should probably say at this point: still haven't told Jones about Rog. Or fired Rog. I know it's bad, but he's not been on shift anyway, and Jones is just so happy at the mo! Can see the change in him. Can't bear to share this crappy news and watch his good mood disappear.

Am just going to handle it myself, I've decided. If I was here solo, this would be my task alone—no reason for me to drag Jones into it to help me. Will fire Rog today. Thought about doing it just now, on the doorstep, but really didn't want to, to be honest, then saw the return address on the top parcel and could suddenly think of nothing else but opening that envelope.

Rog has brought me my sperm catalog.

It's not called that, obviously. The very fancy fertility clinic calls it the sperm donor bank. But it's a big glossy catalog full of men's profiles, and any one of them could be the father of my child.

There are no photos, but even so, it reminds me of flicking through a dating app—except I don't have to talk to these people. Or fall in love with them. Or let them break my heart. They can't hurt me, they can't let me down and they'll never leave me.

And looking through this catalog brings me a step closer to the dream that I fought to hold back for so long. All the little elements that I'd catch myself thinking about when I wasn't strong enough to shut the longing down. A first flicker of movement in my belly. A first cry. A first grip of a hand that I'll hold through a first feed, and first steps, and first heartbreak—a hand I'll hold as long as they need me to, whenever they need me.

Even writing it makes me cry, right here on these pages, but this time I'm not crying because I'm scared I'll never have all those firsts. I'm crying with hope.

I can joke about sperm catalogs and make out like it's all fun and easy but in truth this feels so monumental I can hardly bear it. My test results were good; I have the money. With help from one of these beautiful men who donated their sperm, I can probably have a baby. It won't be easy—have enough friends who've gone through fertility treatments to know that, and I've seen single mums struggling through those early months with a newborn on their own, but . . . I also know without a shadow of a doubt that it'll be worth it.

There are no words, really, for the way I want this. I've imagined each of those small steps so many thousands of times, always knowing that my chances diminish by the day unless I find the mythical man for me before it's too late.

But here I am. Single, independent. And closer to my baby than I've ever been.

Was going to fire Rog as soon as I headed to the shop, I really was. But got there to a stressed Marly: Rosie was out of action with bad cramps, so we were needed on the farm! We left Toby in charge at the shop. (Spoiler alert as I am writing this at the end of the day: he survived! Which, let's be honest, it did not look as if he would when I suggested the idea.)

We were enlisted to clear rocks from Pipit Spinney, one of my favorite spots on the farm. It's this wedge-shaped little field that's too small to be much use—you can hardly get a tractor in there—but I love it because it has the most amazing sea view, and because it's surrounded by wild hedgerows packed with flowers and mini-beasts. This morning I swear I saw a stoat, which I thought was an extinct animal, so got very excited about it until Marly told me "they're like bloody rats, don't encourage them," as though maybe I'd make them too big for their little stoat boots. She didn't let Ginger catch it, though, which is about as close as Marly gets to having a soft spot for something.

Anyway, Jones and I rolled our sleeves up (or, more accurately, tucked our trousers into our socks) and waded into the post-pig mud to clear the stones. It was totally backbreaking work, and Jones was obviously better at it than me because he's a big muscular man and I'm very much not that. But was also surprisingly lovely. Ginger wagging between us, the smell of freshness and roots and reality in the autumn air . . . Gorgeous.

Brianna rang me while I was there. I stepped out of earshot to take the call, finding a tree stump where I could sit down.

"Hey! Ooh, wow, it's nice not bending over for a minute."

"Hello," Brianna said, "what have I interrupted?"

"Moving rocks!"

"Moving . . . Never mind. I saw your short list—are you seriously considering letting a man called Keith put his sperm into you?"

"Bri! He won't be putting anything anywhere, it's a medical procedure, very straightforward, very nonsexual, and also, he's not actually called Keith. I just gave them all names so I don't get the contenders muddled—they're just called, like, Donor 1989 or whatever."

"Oh. Why would you choose Keith? Nobody fancies Keith."

"I don't want to fancy him," I said, a little impatiently. "That's the joy of this! I'm not required to sleep with him at all!"

"Are you still very anti having sex with anyone?"

Found myself gazing at Jones across the field as she said this.

"Sex is not relevant to the sperm conversation," I said. "Once again, Bri, this is the point."

"No, I get that, I've segued."

"Seamless, as always."

"What if you do meet someone one day? What if they mind that Keith's your baby daddy?"

"Then they'd need to work on being a bit more open-minded, wouldn't they?" I said. "Seriously, though, I don't want to think about meeting someone or falling in love. I'm done with that. I want to do this alone, for me."

My voice broke a bit on that last word. God, authenticity is embarrassing.

"And you know I love that for you," Brianna said. "But please. Not Keith. He's a Pisces, anyway—it would never work."

"It doesn't have to—"

"I'm teasing, I'm teasing." There was a beat. "Do you think, if you met someone who really wanted to be a father . . ."

"Your obsession with me having a traditional family structure is giving me the ick."

"It's not about that. You know I totally support you in becoming a single mum. I just don't know that I want you to write off romantic love forever as part of this decision."

"You're just way too happily married to talk to about this. It's hard to find someone who's as perfect for me as Stu is for you, and I'm done with waiting on that miracle to occur before I get to have a baby. I know some people are lucky and get pregnant well into their forties, but I'm scared, Bri—I might not be one of those people. And honestly, I don't want to wait until then anyway. You know what it feels like, wanting a baby—how overpowering that feeling can be."

"Well, what if your little one is five and then you meet the love of your life?"

"My little one is going to be the love of my life!" I chirped, then I toned down the Cheerful Charlie voice—am really trying to give up on all that fake stuff. "I'm just not thinking about romantic love right now."

"I get that. Believe me. You know I love my kids more than life itself. But I also love my husband, and it's not either-or, that's all I'm saying. You've got more than one love story in that big smushy heart of yours."

"My heart is not smushy. Smushed, maybe."

"Oh, please. You sound happier than you've sounded in years. Are you telling me you're still heartbroken?"

Hmm. Didn't answer for a while.

"Having a little poke around in that chest cavity, are you?" she asked, after I'd been quiet for a bit too long.

"Gross. No, I haven't really thought about romance for a while, I guess. So I'm thinking about it."

Was actually buying time. The whole chat had shaken me a bit.

"I guess . . . if . . . one day . . . someone who really, honestly wanted children, and would love mine like their own . . . God, it feels weird to even say it. But yes, I suppose it's theoretically possible I could date this theoretically open-minded man who wants kids. Or, specifically, wants my kid."

"There we go," Brianna said with satisfaction. "She's ready to love again, ladies and gentlemen."

Of course will not be loving again right now, as discussed. But what she said about being happy . . . I am, actually. The grief is still there, the loss, the guilt, but it doesn't press on me the way it did. Doesn't . . . suffocate me. I've been so busy, so preoccupied, so focused on my new goals—I haven't even noticed that the broken heart I thought I'd carry forever has been quietly mending.

No more delaying. Am on a Rog hunt.

Ugh, my stomach's churning. Don't want to do this. He's going to hate me, for starters. Rest of the team will, too, and the committee—everyone loves Rog. But what else can I do?

At least I've managed to keep Jones out of it. Feel quite proud of myself, really. Am not naturally inclined to be Bad Cop, but am being brave and taking one for the team.

Hmm. Bad afternoon. Jones did not see it that way. More when I have a chance to write.

Eventually tracked Rog down on his tractor on the way to one of the polytunnels up at the northern end of Bramblebay, where they're still picking the last of the strawberries.

"Rog, we need to talk!" I shouted up at him over the roar of the tractor's old engine.

"What's that?" he yelled down at me.

"We need to talk! Can you turn off the engine, please, Rog?"

"What do you want with Benji?"

"What? No, the engine, Rog."

"Benji's a good dog, but he's not much help with the sheep—is it Kim who sent you?"

"No, Rog, I'm just—could you turn off the engine?"

"Tell Kim to try Baptiste's collie, he's not bad in a pinch. I'm on my way to the strawberries!"

"Right! Can you . . ." I was doing a very awkward jog to keep pace with the tractor. "Can you spare a minute?"

"Do you want to climb in?" Rog said, finally stopping. "Can't hear you all the way down there!"

Hitched up my skirt and climbed the steps to the tractor cabin. It was surprisingly snug and cozy in there, though as soon as we started moving, the juddering motion made my teeth chatter.

"Sheep emergency, is there?" Rog said, flashing me a gold-toothed smile.

"Sure," I said, giving up. "Thanks for the sheepdog advice. While I have you, can we talk about something else, please?"

"Oh, hello, another Charlie Jones!" Rog said, waving enthusiastically to Jones, who was cycling toward us, standing up in his saddle, peering into the cab of Rog's tractor. He looked a little surprised to see me. Had never seen Jones on his bike before, though it lives propped up by our front door. A little lurch of emotion went through me at the sight of him in his helmet, looking for a split second like he was someone else entirely. Least he was wearing one, though—loads of islanders don't.

"Charlie? What are you doing?" he called. Or at least, I assume that's what he was saying. Rog wasn't wrong—it was hard to hear up there. I asked Rog to turn off the engine for a moment.

"I've been calling you," Jones said, dropping one foot to the track as he came to a stop. "We need you back at the shop. Red's had to duck out for a bit."

"Why?"

"She's . . ." Jones's eyes flicked to Rog. "Can you come down?"

I sighed—had really geared myself up for the hard conversation with Rog—but dismounted again. Jones immediately took my arm to pull me aside. He was windswept from cycling, and the smell of the island breeze had caught in his jumper. I resisted the alarming urge to breathe him in.

"She's crying," he said grimly.

"Red?" I said, horrified enough to stop checking out Jones in his jumper. "But Red's so . . . cheerful! That's like her whole personality!"

"I'm not sure cheerful is anyone's whole personality."

"Maybe that's where I went wrong when I got here."

Jones laughed, then said "What?" when I looked at him in surprise.

"Look at you, laughing at my jokes. You barely cracked a smile week one here."

"Well, you got funnier," he said, the corner of his mouth twitching.

The way his eyes crinkle when he smiles . . . I had to look away. The conversation with Brianna was still fresh in my mind, and it was such a little thrill to make this shadowy, complicated man laugh.

"Did you need something from Rog?" Jones said.

"What? Oh, shit."

Rog had set off again. I yelled his name and chased his tractor down the track.

"Can't stop, Charlie! I'm already late after sorting the plumbing at Karyn's place!"

Could well believe that. Rog is <u>always</u> late.

"What do you need Rog for?" Jones said from behind me.

I sighed, slowing to a walk. "Don't ask. You don't want to know."

"Is it shop business?"

"Yes. I wanted to keep you out of it until it was done, so you didn't have to bear the brunt of everybody's outrage, too, but . . ." I stopped walking. Found myself actually quite desperate to share the burden. "I need to fire Rog."

Jones stared at me as Rog chugged off into the distance behind us. "You're going to fire Rog? One of our four employees? Without discussing it with me first?"

"Trust me. If you knew what I know—"

"Which I don't."

"Well, I just thought—"

"What happened to trusting each other?"

"This isn't about trust! I just didn't want you dragged down into all this. Galoshes already hates me, but she's all right with you, and you've been really getting somewhere with the coffee and biscuits thing, and if you were part of this—"

"She might get the mistaken impression that we're jointly managing the shop?"

"She might blame you!"

"This <u>is</u> about trust," Jones said grimly. "You don't trust me to be able to handle it. Are you even going to tell me why we're firing a good man who works hard and does a great job?" He paused. "Sometimes? If he turns up?"

"I saw him stealing, Jones. That's why the till never balances at the end of the day."

Jones was silent for a moment. "You actually saw him?"

"Yes. He took a couple of twenties out while he was cleaning and locking up."

Jones breathed out slowly. "All right. I'll talk to him."

"Talk to him?"

"Get his side of things."

"Are you serious? Do you not believe me when I say I saw him stealing?"

"I believe you thought you saw that. But I also believe in giving people a chance."

"So do I!" I was so frustrated I could have cried. "But I also believe what I saw!"

"Leave the Rog situation with me," Jones said. There was no crinkling around the eyes now. "Why don't you focus on Galoshes instead? She's been dismantling all your autumnal decorations while you were out."

"She's— What?"

"Yeah. She knows you're too scared of her to bollock her for it, I imagine."

Jones was angry. I've only seen him properly angry once before—that moment when we were drenched by the lighthouse, when I told him he was an entitled man used to getting what he wanted. But this time, there was no danger of this ending in a kiss. His arms were folded tightly across his chest and his glower was fierce. I was having to fight to keep from crying. Had gotten used to the warm, caring Jones—hadn't realized how much he'd changed until he was back to this scowly, shut-off stranger again.

"Your issues with Caloshes are getting in the way of progress in the shop. She's not going to agree to anything until she believes we're good people who aren't trying to turn the shop into some gimmicky tourist trap. I'm doing what I can, but the fact is you're fifty percent of this, she doesn't trust you and we have two and a half weeks to get that shop to a place that justifies two salaries. Sort it, please," he said, climbing back on his bike.

"Jones—"

"I'm done," he said. "Unless there's anything else you've not deigned to tell me because you think I can't cope with it?"

"What? No, no, it wasn't . . ."

He was already cycling away.

FROM: Charlie Jones
TO: Charlie Jones
SUBJECT: Day forty-three sober

Fuck, I'm angry.

I hate being angry.

It makes me want a drink.

FROM: Charlie Jones
TO: Charlie Jones
SUBJECT: Day forty-three sober (cont.)

I'm back at the stables now. Charlie's out somewhere—avoiding me, probably. I wish I'd been calmer when she told me about Rog. I keep seeing her face when I snapped at her. She looked hurt, and disappointed, and . . . anxious. Which I *hate*.

But I also hate being treated like I can't cope. The wolfish voice in my head thinks I can't cope, either, at least not without a beer or two, and it's hard enough ignoring that all day without Charlie acting like one small problem will make me fall apart.

Look at you, though, the voice says. *A little argument with your coworker and you can feel the darkness creeping in again. You're this close to having a drink.*

But the darkness *won't* close over me today. And I've *not* had a drink. I've lit the log burner—a fire is just the right kind of high-maintenance—and I'm mainlining Doc's custard creams. Sugar, keeping busy, and learning my lesson. If I really saw Charlie as a coworker, I wouldn't care nearly as much about her opinion of me. I need to put my walls back up—I need to concentrate on what I came here to do, and focus on my future.

The shop profits aren't high enough to justify two comanager salaries from October yet. And I've been ignoring the possibility that we won't get there, because frankly I've not wanted to think about it. Charlie and I are a team now, we're . . . well, we're whatever we are, friends, I guess, if you can call someone a friend when you want to stare at them all the time.

But I need to face reality. If we don't step things up a gear, there will only be funds for one of us to stay on. And I need to ask Marly exactly what that decision looks like, because that person has to be me.

First off, though, I need to speak to Rog.

CJ

FROM: **Charlie Jones**
TO: **Charlie Jones**
SUBJECT: **Day forty-three sober (cont.)**

I eventually tracked Rog down—he was still at the polytunnel, picking late into the evening with Marly and a few of the remaining summer workers.

A lot of people have assumed the worst of me, over the years. It's the ogreish looming, probably, the fact I'm not much of a smiler. So I'm not going to do that to Rog. I'm done with the darkness, the pessimism—when I'm not depressed, I'm a person who hopes for the best and looks for the good. So that's what I did in the polytunnel this evening.

I just asked him, straight up.

"Rog, did you take some cash from the shop till the other day?"

"Hmm? Oh, yeah, probably," he said distractedly. "For the extras fund. We always take it out the farm shop till—all one business, isn't it? It evens out, that's Rosie's logic."

"That's . . . Rosie's . . . logic?"

"So you know there's always a few B&Bers who don't pay, right? Like Red?"

I did not know this. My face said as much. Rog rounded on Marly, who glanced up briefly over her row of strawberry plants.

"You didn't tell them that?"

"Did they need to know?" Marly asked, head back down.

"Yeah!" Rog said. "They've seen me taking cash out the till and they think I'm nicking it!"

Marly stopped. "Oh. Shit. Sorry. He's not stealing it. You picking over there, Jones, or just having a yarn?"

"The till never balances," I said, pinching a few strawberries and putting them in Rog's container.

"No, well, it wouldn't," Marly said, "because when we need petty cash for the B&Bers who aren't paying rent, you know, for snacks, treats, extras, we just take it from the till."

"You can't do that," I said. "It's an accounting nightmare."

"Accounting is a nightmare anyway, and it's much easier than going all the way to the cashpoint in the post office."

I didn't even know where to begin with this, so instead I asked why some people at the B&B don't pay.

"Rosie," Marly said, as though no more explanation was needed. On seeing my bemused expression, she sighed, hands a blur as she moved her way down the line of strawberry plants. "Her parents did it—any young person in trouble, having a tough spell, they'd have a room at Bramblebay Farmhouse. When we decided to convert the place into a B&B, it was really important to Rosie to keep up what her parents had started, even if we were mostly putting in the extra bedrooms to try to make some money. So there's always at least one person there who's on reduced rent, no rent, whatever—Rosie decides. It's entirely at Rosie's whim. Completely nonsensical."

And very Ormer.

"That's actually lovely," I said.

I still have no idea how both Charlie and I ended up getting this job, and Marly and Rosie having something to do with it is top of the list, but how can I think badly of these women? How can I think they'd create this messy situation on purpose?

"Anyway, I'm the farmhouse guardian," Rog said. "I'm the one people call if there's trouble. Or they need a snack."

"Of course you are." I sighed, trying to refocus. "From now on, you don't just take random amounts of cash out of the till. We need to document where all the money comes from and goes to. Is there a business account for the B&B?"

"Right, someone said 'business'—I'm out! Can't be doing with the business talk!" Rog declared, moving off down the polytunnel, hefting his tub of fresh strawberries.

"Rog, you're a business owner," I pointed out. "In fact, you own about a hundred businesses."

"Stop saying 'business'! I just do odd jobs!"

I wonder what Rog's tax return looks like. I bet it's an interesting read.

"I'm done, too," Marly said, stretching out her shoulders. "Rosie's out this evening with Charlie—fancy a nonalcoholic cocktail at the farmhouse? What?" she added, at my surprised expression. "Do I not seem like a nonalcoholic cocktail woman?"

"Not really," I said. "Sorry."

"Well, we all have different sides to us, Jones, don't we? Virgin sex on the beach?"

It ended up being an unexpectedly nice evening, the sort of spontaneously enjoyable night that I would've thought could only happen with alcohol. We sat with Ginger in the snug room that Rosie and Marly use as their living room—the main one is given over to the B&B guests. It was cozy, packed with a sofa set that didn't really fit, dotted with family photos.

"All Rosie's," Marly said, when she saw me looking. "My family and I aren't really on family-snap terms."

"I'm sorry."

"Don't be. It's not the lesbian thing, they're not homophobes, they're just narcissistic wankers." She nodded to the biggest photograph, in the center of the mantelpiece—a young couple, eighties clothes and hair, big smiles. "Rosie's parents. I wish I'd known them. By all accounts they were *not* wankers. It's kind of sad to know I could've had an extended family if the Nicoles had lived—a good one."

"They do look nice," I said. "Very . . . parental."

"I know exactly what you mean. Like a stock photo of a good mum and dad. It's the kind eyes," Marly said, stroking Ginger's ears as she examined them. "And the way they're holding each other. So much love." She sniffed. "My parents were childhood sweethearts, too. Definitely didn't end with a marriage like that. Yours?"

I wasn't sure quite what to say. "Complicated," I told her, in the end. "Though I didn't really realize how complicated until recently. Funny what you accept as a kid, isn't it? You assume your life is the norm. But they screwed me up more than average, I'd say. We're not estranged or anything, just . . . not close."

"Sorry to hear it, mate."

"You know, you do have another family, now," I said, a bit tentatively. "Here on the island, at Bramblebay, with Rosie. You've built your own one."

"True." She gave me a fleeting smile over her glass. "What about you? Is that your plan—build a family here? I've seen you eye-flirting with Charlie."

"Charlie and I aren't talking right now. And if you saw any eye-flirting, that'll be the last of it."

Marly sat up, interested, and Ginger mimicked her so precisely I couldn't help smiling.

"Really? What happened?" Marly asked.

I explained that I'd caught Charlie in Rog's tractor, moments from firing him. Marly found it hilarious, annoyingly. Her guffaws of laughter really took the sting out of my argument that Charlie had behaved abominably.

"Ah, she was trying to be nice," Marly said, waving it off. "You wouldn't care so much if you weren't obsessed with her."

I protested this; Marly silenced me with a look.

"I've wanted to ask you what happens if we can't justify both our salaries," I said instead. "How will you choose who stays?"

Marly waved that off, too. "Let's cross that bridge. I suspect the answer will become obvious pretty soon."

"What do you mean?"

She looked at me shrewdly. "Just know I'm rooting for you."

We moved on to discussing something else, though now I'm home I'm realizing how uncomfortable that made me. Was she saying I'd get the job over Charlie, if it came to it? I should be pleased, obviously. But I can't help thinking it doesn't seem very fair.

CJ

FROM: **Charlie Jones**
TO: **Charlie Jones**
SUBJECT: **Day forty-four sober**

Charlie didn't get home until after midnight. I'd left the farmhouse around eleven, but I wasn't in bed, I was just watching the fire die down, drinking endless lemonades, writing that last email and ignoring the voice telling me it wouldn't be a big deal to have a glass of wine.

"I spoke to Rog," she said. Her tone was muted. "I'm really glad he wasn't stealing."

"Mm. Me, too."

We said nothing for a while. I didn't let myself look at her. I just fiddled with my lemonade bottle and stared into the fire. If we didn't live together, there was no way we'd have spent any time together this evening. Everything still felt raw.

"Did you figure out what's going on with Red?" I asked into the silence.

"No. She'd pulled herself together by the time I got there. She says she's fine. I'll get to the bottom of it eventually. I mean—we will."

Her voice wobbled a little. I couldn't help it: I looked at her then. I thought of Marly laughing at me, telling me I wouldn't care so much about the Rog thing if I wasn't obsessed with her. Charlie had her hair pulled up in a clasp, and there was a little worried frown just visible beneath her fringe. Despite the day we'd had, I wanted to smooth it away with a kiss.

It occurred to me that I'm so rarely angry, and when I am, it's almost always with myself. What had hurt about Charlie's behavior was the fact she'd confirmed something I loathe about myself. And that it had been Charlie, of all people, to do this—the person whose opinion I have apparently come to care about immensely. The woman I am—look, let's be honest—obsessed with.

Fuck.

Charlie met my eyes and took a deep breath in and out.

"I'm sorry," she said. "I shouldn't have assumed the worst about Rog. And I shouldn't have tried to handle it without you. I thought I was being mature and taking responsibility. Challenging the anxiety by taking on something everyone would dislike me for."

"There're two of us. You don't *have* to take all the responsibility," I said, but in truth the anger had gone out of me. And I liked that she'd apologized like that, without messing around or diluting it. Just a sorry and an explanation.

She moved around the sofa and perched on the arm. I could smell her perfume—it's rich and floral, too complicated to pick out one particular scent, and it lingers around this place all the time. Getting a proper hit of it made me close my eyes for a moment.

"It's just been so nice seeing you happy lately," she said. "I didn't want to wreck that. Though . . . I did, in the end."

"I don't need you to look after me, Charlie. I actually need to know I can cope, I think, without any crutches at all. No alcohol, nobody who I lean on to keep me going . . ."

"There's a big difference between leaning on alcohol and leaning on a friend. And I never thought you couldn't cope, I just wanted things to be good for you, that's all."

I felt a little shot of pleasure when she said that.

"Good, for me, is being someone who's an equal, not someone who needs babying, or looking after," I said, resisting the urge to ask, *Why do you want things to be good for me? Do you find yourself thinking about me all the time, the way I find myself thinking about you?*

She nodded. "I get that. I'm sorry."

Again, there was a lovely simplicity to that. I've never had an argument end quite like this one. I tried to give her back the same.

"I'm sorry for what I said about Galoshes. That doesn't have to be on you—it's not your fault she's so unreasonable with you."

"No, you were right, though. It's such an obstacle for us. I need to find a way to make her like me."

"No, you don't. You need to find a way to show her she should respect you. You're a pretty impressive person," I said softly. "Shouldn't be hard."

"Ha. I don't feel it when I'm around her. I just feel . . ." She pulled a face. "Anxious."

"Still feel new saying that?"

"Still new. Speaking of." She slid her foot across the sofa to nudge the empty bottle of lemonade in my hand. "Well done."

"Thank you. I've had four, and two mocktails at Marly's."

"Wow. You're well hydrated."

I told her yes, I was, and also high on sugar, and possibly lemons.

She laughed. "Does it help? The lemony sugar?"

"Sort of. You can't avoid yourself with a bottle of lemonade. Not that alcohol really lets you do that. It's just a trick of the light. You still end up face-to-face with yourself in the end, you're just doing it with a hangover and no idea what you did last night."

"Ah, sitting with the uncomfortable sensations instead of avoiding them. Yes. I'm trying this. I've been reading about anxiety."

"Yeah?"

"It's good. I feel hopeful. Maybe I won't always feel so afraid."

"Have you thought about medication?"

"I have. I think it's not for me right now. But I'm not ruling it out. I'm trying the Ormer method of managing the mind."

"Which is?"

"Fresh air, proper food and talking the bad stuff out loud to anyone who'll listen, which is probably everyone because this is an island full of eavesdroppers. And if those tricks fail you, go and pet one of the cart horses."

"I'm sure the National Health Service will be prescribing cart horses in no time."

She smiled, and then yawned, covering her mouth with her hand. "I should get to bed. Sleep is part of the Ormer method, too. I'm in the little room, right?"

I didn't want her to go to bed. I wanted her to stay here and talk to me all night, or at the very least to go to *my* bed, to slip into the double with me tonight. Every night.

Completely fucking obsessed.

"Before you go . . . Coming back to the trusting-each-other thing," I said, trying to gather myself.

She paused on her way toward the bedroom door. "Yeah?"

"It would be a lot easier if you didn't lie to me."

Her eyes widened slightly. "I didn't lie to you."

"You didn't tell me what you saw Rog doing. If you had . . ."

"I get I did the wrong thing. But I wasn't being dishonest. There's a difference between withholding something and lying, Jones."

I let her go with that, but I pondered it for a while. *Is* there a difference between withholding and lying? I'd have said yes, once, but now I'm not so sure. A lie is a lie, right? However you tell it, or don't.

Which makes me a total hypocrite, doesn't it?

CJ

Sunday September 21st 2025

OK. So, in the interest of talking the feelings out loud to anyone who will listen, including my own diary: my anxiety has been bad since the argument with Jones. Feel like the whole of my insides are sort of poisonous. Churning and swilling around like something toxic in my belly. And my brain's full of panicky white noise, and I'm just <u>worse</u> at everything right now, which makes me more anxious, because I get anxious about being bad at stuff, so here I am, swan-diving into a vicious spiral.

Right! Cheering up now!

Sorry, I'm actually done with this fake positivity. This is my diary, for God's sake. Who am I pretending <u>for</u>?

Guess it was naive, really, thinking this place could be my dream life. Your dream life isn't a place, it's not a job, it's not a persona you give yourself: independent mama-to-be in her Boden dress! It's a dream. Not real.

The fear's real. That's about it.

Tuesday September 23rd 2025

Hey. It's me again. Charlie Jones, instead of a terrified little fawn-type creature wandering around in her clothes.

It's good to be back. The feeling is still there, but I can see glimpses through the clouds now. The world doesn't look totally terrifying, all is not lost—I know I'm OK, even if I don't completely feel it.

What's set me off (kind of hate this phrase—is very "hysterical woman"—but can't think of a better one) is what Jones said about Caloshes. Specifically, the fact that my issues with Caloshes are the reason the shop isn't making more money.

Truth is, if Caloshes liked me, we would already be serving Doc's biscuits and fancy flat whites. We'd have autumn decorations that weren't constantly being rearranged, and stock laid out the way we wanted it, and staff who actually listened to us.

I've tried so hard to impress Caloshes, but I'm still failing, and because of that, I'm either going to lose my job here in two weeks' time, or . . . Jones is.

What would he do? Would he go back to the mainland? There are so few jobs here out of season—what else could he do?

So . . . yes. The anxiety is a little quieter now that I've figured out where it's coming from, for sure. But the truth is, I'm still scared.

Let's focus on the good things.

* The catalog of donors. That letter from the London fertility clinic, explaining how encouraging the results of my tests were. The possibility of a future I can build all on my own.
* The cows. Have formed a weird bond with a few of them, who often come over to eye me on the walk to the shop.

They don't ask anything of me, they just hang around, like they know I might want company. It's kind of sweet.

* The autumn sunshine. Crisp blue island skies. Birdsong at dusk. Ormer, basically—the clean air, the open space, the earth beneath my feet.
* Jones. He knows I'm not myself at the moment. He doesn't try to talk to me about it—just does little things to make my life easier. Handles the early-morning deliveries at the shop so that I can go for a run when I wake up. Quietly stores my leftovers in the fridge if I don't eat a proper meal in one sitting, because he knows sometimes I can manage a second try later when the anxiety's loosened up a bit. And yesterday he just . . . put his hand on my shoulder. He didn't say anything or do anything, just put his hand there. We hardly ever touch except by accident. I don't dare—I know I'd like it too much. It was strange how affecting it was, having his hand resting on my shoulder. I've never had someone just accept how I'm feeling that way before. Whatever the reason we ended up living this strange, shared life together, I'm grateful for him—even if he is an extremely troublesome distraction.

Have been thinking. Wonder if part of the reason my anxiety's got worse lately is that I'm feeling a bit . . . guilty. And not just about the job stuff—about the people here.

I knew when I decided to come to Ormer that I'd have to hold parts of my past back from the community I hoped to join here. Wanted new friends, new neighbors, and it didn't bother me that I'd have to keep the odd thing from them, because we all do that, right? Even Brianna doesn't know everything about me.

But now I'm here, it's different. Have ended up sharing so much of my real self with people—just last night Rosie and I went to the pub and ended up swapping notes on the ridiculous shit we both worry about, and it was so lovely. Came home feeling the best I have in ages. Guess I hadn't counted on wanting to share myself (my real self?) with so many of the people here. After all, never did much of that back home.

Also hadn't counted on Jones.

It's even harder to hold myself back with him than it is with the others. He's a proper empath, I think—he hurts when you're hurting, he cares. Can see why he turned up here determined to keep everyone at a distance. If you let people in that way, just by nature, then it must be extra painful when they let you down.

But look at this conversation we had at dinner tonight. This is classic Jones. Planned to chat about the shop—"what's up with Red and Toby" was top of my agenda—but instead we ended up talking about what it means to be a good person. The man cannot do surface-level. It's deep chat or nothing. Here, look:

"Do you believe in karma?" he asked me, spooning the rice onto our plates.

Had made korma, which was, genuinely, how this had come up.

"Not really. I think things happen for a reason, though."

"What reason, then?"

This made me pause.

"I think people maybe . . . get what they deserve." I winced as I said it. Wasn't necessarily a nice thought.

"Isn't that karma? The idea that your luck is influenced by your good and bad decisions in the past?"

We made our way to the table. Outside it was already dark—the evenings are drawing in now, and we'd closed the curtains on the long windows that line one side of the stables, to keep it cozy.

"I guess I like to think I'm not just the decisions I've made. That maybe even when I was making bad ones, I was still a good person."

One of the things I love about talking to Jones is that he never sidesteps or tries to laugh things off. He absorbs what I'm saying and really thinks about it, every time, no matter what it is.

"I wish I had your faith in yourself."

This took me aback. He saw my expression.

"I know you say you don't know who you are these days. But you do believe you're a good person," he said.

"I guess . . . I do. Actually. Deep down. I know I've made a lot of mistakes, and my brain does annoying stuff that I hate, but I think generally, my intentions are kind."

I watched how this landed with him.

"Your intentions," he repeated.

"Right. I mean, what <u>is</u> good and bad? Everyone has different ideas of it, don't they?" I shrugged, reaching for a paratha, hot from the frying pan. "I've been thinking about this a lot lately. I spend a huge amount of time trying to work out what other people think of what I've said and done, but really, that's not a sensible way to work out if those things are 'good' or 'bad,' because you'd never get the same answer. Caloshes thinks I did the wrong thing suggesting Toby run the farm shop solo on the morning when we were helping out on the farm; Toby's mum thinks I did the right thing."

"You definitely did the right thing."

"Well, that's your opinion, too, but thanks. What I'm saying is, I know my intentions were to help Toby see his potential, and push him—gently—into building his confidence. My intentions were kind. I won't get everything right, obviously, and if it had gone wrong I'd have felt really sorry about it, but I wouldn't think that decision made me a bad person."

After a long silence, Jones turned his face away.

"Are you OK?" I asked.

He wiped his eyes.

"Oh, God, sorry—did I make you cry?"

He shook his head and then, laughing at himself, nodded. And I just fucking melted. This man. I never knew it could be sexy to see a guy cry, but it was. Something about the combination of hard muscle and the way he turned his face away, the vulnerability in someone so strong . . . It made me want to crawl into his lap and hold him, get closer, get as close as can be.

"I just needed to hear that," he said hoarsely. "Thank you. It made me feel . . ."

"Sad, apparently," I said, pointing to his tears. Trying to break the tension. Anything to stop me reaching for him.

"No," he said. "It made me feel like I could let something go."

Jones and I have both very pointedly left our pasts in the past. That's fine when you're being rivals, or frenemies, or coworkers, or even friends, which I think is where we've got to, now. And it's fine in a crush, too—I fancy Jones, but I don't need to know what he was like when he was growing up.

But as he scrubbed the tears from his cheeks, I realized I really wanted to know what he needed to let go. I wanted to know everything. Past, present, future.

And that . . . that's a major worry.

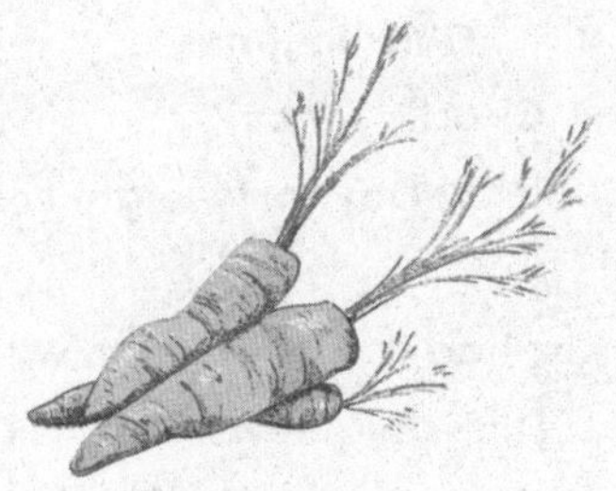

FROM: **Charlie Jones**
TO: **Charlie Jones**
SUBJECT: **Day forty-seven sober**

Acknowledging the Charlie obsession has not helped with the Charlie obsession.

She's in the bath right now. "I'm just going to chill and read," she said, drifting by with a paperback, and then she undressed on the other side of the door and slipped into the water with a long, soft sigh.

We won't live together, soon. Whatever happens, come October 6th, one of us will move out—if we're both staying, it'll be easy to find accommodation elsewhere by then, with tourist season ending. A bit of space between us should be a good thing. It'll help with the obsession, surely. But it doesn't feel like a good thing.

I spend almost every minute of my day with Charlie, and honestly, I don't know how I'll be able to handle a minute less of her.

CJ

FROM: **Charlie Jones**
TO: **Charlie Jones**
SUBJECT: **Day forty-eight sober**

I just had a conversation with Toby.

This is big news. Toby is an astonishingly accomplished conversation dodger. He has done hours—days—of shifts with me and has still managed never to utter more than five words at a time in my presence.

It's not that he's unfriendly—he's just very shy, I think. Everything I know of him is impressive: rumor has it he's doing well in an Open University course, and he's a runner, and we occasionally cross paths around the island when I'm out mountain biking (though he does often turn around when he sees me and run the other way). Most impressive of all, though, he's a hugely gifted artist. Marly showed me the mural he's painting at the farmhouse when I was there the other night, and it's incredible—this massive stylized depiction of the Nicole family's history on the island right through to the present day.

Anyway, today, Toby came to *me*. He sidestepped over from behind the till while I was sorting the fridges and cleared his throat. I was so surprised it took me a while to realize he didn't just want me to move out of his way. Toby's hair was, as usual, gelled to cover as much of his face as possible; I could see about half an eye.

"I need some advice," he whispered.

"Sure. What can I do for you?" I said.

"I don't know if you've . . . noticed . . ." Toby trailed off, playing with the laces of his hoodie.

I suggested we could sit down in the sunshine, grab a hot drink. As we are—famously—not yet up and running serving coffees, we're all still making our own in the back room, and the picnic benches are languishing, generally used to store things or lean bikes against.

Toby remained completely silent as I made us both a coffee and we sat opposite each other on one of the benches. It was warm enough to sit out here, just—there's a bite in the wind, now, and I was grateful for the latest of Galoshes's hand-knitted jumpers I'd acquired. Everyone knows Charlie has changed her look since getting here—the sweet ribboned dresses are long gone, and she's always in a pair of chunky boots under some sort of long skirt or her favorite jeans—but I have, too, really. I am very much a woolly jumper man these days.

"So what's up, Toby?"

"You may have noticed . . . some tension . . . between Red and me."

I said something vague like, Oh, really? As though I didn't have this very issue written on my to-do list.

"The thing is . . . the only person I can talk to about stuff is my mum," Toby said, his voice getting smaller and smaller. "Well . . . my mum and Red. Before. But . . . something changed. And I have . . . no idea what."

"With Red?"

He nodded.

"You guys were friends? Or more than friends?"

"More than friends," Toby said, in such a quiet whisper I had to duck forward to hear him.

"Really!" I said, then tried to dial down the surprise.

Why *was* I so surprised? Toby is a good guy, and I'd have guessed that Red is just the sort of person to see through things like shyness and bad hair to spot herself one of those.

"I know," Toby said miserably. "We had the most amazing few weeks together when she arrived. We stayed up all night talking, camped under the stars . . . I've never been so happy. She made me feel . . . enough. More than enough." He hung his head. "Then she stopped talking. And I figured . . . she'd just seen sense . . . and gone off me. But she won't . . . even look at me. I think she's . . . upset . . . but I don't know what I did . . ."

"Have you asked her?"

He blinked across the table at me. What I could see of his face was a picture of desolation. It was a helpful reminder that while life in your thirties has its challenges, anything beats being a teenager.

"Any time I try to speak to her . . . she just runs off. And she leaves all my messages on read. I don't know . . . what to do . . . but you seem . . . you know, you seem like you've probably . . . dated loads of women . . ."

I choked on my coffee.

"I mean, I have dated some women," I said. "But I wouldn't say I'm an expert in romance. I am single, for starters."

"Right, but . . . you're good at talking to everyone . . . and Charlie always stares at you when you're not looking . . . and I'm pretty sure the girl tourists hang out in the shop more when you're around . . ."

I was keen for him to elaborate on this.

"Like that one earlier . . . who was trying to choose a yogurt for like . . . ten minutes? Oh, you meant Charlie? Yeah, she's always looking at you, and finding reasons to be near you, that kind of thing . . ."

This delighted me far too much. With a great deal of effort, I returned my attention to Toby's love life and suggested he could write Red a note.

"A note?" He stared at me, perplexed. "But I don't . . . I don't even know what I'd say."

Which is how I ended up helping a nineteen-year-old write a love letter this afternoon.

And now, ridiculously, I'm off to deliver it. Toby went wide-eyed with terror at the thought of pushing it under Red's door at the B&B, so I took pity.

I'll write again soon, when I'm done playing Cupid with the staff.

So much for not getting emotionally involved . . .

Bye for now,
Charlie Jones

FROM: **Charlie Jones**
TO: **Charlie Jones**
SUBJECT: **Day forty-eight sober (cont.)**

Here's how that went.

"Jones," Marly said in surprise when she found me on the farmhouse doorstep.

Ginger shot out from behind her, colliding with my shins in her enthusiasm to say hello. I scratched her ears.

"Sorry, I know it's late. I need to hand deliver a love note. Is Red in?"

"*Red?* No! What about Charlie? Red's way too young for you—Charlie's a proper grown-up. She could handle you. Here, Ginger, it's only Jones, have some composure, girl."

"I'm not giving Red a love note from *myself*, Marly. For one thing, I'm her employer."

"Oh. That, too."

"It's from Toby."

"*Oh*, that lovesick little pup—I wondered why he'd stopped coming around. They had a falling-out, have they?"

Marly opened the door and let me into the hall, Ginger racing ahead of us. The fire was crackling in the living room—their first of the season, Marly told me—and there was a large cast-iron pot bubbling on top of the Aga stove in the kitchen.

"He's not sure what happened, actually," I told her. "Red kind of ghosted him."

"You can't ghost someone on the Isle of Ormer. It's impossible. The old guy who used to own the tourist tat shop tried to do it to Rog to avoid paying him for something, and news got around so fast it was discussed at the next night's parliamentary meeting."

Intrigued, I asked what happened to him.

"I told you when you arrived, Jones—we look after our own here. And we have our own rules."

"Swimming with the fishes, is he?"

"Ormer Parliament created a new law just for him. They made it illegal to sell figurines, just for a bit. Don't laugh, he'd have rather been thrown in the ocean, I reckon. The man had a shop full of china he had to ship back to the mainland. Anyway, Red's working at the pub tonight," Marly went on, looking down at the envelope I was holding. "You want me to take the note for her?"

"Toby asked me to push it under the door. I was given very specific instructions."

Marly grinned. "Third door on the left as you go up." She headed back toward the kitchen, Ginger at her heel. "Come by for pudding once you're done playing postman—Karyn's been testing new chocolate pots, Rosie wangled all the duds for us!"

I headed up the stairs. And look, it's not that I went snooping. I just did some math on my way down the corridor. I know everyone who's staying at the B&B at the moment—they're all long-term guests and they stop at the shop now and then. There's Red, then a couple of older guys who served in the US Army and struggled to find their feet afterward, an octogenarian living out her dream of island life, a lawyer just out of a nervous breakdown, and that's it.

Five guests. But as I walked along the corridor, I noticed six rooms. There was another door, labeled *Private*, which I assumed led to Rosie and Marly's room, and then the bedrooms were all numbered, with B&B-style room names. 1. Fritillary, 2. Kestrel, 3. Minke, 4. Fulmar, 5. Gannet, 6. Puffin. A small name card had been added below each room name with the guest staying there, in Rosie's curly handwriting. But Puffin room had no guest, and the door wasn't clicked into the frame.

When we first got here, we asked Rosie if there was a spare room, and she said no. Marly promised she'd tell me as soon as anyone moved on from the B&B, since their booking system is "unofficial," which I think means it only exists inside Rosie's head.

So I was surprised to find a seemingly unoccupied room. And it was so easy, as I walked past, to give the door a gentle push and check inside.

The double bed was made, but untouched. There were no personal possessions visible, just a clean towel waiting on the chair beneath the window and a little stack of books on a shelf by the bed, with titles like *The History of Ormer*, *The Channel Islands Through the Ages*, *Ormer Families*. It looked like the perfect B&B bedroom, waiting for its guest.

I pulled the door closed and made my way to Red's door, kneeling to push Toby's note beneath it. When I headed back downstairs, I went into the kitchen to find Marly with her holey socks up on the dining table, eating a chocolate pudding from what looked like a recycled yogurt pot.

"G'day," she said. "Mission accomplished?"

"Yeah, thanks." I took the pudding she nudged my way. "It's lovely up there. I've never actually been upstairs before."

"Oh, thanks—all Rosie. I'm not really the decor type. Give me a tractor any day. Hard to believe she's the one with the farmer genes, sometimes."

I considered finding a subtle way to ask the question, but honestly, Marly's my friend, she's a straightforward person and I'd so much rather be open with her.

"Who do you guys have staying at the moment?" I asked.

Marly ran through the list of names.

"Five people. But six rooms?" I said.

I kept my tone as light as possible, but still, she stiffened.

"Puffin's not available."

I just about swallowed back on saying *It looked pretty available*—I didn't want to confess to looking behind a closed door.

"You keep a whole room empty?" I said instead. "Why?"

"It's not empty. It's . . . reserved." She sighed. "I know how it sounds. You need a room, we have a room spare . . . But I can't give you Puffin."

I told her I get it—it's none of my business. But the pudding kind of stuck in my throat.

Marly looked at me for a long moment. "It could be your business," she said. "I know Rosie said you can take as long as you need to open up to us about why you're here, but it's been almost two months, Jones. It's time to find out who's the best fit here, do you understand me? You or Charlie?"

She was giving me this look. As though she was trying to tell me something without saying it.

"Sorry, what? What does the shop have to do with the empty room?" I asked.

"No, nothing. It's not about the shop. It's about you."

"Me?" I backtracked. "What do you mean, me or Charlie—we're hoping we can both stay, aren't we?"

"Forget it, Jones," Marly said, getting up and chucking the yogurt pot in the sink. "You want to carry on playing games, then carry on playing them. But keeping your cards close to your chest might not be the best way to manage the hand you've been dealt."

She just walked off after that, leaving me to show myself out. I stood for a moment in their farmhouse kitchen, absolutely bewildered. What game did she think I was playing? What did she mean, *It's about you*? And what the hell did an empty room at the B&B have to do with me and Charlie?

So long,
Charlie Jones

Guildford, four months earlier

Charlie's phone rang. It was Oliver.

"Just checking in," he said, clearing his croaky throat.

Every time Charlie answered the phone and heard Oliver's voice, a shadow of what she had felt that day in the Brecon Beacons would move through her. *Fearne calling*, her phone had said.

She had known somebody was dead, or dying—she had seen the medics from the air ambulance unloading the stretcher as she reached for the phone on the car seat. There had been an unspeakable, sickening moment of suspension as it rang. The truth hadn't quite been true yet, at least not for Charlie. In that instant, she'd thought, *Thank God it wasn't Fearne.*

But the panicked voice on the other end of the line had been Oliver's. He had used Fearne's phone—in the tangle of their crash among the trees, it was the only one that he could find.

Oliver had lived.

And Fearne was gone.

Her dearest friend, that effervescent bubble of a human being, who had been her sister, who had taught her what it felt like to be loved. She was dead, and Charlie woke up every morning thinking the knowledge of it might be the end of her, too.

“Charlie?” Oliver said now, his voice still scratchy. “Are you OK?”

Charlie was standing in the middle of Fearne’s flat. She was clearing the place out. Fearne’s family lived in Cornwall and had left shortly after the funeral; they had each chosen sentimental items, but Charlie had insisted that she would take on the burden of clearing the apartment for them. Bri was on her way over to help soon. She hadn’t known Fearne like Charlie had—they’d never quite gelled. Both such strong personalities, perhaps, that a room couldn’t hold the two of them at once. But Brianna was a person who showed support by showing up, and Charlie couldn’t seem to shake her off at the moment.

“I’m fine,” Charlie said, staring down at all of Fearne’s pots and pans. The woman never cooked—why had she owned so many saucepans? Charlie sipped her thermos of coffee and rubbed at her blurry eyes. “I should be the one checking on you. How’s your arm?”

He’d fractured a bone in the crash; his arm was in a sling, and there was something schoolboyish about it, this strapping man with his arm in its little bandage hammock.

“It’s fine. It’s whatever. I don’t deserve looking after.”

She frowned. “That’s crazy, Oliver, no.”

“It should have been me,” Oliver whispered.

“Oliver . . .”

Every time he said this, her stomach swooped with guilt. Did he know what she’d thought? Was that moment written on her, the split second in which she’d wanted him dead?

“It was my fault,” Oliver said, his voice thick with tears. “It was my fault she died.”

“It wasn’t your fault,” she said forcefully into the phone, using her other hand to sift through saucepan lids.

Oliver could not seem to hear this enough, and his absolute conviction that somehow he could have saved Fearne sometimes rubbed off on Charlie. She would find herself thinking perhaps *she* was to blame. She'd been reading Berty's texts when Fearne had crashed. Sometimes she thought that was simply bad karma—she had let her ex in and was being punished. Sometimes she imagined that she'd missed something important on that hillside, something that could have saved Fearne. She could have called the air ambulance instead of Oliver; perhaps he could have used his hands to stabilize Fearne's spine, and then she would not have died. *You killed Fearne*, she would think to herself. *You basically killed her yourself.*

These sorts of extreme thoughts were not new to Charlie. They sidled into her brain and took up residence now and then. *You're a piece of shit*, her inner voice would say out of nowhere, often at three in the morning, when her defenses were at their weakest. *Everyone will see it eventually, and they'll all leave you. It's what you deserve.*

The thoughts had worsened since Fearne's death. Sometimes they sounded like Berty: *There's something very wrong with you*, she'd think, and she would almost hear his voice telling her so in the dark.

People who met Charlie would never, ever expect that she sometimes wondered such things. She seemed bubbly and fun. Obliging. A bit of a loose cannon, a bit scatty, kind of high-intensity, but certainly not *mad*. And Charlie felt sure that only a mad person, or a very bad person, could think the thoughts she did in the middle of the night, so every morning she forcibly forgot them, brushing them away as she combed her hair and styled her fringe. By the time she had her morning coffee, she was Charlie Jones again: sweet, fun and perfectly normal.

Brianna finally arrived at Fearne's flat two hours late, a tornado with bin bags and cleaning products. She looked Charlie up and down in Fearne's hallway.

"I knew you wouldn't be looking after yourself."

"Hi, Bri," Charlie said wearily.

"I don't know if you just don't want me in your life at the moment, or whatever, but you've dodged way too many of my calls over the last six months," Brianna said grimly, as she pulled Charlie into a fierce hug. "And I am not a person who can handle being ignored. I'm leaving the assistant director in charge for this, and he couldn't find his way out of a wet paper bag, so you better actually talk to me or I'll have ruined Friday's episode of *Eastside Close* for nothing."

Brianna pushed past Charlie and began to sort Fearne's belongings into piles. Charlie winced every time she touched something.

"You need some fresh air. You look terrible. Are you eating? Sleeping?"

"Not you, too," Charlie said, before she could stop herself.

Last night Oliver had been fretting about her again—she'd forgotten their plans for the day, and then she'd left the light on in her car and run the battery down. But wasn't she allowed to be a little all over the place right now? Everyone was always so hard on her.

And Bri was the worst. Her judgmental concern about Charlie's well-being had always been much more irritating than Oliver's soft questioning ever could be. Charlie flashed back to the conversation they'd had when Charlie had first begun to distance herself from Brianna. *You seem like a bit of a mess*, Bri had said, in that blunt way of hers. *There's nothing in your fridge—just wine and margarine. And when did you start wearing odd socks? Is that a fashion thing?*

"Oliver still fussing over you?" Bri said shrewdly. "How's he doing? He and Fearne were good friends, weren't they?"

"He's . . ." Charlie wasn't sure what to say. Oliver seemed to be withdrawing into himself; every time they spoke, he was a little duller, his eyes a little blanker. "He's struggling. He was there with her when she—when Fearne—when she died."

"Christ," Brianna said, pausing midway through bagging up a bunch of Fearne's pom-pom cushions. "Poor man. That must be hard for you as well, though. Are you having to look after him, too?"

"I don't mind. I love him."

Brianna looked slightly surprised.

"Wow, right," she said. "And you want the same things?"

This question threw Charlie slightly, and Brianna—of course—noticed.

"The kids thing," she said. "He knows how you feel about it?"

"We've . . . It's not come up yet."

"Charlie . . ."

She felt ashamed.

"It was too early to begin with, too casual, and then . . . We've not really been in that place . . ."

"But you do think you're good together?" Brianna asked. On Charlie's exasperated, exhausted look, she softened. "I'm worried about you. And I'm worried he's not helping. I wonder if you need a fresh start, Charlie. Is this guy really the person you need?"

"He is. He's the right person for me."

But even as she said it, it felt wrong. Fearne was the person she needed, not Oliver. And there it was again, the blast of guilt. Berty popped into her head, just to hammer the feeling home.

She doubled down. "Oliver's perfect," she said, reaching for a bin bag. "He's everything I want, all right?"

The week after Fearne's funeral, Oliver had gone to bed, and he barely got up in the weeks that followed.

It was not simply grief. Charlie knew that, because surely there could be no grief heavier than hers, and *she* was not rotting under the duvet, sullen and unresponsive. Brianna told her Oliver was depressed, but Charlie couldn't quite believe that—she knew you weren't meant to think things like this, but she felt Oliver was just not that sort of *person*. He was scrappy and resilient and determined. He was surely suffering from something else, something physical. She didn't know, because he hardly spoke.

Still wracked with grief herself, she cared for him with great tenderness, as though she were enacting a montage of a Kind and Supportive Girlfriend. Unfortunately, nobody was watching; the reality was exhausting, and she often found her kindness wearing thin. She would sometimes leave his house and sit on a particular bench opposite, let her head collapse forward onto her knees and simply sob.

But she kept going. She imagined Fearne often—they'd known each other so well Charlie hardly needed Fearne around to access Fearneness these days, and that trait became half blessing, half curse. She would feel Fearne behind her, standing on tiptoe to rest her chin on Charlie's shoulder, or would hear her cackling laugh from nowhere. It was beautiful and excruciating every time she caught a trace of her.

Oliver had these moments, too. They talked about them sometimes, on his better days. It was this that kept her coming back—the fact that he understood. And perhaps the guilt, too. The knowledge that some deep, awful part of herself had wished for a moment that he'd died on that hillside. That when it came to the fork in the road, the sliding doors moment, she'd wanted the universe to choose Fearne.

"Do you know," Oliver said one day, as they lay facing each other in his bed, "we haven't kissed? Since Fearne died?"

The room was filthy. Charlie cleaned the house often, but Oliver filled it with mess again: uneaten food, unwashed clothes, unopened post from races he'd entered before Fearne's death. Charlie hated being in his house now—hated being with him, sometimes, if she was truly honest with herself. It was so hard to remember the sexy, understated, self-confident man he had been.

"Oh," Charlie said. "I . . . I guess we haven't."

"Do you still love me, do you think?" Oliver asked.

His tone was curious rather than pained. After a moment, he took her hand from where it lay on the bed between them.

"It's OK," he said.

"I must love you," Charlie said, and she was shocked to find her eyes filling with tears as she said it.

"I'm so sorry," Oliver whispered. "Looking after me like this has been hard for you. Of course you've fallen out of love with me."

"Oliver, God, don't," she said, beginning to cry. "I *do* love you."

"In a way," he finished for her. "You love me in a way. But not in the way that you loved Berty."

She shut her eyes tightly, squeezing two tears onto the pillow beneath her.

"You've done so much for me," Oliver said, wiping her tears away. "Especially these last few weeks. But you don't have to stay with me just because I'm . . . like this. You can leave, Charlie."

"I don't want to leave you," Charlie said, and she meant it.

True, she didn't love him with the fiery endlessness with which she had loved Berty. But she did care for him, and she owed him, too. Or was it Fearne she owed? Whoever it was, she felt a deep, cosmic obligation to keep returning to this squalid place.

"Can we stay together like . . . friends?" she asked, and then cringed at herself. "I just mean that I still want to help you get back on your feet, and talk to you about Fearne, and still see you . . ."

It occurred to her only as she said this that it might actually be true.

"I want you in my life," she whispered.

Oliver smiled. A tiny, Oliver smile, the first she'd seen in several weeks.

"Well, I like being in your life, Charlie. So that works."

It did work, sort of. They fell into a routine as Oliver began to recover, a kind of mutually supportive grief. They would stay up late on his tiny balcony over the A road, drinking toasts and sharing stories of Fearne. Charlie would go to work the next day and try to turn the shop she'd built with Fearne into something that could exist without her.

But Charlie couldn't shake Brianna's words from the night at Fearne's flat. *I wonder if you need a fresh start, Charlie.*

When Fearne was alive, they'd sometimes joked that it was Fearne's world, and everyone else was just living in it. And in a sense, it had been, for Charlie. It hadn't particularly bothered her: she loved Fearne, and was happy to let her best friend lead. She didn't mind her days being filled with bikes, and when Fearne's handsome friend wanted to take her out on a date, she didn't mind that, either. But now Fearne was gone, Charlie had been left in a sort of . . . ghost life. Even her job was a dream she had shared with

Fearne. She was estranged from her adoptive parents and had no other family, yet; she had nothing to anchor her but an ex-boyfriend who moved through the same ghost town she did.

She woke up one morning with a pounding head, stared across at her bedroom wall and realized she had no idea what she and Oliver had done the previous night. Had they cooked pasta for dinner? One day was sliding miserably into the next; they were not in the first pit of grief, but wherever they were now was viscous and gloomy, an emotional quagmire. Charlie reached blindly for her phone and began to doomscroll, as she did every morning, but part of her recoiled as she did it. She was looking for escapism, presumably, but where was the pleasure in this? Where was the pleasure in anything, lately?

It was fate, Charlie told herself later. She turned to her usual bookmarked pages—Isle of Ormer property, the Isle of Ormer official site, the community Facebook page—and there it was, advertised in gold letters above an image of the island in its emerald-green splendor.

ARE YOU SEEKING A DIFFERENT KIND OF LIFE?

WOULD YOU LIKE TO JOIN A WARM, FRIENDLY COMMUNITY ON A BEAUTIFUL, SECLUDED ISLAND?

FARM SHOP MANAGER REQUIRED AT BRAMBLEBAY FARM. APPLY TO ROSIE NICOLE, BRAMBLEBAY FARM, ISLE OF ORMER.

Charlie could hardly believe how perfect it was.

She handwrote her application. She stretched the truth a little on her CV—Vintage, Please was not *quite* the resounding success she made it sound—but her cover letter was all truth. She wrote about how she had been fascinated by the Isle of Ormer for many years. She wrote about how it was time, at last, to live the dream she had made so many mood boards about. And she finished her letter by saying that more than anything, she hoped Bramblebay Farm might be her *home*, the home she'd always longed to find.

Wednesday September 24th 2025

Anxiety's not been so bad today—honestly can't say why, maybe it was facing the fact the Caloshes stuff was triggering it? Or maybe it's just Ormer Ormering away around me in its beautiful autumn colors, reminding me that the great big gorgeous world gives no shits about the nonsense knots I'm tying in my own head. The Rosie method—the big-sky method. Whatever the reason, it's an absolute <u>relief</u> not to feel like I want to climb out of my body for a while.

Came home from work and Jones was out. Felt weird. Bit disappointed—he's usually in on a Wednesday night. We tend to have a cozy evening, cook something with a lot of cheese in it, switch the lights out early (have got in habit of going to bed at same time, because of bedroom logistics. We say good night through the door once we're both tucked in—it's all sickeningly cute, and there I lie, thinking about him topless).

Eventually spotted Jones out of the kitchen window. He was gardening. Odd—I've never seen him garden before. Rog and I did some planting out there a few weeks ago (before I almost accused him of theft) and am not actually sure Jones had yet noticed. But there he was, with my trowel, hacking away at something in the soil. Looked hard going. Plus it was almost dark.

By the time I'd gotten my trainers on and headed out to query this new activity, he was sitting on our garden bench, sipping at a coffee with the satisfaction of a man who had Achieved Something. I looked at the flower bed.

"Umm. You dug up all my primroses?"

"What?" Jones said, pausing midsip and giving the flower bed a double take. "What primroses?"

I pointed at the heap of greenery now sitting by the hedge.

"Oh, shit," Jones said, putting his coffee down beside him. "Those weren't weeds?"

"Those weren't weeds," I confirmed.

"Oh no. I'm so sorry."

Shifted his coffee to the side so I could sit down. "Hope that's decaf," I said, peering into his mug.

"Well, it's not whisky," he said slightly distractedly. He was still gazing at the flower bed. "Do you think I can replant them?"

"You could try," I said, eyeing the squished primroses. "What inspired the sudden Monty Don–ing?"

"Bit of a weird day. You know Toby's in love with Red?"

"I did sort of figure, with all the longing gazing."

"They were together for a few weeks," Jones said, reaching down to flip over one of the more distinct-looking primroses from the heap beside us. "They're really not weeds? There aren't any petals, or . . ."

"Not yet," I said, trying not to laugh. "They're not in flower right now."

"You'd have killed me for ruining your flower bed six weeks ago," Jones said, looking up at me with a little smile as he straightened.

When I first met Jones, he was so <u>heavy</u>. Heavy brow, heavy shoulders. These days, he's lighter. There's still a shadowy quality to him—a sense of complexity, maybe—but it reads as maturity rather than messiness. I remember when I first saw him at the harbor, I thought his whole vibe was very "I'm a hot mess, try to fix me." Now it's more, "I've got layers, want to see?"

"I'd only have minded because I'd care so much what Rog would think about us wrecking the flower bed he built. And what the rest of the committee would think when they walked along the track and saw our garden."

"Ah, and you're done trying to impress people now?"

"Absolutely," I said, having just spent my day relentlessly trying "casual chat" with Caloshes (my latest unsuccessful tactic for winning her over). "Did you say Red and Toby were together?" I asked, rewinding.

"I know. An intense summer romance, apparently. All sorts of grand promises made. Then Red just stopped replying and started avoiding him whenever possible. It's been driving him crazy."

"That doesn't sound like Red. She wouldn't mess someone around like that."

"That is actually not the mystery of the evening," Jones said, chucking the remnants of his coffee into the grass. "I went to the farmhouse to drop off a love note for her from Toby—"

"I'm sorry, you what?"

Jones looked distinctly embarrassed, which made the whole thing even cuter.

"Look, it's a long story, the boy was very upset . . ."

"How's the grumpy island hermit act going for you, by the way?" I asked.

He leaned his shoulder into me, a teasing nudge. All very friendly and PC, but my body didn't think so. My stomach went swoopy. I leaned back, just a little—prolonging the moment, maybe turning it into something else. Sitting shoulder to shoulder with him in the darkening garden, I found myself thinking, I don't just want him. That swoop in my stomach, it's pure, undiluted longing.

And honestly, I thought that feeling was gone for good. Thought I'd grown out of it, had been through too much. Surely you can only want someone like this when you don't know how easily they could hurt you.

I pressed my shoulder to his and savored it, and all the while I was thinking . . . Oh no.

"So, yeah, there's a spare room at the B&B, but they won't let us use it," Jones was saying, moving away slightly, breaking that connection between us.

"What?"

I was busy having my terrifying epiphany: Jones, my job-stealing knitwear-wearing deep-chatting roommate, had shifted from the category of "distractingly hot guy but obviously won't go there" to "major, major problem." Because you can't ignore a stomach swoop like that. It's rare. It's precious. It demands your attention.

"A whole empty room. And Marly got so weird about it. She started talking about the shop, and us, as if me being told about the room was conditional on me telling them stuff about me, and my life? Then she got sort of pissed off at me."

"Sorry," I said, catching up, "there is a spare room? But we can't have it? Why not? Do they not trust us in their house?"

So weird to think we could've potentially stayed on the island without being housemates. Imagine not saying good night to Jones through the wall every evening, or brushing against him as we pass in the kitchen, or talking the way we do over dinner sometimes, the way I've never talked to a man before. Don't think I actually knew men could be as interesting as Jones.

"I have no idea," Jones said. "I've been out here ruining your flower beds trying to think it all over. Do you think it has something to do with the job mix-up? Somehow?"

"The room? How could it?"

"I really don't know," he said.

He paused for a moment, looking at me in the darkness. I shivered.

"What will you do, if we can't get the shop running a better profit by harvest festival?" he asked softly.

"We will."

"We really might not."

I looked away. "We will. I've got a plan with Caloshes. You'll see."

He seemed relieved. Which just demonstrates the problem with the stomach swooping. Because I don't have a plan with Caloshes at all—just didn't want him to worry. The sort of shit you do for a person you like way too much.

Thursday September 25th 2025

New day. Have pulled myself together and stopped lusting after my inconveniently named roommate. Well, not stopped, but have redirected my brain to other, more productive avenues. Don't know what I was thinking last night—I've let this crush get too far. No more sexy daydreaming about Jones. The plan is solo motherhood. There is no way to do that with a man in the mix.

Helpfully massive job crisis to deal with anyway—it's less than two weeks until harvest festival, which means the Caloshes problem needs sorting now.

Have decided to tackle this one element at a time. The most pressing issue is not the in-my-face insubordination, it's the fact that she's blocking the coffee and biscuits. We're losing precious days to prove the concept—we're almost out of time. Had a brain wave on my run this morning, though. One thing I learned in my old job is that a woman who feels powerful will relax. And I think Galoshes feels powerless right now. So as much as I want to show her who's boss, and force her to do as she's told . . .

"How would you do it?" I asked, sitting down opposite her as she ate her lunch on one of the farm shop picnic benches.

She looked startled, and then irritated. Not surprising. This was absolutely an ambush.

"This is my lunch break," she said, taking a very deliberate bite of her pasty.

"Then you can have the time back. I want to know how you'd do it. How could we introduce coffee and biscuits at the farm shop, but do it the Ormer way?"

Her chewing slowed a little. She swallowed, looking at me with narrowed eyes through her pink-rimmed glasses. I bit down on the anxious impulse to tell her not to worry and that I'd come back later. There was no later. I was out of time.

"The Ormer way? Do you even know what that means?"

"No," I said. "Not really. I would really like to, though."

"Well. I suppose I'd offer discounts for locals, so they could afford it, too."

"Good idea."

She looked at me suspiciously.

"What else?" I asked.

"When they used to serve drinks down at the post office, some of us would just wander over with a mug."

"Bring your own mug—love it."

"And the coffee wouldn't be some fancy forty quid a bag stuff. Just normal coffee."

Winced a bit at this. But fine—we can still put some nice farm-shoppy touches on the flavor description on the chalkboard. "Amber tones," "cinnamon-edged," that sort of thing. I mean, who's to know? It's like wine, everyone's just making it up.

"And any leftovers go to those families on the island who need it. We all know who they are. No fuss, we'd see it gets to where it should go."

"I'd need a little more detail on that, but absolutely, we would want to avoid waste anyway."

Caloshes put her pasty down. "Are you serious about this?"

"I'm serious about this. I realize we've been a bit heavy-handed here. This isn't just a shop, it's a community center. We need to make sure the changes reflect that, as well as making money."

Caloshes folded her arms. "And tell Doc to tone down the wankery."

I burst out laughing. "I might word it differently, but all right—we'll keep it simple to begin with, shall we?"

After a long, agonizing moment, Caloshes nodded once.

"Really?" I said, my voice a bit too shrill. "You won't block us at tonight's meeting?"

"I wouldn't block you," Caloshes said, affronted.

"Right . . ."

"But I think Baptiste's objections on animal rights grounds might be revoked, now you mention it."

"Animal rights?"

"All that butter."

I laughed again. Caloshes remained entirely straight-faced, adjusting her glasses, but there was maybe a hint of warmth in those eyes. Progress, definitely.

Just read back over all this and feel so great about it. Have got somewhere with Caloshes! She still doesn't respect me, of course, but who cares? (. . . I care. Enormously. Find it hard to think about anything else, actually. But progress is progress, and at least now while I'm obsessing about impressing Caloshes I can do it next to the Bramblebay Farm Shop coffee machine.)

Next job is harvest festival planning. Ormer does harvest festival in a big way—there's a tractor procession, orange leafy wreaths on every door on the Rue, the chocolate shop sets up a stall on the harbor selling gingerbread and pumpkin-spiced hot chocolate . . . but Bramblebay Farm has never been involved.

Which is ridiculous. We should be at the heart of harvest festival. We're a farm! There is no harvest without us! So, buoyed up by coffee and biscuit success, am plotting new festival schemes while Red manages the till. Thinking donkeys should be involved. More soon.

Returned to the shop floor to find Red nowhere to be seen. That girl does a disappearing act like nobody else—often find she has vanished when Toby is around, and then reappears as though she was never gone—but nonetheless was quite surprised. She was supposed to be in charge while I stepped out to think about donkeys.

Then heard the sound of sniffling. Crying, unmistakably.

Crept toward the till. Red was crouched behind the counter, curls falling forward, shoulders shaking with sobs.

"Oh, Red, what is it?" I asked, coming around the counter to duck down beside her.

She jumped. "Shoot," she said, tugging her sleeves over her hands to wipe her face, expertly dodging her piercings. "I'm so sorry, Charlie, I was just taking a minute, if I'd heard the door open I would have . . ."

"Don't worry about it. Hang on."

Hopped up and flicked our sign to CLOSED. People could wait a minute for their pumpkins and leeks.

"What's going on, honey?"

She was sitting cross-legged on the floor now, staring miserably at her own feet.

"Please talk to me. Are you OK?"

"I'm fine." She wiped her cheeks again. "I'm so sorry to be making such a fuss."

"Please don't say that. Do men make a fuss?"

She paused for a moment. "No, they never do, do they?"

"Right! So we're not doing that, either. You're upset. I'm sure you're upset for a good reason. Even if the good reason is 'my hormones are doing a mad dance today because my period is due.'"

That got me a little smile. I leaned to pinch her a pack of travel tissues from by the till. Would put them through later. Or just steal them, maybe, since apparently we are all quite chill about borrowing from the shop when need be.

"I can't talk about it," Red whispered. "There's nobody I can tell. I've not spoken to my parents since they kicked me out, and my brother lives on the other side of the planet, and he never picks up when I call him anyway . . ."

Leaned in to hug her, and let her cry into my shoulder.

"I promise I've known my fair share of everything going dramatically wrong, and I'm a great listener. And a <u>great</u> keeper of secrets. I won't tell a soul anything you don't want me to tell."

She pulled back slowly and reached for the pocket of her hoodie. Her hand stayed there, clutching something.

"I don't know what to do," she said miserably.

"That's OK. Maybe I'll know."

"I can't say it."

"That's OK, too. You can write it down. Mime it. I'm excellent at interpreting all forms of expressive dance, too."

Was staring at the hand in her pocket—felt sure that when she brought it out, saying anything wouldn't be necessary. Could see her loosening up a little. After a long moment, she gave me the bravest wobbly smile as she pulled her fist from her hoodie and showed me what was inside.

A pregnancy test. Two lines.

My heart did a small, guilty hiccup. But just a small one. Six months ago, seeing a positive pregnancy test in someone else's hand would have made me wretched with jealousy, then full of shame at not being able to feel joyful for them. Then would descend into panic as I went through the same old cycle of thoughts: what if I'm not with the right man, what if he'll never want kids with me, what if I never have this? Then I'd probably spend a day trying to convince myself I didn't want it that badly anyway, and there was plenty of time, and it was <u>fine</u>, I was <u>fine</u>, it was <u>fine</u> to wait.

I know myself so much better now. If I'd realized back then how anxious I can get about other people's opinions of me, I'd have clocked that I'd spent the last decade tiptoeing around wanting kids in case I freaked out my boyfriend or he thought I was being (God forbid) Too Much. I'd have recognized that I <u>do</u> want a baby, a lot, and don't want to wait.

Sitting there with Red, it was easy to let the envy pass through me and drift away again, because I understood it. I've forgiven it. Even better: I've taken this choice into my hands. No more subtle hinting and desperately hoping. No more letting a man decide when it's time. I'm doing this on my own. I'm in control.

So I smiled at her. "Red," I said softly. "You're pregnant."

She burst into another flood of tears, leaning into me again. It was a totally awkward mess of a hug, but she didn't seem to mind, so I held her as best I could on the shop floor and let her cry.

"Oh, honey . . . Do you not want—"

"I do. I want to have the baby," she whispered into my shoulder. "But . . . Charlie . . ."

Ding! went the little bell above the shop door.

We sprang apart in a flurry of tissues. I tried to stand, ended up getting stuck under Red's knee, bashed my elbow on the counter, belatedly realized her hair was caught in the button on my shirt collar, and by the time this impromptu game of Twister was over, Marly was there, leaning over the counter, staring down at us with a perplexed expression.

"Are you two . . ."

She trailed off. Her gaze had landed on the pregnancy test lying on the flagstones between us.

I looked at Red's face. In the split second of silence, she gave a tiny, pleading, desperate shake of her head.

I turned to Marly. "That's mine," I said. "Sorry. That's mine."

Swiped it up and shoved it in my pocket. Silence stretched.

"If you could just pretend you never saw that, I'd appreciate it," I said to Marly.

The enormity of what I'd just done was sinking in. Marly was studying our faces. Red's was tearstained, while my makeup was presumably unsmudged.

"Red found the test in the bathroom," I said. "She was upset because she didn't know whether to speak to me about it."

This was actually totally excruciating. Yes, I've made peace with the envy, but pretending to be pregnant when it's something I want so badly my heart aches . . . that's a whole other ball game.

"Charlie . . . there's no midwife on the island," Marly said to me, her eyes serious. "Doc Laurry is lovely, and brilliant, but he'd be the first to say he doesn't specialize in women's health. We don't recommend anyone stays on the island if they're pregnant."

Ah. I glanced at Red. Her hands were twisted together and her bottom lip was shaking.

I knew she was staying at the B&B, earning her keep by working here. Knew she couldn't go home to her parents. And I guess I knew why she didn't want Marly to find out she was going to have a baby.

Which meant that for now . . . I was going to have to keep up another lie.

And this lie . . . Oh, this lie <u>hurt</u>.

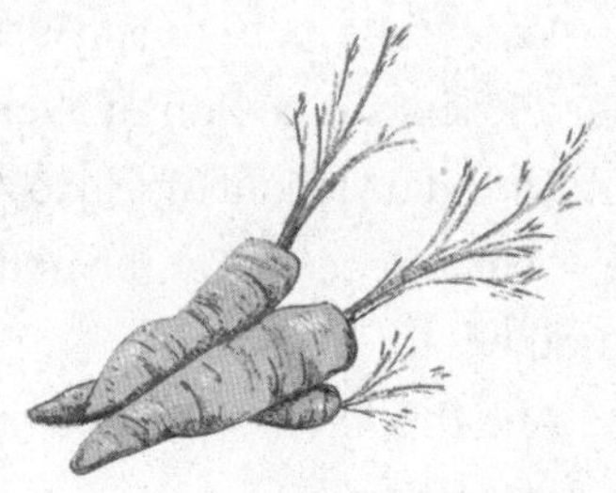

FROM: **Charlie Jones**
TO: **Charlie Jones**
SUBJECT: **Day fifty sober**

It was a clear day today, blue skies and orange leaves. Rosie insisted on Marly taking a Friday off, and Charlie was managing the shop, so Marly and I decided to cycle down to the beach by Hoard Cave, one of the spots on the island I wanted a closer look at. Red had told me that pirates used to stash stolen goods there; I had visions of chests of gold coins.

Marly said nothing about the spare room. I didn't, either. I just wanted a ride with my friend, mix-ups and mysteries put aside. She was quiet, though, like something was preoccupying her.

"Have you seen Charlie today?" she asked eventually, as we left our bikes on the gravel and began to pick our way across to the cave.

It was only accessible at low tide, but thankfully I am well aware of the tide times these days—or at least, I have an app for that.

I told Marly I'd seen Charlie at breakfast, leaving out the part where my heart soared because Charlie ate the whole bowl of overnight oats I'd made for her. She's not felt able to eat a meal in one go for ages. She slept properly last night, too. I love it when she's less anxious. There's a strange kind of satisfaction to it. It's like watching your football team winning the game. *Fuck you, anxiety*, I thought, as she smiled at me over her mug of coffee. *My girl's going to take you down.*

I realized Marly was giving me a slightly odd look. She said she'd seen Charlie yesterday, and that she'd "had some stuff to tell her."

"Really? What stuff?"

She scanned my face for a moment before staring out to sea.

"Some stuff about the harvest festival. The whole barn dance plan."

I had to ask her to repeat this, for obvious reasons.

"Barn dance. It's a fun idea. Very tourist friendly, and a good use of the old sheep barn."

I had a lot of questions at this point. The old sheep barn with only half a roof? Had we looked into insurance for this? Had anyone confirmed that the barn would stay standing for the duration of a barn dance, however long one of those was?

"Charlie thought a harvest festival barn dance would encourage people to bring the celebration up here, spend some money at the farm shop. Jerry's got a folksy, country sort of band, they'll do the music—"

"Jerry the milkman? The constable? Who runs the secondhand book trailer?"

Yes, apparently.

"What even is barn dancing? I'm not actually sure."

"Oh, you know," Marly said, pausing briefly between the rocks to do some kind of country-and-western-style jig on the sand. There was a lot of arm-pumping involved, as though she was trying to inflate an air bed. "Someone yells out the moves, everyone joins in . . ."

"This sounds terrible," I said, with genuine horror. "Enforced dancing? And you think this is a good idea?"

"I'm not going to be bloody dancing, am I?" Marly said. "I'll be working at the bar. But Rosie's in love with the whole plan. There's also something involving a donkey, but I'm hazy on the details."

I asked who on the island has a donkey, and Marly said there were some wild ones on Little Ormer, which did not fill me with good feelings about whatever Charlie had planned. We were almost at the cave now, its entrance a dark shadow on the cliffs ahead. Marly swung her rucksack from her shoulder and chucked me an old-fashioned, clunky flashlight.

I approached the cave, the beam of my flashlight catching the shine on the wet sand inside. Our feet left thick, sludgy footprints as we stepped in, heads ducked.

It got dark quickly. The sound of slow-running water echoed around us.

"Keep going," Marly said when I faltered, seeing the cave narrow to a slit just about wide enough for one person.

"What, down there?"

"You want to see the hoard? Or not?"

I didn't know what that was, but I knew I wanted to see it. Marly nudged me in the back with her flashlight and I twisted to squeeze through the gap. There was an inch of water between the stones under my feet now, and we were dropping; I had to cling to the rocks around me as I climbed down the narrow passageway. The wet boulders beneath me were streaked in strange colors, rusty blues and pale greens. Eventually the walls of the cave began to widen on either side, and then it opened out again into the most extraordinary cavern.

I shone my light around. The walls of the cavern were dotted with the strangest alien-like creatures—anemones, Marly told me. They looked like hundreds of giant red gemstones, or boiled sweets stuck to the cave walls, shining wet and vibrant. It was an amazing sight. We stood in hushed silence, gazing around us.

"It never gets old, this place. You get it, I know you do. The island's home for you, isn't it?" she said eventually, her voice echoing quietly through the cavern.

"I think it might be, yeah."

She smiled. "Want a picture? Here, give me your phone. I left mine at the farmhouse."

She took a moment fiddling around trying to open my camera app.

"You all right there, Grandma?" I said.

She took revenge by taking a candid shot that I can confirm, now that I've got my phone back, was extremely unflattering.

"There you go," she said, handing my phone over.

I frowned. She looked distracted again. Disappointed, even, as though I'd said something that she'd hoped I wouldn't say.

"Sorry, the grandma thing was a bad joke," I said, suddenly thinking of all the ways it might be insensitive. Rosie and Marly didn't have any children, but perhaps it was a painful topic for them; for all I know, she might long to be a grandma one day, but it isn't in the cards for her.

"What? No, jeez, I don't care about that. Come on, let's get back before we're drowned by the rising tide, shall we?"

I followed her out of the cave.

When I first met Marly, she really didn't strike me as the mysterious, unreadable type. She was so straightforward. But lately I feel like half the time I don't understand what she's trying to tell me.

And the strangest thing is, as I walked behind her, back through the cave, my light caught on her back pocket, and the unmistakable shape of her phone. So she didn't leave it at the farmhouse at all.

Why would she lie?

I feel a bit low this evening, which is unfair, really, because who am I to judge Marly for holding things back?

I'm starting to see everything so differently from when I first arrived here. Secrets don't feel harmless anymore—I'm not sure how I ever kidded myself they were. The idea that I can leave the past behind seems increasingly ridiculous now that I'm sober. I'm finding myself constantly looking back to the man I used to be, and the thought of *never* telling anybody here about my life before they met me . . . it doesn't feel freeing. It feels like a new kind of burden to carry.

Especially with Charlie. I just read this email through and saw I'd called her *my girl*—I didn't even notice myself typing it. It didn't feel strange. It felt true.

Maybe it could be, if Marly and Rosie let us both keep our jobs? If Charlie and I are just coworkers, not competing for anything, not living together . . . could it happen then?

I'm not sure how she feels about me now, but Toby says she stares at me. And there was that kiss, in the rain, at the lighthouse . . .

I don't know. I can't believe I'm even letting myself consider it—I came here so determined to keep *everyone* at a distance. But honestly, these days, I spend most of my time longing to pull Charlie close.

Night,
Charlie Jones

Sunday September 28th 2025

Feel powerful urge for a list. Always a sure sign I'm stressed-out. Here's the situation:

* Red thinks she's about ten weeks pregnant.
* Toby is the father. (Poor confused Toby—but more on this soon.)
* Red needs to see a midwife.
* Red doesn't want Marly and Rosie to know she's pregnant, because she's worried they won't let her stay at the B&B.
* Toby doesn't know Red is pregnant.
* Marly thinks <u>I'm</u> pregnant.

Red's pretty overwhelmed right now, so I didn't want to go too hard on the whole "You need to see a midwife! You need to tell Toby! You need to tell Marly!" stuff. But she does, she does, and she does. Can't go on with Marly thinking I'm pregnant—it's too hard. And there's only so long that I can be all that Red needs here.

Pouring with rain today—have just ducked into the pub to write this out. They've lit the open fire, so I'm drying off here, waiting out the weather, figuring out what and how to tell Jones about today when I get home.

It's been an intense afternoon.

Red asked me over to the farmhouse to help her sort her head out, as she put it. We sat on her bed—"Is this weird?" she asked. "Being my boss and seeing how messy my bedroom is?" I explained that being a boss is not the same as being your mum and I really don't care about the state of her bedroom as long as she knows how to sell an onion that's slightly past its prime. Though it really was a state in there. Clothes and shoes everywhere, Chappell Roan posters stuck to the walls with dried-out poster putty, several plates growing new species of mold.

"I don't know how to tell Toby," Red said, fiddling with an envelope.

"Oh my God, is that the love note?"

Very nearly finished this sentence with *that Jones wrote*—saved it just in time.

"How do you know about that?"

"Just . . . Toby mentioned it to Jones."

"He did?" Red's eyes were wide. "What does he think is going on? He must be so confused. But he's so young, Charlie—he's nineteen. He still lives with his mum! I can't tell him he's going to be a father." The last word was said in a whisper.

"He only lives with his mum because rentals are really limited on this island," I said, pointing a finger at her. "And you're young, too!"

"I'm twenty-three."

Said with gravity, as though announcing that she was in fact middle-aged.

"He's a kind, sensible guy, Red, and he loves you. I think you should tell him soon, especially if you're sure you want to have the baby."

"I am sure," she said solemnly, and she pressed one hand to her stomach, which made mine turn over.

"Good." Took a little moment to collect myself, then plowed on. "And you love him, don't you? Don't you want him to be part of all of this?"

"Right now, it's . . . mine," she said, so quietly I almost couldn't hear her. "Like a little precious secret. Once I tell him, it'll be a problem, won't it?" Her eyes filled with tears. "We'll have to work out what to do, how to manage, I mean, we have no money, neither of us have a place to live that's ours . . ."

"Could you live with Toby's mum?" I suggested.

"I don't know! I don't know, and I just . . . don't want to think about it all right now." She looked down at her hand, pressed to her belly. "For now, I just want it to be my precious secret. Does that make any sense?"

I sighed. Because yes. It made total sense to me.

Left her with a (fresh and clean) plate of biscuits from the pantry downstairs, a large bottle of water and firm instructions to stay hydrated. On my way down the corridor, couldn't help stopping outside Puffin room. The door was clicked shut now—Jones said it was ajar when he came by. But I'm not as scrupulous a person as him, let's be honest, so I peeked inside. Then stepped inside, and closed the door behind me, because if you're going to snoop, you might as well actually do it properly.

Why was that room empty? Whose had it been, or who was it waiting for? And did that person have something to do with the mix-up that brought me and Jones here together?

I moseyed around, doing the sort of random low-key "searching" that someone might do for approximately five seconds on the telly before zoning in on the spot in the room where all the secrets were hidden (Look, a book sticking out on a bookcase!). Didn't work, unfortunately. Everything was very nondescript. The room was decorated pretty neutrally compared to the B&B as a whole, as though it was waiting for someone to bring their character to it.

Headed for the little stack of books on the shelf by the bed. They were all about Ormer—hardly surprising for a guest room on the island. Tugged out The History of Ormer and flicked through it, and finally got my TV-detective "bingo" moment.

There were a few sheets of paper folded in the center of the book. I opened them up. The pages were typed, with photographs dotting each one.

It was a list of people, each with a picture beside them. And every single person on the list was called Charlie Jones.

Got home to find Jones fast asleep on the sofa, in front of the crackling log burner. Was slightly shocked by how impossible it was to hold back a smile at the sight of him, especially given pounding anxiety after B&B discovery. With his hair messy and his checked shirt unbuttoned enough to show the hair on his chest, the firelight caught the sweetest side to him.

"You're home late," he said, cracking an eye open.

"And you're not even using the bed. If you were willing to take the sofa, why did we have that argument about sleeping arrangements when we first arrived here?"

"You stole half my new life. I was irritable." He yawned, stretching. "Where were you?"

Dropped my bag on the floor by the sofa (have decided that, since Jones leaves everything on the floor and cannot be trained out of this, I will just start doing the same. If you can't beat 'em, etc.).

"You stole half of my new life, thank you," I said, but I was thinking of the list, the other Charlies. Seemed like the two of us ending up with half a new life wasn't a coincidence at all. "Budge up," I said.

Jones shuffled along the sofa, swinging his legs around so there was room for me. He smiled as I sat down beside him, then frowned.

"You're feeling anxious?" he said. It was only half a question—he already knew the answer. He laid one steadying hand on my arm. "What can I do?"

God, I could have wept at the loveliness of that question. It was impossible to resist the urge to lean onto his shoulder, so I let myself rest my head there and closed my eyes.

"I went to the room," I said.

"At the farmhouse?"

"Mm. And look." I shifted to pull out my phone. I'd taken a photo of each page of the list before putting it back where I'd found it.

Charlie Jones from Wisconsin, Charlie Jones from Paris, Charlie Jones from Llandrindod Wells . . . all with their little profile pictures beside them. Some had more information beneath their name:

* likes dogs
* one of four siblings
* works in banking

"What the fuck?" Jones breathed, scrolling down to the page below. "This was in that room? At the farmhouse?"

I nodded.

"What the <u>fuck</u>?" he said again. "What does it mean? Why . . . are they obsessed with Charlie Joneses?"

"A Charlie Jones fetish is currently my top explanation," I said. I wasn't even joking. "They didn't contact <u>you</u>, did they, about the job? Like how they recruit people for <u>Love Island</u> from TikTok?"

"What? No, I just . . ." He looked back down at the list on my phone, his brow furrowed. "I never spoke to Rosie or Marly before we came to the island."

"Well, me neither."

"But they knew who we were," he said slowly, and then paused. "Except they didn't. I'm not on here. You're not on here, either."

"Nope."

He kept flicking through the pictures, searching each page in turn.

"What does it all mean?" He rubbed his eyes as he handed my phone back.

I tucked my feet underneath me. "You know those big dog gatherings they do? Five hundred cocker spaniels all in one place?"

He started laughing. "That, but for Charlie Joneses?"

"Right. There are four hundred and ninety-eight more of us on this island right now, waiting for the big meet-up."

Was still close to him from leaning on his shoulder. Our knees were touching, our bodies turned toward each other. It was lovely—too lovely, dangerously lovely—but the anxiety was still roiling in my stomach, and it wasn't just the business with the farmhouse and the shop. The more I get to know Jones—the more I fall for him, if I'm truly honest with myself—the more I find myself coming back to that question of my intentions.

When I arrived here, my intention was to start a new life. It was nothing to do with anybody else, I reasoned—it was <u>mine</u> and my future child's, and any truths I decided not to share wouldn't hurt anybody. They were just part of the fresh start. Nobody here had a <u>right</u> to know about who I was before I got here, except Marly and Rosie, but as long as I'm doing a great job at the farm shop, I can keep the guilt about that at bay.

But the closer I get to people—to Jones—the harder it becomes to say that my intentions are entirely positive. If I'm being truthful, I'm now hiding parts of myself because I'm afraid of how everyone will feel about me if they find out the truth.

"Shall we have one of your honey and chamomile teas?" Jones asked. "Forget about the whole weird situation for a while? I don't want to talk about it if it's making you feel more anxious."

He gave me the ghost of a smile, eyes crinkling, and my whole body warmed in response. Reminded myself very sternly that I didn't come to this island for the tingly, glowy feeling I get when Jones smiles at me—I came to this island determined to leave men aside.

Just hadn't counted on a man like this one.

"It might be nice to talk about something else for a while," I said. "Mostly because we can't do much about this, can we? We can't ask Rosie or Marly without confessing that I went poking around in their guest room."

"When you first turned up here, I would never have thought you had that in you."

"Ah, when I was Fake Charlie? Yeah, well, you can definitely claim some of the credit for me embracing my true self: the snoop."

"I barely did anything. Just pissed you off in the rain one day."

"You goaded the good girl out of me."

His smile was slow and a little sweet. I wondered if he could talk about that night without thinking of the kiss in the rain. I definitely can't. Can't even write about it now without going there. His body hard against mine, his lips slick with rainwater . . .

"I like you a lot better when you're not behaving yourself," he said, stretching his arm across the back of the sofa.

My breath quickened. Glanced at his crinkling gray-blue eyes and then looked away hastily, because that felt like a very risky place to look. His gaze wasn't just soft and sweet now. There was heat there.

"Does getting nastier really count as personal growth?" I said, through a laugh.

"You're never nasty."

"What am I, then?"

It was a dangerous question, and I knew it. But I wanted to hear what he thought of me. Wanted to catch him in this moment—sleepy, walls down, knowing smile on his face—and hear him say what I suspected we both knew.

There was something here. It had grown slowly, like the two of us, and it was absolutely going nowhere, couldn't go anywhere. But it felt so good. I looked away, my gaze finding my handbag. I keep the catalog of donors in there—don't want to leave it lying around the stables. Stared at the bag and tried very hard to remember exactly why flirting with Jones was such a bad idea.

"You're thoughtful and kind," he said softly. "Funny, too. You get the best out of people. You're scared, sometimes, and you do the thing anyway. You're brave. And you're so beautiful that I want to stare at you nonstop. I thought for a while if I looked enough, I'd get you memorized, and I could quit, but it really hasn't worked that way."

I kept my eyes fixed on that handbag. It began to swim in my vision.

"One all," I said. "You made me cry, this time."

He reached out to squeeze my ankle. His hand lingered, then, when I didn't pull away, it stayed. The way I was sitting, knees to the side, legs tucked, meant his knuckles were tantalizingly close to my upper thigh. I wanted him to move, just a little. Imagined him stretching out his fingers, climbing his hand up the curve of my hip and gripping me there.

"Charlie. I never thought . . ." His voice was husky.

The look in his eyes sent a feeling through me, a kind of inversion of the anxiety: a firework, but a good one. I looked down at his hand on my ankle. Slowly, fully in the knowledge that I shouldn't, I slid my hand over his. Just this—his hand on me, mine on him—was enough to send desire beating through me. It was becoming so bloody hard to remember why we shouldn't do this. Had a wild vision of telling him, *I want a baby*, and of him saying, *I want a baby, too, right now, let's have a baby together*, but of course it was crazy. It would never happen like that. I know exactly how it would go: I'd fall for him, then either scare him off or let him string me along for far too long, and all the while I'd lose yet more precious time.

"Charlie," he said again, his voice deeper. Almost a warning.

Knew I should let go of his hand. Move away. Keep my eyes down.

Instead, I looked up and met his gaze. Saw pure, raw longing there, and felt it surge through me in response, and knew I was done for. Reason was gone. There was nothing I could do except lean forward to kiss him.

He moved in the same moment. We met halfway, lips fierce as we collided with a searing kiss. My hands were in his hair, tugging and clawing, and his fingers worked their way under my jumper, searching for skin, finding it. He gripped my hip. I lay back, pulling him over me as we kissed harder. Wild and messy. He ground against me, just once, and I cried out—I was already lost in it, lost with him.

I honestly don't know how long it was before I saw sense. He said "Charlie" again—moaned it, his lips against my neck. That was what pulled me up short.

"Jones," I said breathlessly.

He stopped instantly. Heard something in my voice, I guess, or felt it in my body.

"You OK?" he asked, smoothing my fringe back from my forehead.

I could feel his chest heaving against mine.

"I just . . . I can't," I said, and he was already moving off me, straightening his shirt, shoving back his hair. His eyes were warm and kind, but he gripped the sofa cushion as he settled back into it, as if he needed something to hold him steady.

"I'm sorry, I didn't mean to get . . ." He took a breath, running a hand over his face. "I was trying to tell you, I never thought anyone could make me feel . . ."

I said his name again, pulling my knees up to my chest. His eyes searched my face.

"No?" he said. "You don't feel the same?"

His voice cracked a bit. Felt like my heart might crack, too, but I said what I needed to say, because I had to.

"I can't," I whispered. "Not right now. That's not what . . . I'm not in a place where I can . . ."

But I found myself reaching out and lacing my fingers over his again, filling in the gaps. His expression was full of yearning. I love how Jones's emotions are always right there in his eyes: the anger, the sadness, now the hope. I was full of yearning, too, still am right here with my notebook in my bed, but the resolution I'd made was loud in my mind. No more men choosing my future for me. No more letting them decide.

"I can't do this right now," I whispered instead. "I'm so sorry."

"OK. Of course. That's OK."

I knotted my fingers more tightly through his, my whole body aching. Didn't mean to kiss him again, but we were so close, and everything that had just happened was right there, like a note still hanging in the air.

This kiss was light, barely there, but it instantly lit that blaze in me again. My heart beat in my throat. He lifted a hand to my hair but hardly touched me this time, fingertips as light as his lips on mine. I let out a noise, the sound of that yearning in my chest. His thumb slowly traced my jaw and the sparks went all the way to my toes.

"I won't—I won't do that again," Jones said, pulling back slightly. "I'm sorry."

"No, I'm sorry. I just . . . I wish I could, but I can't."

The whole conversation was half silence—neither of us managed to finish a single thought. And all the while I was on *fire*. I ran my thumb across the back of his hand, tracing the freckles there, trying to steady myself. Wanted to say *Maybe one day*, but that wouldn't have been fair. Wanted to say *Please have a baby with me*, but that would be ridiculous. Wanted to say *There's so much I'm not telling you*, but what would be the use in that?

So we sat there, silent, hands touching, both flushed and breathing fast. I wondered what he wasn't saying, either. All the gaps and the holes and the fears we couldn't let go.

"I'm glad we're here, all the same," Jones whispered. "Both of us, I mean. I'm glad our paths crossed the way they did."

"Me, too," I said quietly. At least I could give him that much.

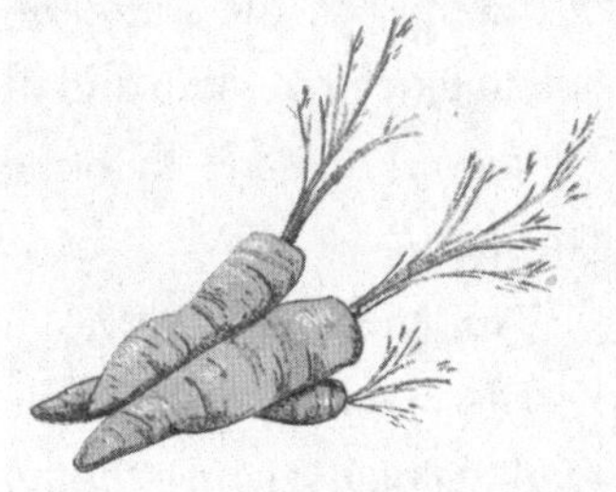

FROM: Charlie Jones
TO: Charlie Jones
SUBJECT: Day fifty-three sober

I can't write about last night.

I can't write it all down here. It's too intimate. I can't even write down why I can't write it down.

But I can say that I haven't stopped thinking about it for a single second since.

The problem with living with the woman you're falling in love with is that once you've decided not to kiss again, or not to do all the other things you want to do, you're still just both there. Together. She took herself off to bed first, afterward, but popped back into the kitchen to get a glass of water in those pajamas, the pale blue ones with the little shorts, and I felt like I was going to go mad if I didn't touch her.

Right now, she said. *I can't do this right now.*

Is it reasonable to feel hopeful after that? Or am I being delusional? To me, *not right now* conveys a possible *yes right now*, one day. She's been very open about the fact that she turned up here grieving and brokenhearted. I don't mind waiting until she's ready, if that's what she wants.

Is it what she wants, though?

Bye for now (see—it implies that I'll be back, doesn't it?).

Charlie Jones

FROM: **Charlie Jones**
TO: **Charlie Jones**
SUBJECT: **Day fifty-three sober (cont.)**

Reading over the below, I think perhaps that email was even more embarrassing than it would have been if I'd detailed everything that had happened on the sofa with Charlie. I am thirty-seven. I am an adult. What am I doing? What would I advise Toby to do?

I just need to talk to Charlie and finish a sentence. I need to ask her what she needs from me right now, and whether after *right now* is over, there's any chance she might want . . . I don't know. Me, I guess. She's gone to the shop for the early shift, but we're meeting to discuss harvest festival this lunchtime, so I'll see her then, and have time to talk to her properly afterward.

It doesn't have to be all fraught and angst ridden. We just need to have a grown-up conversation. There are a lot of things to consider here. Our living situation. The job share. The bizarre list of Charlie Joneses from the Bramblebay Farmhouse spare room. I need to keep a level head.

. . . But I can't stop thinking about last night, that's the problem. I honestly cannot stop the memory of it from appearing in my mind, over and over, every beautiful second of it. I've been sitting here with my laptop on my knees, in bed, getting absolutely fuck all done, and it's absurd. My head is not level. I am not feeling like a grown-up at all. I'm feeling like a teenage boy, and I don't know what the hell to do about it.

So long,
Charlie Jones

FROM: **Charlie Jones**
TO: **Charlie Jones**
SUBJECT: **Day fifty-three sober (cont.)**

Let me recount the harvest festival meeting, explosive secrets and all.

The rain was thick and heavy; everyone arrived at the farm shop dripping, then shed all their waterproofs at the door.

"Change is coming," Galoshes said ominously. "You can feel it in the air."

"What a depressing spin on autumn," Charlie said.

"Can we talk about my squash bobbing idea?" Red asked.

"You know I'm all for the harvest theme, but can't we just do regular apple bobbing?" Charlie asked. "Apples are autumnal, too, aren't they? I mean, you mull them—that's basically the test."

We were standing in the middle of the shop, the rain coming down on the roof with that satisfying pitter-patter that always makes me think of camping. Charlie was dressed in a long skirt and a woolly brown jumper, her hair pulled up in a clasp; she looked fresh-faced and beautiful, and every time I glanced at her, I knew she could feel it. It was something in her posture—her usual poise was just a little more self-aware. I had to swallow my smile as her cheeks pinkened under my gaze. *She doesn't want a relationship right now*, I reminded myself. But I'm a patient man. I can wait.

This is the problem with hope—once it kicks in, you can't shut the bloody thing up.

Meanwhile Red was waving a round zucchini under my nose. "Is that not the most autumnal thing you ever did see?"

She seemed much happier than she had been last week, though I've had no update from Toby. He was still gazing longingly at her from where he stood beside Galoshes, so I assumed their relationship issues remain unresolved. I found myself thinking, *Why don't they simply talk to each other?* and then remembered that I, too, have absolutely no idea where I stand. I was probably gazing longingly at Charlie, too. Maybe you never grow out of being foolish when you're in love. I can't decide if that thought is depressing or lovely.

I tried to return my attention to the zucchini situation and asked Red if she meant it was autumnal because it was yellow.

"It's just *fun*. Vegetables in unexpected shapes are fun. And apple bobbing is so done. We want to do things the Ormer way!"

"I like apple bobbing," Toby offered. "And I'm . . . pretty Ormer. Seventh generation."

He blushed beet red, and I gave him an encouraging look. When we first got here, he'd never have spoken up in a meeting like that.

"You'll *love* squash bobbing then," Red said, very brightly, though without looking at him. She deflated slightly as everyone remained in puzzled silence. "All right, I'll be straight up with you. Rosie planted way too many of these, and nobody's buying them, so she's bribing me to win you around to the idea, OK?"

"Ah. Did Marly by any chance advise against this crop?"

"I suspect so?" Red said, trying to suppress a grin.

I grinned, too, and then my smile dropped—I remembered that list in Marly's spare room, and the fact that my friend was hiding something from me. A few weeks ago, it would have been proof that I was right about keeping my walls up—and it's true that the whole business would hurt a lot less if I'd kept Marly at a distance. But I don't think I ever *could* have. That plan was never realistic. I am not a man with walls, and I just have to live with it.

"Out of interest, what was Rosie's bribe?" Charlie asked.

"She said she'd let me drive her tractor."

Charlie laughed. "Honey, sort out Rog's dodgy Wi-Fi and he'll let you borrow one of his for a week," she said.

Rog, of course, was late for this meeting—something to do with delivering a trailer to a sheep farmer, or possibly it was the sheep he was delivering, I forget. When Rog calls me to make his excuses, I generally just tune out these days.

"He's been bugging me to go around and fix it since I got here," Charlie told Red. "Apparently I look 'tech savvy.'"

"It's the fringe," Red said.

"Right? I cut it in myself, you know."

This was an excellent excuse to stare at her, under the guise of examining her hair. Though, now that I was actually looking at it more closely, I noticed that her roots were peeking through—I hadn't realized she wasn't naturally brunette, but the hair at her parting was pale.

"No way! Do you have a before and after?"

Charlie paused at that. "Maybe somewhere," she said. "Next on the agenda: donkeys."

Charlie was definitely avoiding my eye. Unlike Toby, I actually saw this as an excellent sign. You don't avoid somebody's eye if you still see them as a friend. You avoid someone's eye if *not right now* means *maybe soon.*

"Don't be daft," said Galoshes. "You'll never catch 'em."

"I was talking to Baptiste about it, and he said those donkeys aren't actually wild—they're domesticated but broke out of someone's garden one day and never came back."

"Are you suggesting we offer donkey rides?" I said, with horror. "On semi-feral donkeys?"

"No, no! I just want them in the field behind the sheep barn where the dance is happening, for the photo opportunities. Tourists love an animal, and the pigs are already occupying West Hilly Field—we just need a good shot in the other direction."

"Dance?" Galoshes said, with suspicion. "What dance?"

"The barn dance," Charlie said. "And before you tell me you hate the idea—"

Galoshes promptly confirmed that she did indeed hate the idea.

"I have the perfect job for you," Charlie told her.

"I refuse to do it."

"You don't even know what it is."

"I'm not doing it, whatever it is."

Charlie's eyes flicked to me. I watched her take a deep breath, and then return her gaze to Galoshes.

"Galoshes, until October the 6th, I am your boss," she said.

"Half of my boss," Galoshes said. "The smaller half."

"In what—" Charlie gathered herself. "That means that until Monday, I have the power to fire you."

"You wouldn't dare," Galoshes said immediately.

"When I first came here, no, I wouldn't have dared. But I've come a long way, and learned a lot about myself, and frankly,

I've tried everything. I've cajoled you, included you, placated you, and you still won't treat me with even a gram of respect."

"I said yes to your biscuits, didn't I?" Galoshes said.

"That was a start," Charlie acknowledged. "But doesn't actually make up for the constant insubordination."

"You've tried the carrot, now for the stick, eh? I don't buy it. You wouldn't fire me."

"Please. Give me a final straw. Give me one last reason." Charlie's voice dropped deeper. "And see if I'll do it."

There was a long, tense moment. I was having to fight extremely hard not to smile. Charlie looked magnificent—chin lifted, shoulders back as she stared Galoshes down. The little tremor in her bottom lip was only mine to see, and I wanted to kiss it slowly and tell her how proud I was.

"What exactly is the job?" Galoshes said at last.

"Dance caller."

"What?" Galoshes said, with menace.

"You would be the person telling everyone at the barn dance what to do."

Galoshes paused.

"Everyone?"

"Everyone. You shout, they dance. So, shall we try that again? Galoshes, I've got a job for you at the barn dance, would you like to hear about it?"

"Yes. Please," Galoshes said, after a very long moment.

Charlie smiled, and something seemed to soar in my chest. I don't think I've ever felt pride for another person like that. I love that I know how big this was for her, and that I get to see her triumph over it—that I'm the one person who knows she's just proven how fucking brave she is.

"Wonderful. You'll make a fantastic caller. I'll send you some links—"

"I won't look at 'em," Galoshes said, and then, on Charlie's look, "Not because it's you, just because I don't do the internet."

"I'll . . . I'll show you them," Toby offered, blinking fast. "If . . . you want?"

"Wonderful," Charlie said. "Great teamwork, guys. Now, I have to shoot. I'll see you all in the morning."

"You won't be home for dinner?" I blurted.

I realized, from the interested look from Galoshes and Red, that this was perhaps not something I should say in front of all the staff. They knew our living situation, but probably didn't imagine we ate dinner together every night, because that would be . . . coupley. Charlie met my eyes for one quick moment and then looked away again. Definitely flustered.

"Not tonight," she said, already on her way toward the door. "I've got three hours' worth of dances to choreograph with Jerry and the Merry Milkmen, so don't wait up!"

So much for talking. I sighed, then noticed Red watching me with a shrewd look on her face, and tried to pull myself together. *Don't wait up* probably gave everyone the wrong impression, too. I cleared my throat and asked Galoshes to give me a hand moving the boxes of new coffee beans from the shop floor to the back room.

"This is the ridiculous 'autumn spice' blend?" Galoshes grumbled, as we started stacking them. "If one more thing in this shop has 'autumn' slapped on it, the whole barn will turn into a bloody pumpkin, I swear. What happens when autumn finishes? Will it be like this in winter, too?"

"Halloween first, I imagine."

Good to know that Galoshes's new respect for Charlie wasn't going to put a stop to the whinging. It wouldn't be Bramblebay Farm Shop without the constant background noise of Galoshes complaining.

"I don't know what's got into that Charlie," Galoshes said, shifting a box with a very loud groan. "Maybe it's the pregnancy hormones, but she's finally grown some balls, so to speak!"

I froze. Galoshes headed off through the back-room door, turning when she clocked I hadn't followed.

I don't know what I said, exactly. Something shocked. Something like, *Charlie's not pregnant*, or *No, she's not*, or . . . the kind of nonsensical, desperate thing you say when the future you've just started to dream about abruptly falls apart.

"Oh," Galoshes said, seeing my expression. She glanced behind her to check the rest of the staff were out of earshot. She actually looked slightly penitent, for once. "I overheard—Rosie did tell me not to tell anyone, and she's not even twelve weeks along yet. But I thought you of all people would know, what with you two living together and all."

Well, now I do know.

And obviously this changes everything.

So long,
Charlie Jones

London, two months earlier

It was late July. Jones and Aspen had weathered a wet, argumentative spring together, full of serious life matters—the funeral of an old friend of Jones's, the falling-out between Aspen and her mother, a problem with Jones's hot-water tank. Grown-up things, as though they were aging faster than they should be.

Their relationship felt right *just* enough of the time. When Jones's commitment wavered, Aspen's eyes would suddenly sparkle again, and she'd tug him to bed, and he'd forget everything but the fun of her. There was something so sexy about seeing Aspen rumpled and laughing—she was generally put together and efficient, but in Jones's bed, she was deliciously disheveled.

As the months slipped by, he thought often of the day when Gloria had given birth in the back of that Uber. The baby's tiny, alien feet, its unearthly cry. The feeling that had grown in his chest, strange and suffocating, too complex for him to understand.

He eventually figured it out in the queue for the tills at the Co-op one day. The woman in front of him had a toddler dragging at her hand and a baby perched on her other hip; she looked off-balance, and he wondered if he should offer to hold something for her, before realizing the only thing he could take from her was a child.

He stared at the baby, then the toddler. These small, needy people, these little agents of chaos. He thought of Gloria's newborn with its tiny bloodstained hands, and he realized—*I do not want a child.*

It was something to which he had never given a great deal of thought. He was still young, midthirties; he had been in a marriage where kids weren't in the cards, so the question had been irrelevant, and Jones never dwelled on things that weren't relevant. As a single man, before he had met Aspen, the thought had crossed his mind—*Perhaps I will end up having kids one day.*

But he did not want a child. That was what that feeling was. He had looked at the tiny baby and felt sure of it, and the nasty, uneasy sensation that had followed was a sort of shame. It wasn't that he didn't find the baby cute. He just knew he didn't want to be a father, in the way one knows these things—that you love someone, that you need a glass of wine, that you've forgotten something important. It was simply not for him.

Which was fine. No need to feel shame about it, he told himself. But still the shame persisted, and he could not say why.

The reason became clear a week later in a sun-bleached St. James's Park. He and Aspen were picnicking, as she called it—overpaying for small pots of things that did not go together, ideally from Marks & Spencer. But when Aspen arrived, she was not in her trademark scrubs or loose skirt and silk top—she was wearing a baby.

"Hello," Jones said, staring at the child in the sling on her front.

"I know," Aspen said, already starting to laugh. "Surprise!"

An elderly couple nearby glanced over and smiled. He and Aspen looked like a perfect young family, Jones realized with a jolt.

"My sister had a childcare crisis, so we've got a little gate-crasher on our hands."

"Ah. This is baby Mabel?"

"This is baby Mabel," Aspen said, kissing her niece's head.

"Right. Well, shall we sit? Can you sit?"

Jones did not like how much this had thrown him. Aspen looked happy—happier than usual—and she was so competent handling the baby that he could suddenly see her as a mother.

As Aspen busied herself finding a shady spot for Mabel to kick about in, Jones realized with dawning horror that the shame he felt was not because he didn't want to be a father. It was because he suspected Aspen wanted to be a mother.

At first, he had stayed with Aspen because it was the kind thing to do. She'd been grieving; she said she needed him, and he didn't want to hurt her. But was it still the kind thing? He watched Aspen tickle baby Mabel's tummy and closed his eyes for a moment.

"Aspen," he said.

Jones knew he had his faults, but he liked to believe he could tell right from wrong. And this was not right.

"Do you want to have a baby?"

She looked up at him, crouched over the baby, her necklace dangling in front of Mabel's nose. The expression on Aspen's face was heartbreaking. It was as if he had made some sort of beautiful announcement, had told her the best news in the world. She looked *overjoyed*.

"I mean, yeah. Yes. Do you?" she asked, sitting back on her haunches.

"I'm so sorry," he said.

He was wrong: *this* expression was heartbreaking.

"What?" she said.

"I'm really sorry. I don't want to have a baby."

"Oh," she said, putting a hand on his thigh. "God! We're not talking about right *now*, are we? I know you don't want a kid right now. We've talked about this."

He frowned. Had they talked about this?

"Early on, before we made it official?" she said, returning her attention to baby Mabel, who was kicking her fat heels on the picnic blanket. "That night we had ramen at yours. We talked about Conor fainting when his wife was giving birth, and you said you can't imagine yourself being a dad *right now*."

"What?" He vaguely remembered the takeaway, but couldn't recall this conversation at all.

"Yeah! And I'm not putting any pressure on." She smiled—a little tightly, he thought. "Not right now is fine."

"But, Aspen . . . I'm not saying not right now. I'm saying I don't want kids."

He had kept his voice gentle, but her eyes instantly filled with tears.

"I'm so sorry," he said. The shame swirled in his stomach.

"You don't have to decide now!" she said, blinking fast. "I was a no, too, in my twenties."

"But I'm not in my twenties, Aspen. I'm thirty-seven. And I really feel sure about this."

"How *can* you be?" she said, her voice rising. "You were a not-right-now like, six months ago. What happened?"

"I don't even remember saying that. It was just a throwaway remark, I guess—like, wow, imagine being a dad at this point in my life. I don't know. I honestly don't remember it."

Aspen picked up Mabel, holding her in her lap like a shield. Her tears spilled over; she swiped them away with frustration.

"A throwaway remark," she said bitterly.

"I mean, I assume so? I don't remember. I'm sorry."

"Do you remember what I said to you when we first met?"

"What?"

"I told you not to waste my time."

Aspen struggled to her feet with Mabel in her arms. She began thrashing around with the sling, trying to get Mabel in; Mabel frowned, then squawked in protest, then began to cry.

"Can I help you?" Jones said, getting up clumsily.

"No," Aspen said, and her voice was like steel. "No, you really can't."

"Aspen, please, don't be like this. I love you," he said, a little helplessly. He felt awful.

"Do you really?" she snapped, fixing the last strap around Mabel's shoulders. "Or are you just fucking incapable of being alone?"

Friday October 3rd 2025

Brianna just rang. Having resulting loss of mojo. Feel quite peeved.

"Have you booked an appointment to get it on with Keith?" she said.

Was walking down the Rue, heading for the chocolate shop—we were out of pumpkin spice truffles, because whatever Galoshes thinks, seasonal is seriously selling. The coffee machine has been up and running for a week now, and we're the busiest we've ever been, despite peak tourist season coming to an end. Doc's biscuits are flying.

"Keith the sperm guy!" Brianna explained, when I asked her what the hell she was on about.

"Oh. Didn't we decide against Keith?"

"Right, well, whoever, whichever father you settled on."

"I've not booked my first proper appointment at the Guernsey clinic yet," I said. "And you don't just get to wander in and grab a pot, if you know what I'm saying—there are a bunch of things to do first."

"You've not booked it?"

This was full of subtext.

"You know I did the initial stuff and got myself checked over before I even got to the island," I said, swinging open the door to the chocolate shop. "It's not like things aren't in motion."

Karyn gave me a gratifyingly cheery wave.

"I just thought you would be raring to go, now that you're feeling so much better in yourself, and you're sure the island is where you want to do this . . ."

"I was. I am! I am."

Grabbed all the pumpkin spice truffles, piled them under my chin, and made my way to the till with my phone wedged to my ear. The signal down this end of the Rue was always terrible, and Brianna's voice crackled as she said, "You're not having second thoughts, are you?"

"Of course not!"

"Not getting distracted by the cute boy you kissed last weekend?"

"*No*," I said, a bit too loudly. As though I hadn't spent the entire week daydreaming about making out with Jones on the sofa. "Sorry," I mouthed at Karyn, who had jumped a little. "Bri, now isn't a good time. I'm still totally committed to the plan, all right? I've just been busy. And I'm probably going to lose my job in a minute."

"Fair point," Bri said. "What *is* your plan to support your future child when your cut of the inheritance runs out?"

"Wow, you're fun today! Let me call you back," I said, hanging up and dropping the phone on the counter. "Sorry, Karyn. All these, please."

"Ah, I remember those days," Karyn said with a smile as she tapped away at the till to apply the farm-shop discount. "When you just *have* to have something! Glad my truffles are hitting the spot. It was always capers, for me."

"Right," I said, checking the message that had just popped up on my phone screen. "Wait, sorry, capers?"

I shouldn't have called you from work, I'm in boss
lady mode and went too hard. My question is, do

you think you're going to wait and see if things get serious with Jones, instead of pursuing this solo? Do you even know if he wants kids? Isn't he Mr. Island Hermit—didn't he turn up determined to be alone . . . ? I'm worried I've pushed you in the wrong direction by wanging on about how you still have room in your life for romantic love. Xxx

"I just loved them! Here you go, sweetie," Karyn said, sliding a large paper bag across the counter.

Thanked her (ignoring weird caper chat—the woman is a committee member and just called me "sweetie" and smiled at me, so if she wants to talk about obscure tiny vegetables that's fine with me) and made my way back to the farm shop with the truffles, mood distinctly dampened. Was Bri right? Was I delaying on starting things with the fertility clinic? Thought that by shutting things down with Jones, and keeping my plans a secret, could keep myself safe from that temptation. But maybe even that wasn't enough.

Despite all my resolutions . . . am I letting that daydream of a love story with Jones get in the way of the real dream I came here to find?

Jones also being weird today.

"Are you OK?" he said, when I returned to the shop. "You look a bit flushed. Do you need to sit down?"

"Pardon?" I said, unpacking the truffles. "Oh, no, I'm fine, I'm just in too many layers."

I'd called the fertility clinic on the way here—they had an opening on Sunday, so I'm all booked in for then, and was feeling quite weird about it. (Still am, TBH.) Also pretty sure I get flushed every time I'm in Jones's presence now—have been avoiding him so scrupulously this week that I've hardly put it to the test.

"Do you want to go home and change? I can stay a bit longer if you need me to. Or get you something from the stables and drop it back on my way to Rog's cart?"

"What?" Risked a suspicious glance his way, then checked my outfit. "Have I been shat on by a bird or something, and you're too polite to tell me outright?"

"Please do not say 'shat' in front of the customers," said Caloshes, who had appeared just in time to see me disgrace myself in some way, as she is wont to do.

"There aren't any customers right now, Caloshes."

"Not with you swearing like a sailor, there aren't."

Decided to rise above. Even Caloshes could not pretend I was putting customers off—this was a rare moment of calm in a hectic week of us all crash-coursing barista training (watching a lot of videos about milk frothing) and trying to keep up with the demand for Doc's already-famous chocolate and cherry biscuits.

"Rog's cart?" I asked Jones.

He was looking particularly gorgeous in a checked shirt and jeans haphazardly tucked into mud-caked brown boots. He's started wearing his hair swept back from his face—it's a lot longer than it was when he first arrived here. It's a <u>very</u> good look. Whenever I've seen him this week, can pretty much only get through it by reciting to myself, <u>He is not the plan, he is not the plan, he is not the plan</u>.

<u>He'd make a really hot dad</u>, went a very bad voice in my head.

"He's going to teach me how to drive a horse and cart," Jones said, looking an adorable mixture of embarrassed and delighted.

"What! What for?"

"Well, I can't drive a tractor."

"I wouldn't worry about not having a special tractor license, Jones—this is Ormer. Haven't you seen the licensing prices?"

Pointed to the sign that had once lived stuck inside the farm shop window, now pinned to our community noticeboard. Toby's idea, actually—sweet, conscientious Toby, who still has no idea he's going to be a father.

The sign reads:

GET YOUR LICENSES FOR 2025 NOW.
Available in the Constable's Office 2 p.m.–4 p.m.
Tues and Weds.
Carriage Driving: £12
Tractor: £15
Firearms/shotgun: £5

Whenever I see it, it reminds me how this island looked when I first arrived on the Rue in the dust and sunshine. A tiny Wild West.

"I don't actually have a driving license at all, though," Jones said sheepishly.

"You don't drive!"

He shook his head.

"I wonder whether Jerry would ask."

"You'd hope."

"But . . ."

"Yeah. Probably not."

We grinned at each other. Uh-oh, prolonged eye contact. Absolutely deadly. I looked away instantly, but he'd already made me go hot again. Was thinking about the way he'd felt on top of me, the hungry kisses against my neck, my jaw . . .

"I'm making us stew tomorrow," he said, with a decisive nod. "Lots of vegetables. Maybe some cavolo nero. You look a bit peaky.

You need to make sure you're getting enough iron, and since you don't eat meat . . ."

Am slightly surprised—not by the comment about iron, because you get this about twice a week if you're a vegetarian, but by Jones's sudden interest in my diet. Cannot decide if this is oddly paternalistic or quite sexy. Probably a highly problematic combination of both.

"Have you had your booking appointment with a midwife yet?" Marly asked me when I arrived at the farmhouse to see Red a few hours later.

Was still quite grumpy. Has been that sort of day. Cannot seem to win: am either getting flak from Bri for being insufficiently pregnant or from Marly for being pregnant and not doing enough about it. Hate this lie. Want to be up at the B&B checking on Red as much as I can, but that means being around Marly and Rosie, who both keep mothering me and my painfully nonexistent baby—Marly has obviously shared with her wife, which I do get, but only makes this harder. Rosie and I are friends, and now I'm lying to her as well. More lying.

Though, since finding that bizarre list of Charlie Joneses, am pretty sure she's lying to me about something, too. And I've still got no plausible explanation as to what.

When did everything get so messy? It's all lies and secrets and people pretending to be things they're not. Where's my beautifully simple new life gone??

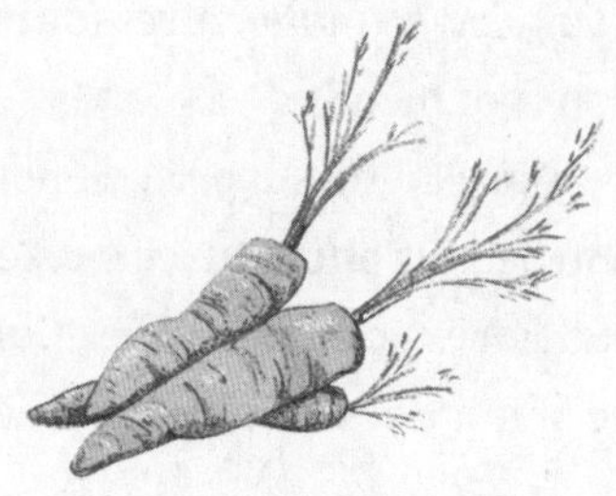

FROM: Charlie Jones
TO: Charlie Jones
SUBJECT: Day fifty-eight sober

Pregnant. *Pregnant.*

It's been almost a week since I found out, and I'm really not sure I'm any closer to processing this. Meanwhile harvest festival is occupying every waking thought that isn't dedicated to Charlie, because she has the most ambitious plans for this barn dance, and I have become a person who cannot say no to her. So anyway, I'm off to try and catch a donkey now.

So long,
Charlie Jones

FROM: Charlie Jones
TO: Charlie Jones
SUBJECT: Day fifty-eight sober (cont.)

I'm covered in mud, freezing and have a very large bruise on my shin. I think Galoshes filmed everything, so that's great.

Anyway, there is now a donkey in the appropriate field, looking very photogenic. Well done me.

Christ, I want a drink. I'm trying so hard here, but I feel as though all the connections I've made on this island aren't even real. Marly's got a completely bizarre list of Charlie Joneses in her spare room and we can't work out why. Charlie's pregnant—presumably the father is someone I know here, or a tourist, because Galoshes said she's not even twelve weeks along yet, so it must have happened while we were both on the island, and I just . . . I don't know if I can handle all this.

I was with her all the time in those early weeks here. I keep going over and over every day. When *could* she have met someone? Who the hell could it be?

I need to go and shower. And then what? The evenings have been so hard this week. I don't trust myself to go out. The pub will be warm and easy. I can imagine how good a beer would taste right now—I'm sure I'd feel better within just one sip.

At least there's nothing alcoholic in the house. If I just stay here, I think I'll be OK.

Bye for now,
Charlie Jones

FROM: **Charlie Jones**
TO: **Charlie Jones**
SUBJECT: **Day fifty-eight sober (cont.)**

I was just out of the shower, having finally removed the mud from my ears, and heard someone hammering on the door. I ran down in my towel and yanked the door open to find Marly on the doorstep with her arms folded and Ginger wagging at her heel.

"Just tell me why you came here," she said, as Ginger surged at me. "I've been rooting for you, mate, I really have, but it's harvest festival in two days and it's crunch time, buddy. Why did you come here?"

"Is this urgent? Or can I go and put some clothes on?" I asked, trying to pet Ginger without losing my grip on the towel.

I was feeling so strung out—I'd spent the whole shower thinking of all the reasons why it would be perfectly fine to go to the pub tonight.

"Yes, it bloody well is urgent. You're upsetting my wife!"

"What? How am I upsetting Rosie? Will you just come in, Marly? I'm freezing."

"You honestly have no idea why I'm asking you this?" she said, putting her hands on her hips.

"No! I don't have a single clue! Can you tell me what's going on?"

"No!" Marly yelled, yanking off her flat cap and slapping it against her leg. Ginger jumped, returning to Marly's heel. "Not unless you *know*, I can't! Rosie has been very clear on this, and she'll kill me if I push you, so you have to say it *first*, Jones!"

"Say what first? What are you talking about?"

"You really don't know?"

"I really don't know."

She dropped her head. "Fuck," she said, turning away. "I so hoped it was you."

What is going *on* around here? Secrets and lies, secrets and lies. The future I'd dreamed up here suddenly looks so unrealistic—did I really think I could have something that good?

I mean, Charlie's *pregnant*.

I just don't know if I can deal with all this without a drink. Maybe I could go to the pub and have a lime and soda, or something? I need to be somewhere warm and busy, with *people* around. Yeah, I might do that—better than kicking around alone here, right, waiting for Charlie to come home?

To be honest, I might just go and have one drink at the pub—I think I could handle one these days, and it would make this all feel a hell of a lot easier.

Bye for now,
Charlie Jones

FROM: **Charlie Jones**
TO: **Charlie Jones**
SUBJECT: **Re: Day fifty-eight sober (cont.)**

Hello! Hi!

OMG, she writes back!

That last email of yours had me freaked, my friend, so here I am, replying. I know, I know, we had a rule, but that was designed to snap us out of the weird codependent thing and we're totally snapped out now, so I'm declaring replies permitted. New lives are all very well, but sometimes you need an old buddy who gets the context, you know?!

Because holy shit, you have a lot going on over there.

But you're so strong. I know you've got this. Look at the subject line of this email. You made it this far. Can you really bear the thought of going back to zero? If you're reading this in the pub: get out. Go, now, walk out the door into the fresh air, take yourself down to the beach, and remember that you only need to stay sober for another five minutes, and then another, and so on. You can do anything for five minutes.

Listen, I've been thinking for a while about coming out to the island. And guess what: you've freaked me out enough that I've only gone and decided to actually do it! I've booked a flight. I've booked a ferry. That's right, Mr. Jones (LOL, still so weird)—I'm coming to see you!!

Stay strong, my friend. You've got this.

With love,
Charlie x

Guildford, nine weeks earlier

One day, Charlie returned home from Vintage, Please to find that Oliver had let himself into her flat.

This was not in itself unusual. They still had keys to each other's places, still hung out most nights, might let themselves in if the other person wasn't home yet.

More surprising was the state of chaos around him.

He was sitting on the floor at the end of her bed. Half the clothes from her wardrobe were strewn across the duvet; he'd upended some old shoeboxes, sending the heels she'd worn in her twenties splaying across the bedroom carpet like snapshots of old nights out.

"What the hell?" she said, standing in the doorway. "Oliver?"

"Brianna called me," he said. "I'm freaking out about you."

For the last month, Charlie and Oliver had settled into a sweet, platonic friendship that was in some ways more intense than their relationship had ever been—sometimes they would still sleep in bed together, or hold hands, and often they would cry in each other's arms. He knew about the job she had been offered on the Isle of Ormer, and he'd encouraged her to go. It had been a long time since he'd fretted about her the way he used to, when they were a couple. So what the hell was this about?

"What did Bri say to you?" Charlie asked carefully.

"I can help you," Oliver said. "You can talk to me, Charlie."

"I know I can," she said. "What did Brianna say?"

"She said . . . to look around the flat for anything you might be trying to hide from us."

Charlie was shocked to feel a spike of fear—until that moment she'd genuinely felt she had nothing to keep from him. His steady, beseeching gaze told her he saw that truth in her face. She smoothed down her canary yellow dress, busying herself picking up high heels. Her head was suddenly buzzing. It was very important that she did not think too hard about this.

"Wow, I've not worn these since . . . Oh, way back—before I was even married. Berty used to love them."

"Charlie . . ."

Charlie could feel that inner voice trying to elbow its way into the room. *You're awful, you're a piece of shit. Oliver is going to find out, and he's going to stop caring about you, just like Berty did. Just like your parents did.*

"These crystals on the straps! So adorably 2010. I probably wore these with a bandage dress."

"Brianna says . . . She says you're not OK, Charlie."

Oliver stood and made his way through to the kitchen. Charlie's heart began to hammer as he started searching through the cutlery drawer, then the cupboard of mugs.

"Oliver, stop it!" She grabbed his arm as he reached for the cupboard under the sink, but he shook her off and opened it.

He pulled out the cardboard box behind the cleaning products.

Charlie let out a sound so thick with shame it was almost animal—a whimper, a mew. With teeth-gritted force, she pulled herself together.

"That's no big deal, Oliver! It's just my backup box. It's just where I keep spares."

His expression was grim as he placed the box on the kitchen table and took off the lid.

Three half-empty bottles of spirits lay inside. Vodka, gin, whisky. She'd hated the taste of all three of them, once, but these days she wasn't fussy.

When she had first begun the backup drinks box, Charlie had congratulated herself on her forethought. She was notorious for running out of alcohol—for running out of everything, actually. It had been a favorite inside joke with Fearne—whenever she came for dinner, she'd message beforehand to say, *What've you not got enough of, then? Want me to pick up some milk? Bread? Eggs?*

And running out of wine was the worst. The evening would just be getting started—they'd just be warming up. Who wanted to pop out in the rain to the corner shop then?

At first it had been two bottles of wine. A red, a white. Then she'd drunk those herself, on a couple of evenings when setting up the shop had been stressing her out and she'd needed something to help her relax. So she'd replaced them a few times, and then, when that had become tedious—she would still end up running out—she'd opted for gin. It was more space efficient.

"I can't believe I didn't see it," Oliver said, closing his eyes. "You've been . . . Oh, God, I used to worry about you so much, but I never thought . . . The slurring, the forgetfulness, all the times you insisted on bringing coffee in your own thermos from home . . ."

Charlie would do almost anything to escape from this conversation. She stared at the kitchen window, contemplating jumping from it.

"It's my fault," Oliver said, sitting down unsteadily. "I should have noticed. Of all people, I should have noticed. But I've been drinking too much, too, since Fearne died, probably even before then, really, and I just . . . I'm so sorry, Charlie. I let you down."

Charlie leaned forward on the table, looking at the backup box. Her heart seemed to be beating behind her eyes, a pulsing, awful thump. She'd had a drink already today. There was a backup box at the shop, too.

She was not surprised that Oliver hadn't noticed her drinking—she was extremely good at hiding it. In fact, much of the time, even she could go about her day without looking directly at it. It took a lot of mental effort, but it was possible.

Oh, God, she thought, and there was the voice, the one that came to her at three a.m., when the night stripped her bare and she could not hide from herself. *You're a disgusting addict. You're useless, you're worthless. No wonder nobody wants you.*

You're an alcoholic. You have to stop drinking.

"It's OK, Charlie," Oliver whispered.

She began to cry.

Berty had said it, too, when he'd left her. *I don't know what else to do, Charlie*, he'd said, as he'd packed up his suitcase, face red with crying. *I'm so sorry. But you're an alcoholic. And I can't be with you unless you stop drinking.*

Oliver, by contrast, had made it so easy. His friends from the downhill-racing scene were fun—thrill-seekers and adrenaline junkies—and her drinking seemed tame in his context; he was chill, flexible, had always been happy to stay at his place if she wanted him gone. He also, crucially, did not know her the way Berty did, so the drinking had been much easier to hide.

She'd thought that was why the universe gave him to her—to make life easier, softer, more fun. But as she slowly lowered herself down into the chair opposite and looked into those gray-blue eyes, with the crinkles at the corners, the thought occurred that perhaps the universe had brought Oliver to her for *this* moment. The moment when more than anything she needed a kind friend who knew what it was like to be ashamed and miserable.

"I'm so sorry," she sobbed, laying her head on her forearms. "I'm so sorry."

"Why are you apologizing? Charlie, shh, it's OK."

He leaned across the box to stroke her hair. The kindness almost undid her. For a very long time, almost all of Charlie's mental energy had been consumed by the dance of denying her addiction. Those awful, truthful three a.m. moments, when she had lain in the darkness and known she should stop drinking alcohol, had become harder and harder to delete each morning. Every time she reached for her favorite gin glass—the tumbler that sat just right in the palm of the hand—she faced the cognitive dissonance that came with very badly wanting to regain control over her life, and very badly wanting a drink. It was exhausting. And now, at last, she was letting some of that go.

Oliver let her cry. Eventually she lifted her head and looked at him through swollen, bleary eyes.

"Thank you," she said hoarsely. "For being so kind."

"Here's what we're going to do," he said, squeezing her hand.

At some point in the last half hour he had removed the box from the table; Charlie felt a wild lurch of panic at the thought that the bottles might be gone, until she spotted them on the floor by his feet.

"You're going to go and talk to a doctor about quitting alcohol. I am, too. You're going to go to the Isle of Ormer, to that amazing farm you showed me, and . . ."

He trailed off; Charlie was shaking her head.

She wanted that more than anything—more than Oliver could possibly know. But she wasn't ready for her dream life, her family. This wasn't how the Isle of Ormer chapter was supposed to start.

"I can't go. I don't want to take it. The job."

"But you've been so excited about it," Oliver said, frowning.

"No." She shook her head again. "I need to sort myself out. I can't go right now. It's not the right time. You're right: I need to stop drinking." She could barely get the sentence out, it terrified her so much. "That has to be the priority. I can't go now."

"You're sure? It's such an amazing job, Charlie—it's a once-in-a-lifetime thing, isn't it? A total fresh start, in your dream location . . . You've been fascinated with that island ever since I've known you, and I doubt many chances come up to work there. Maybe it would *help* you get sober."

She stared at him across the table. He looked exhausted, too, she realized. And he'd just told her he was also drinking too much. He had lost not just a close friend but his passion—he hadn't been on a bike since Fearne's death. He'd had a truly awful time, too.

"I'm sorry," she whispered again. "You deserve so much better than all this. Than me."

"What do you mean? Charlie . . ."

"You know, we were so badly suited," she said, wiping her face. "You're so driven and determined, and I can never stick to anything. You're all cool and understated, and I'm . . ." She gestured down at her outfit: a yellow seventies dress she kept meaning to shorten, but never got around to sorting. "And you're *steady.* You'll be someone's rock. A family man, maybe. You know I don't even want kids?"

Oliver's surprise was evident. "You don't?"

"I never did. Berty and I were on the same page about it from the start, so I guess I . . . I didn't think to bring it up with you, and . . ." She was making excuses. She swallowed and lifted her chin. "I should have told you straightaway. I'm sorry."

"Right. Huh. Well, I guess I didn't bring it up, either."

"You want a family?"

"I do," Oliver said after a moment. "When I feel like I'm good enough for one."

"I want that for you. I want you to start over, and figure out who you could be without me and Fearne and booze, and meet somebody who's the perfect fit for you . . ."

She was crying again, partly for Oliver, and partly, she realized, for Berty. Brianna had finally caved and given her all the details of his new relationship, and it broke Charlie's heart to know that he had done exactly that—left her, found himself, found someone who fit him better.

She stood, needing to escape the table and all its intensity, and wandered to the fridge, where she had pinned the handwritten letter that Rosie Nicole had sent her, offering her the job at Bramblebay Farm Shop. *Dearest Charlie,* it began. *Thank you so, so much for your application. I was so thrilled to read it.*

Brianna had laughed at it when she was here last, reading out the charming instructions on how to get to the farm—*Head for the dairy, but be sure to turn right before you reach the field of Jersey cows.*

"*This* is the job offer? That's it? You just turn up with this letter and say 'Hi, I'm Charlie Jones'?"

"I wasn't even going to bring the letter," Charlie had said, with a grin. "I don't think they have an HR department, Bri, I think this is about as official as it gets."

"Fuck me," Bri had said, snapping a photo of the letter. "Might nick this note off you and take it myself. I quite fancy an idyllic new life. Hello, I'm Charlie Jones! Honest!"

At the time Charlie had been giggly and playful, laughing along—drunk, unbeknown to Brianna, though perhaps that was when she'd guessed at it. Fearne hadn't known, either. Lovely Fearne, who had always been drunk on life and never thought it was strange when Charlie was a little giddy, too.

Charlie stood in front of the fridge now, running her finger across the signature on the bottom of the letter. *Rosie Nicole.*

Brianna's words popped back into her head. *That's it? You just turn up with this letter and say "Hi, I'm Charlie Jones"?*

Charlie glanced over her shoulder at Oliver. He looked so broken. Did anyone need a fresh start more than him? And if he were there, at the farm, becoming part of that community . . . then she wasn't losing this chance altogether. She could live it vicariously. If she let Oliver take the opportunity instead, then she could ask him to tell her *everything*, and that way when the time came, when she was finally ready, she'd be so much more prepared.

"I've got a crazy idea," she said. "Hear me out, OK?"

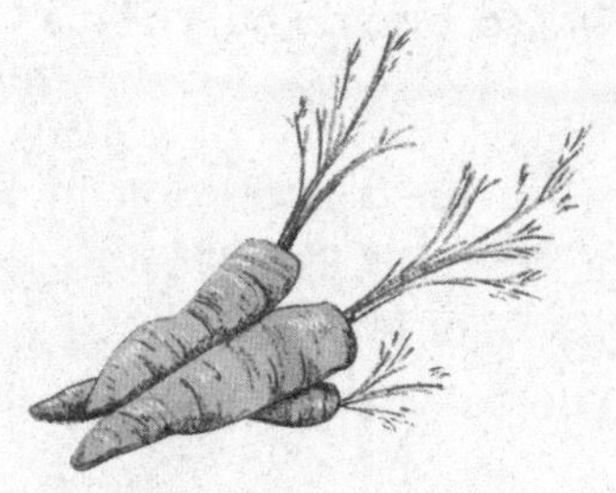

FROM: Charlie Jones
TO: Charlie Jones
SUBJECT: Are you actually coming to Ormer???

Are you actually coming here, because if you are, we really need to get our story straight. I mean, you cannot tell everyone you're called Charlie Jones. You know that, right?

PS Thank you. I left the pub. I went to the beach. It helped.

FROM: Charlie Jones
TO: Charlie Jones
SUBJECT: Re: Are you actually coming to Ormer???

Hello, queen of subterfuge here. You dated me for a year and it took you that long to realize I drank gin most mornings. I think I can handle hanging out with your new friends without giving the game away, Oliver.

PS Well done—I knew you would!!

FROM: Charlie Jones
TO: Charlie Jones
SUBJECT: Re: Are you actually coming to Ormer???

OK, so, also do not call me Oliver.

FROM: **Charlie Jones**
TO: **Charlie Jones**
SUBJECT: **Re: Are you actually coming to Ormer???**

LOL! Yes, of course! Starting now, I'm on it, JONES. Who shall I be? I've always liked the name Absurdia—Fearne and I went to the circus once on a school trip and the woman who walked the tightrope had that name, and I've loved it ever since.

I'm so excited. You know I've been ADDICTED to your emails (a healthier option, though, right?!)—meeting everyone is going to be like meeting celebrities. I wonder if Rog will sign my boobs.

FROM: **Charlie Jones**
TO: **Charlie Jones**
SUBJECT: **Re: Are you actually coming to Ormer???**

You cannot call yourself Absurdia. That's a totally weird name. You need to *not* draw attention to yourself. Which flight will you be on? What's your ferry?

FROM: **Charlie Jones**
TO: **Charlie Jones**
SUBJECT: **Re: Are you actually coming to Ormer???**

Flight details and ferry details attached! Can't wait to see you, dear friend xx

FROM: **Charlie Jones**
TO: **Charlie Jones**
SUBJECT: **Re: Are you actually coming to Ormer???**

Charlie, you're going to be here *tonight*? I haven't sorted you anywhere to stay!

FROM: **Charlie Jones**
TO: **Charlie Jones**
SUBJECT: **Re: Are you actually coming to Ormer???**

Can't I just crash on your sofa at the stables? I know it's a bit of a squeeze with your excellently named roommate living there, too (DYING to meet her), but you know I'm not fussy. Since I've stopped drinking I sleep like a LOG, by the way—who knew the whole insomnia thing was totally alcohol related! I thought it was meant to HELP you sleep. No more 3 a.m. self-hating for me, though! Aren't you proud?

FROM: **Charlie Jones**
TO: **Charlie Jones**
SUBJECT: **Re: Are you actually coming to Ormer???**

I'm really proud. You know I am. But you cannot sleep on my sofa. Things with Charlie . . . as in, Ormer Charlie . . . are really new and positive right now, and my ex-girlfriend turning up with a ridiculous fake name is definitely likely to throw a wrench in the works. I'm going to find you a place to stay, though—there must be somewhere, we're coming out of high season now.

This is such a mess, Charlie. The lies I told to get here seemed so harmless when we were cooking it all up in your kitchen, but I'm falling in love with this woman, and I just don't think I'm a person who can build a genuine future without sharing the past. I can hardly bear to type it, but as I was sitting on the beach last night I realized . . . part of the reason I'm feeling shitty again is because I *know* I'm doing something wrong now. And I have to make it right.

I have to tell her how I ended up here, being Charlie Jones. How I was desperate, lost, didn't stand a chance at quitting drinking if you and I kept living the life we'd been living together, with Fearne's absence at every turn . . . How you gave me the fresh start you'd found for yourself, and said I could just call myself Charlie Jones, and it sounded so easy, kind of fun, really, the sort of thing Fearne would find hilarious . . . Oh, God, it looks even worse than I thought now I've written it all out.

I *do* have to tell Charlie, don't I? I've been dodging that truth for weeks, but your email saying you were on your way was a total shock to the system. I've lived as Charlie Jones for two months now. Sometimes I almost forget that you're real, and I'm not.

You know I'm looking forward to seeing you, but I have to ask . . . are you coming here to take it all? The job, the new life? This is a really awful, unacceptable thing to say, but I don't know if I'm quite ready to give it back. I love it here. I'm sober, I've got friends, I'm falling for someone, I'm *settled*. Fucking hell, I *like* myself when I'm Charlie Jones. This whole crazy plan of yours actually worked—I *am* Jones to all the people in my life here. I have made a proper, genuine fresh start.

I'm so sorry. I know I owe you so much. If you want the name, the job, it's obviously yours to have back. I'll confess it all to everyone right now if you need me to. But I'd really love to be able to stay here on this island, somehow. If we can find a way. If Charlie can ever trust me when she knows the truth.

FROM: Charlie Jones
TO: Charlie Jones
SUBJECT: Re: Are you actually coming to Ormer???

OMG, Oliver, I don't want to take your new life away from you! I'm SO happy you're doing so well. And I know that when I gave you this opportunity (and my favorite cap) I was giving it to you for good (though actually I really miss my CJ cap so maybe I could have that back. Kidding. Kind of. It just REALLY goes with my brown leather jacket!).

So yeah, no, I'm not trying to steal this life from you. I just want to come and be part of it. You can keep being Jones the farm shop manager if you like. Maybe you can just employ your old mate Absurdia.

That said, I think it's a great idea for you to tell new Charlie about your real name. It's only a name, anyway—like I said when we decided you'd take the job, you're still you! You're just borrowing my helpfully unisex name, given to me by parents who weren't even my real parents and never loved me anyway. 🙃 And if you're feeling bad because you didn't *technically* earn the job, well, we all know my CV was pretty fictitious anyway, and yours would have been way better. You've done a million retail jobs alongside racing and you were always amazing when you helped out at Vintage, Please, plus pub work is still customer facing, so your last job was pretty relevant, too. So . . . nothing to feel bad about.

I'm sure new Charlie will get it. If not, you can always file a petition to have your name changed and then you're not even lying about it, LOL. But yeah, maybe tell her soon.

I have a cool idea on accommodation. Couldn't I just crash in the spare room at Bramblebay Farmhouse, at the B&B?! What was it called—Puffin room? I'll basically just want somewhere to shower and sleep after all the traveling. You don't even have to tell Rosie and Marly I'm there tonight, I'll be quiet as a mouse. Just leave me with some good snacks, go tell the woman you love that you love her and you're actually called Oliver (no biggie) and then let me come and join the fun tomorrow morning!

Can't wait to meet your new Charlie Jones. As if you fell in love with another one. What are the chances?!

C x

Saturday October 4th 2025

Spent the afternoon with Red—am now pretty desperate to get her to see a midwife, and tell <u>someone</u> else she's pregnant. Starting to feel horribly guilty. Marly keeps talking to me about leaving the island and I can't explain why that's really not necessary, and meanwhile Red still hasn't had any of the checkups she needs at this stage of her first trimester, and I can't figure out how to help her without telling someone. Ugh.

Anyway, was really looking forward to the hearty stew Jones said he was making us tonight. But came home to find the stables cold, dark and empty. No idea where he is. Have got the log burner going and am currently in the bath, with lots of bubbles, making the most of having the place to myself. But I'm a bit . . . sad. Don't think of him as a guy who promises to do something and then doesn't follow through.

A helpful reminder to stay focused, really. Fertility clinic appointment tomorrow—my journey starts here. <u>My</u> journey. Am thinking of Red, hugging her knees on her B&B bed, agonizing over how to tell Toby about the baby, wondering what he'll say, what it'll mean for their relationship, and am reminded of exactly why I didn't want to hand that kind of power to a man.

Sunday October 5th 2025

Currently on the crack-of-dawn ferry to Guernsey. Feels very wrong watching Ormer shrink away behind me. The reverse of my first entry in this diary, the first day of my new life. Which is ridiculous! I'm not leaving, nothing is coming to an end. Just have an appointment—an exciting one. I guess being here on the deck is reminding me how much Ormer feels like home now. Don't ever want to have to leave.

On the way back now, and my head is <u>full</u> of that awful anxious white noise feeling, but let me try to write a bit about what happened in Guernsey.

It was so busy and hectic after life on Ormer. Cars seemed to be traveling at a hundred miles an hour, and the shop fronts seemed so bright and garish, the other boats in the harbor so gigantic. Actually totally . . . hated it. The air tasted sour and nasty to me, and the trees dotting the roadside looked like over-pruned imitations of real ones. God knows what I'd think of London these days.

The fertility clinic was up the hill, about a twenty-minute walk. It was cool inside. There were lots of plants around, the kind with little gray pebbles inside their pots.

"Could you fill out this form for me, please?" the receptionist said.

* Name.
* Address.
* Previous address.
* GP's address.
* National Health Service number.

Stared down at the form and realized how delusional I've been. Those tests back in London were in my old name. <u>Everything</u>

was in my old name. I can play at being Charlie Jones in the strange world of Bramblebay, Windward Ridge and the Pirate's Den pub, but outside of the dreaminess of Ormer's little bubble, there's a system. We have to identify ourselves somehow.

What will I put on my child's birth certificate?

What will I say when she asks about my life before she was born?

What will I tell her when she questions where she's from, when she wants to know about the Joneses?

It hit me right there in the clinic. Becoming Charlie Jones was only ever a fantasy of a life, and I want more than that. I want a future.

Still on the ferry back to Ormer, out on the uncomfortable wooden benches on the deck with my back to everyone so nobody can tell I'm crying half the time.

Just rang Brianna.

"How do you think Mum would feel if I tried to get back in touch?" I asked her.

"Are you kidding me? She'd throw a fucking party! All would be forgiven."

Not sure about that.

"Yeah, she likes to hold a grudge, but not when it comes to you. You were always her little bestie. She calls me every two days to check up on you, you know that?"

"Really? She does?"

"Look, I get why you drew a line with her in the spring—you needed the space to grieve, she was expecting you to be at her beck and call coaching her through it . . . It was a mess. You were right to set some boundaries. But she and I both knew you wanted a family and weren't saying it out loud. I'm sure she was extra clingy and needy because that's the only way she knows how to be close with you. She was trying to be there for you."

"By constantly ringing me to talk about how sad she was that Dad died?"

"I didn't say it was a good method. But I think if you reached out to her now and opened up to her about wanting to have a kid on your own . . ."

"She won't get it. She'll say 'a baby needs two parents' and I'll just feel horrible and completely lose sight of what I think about the whole thing."

"I don't know. You're stronger than you used to be—I don't think that would shake you the way it would have, once. And I reckon she'll get it more than you think. You know, when I had the miscarriage, she told me she and Dad tried for four years before she had you. Hence the age gap between us. She wanted the whole 'two under two' thing, but instead we're five years apart."

"You're kidding. How do I not know this?"

"People don't talk about fertility and stuff. I mean, fucking hell, you were so unwilling to talk about how badly you wanted kids that you moved to an island in the middle of the Channel and told everyone to call you Charlie."

That made me laugh. "That was your idea, thank you very much."

I mean, really, it was Brianna through and through, wasn't it? My bad-influence big sister, who used to pinch us Wispas from the corner shop on Friday afternoons, who got her first job in telly by walking onto the set of Eastside Close and pretending to be a runner.

Look at this, her message had read, with the photo of that handwritten letter. Charlie's been offered this job, but she's just told me she's not taking it! Crazy, right? What a missed opportunity!

Had always loved Brianna's updates on Charlie—classic shameless, boundaryless Bri. When Brianna sent me the picture of the letter, I'd just quit my job in a tearful blur, decided to end yet another failed relationship, dyed my hair and cut myself an extremely high-risk fringe, and was facing the terrifying reality that I wanted a family more than anything, but was once again single.

After years of trying so hard at *everything*, I had ended up with nothing.

What a total dream of a job, I had messaged back. *Can't believe she's giving that up! xx*

Brianna had called me immediately.

"So," she'd said, without a hello, "I have an amazing idea. *You* take it."

"I take what?"

"The job."

"*Charlie's* job?"

"She's taken your man, babe."

"She has not. He's not my man anymore. And as far as I'm aware, he's not her man again yet." I paused. "Is he?"

"OK, well, no, but she's been messaging him. Since before you officially broke up, I'm pretty sure."

"You *like* Charlie. Are you this much of a bitch to all your friends?"

"I just know where my loyalties lie! She's a friend, you're my sister. End of story. Plus she's been the flakiest flake for the last three months since her mate died—"

"Bri! I imagine she's probably been *grieving*?"

"I know, I know, why do you think I've been going around to check on her so much! I am actually officially worried about her, to be fair, but she's refusing to talk to me about what's up, so I've put someone else on the case. Someone more touchy-feely. Anyway, you're not taking anything off her because she doesn't even want it. It's a dreamy new life going to waste!"

"Brianna . . ."

"The first thing I thought when I saw that letter was, Oh my God, it's like these people exist in another time, sending handwritten letters and being like, just rock up and turn right at the cow field! How easy would it be for someone to scam them? And then Charlie says she's not going to take the job, and I'm thinking . . . well, someone should, right?"

"Bri, don't be crazy."

"That is like saying, Water, don't be wet. You know this. But you also know I'm a genius."

"It's immoral! Like you say, it's a scam. That job was offered to Charlie."

"Charlie will have lied through her teeth to get it."

"Then it should go to someone else who applied."

"Or to you. Why not? It's not a scam if you're only trying to do a good job, is it? You'd be great at running a farm shop! It's perfect—you desperately need a fresh start. You might even end up building a life there—a cute little island community could be the perfect place for a single mum . . ."

I remember how a shiver had gone through me when she'd said that. But not a bad shiver, an excited shiver. A decade ago I'd have rather died than be a single mum. It would have scared the hell out of me. But I was thirty-seven. I wanted a baby so badly that sometimes I thought of little else, despite constantly telling myself I was in no rush, didn't mind waiting, blah blah blah. Was the next step really downloading Hinge again, scrolling through all the mediocrity, no doubt settling for less than we deserved? Was it really better for my hypothetical child for me to rush into a relationship with yet another man who'd probably end up leaving me one day?

"I don't even know if they have, like, maternity care on this island of hers," I'd found myself saying. I was already half-gone.

"Are you kidding me? You're always going on about how you hate the medicalization of pregnancy and birth, you big hippy. And what a perfect place to raise a kid! They could run wild on the cliff tops and eat organic stuff from your shop! Ooh, I'm googling, there's a little school there."

"Oh my God," I'd said, melting. "An island school?"

"There's nothing to stop you from doing it. I'll be your reference, if they ask for one."

"What if Charlie's already turned it down? Said she's not coming?"

"She hasn't. I asked. She said something vague about how that wouldn't be necessary—she's just going to flake and not show up, hundred percent. This is Charlie we're talking about. Literally all you have to do is say you're called Charlie Jones," Brianna had said. "You've never liked your name anyway. Come on. It would be *fun*. And rebellious. You've never rebelled in your life, you might like it. You know it's always suited me *very* well."

"Until you got married to a man called Stuart and settled down and had two babies."

"Becoming a boring suburban mum was the most surprising thing I could do by the time I hit thirty-five and you know it. Why are you not loving this plan as much as I am? It's a ready-made new life."

"I couldn't. I just couldn't."

"Why not? I mean, come on, you want to. And have you ever in your life done something because you *wanted* to, and not because you thought it would impress someone else?"

"Wow. Ouch."

Most of the people in my life back on the mainland thought of me as confident, bold, outspoken—not the sort of person who pandered to the opinions of others. But Brianna knew the truth. That's sisters for you, I guess.

Though Jones saw the true me pretty quickly, too. That night in the rain at the lighthouse, when he'd looked me right in the eyes and told me he liked me better when I wasn't faking anything . . .

Anyhow, I'd told Bri that it would have been wrong—it was stealing. But even as I'd said it, if I'm totally honest, the thought of nicking this from under Charlie's nose had been a little satisfying, given the context.

"Who gets hurt?" Brianna had asked.

"Well . . . I guess . . . the people who own the farm and end up with a really inexperienced farm shop manager?"

"Screw that, you have a degree, you've got experience working in retail . . ."

"I worked at Next in my sixth form summer."

"Right! Great! I think you'll be amazing at the job. You have watched a lot of Hallmark movies."

"This isn't how the world works. I can't just pretend to be someone else."

"Please! You've been pretending to be someone else for years. This is a chance to be yourself at last, Aspen."

Just never, ever imagined the lie could get so big.

Am last off the ferry—what you get for hiding away on the deck—and just saw a guy filing off the boat who looked . . . terrifyingly familiar. Got major heebie-jeebies. Am reminding myself that many men wear their cap backward. In fact, Jones was when I first saw him at the harbor all those weeks ago. (Charlie Jones, I mean—Ormer Jones.)

Oh my God, I think it's him. I think it might actually be him?!
I can't believe this. What's he doing here? On Ormer? My Ormer?
Oh, God. It is him.
It's Berty Jones.

London, early August

Jones did not know what he was going to say when he got to Aspen's flat. He felt alternately wronged, angry, guilty and ashamed as the number 43 bus trundled its way through the streets of London. Had he led her on? He'd never said he wanted a child. She'd never told him *she* did. On paper, he was in the clear—but the nagging feeling of shame remained.

And then, in that wonderful way of hers, his ex-wife messaged at just the right moment.

> Hey Berty. I just want you to know that I've quit drinking. I'm seven days sober. I'm so sorry for everything I put you through. I love you, always. C x

He closed his eyes and leaned his head against the bus window as emotion flooded through him. This time even Jones could not mistake it: it was relief, and love, overwhelming in its intensity.

Only now could he admit how deeply he had longed for this moment. Seeing *Hey Berty* beneath her name again seemed almost too good to be true. Jones had ditched his first name at sixth-form college, when he'd gotten tall and good at sports, but he would always be Berty to Charlie. She had known him since secondary school, back when he'd been an awkward scrawny kid and she'd been the beautiful but odd girl who followed Fearne around.

She'd loved him even then, and she still loved him now. *I love you, always.*

He opened the message and scrolled up and down, though he'd long ago deleted their message history in an attempt to stop reading through the beautiful minutiae of their marriage, so the screen barely moved with his thumb. He wanted to keep the message lit there, as bold and bright as his wonderful wife. She had been the pride of his life, with her tumble of unruly dark waves and her little vintage dresses, her endless new projects and her scrappy, wounded, ever-hopeful heart. He had known from the age of fifteen that he would love her forever.

Until the drinking. He closed his eyes again. She was sober. He could hardly let himself believe it. The end of his marriage had been truly excruciating—he had left because he had tried everything he could think of and did not know what else he could do for her, but even so, it had felt like such a betrayal, and more than that, it had felt *wrong.* He didn't *want* to separate. He wanted her, the love of his life, but she was buried inside a new wine-drunk woman who wouldn't acknowledge that she had a problem, and he didn't know how to get her back. Their mood board had hung in the kitchen, dotted with photos of that magical island she had introduced him to a few years ago, of plans for winters spent chasing the sun around the world and summers back on the Isle of Ormer. Walking away from her had meant rewriting his whole life plan, and he hadn't known how to do it.

As the bus pulled up at the stop by Aspen's flat, Jones clicked the screen off, taking a deep, steadying breath. Charlie always knew what Jones was feeling, and what he needed, and it seemed that still held after almost a year and a half apart. He felt dizzy with the urgent desire to see her, aware all of a sudden of the aching hollow inside himself that had remained empty ever since he'd walked away from her.

But he had to face Aspen first.

When Aspen answered the door, he blinked in surprise. She looked gorgeous, as always, but also entirely different: her trademark ginger hair was gone, dyed dark brown, and she'd cut in a fringe. It made her look like a very sexy librarian. Aspen's ability to transform herself was part of the reason that it had taken them a while, when they'd met at Stuart's birthday party, to realize they'd known each other at school. Back then she'd just been the silent, watchful younger sister of Charlie's friend Brianna, with carrot-orange hair and limbs that seemed too long for her, like a crane fly.

As he looked at her now, he noticed with vague wonder that even though he could see how stunning she was, one short text from his ex-wife had effectively killed all attraction he felt for her.

"Hello," she said, with a guarded smile.

"Hi. New hair."

"I needed a change," she said, already walking through to the living room. "Can I get you a drink?"

The formality of it all felt incredibly strange; he'd had sex with Aspen on that sofa, held her while she cried in his lap on that armchair, fixed the baseboard by the TV himself.

"I'm fine, thanks."

They sat. Jones felt almost painfully uncomfortable. He stared at the carpet.

"You were right," he said eventually. "I did waste your time. I'm very sorry. I think . . . I did know you were serious about me in a way I just . . . couldn't be, about you. I wanted to—but I couldn't."

For a moment she just regarded him from the bay window, her tea cupped in her palms. Poised as ever. For all her warmth and charm, there was something unreachable about Aspen. An unimpeachable, flawless outer shell that she'd worn even in grief.

"I so hoped you were different," she said. "You had your shit together. You'd been married, you knew how to commit." She sighed, looking out of the window.

"Why didn't you ever tell me how much you wanted a baby?" he asked, after a long moment.

"I knew you were just out of a very serious relationship with a woman who didn't want children. I didn't want to scare you off, I suppose. I thought that once you were settled in a new serious relationship, you might start to think about having a family, if your partner wanted one. And you made that comment, about not wanting to be a dad *right now* . . ."

"I don't even—"

"Yes, I know," she said, voice sharp. "It was a throwaway remark."

"I'm sorry. It was thoughtless. But you never seemed . . . I just got the impression you were fun and easy about stuff. I honestly didn't think about the whole kids thing until the day with the Uber."

She looked down at her tea for so long, he wasn't sure if he was supposed to say something else.

"You have no idea what it's like," she said at last. "The ticking clock. Wanting a child so much you feel like you're living the wrong life, because all you want is to be a mother, but you date men, and you date men, and men are just *shit*, you know? They *all* fall short. But I kept hoping, and I told myself every time that the next one would be better. And, yes, I maybe . . . wasn't up-front about what I wanted right away with you. But in my *vast* experience of the dating scene, men spook easily, and sometimes they don't know what they want until a woman has shown them."

Jones raised his eyebrows before he could help himself.

"What?" she said. "Tell me—did you know you wanted to get married when you met your ex?"

"I mean . . . I was a child when I first met Charlie."

"What gave you the idea of proposing when you did?"

He thought about it, and then stopped thinking about it, because that was proving Aspen's point.

"This has nothing to do with Charlie, anyway," he said, but he knew instantly it was a lie. If he'd not received that text on the way here, what conversation would he be having? There was a horrible truth in what Aspen had told him at St. James's Park: he did hate being alone. If he couldn't have Charlie . . . He shifted in his seat. Aspen had been a great second choice, and he couldn't say with certainty that he'd have given her up for anything but the possibility of his Charlie coming back to him.

Aspen was watching him shrewdly.

"You never did love me the way you loved her, did you?"

"I . . . I was with her for most of my life, Aspen, it's hard to explain that sort of relationship to . . ."

"Someone like me? Someone who can't make them stick?"

"I didn't say that."

The tension was rising. Jones was beginning to sweat. He had never told Aspen why he'd left Charlie—he'd never told anybody. The drinking had been her secret, and it would have been disloyal to share it. But without it, it was hard to explain the nature of their breakup—how he really had thought there was no hope left for them, but how now that there was . . .

"Well, anyway, you can close off this chapter now," she said. "Your fun year with *fun* Aspen. A year that doesn't matter to you.

A year I'll never get back. You'll go back to her, presumably? Yes, I can see in your face you're already half there."

"I'm not! I'm not. And it's not that I didn't love you, Aspen," Jones said, readjusting his cap. He didn't want things to end like this—he didn't want to leave her with the impression he'd treated her badly, particularly as he was just starting to think with horror that he might have done. "It's more that you're . . ."

"Mm. I get it, don't you worry." Aspen's smile was cold and brittle as she said, "I'm *just* not Charlie Jones, am I?"

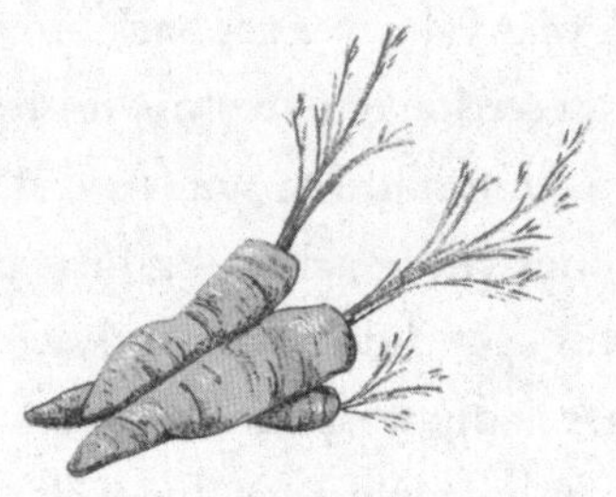

FROM: **Charlie Jones**
TO: **Charlie Jones**
SUBJECT: **Hellooooo**

Hey,

I told you this was a great plan. I've been squirreled away up here in Puffin room all night and all morning, and I promise nobody's clocked I'm here. I've been quiet as a mouse. You were so hilarious last night. It basically took the threat of me sleeping on a random dark bench for you to sneak me in here, and look! No harm done! I told you so.

That said, if you *could* come and get me soon, that would be fab. I didn't totally think through what it would feel like staying in this room, and I've run out of snacks, plus I want to hear how it went when you told new Charlie your real name. Have you found her yet?!

Also, I dodged when you asked about Berty while we were getting me set up here—I'm sorry. I know you and I aren't really standard exes but we *were* together and I felt weird discussing him with you! Which is so daft given you've written me a hundred emails about how much you luuurve Charlie. (I called that long before you did, by the way. "Oh, she's such a nuisance!" he says. "Oh, I wish she wasn't here!" Load of bollocks.)

As soon as you get back from your Charlie-hunting mission I promise I'll fill you in on everything that's gone down between me and Berty over the last couple of months. Short answer is, yes, I still love him, God, so much, and we've been messaging loads, but that's it so far. I'm so scared that if I go back to him I'll fall off the wagon and screw it up again, and how the hell do you know when you're ready?? You know?

Anyway, wow, I can see why you sent me all those emails, this is great, isn't it? Way easier than talking in person. Especially when there is almost no entertainment. Hint hint.

I found the list of Charlie Joneses, by the way, in the book about Ormer. You never mentioned whether I was on there or not. Did it not occur to you that I might want to know? I mean, it was me who got offered your job in the first place . . .

Charlie x

Sunday October 5th 2025

For about five seconds after recognizing Berty Jones, I just stood there on the ferry in the island drizzle in absolute blank panic. My first thought was that he was here on behalf of his wife, coming to get me for nicking Charlie's job. Not sure what "coming to get me" would have involved, but nonetheless, anxiety was through the roof.

"Excuse me," he called, once he'd stepped onto the harbor.

I was just getting off the ferry. Red was there, helping people in her tour-guiding T-shirt; found myself reaching to clutch her arm as I stepped to land. She looked at me, puzzled, as Berty went on, "I'm looking for Charlie Jones?"

"Oh, fuck," I muttered.

Red got the idea and pulled me behind her, out of view. I told her I loved her through the cloud of her curls.

"What's going on, Charlie?" she whispered over her shoulder. "Who is that guy?"

"Which Charlie Jones?" someone on the harbor called back at Berty, to a chorus of laughter.

I realized—shit—half of the island was out here, preparing for tomorrow's festivities. Barn dance is tonight, but main festival kicks off tomorrow, so the harbor was getting decked out in full orange-and-gold glory. Galoshes, Rosie and Marly were there, and I could see at least six members of the committee, even while cowering behind Red. And there was Jones—my Jones, Ormer Jones, looking windswept in an old brushed-cotton shirt as he ducked his head so that Marly could speak in his ear.

"Got a couple of Charlie Joneses about," Rog shouted good-naturedly, taking an armful of gourds from his trailer.

"What did you say?" Berty asked.

"Kind of a funny story, actually," Rog said. "They both showed up for the same job, up at the—"

"Oliver?" Berty said.

Nobody responded to this. He said it again. I obviously had no idea what he was talking about and was pretty preoccupied trying to work out how the hell I was going to navigate this situation (*Why* didn't I just tell Jones about the name thing sooner? Now it was going to be *awful*.) but did slowly clock that Berty was looking in Jones's direction.

And Jones was looking *very* windswept, actually. Maybe more . . . frazzled.

"Look, mate, I can explain," Jones said.

Never heard Jones call anyone *mate* before.

"Oh, so she came here for you, did she?" Berty said, readjusting his cap—always a tell that he's feeling something, an experience Berty has never been particularly comfortable with.

"No, hang on, it's not like that, she—"

"So where is she? Where's Charlie?"

He was looking around now. I shrank back, but it was too late—Galoshes had spotted me.

"There she is," she said.

Berty's eyes settled on me. I saw the exact moment he recognized me—he looked totally astonished. If I hadn't been completely panicking at the imminent public humiliation (actual worst nightmare—in front of most of the committee, in front of Jones . . .) then might almost have been a little bit satisfied.

"Aspen?" he said.

My eyes went straight to Jones. He was stiff, arms crossed over his chest, staring at Berty.

"What the hell?" Berty said to me. "What are <u>you</u> doing here?"

"I can explain," I said, a little desperately.

"You think this woman's called Charlie?" Berty said, turning back to Rog.

"Ain't she?" Kim called. "That's Charlie Jones and that's Charlie Jones." She pointed at each of us in turn.

Berty's face was a picture of disbelief.

"You think that's Charlie Jones, too?" he said, pointing to Jones.

"He's not called Charlie Jones?" Galoshes asked sharply.

Complete hush across the little harbor now. Remember hearing the ferry creaking behind me, and waves lapping against rock, and feeling totally disassociated from all of it.

Berty's expression was dark as he pointed to us in turn.

"You all honestly think that these two people here have the same exact name? They are both called Charlie Jones? You think that's an actual plausible coincidence, do you, and that they both turned up here at the same time for, what . . . no reason at all?"

"Well, it's just one of those weird things, isn't it?" Rog said, after a slightly defensive silence. "Like those stories about people who get swapped at birth or accidentally inherit each other's houses or whatever."

"That man is called Oliver. That woman is called Aspen."

Everyone was staring at us. Anxiety was pulsing through me—could hardly bear it. It was crushing, <u>awful</u>. Wanted to crouch down on the ground in a ball, or perhaps throw myself off the edge of the harbor—not to die, it wasn't about that, it was just about *doing* something to make the feeling *stop*. Needed to get out, get away, go somewhere nobody in the world could see me.

Caloshes marched over.

"You're not Charlie Jones," she said, looking at me.

"No." My voice was croaky. My whole body was trembling. "I'm so sorry for—"

"And you're not Charlie Jones." Caloshes turned back toward ~~Jones~~ Oliver.

"No," he said simply. He wasn't looking at me. He turned to Marly and Rosie. "I'm sorry I didn't tell you. Both of you."

"But," Rog piped up, "if you're not Charlie Jones, and you're not Charlie Jones . . ." His face was crumpled in bewilderment. "Marly and Rosie offered that job to *someone* called Charlie Jones, didn't they?"

"They did," Caloshes said grimly.

"So where the hell's the actual Charlie Jones?" Rog said.

"*Thank* you," said Berty. "Where the hell is my wife?"

Lot of commotion after that. Don't quite know what happened, really—was in my own little hell, the anxiety gnawing at my insides.

Red gripped my arm, the way I'd gripped hers as I'd stepped off the ferry.

"Are you OK?" she said.

"I'm so sorry," I whispered, as everyone around began to speak to me.

"You're who?" . . . "You lied to us?" . . . "Who the hell even are you?"

"Hey, come on. I'm sure you had your reasons. Give her some space!" Red said to the crowd around us, pulling me through so I was closer to Berty, ~~Jones~~ Oliver, Rosie and Marly. I nearly tripped over an absurd heap of pumpkins.

"You're really not called Charlie Jones?" Rosie said to me, and her eyes filled with tears.

"I'm so, so sorry," I said shakily. "It didn't seem like this big a lie when you were all theoretical people, and the farm shop was just some cute idea . . ."

"I'm so sorry," Oliver said.

There were tears in his eyes, too, and he still wasn't looking at me. Anxiety roared through me. What if he hates me now? And who even is he? He felt suddenly like a terrifying unknown, and it made me realize that until this moment he'd seemed so safe to me. Someone I could trust. Now he was a stranger. That night we'd shared on the sofa, all the gaps and silences . . . We'd hidden so much from each other—how could I have felt I knew him so deeply? I'd not even known his name.

And he'd not even known mine.

Did it matter? Don't know, can't tell—even now I'm writing this I'm too churned up to figure it out.

"You're not called Charlie Jones, either?" Rosie asked him, hushed.

"I'm really sorry. I don't know what else to say. Charlie suggested I could step into her shoes and come here, and . . ."

"Charlie did?" Rosie straightened. Her hand tightened on Marly's. "So you know her? The person who actually applied for the job?"

"My wife," Berty said.

Guess we were officially dropping the "ex," then. No surprise there.

He looked at Oliver. "Do you know where she is? Is she OK?"

"She's fine. She's good, actually—the best I've seen her."

Berty stiffened. "You've seen her? Is she here, then? She sent me a message this morning about coming here, but it was pretty random even by Charlie standards and I freaked out that she'd . . . you know."

Not sure what that meant.

"She's safe," Oliver said. "She's OK."

Berty's shoulders sagged.

"So there is a real Charlie Jones? Who wrote me that letter? Who applied for this job?" Rosie said insistently.

"Yeah, yeah, there is," Berty said. He checked his phone, then his gaze turned to me. "And what exactly are you doing here, Aspen?" he said, with uncharacteristic sharpness.

Felt myself flush hot with shame. "It was Brianna's idea," I blurted.

"You know Brianna?" Oliver asked.

"She's my sister. How do you know Brianna? Who even are you?" My voice cracked slightly.

Oliver looked lost. "I'm . . . I'm a friend of Charlie's. That's how I knew Brianna—through her. Did you know Charlie? As in, Charlie Jones?"

"That clears things up," Caloshes said.

"This is Aspen," Berty said shortly. "We dated for a while. When Charlie and I were apart. When you were dating Charlie."

This was directed at Oliver.

"Oh my God," I said, staring at Oliver. "You dated Charlie Jones? As in, the Charlie who's friends with my sister? Berty's ex-wife?"

"Yeah. I mean, Charlie and I have been just friends for a long time," Oliver said—not sure if it was for Berty's benefit or mine. "She wanted this job, but then she . . . changed her mind, and suggested that I could just step into her shoes here. I know it was wrong," he said, turning to Rosie and Marly. "I should never have done it. And once I had done it, I should have told you. I kept telling myself it was just a name, and it didn't matter as long as I was doing a good job . . ."

"It did matter," Marly said. "It really fucking did."

"But this Charlie," Rosie said, looking between us all. "The one who actually applied to work at Bramblebay. Where is she?"

"I'm so sorry, Rosie," Oliver said, just as Berty said, "That's what I want to know."

Berty did a sudden double take at Rosie. "You're Rosie?" he said. "Rosie Nicole?"

"Yes. Yes," Rosie said, clutching one hand to the scarf at her throat.

"Oh, fucking hell," Berty said, removing his cap altogether.

"It's her, isn't it?" Rosie whispered. "Your wife."

"I can't . . ." Berty paused. "She should be the one to tell you."

Rosie looked almost frantic as she turned to Oliver, who was reading a message on his phone.

"Where is she?" Rosie said, letting go of Marly to reach for Oliver's arm. "You have to tell me where she is."

"OK, well, she says it's fine to tell you all, so . . . I'm very, very sorry about this," Oliver said, eyes flicking to the furious-looking Marly. He looked wretched. "But Charlie came to the island kind of spontaneously and there was nowhere available for her to stay, and she suggested . . . She thought maybe she could . . ."

"Jones—Oliver—whatever your name is," Marly said bluntly, "spit it out, would you?"

Oliver swallowed. "The real Charlie Jones is currently in your spare room."

Shocked silence. Then, all of a sudden, Rosie doubled over and began to laugh.

The whole group exchanged glances over her back.

"She's in my spare room! She's in my spare room!"

"She just needed a safe place to stay for the night and I wanted to find, well—you, before you met her . . ." Oliver said, directing this to me.

We had a brief moment of fleeting, precious eye contact before Marly began to hoot with laughter, too.

"All this fucking time! All the investigating!" she said, doubling over beside Rosie and putting her arm around her wife's shoulders. "And now she's just turned up and made herself at home in the spare room!"

"What's going on?" Berty said.

"What's going on," Rosie said, straightening up and wiping her eyes, "is that I have kept a room empty at the B&B ever since my parents died, and I discovered in their will that they had another child. My sibling was put up for adoption ten years before I was born. I've searched for them every single day since I found out. I've always said that when they come home, there will be a room ready for them at the family farmhouse."

"Oh my God," Oliver said under his breath.

"The only thing I know about this person is the name they entered when they signed up for an ancestry app—one of the billions I downloaded and gave my DNA to. We matched six years ago. Full siblings. They deleted their profile, and it barely said anything anyway, but I got the notification, and I've known since then that my sibling, whoever they are, is called Charlie Jones."

I thought of how long Rosie had spent scrolling through my phone on the Night of the Pig, when she asked to borrow it to ring Marly. My heart plummeted. She'd hoped I was her sister, and she was looking for that app on my phone to prove it. Presumably she'd tried to search Jones's phone, too, or Marly had. And that list of people called Charlie Jones, tucked away in a book about Ormer history...

"And then someone named Charlie Jones applied for a job on the farm. Finally, after all these years, I knew they were ready to meet me. The letter I got with their application wasn't explicit, but... 'I think Bramblebay Farm could be my home,' they said."

"Shit," Oliver said. "Charlie asked me to write her emails and tell her everything that I did here. Every single detail. She said she thought it would be good for me to keep myself accountable, and I figured she was probably interested because she's always been obsessed with this island, but . . . I guess you said where you were based in your profile on that ancestry app?"

"I said absolutely everything I could," Rosie said, smiling, her eyes full of tears. "I was desperate for them to find me. And then, after all these years of searching, in among all those job applications, there was that name."

"So <u>that's</u> why you let both the Charlies stay on!" Galoshes said to Rosie, with satisfaction. "I knew we didn't need two bloody farm shop managers."

"When the two of you turned up, I didn't have a clue what to do," Rosie said. "Two Charlies! I didn't understand it at all, but I wasn't about to turn away a Charlie Jones. What if I sent away the person who was my only living family? Only one of you could have written that letter, of course, but the other one had still chosen to come here, and that in itself seemed like it had to mean something. I just couldn't work it out. One of you had to be an imposter, but it could just as easily have been the person who wrote the application, so that wouldn't help me. I had to get to know you both, and try to figure it out. It's been so hard, spending time with you, hoping against hope but also knowing that you might be a fraud, with any number of possible motives for pretending to be a relation of mine . . ."

"I'm so, so sorry, Rosie," I said. "I had no idea the lie would cause you so much pain."

Rosie gave me a small smile. "I suppose you couldn't have known. But I wish you'd told me the truth. I was hoping . . . I hoped it was you."

So <u>awful</u> to know that while we've been becoming friends, she's been hoping I'm family. Can hardly bear to write all this down. Am just so ashamed of myself.

"Everything we shared," I told her, "it was all real. It was all me. I hope you can forgive me, Rosie."

Rosie wiped her eyes. "I'll try, of course, I just . . . This has all been so intense, the hope, the wondering."

"Come on," Marly said, tugging Rosie's arm. "Let's go home. Let's meet your Charlie Jones."

Guildford, yesterday

Charlie Jones had spent most of her life waiting to be ready.

When she found out that her adoptive parents had lied about the death of her birth parents, back in 2019, she thought it might be time. Spurred on by grief and fury, she even signed up to the Who-Might-I-Be app—she did the swab and everything. But the moment she found her sister, the moment she saw Rosie's beautiful smiling face on her profile page, Charlie panicked.

She wasn't good enough yet. Her finances were a mess; she and Berty were still living in a tiny, rented flat in the gray pocket of London where they'd grown up, and she hated her job on the tills at Sainsbury's, and she wasn't *cool* enough yet, she wasn't long-lost sister material.

Charlie's adoption story was so unlike all the beautiful ones she would stalk on social media. Winny and Simon Morrissey had adopted Charlie as a last-ditch effort to save their marriage, and it had not worked. But neither of them would leave, then, because of Charlie—they felt it would be wrong. As a result, much of the time, everybody involved felt painfully unloved, none more so than Charlie, who learned at every turn that she was a much-resented inconvenience.

She had always believed her birth parents were dead—her mum and dad had told her as much from birth—so she would not let herself dream of finding them. But the Morrisseys had almost no relations, just a few distant cousins and an aunt who couldn't travel, and Charlie always longed for a *family*. A sibling, maybe. She felt deep in her heart that she had one out there somewhere, a person who would understand her in a way that nobody ever had, not even Fearne, not even Berty.

And then she'd learned that her birth parents had lived until 2019. All along, they'd been out there, alive and real—a truth her parents only told her once it was no longer true. The Nicoles died in a car accident when Charlie was twenty-eight.

The rage Charlie had felt was unlike anything she had experienced before. How *could* her parents have kept this from her? They had stolen something priceless; they had robbed her of a chance to understand the story of how she came to be. She couldn't forgive it.

Her fury was the fuel she needed to cut herself off from her adoptive parents altogether. Aside from a few reconciliation attempts they'd made over the years, they had not spoken since. It was around this time that drinking slipped from something fun to something necessary, and finding her blood relatives shifted from a childhood fantasy to Charlie's greatest life goal. She became obsessed with becoming worthy of them—it was suddenly imperative that she leave her job and do something *cool* and unusual, and when Fearne suggested they turn Vintage, Please into a reality, Charlie jumped on it. She felt like a blank page; she had to make something of herself.

Because the only thing equal to the powerful desire to find her birth family was the overwhelming fear that they wouldn't want her back.

She had screen-grabbed Rosie's profile the second they matched on the Who-Might-I-Be app, and then instantly deleted her account. She must have opened that screenshot a hundred thousand times. Her fascination with the Isle of Ormer had begun there—she'd learned all about the Nicole family, *her* family, and their long-standing history on the island. Berty and Fearne had encouraged her to reach out countless times, or even just to visit Ormer without declaring who she was, but Charlie would always say the same thing. *I'm not ready.*

But how does a person know when they're ready? When would Charlie ever be good enough?

She had come so close when she'd seen the farm shop advert. A *job* on the very farm her sister owned—it was too perfect an opportunity to miss, and it came to her when she was so close to rock bottom. As though Rosie was already looking out for her.

She applied. She got the job, thanks, she thought, to her rather inflated CV—Charlie had always been good at a positive spin. And she had planned to go, she really had. She knew Fearne would have wanted her to; Berty had moved on with Brianna's pretty little sister; there was no joy left for her at Vintage, Please without Fearne.

But then Oliver found the backup box underneath her sink, and Charlie finally faced the truth that she had a problem.

And that meant she was *definitely* not ready.

How about now, though? What about October 4, 2025, when she was more than two months sober, when the contract on her flat was coming up for renewal and she had the perfect opening to move elsewhere? Vintage, Please was doing better online than in-store these days; she was glad she'd kept it going, but was considering giving up the brick-and-mortar shop and moving the business to online only. She could manage it from anywhere if she did that—even from a tiny island in the middle of the Channel.

For the last two and a half months, Charlie had woken up, wanted a vodka orange and made herself a cinnamon syrup–laced coffee instead. She had fought through the early shakes and cravings; she had gone to her AA meetings, wept on the phone to her sponsor, joined an online sober community, and through all of it, she had marveled at herself. She had never thought she was a particularly strong person. Who knew she had this kind of staying power?

Every day, she had allowed herself a few messages to Berty—a reward at the end of each sober evening. He was impatient to meet up, but she had set herself a goal: three months sober before she could see him again. She had to earn it.

She had read Oliver's emails over and over, gleaning every detail she could, and said to herself, *Maybe next month I'll visit him on Ormer. Maybe next month I'll be ready.*

She might never have gotten there, if it hadn't been for that peculiar *other* Charlie who had turned up in Oliver's emails. The brave, beautiful one with slightly bendy morals who had searched that empty room at the farmhouse and found a list of Charlie Joneses. That particular email from Oliver had given Charlie the first clue that her sister knew her name.

She had deleted her profile so fast all those years ago. Within *seconds* of the match being made. Frenzied googling told her that once her profile was gone, there was no way for Rosie to know they'd matched, unless she'd happened to be in the app at that precise moment. But the list of Charlie Joneses in Rosie's spare bedroom told Charlie the one thing that she longed to hear more than anything.

Her sister wanted to know her.

Sunday October 5th 2025

We did try to streamline the meeting-Charlie group. Galoshes, for instance, seemed a superfluous addition, as did I, if we're honest, but Marly said a firm "She's coming, too" when I suggested hanging back. Rog insisted on joining in, because who else would drive us there? And Red just needed a ride back to the B&B to change. Was a bit of a squeeze in Rog's trailer. Felt very close to a lot of people who were quite annoyed with me.

Should've known there was no such thing as a ready-made new life. The past doesn't disappear just because you hit restart.

On the plus side, astonishingly, I hadn't fallen apart. Anxiety was almost unbearable. But actually, my great big worst possible thing was happening: <u>everyone</u> thought badly of me right now. I was completely exposed to their judgment. And I hadn't run. Had said sorry. Had let everyone feel what they needed to feel without trying to justify my actions or wriggle my way out of it all somehow. I was sticking around, sitting with the discomfort (understatement. Feel like I want to claw the dread out of me) and I was going to do my best to make it right.

"So, let me get this straight," Berty said to me, leaning forward to rest his forearms on his knees as Rog fired up the tractor engine.

"Brianna told you that Charlie had gotten a job offer working in a farm shop here, but had decided not to take it. So you thought it was going spare . . . and decided to pretend it was yours?"

"It sounds very bad when you say it like that," I said. My voice shook. "I really didn't think it would do any harm."

"What about us?" Marly asked.

I cringed. "I promise you, if I'd sucked at this and the farm shop had made no money, I'd have left. That was something I told myself from the start. I would only stay if I genuinely did a good job."

Which had not helped with the anxiety about getting the committee on my side.

"Well. Fair play. I checked the ledgers in the back room yesterday. This week, the shop is making more than twice what it made this time last year, and bringing in the biscuits and coffee has made a massive difference."

There was a shocked pause. That interjection had come from Caloshes.

"What?" She shrugged, lifting her chin in my direction. "I've always known there's something off about her. Now I know what it is. We've all done shit we're not proud of here, haven't we? Ormer's swimming with people who wanted to start over, and nobody wants to start over because they've made such a great go of it the first time. She lied, but the only harm she did was something she could hardly have guessed would happen."

"And in fairness, Charlie herself had the same idea as Aspen," Oliver said.

The sound of my real name in his voice made the hairs stand up on my arms.

"That's why Charlie gave it to me," he went on. "It was the ideal opportunity for a fresh start. I should have thought of it, actually—

the idea that you and I came to the job via the same route," he said to me. Another fleeting moment of eye contact, enough to make my cheeks heat. He was the only person I wanted to look at me. "The job and the name were ripe for the taking, so . . . two of us took them."

"And Charlie wanted you to do this? She suggested it?" Berty said to Oliver.

Could see how much it was all pissing him off. His jaw was tense and he was back to fiddling with his bloody cap again. He told me once that his ex-wife thought it looked cool when he wore it backward—might explain why I always found the affectation so annoying. In retrospect, Berty had talked a <u>lot</u> about his ex-wife.

"Look, there's nothing to feel insecure about—she and I are just friends," Oliver assured him, "and we have been for a long time. Ever since Fearne died."

Was Fearne the person Oliver had spoken about on the beach that night? The one he'd lost? After weeks of knowing so little about his past, I was suddenly immersed in it, and it felt so surreal. Like starting again, or . . . the opposite, I don't know.

"I suspect Charlie hoped I'd tell her all about you, actually, Rosie," Oliver said.

"Did you?" Rosie breathed.

He smiled one of his tiny, warm smiles, and nodded.

"I can't believe she's here," Rosie whispered. "I can't believe she's ready to meet me at last."

Had been very much in the moment until this point—there's only so much you can absorb when you're <u>this</u> anxious, and, if we're honest, this confused. But it suddenly hit me that I was on my way to see the real Charlie Jones. We'd met back when I was a kid and had chatted briefly at Brianna and Stuart's wedding, but I didn't <u>know</u> her particularly. Had always thought she seemed fun and dressed well. Since dating Berty, I'd added a few more opinions, many of which were probably a bit unjust, but it's hard to think pure, kind thoughts about the ex-wife of your boyfriend, especially when a little buried bit of you knows he's still in love with her.

Realized she would probably be pretty angry when she discovered I'd stolen her job. And her name. Doubt she liked me much before even getting to that stuff, for all the same reasons I'd not particularly liked the idea of her, either.

"Oh, God," I whimpered, very quietly.

"Are you doing OK?" Red asked beside me. "It's all out there now. It must be a bit of a relief, right?"

"Oh, oh," I said, turning to her and clutching her hands. It wasn't all out there yet. "I'm a midwife."

Her eyes widened slightly.

"As in," I backpedaled, before I revealed Red's pregnancy to the whole trailer and thus pissed off the one remaining person who seemed to like me, "I've wanted to tell you that for ages, because we were talking, weren't we, about how Doc Laurry should hire a midwife on the island . . ."

Glanced at Marly, who was looking at me with a slightly warmer expression. Suppose she thought that was why I'd decided to stay on the island when pregnant even though there was no qualified midwife here. And that had been the idea—it was the reason I felt comfortable planning to start a family on the island. It would've been lovely to explain that and be free of all the lies, but this one wasn't mine to dispel.

"Right! We were talking about that!" Red said, a bit too loudly, as though she was performing in a pantomime. She really was a terrible liar.

"You're a midwife?" Oliver said.

He was looking at me wonderingly. My stomach flipped when our eyes met, just like it always did back when he was Jones. Guess my body hadn't got the memo that this man was a stranger now.

"I am," I began, and then I stopped short, because a thought hit me.

Charlie Jones didn't want a baby. Brianna had told me that as soon as I'd started dating Berty—she'd known how badly I wanted a family before I'd been ready to admit it to myself.

Oliver had been in a relationship with Charlie before coming here. Does that mean he didn't ever want a baby, either?

Not that it matters. This is exactly why I wasn't getting involved with ~~Jones~~ Oliver. No men, nobody else's opinion to consider.

But judging by the way my stomach plummeted when I remembered that Charlie Jones had never wanted a baby . . .

I've been considering Oliver's opinion already, without even noticing.

For fuck's sake. When will I learn?

When we arrived at the farmhouse, there was a bit of kerfuffle in the corridor outside Puffin room as everyone faffed about deciding who should be the one to knock on the door. In the end, we assembled in an impromptu ranking of how important it was for us to see the real Charlie Jones, and it went like this:

1. Berty (worried ex-husband clearly itching to reproclaim his love)
2. Rosie (probably long-lost sibling, but too nice to tell Berty this meant she should definitely go first)
3. Marly (supportive sister-in-law who has put up with a lot of Charlie Jones–related trouble)

4. Oliver (?? Ex-boyfriend, now very good friend, apparently? Not that I should care, etc.)
5. Galoshes (pushy)
6. Me (hiding)

Red and Rog stayed in the kitchen to make a round of tea. Tried to stick around with them, but Marly looked daggers at me and said, "Nobody ever sorted their life out by hiding in the kitchen." So I watched in sickened anticipation as Berty knocked on the door of Puffin room and called a soft, "Charlie?"

Would she recognize me? If Oliver had been filling her in on everything going on here, he'd presumably mentioned the other Charlie Jones. She'd probably not worked out who I was, either—the only person who could have cleared it all up was Bri, I suppose, as she's the one person who knew us all. Plus her husband, Stuart, whose birthday party I'd been at when I'd gone home with Berty.

Wiped my sweating palms on my trousers and considered becoming a person who prayed. Though, I thought, what exactly was I praying for? That Charlie Jones wouldn't think badly of me? Of course she would. She should, frankly.

For a second out there in the corridor I imagined the whole thing from Charlie's point of view. She was here to meet her sister. She was about to see her ex-husband for the first time since . . . that funeral Berty went to back in the spring? That was the only time he'd told me he'd seen Charlie since the separation. So this was a big day for them.

I, meanwhile, was a woman who'd dated her husband while they were apart—a temporary blip in their love story. I did not matter.

It sounds so obvious, but the thought totally floored me. Suddenly properly understood what Rosie had been saying that night we'd stargazed together. I spend all my time wondering what everyone thinks of me, when the reality is they're hardly thinking of me at all. Yes, Charlie likely won't be best pleased to hear what I've done. But how freeing to realize that actually, I'm a tiny speck in the great big tapestry of her life, and this moment right here with Rosie was her story, not mine.

Isle of Ormer, now

Charlie was sitting cross-legged on the bed, staring down at three pages of Charlie Joneses. There were tears in her eyes.

It was Rosie's handwritten marginalia on the printout that had gotten her. The little notes about each person she thought was a contender: Charles from North Yorkshire (*the nose??* she'd written beneath his photo), Charlotte from Geneva (*moved there aged 18, born in London*). It was heartbreaking and beautiful all at once. Little did Rosie know that searching for similarities like this, obsessing over the details, creating this room in preparation for the moment—all of these small acts *were* the similarity. This was absolutely something Charlie Jones would do.

She knew they were coming—Oliver had messaged ahead—but when she heard Berty's voice on the other side of the door, she felt suddenly paralyzed. *I'm not ready*, she thought, *Oh, please, I'm not ready.* The door swung open in the face of her silence, and there he was: brow furrowed in concern, cap backward, polo shirt a little too tight. He always did shrink things in the dryer, she found herself thinking—even at a time like this, Charlie's brain would not entirely dedicate itself solely to one single thing.

"Berty?" she whispered.

It was too good to be true. She was not allowed to see him yet—she was not three months sober. But here he was, her gorgeous giant of a husband, in the Nicole family farmhouse. It was a scene she had painstakingly created on her mood board and thought of every single day. The farmhouse, the love of her life, and behind him . . .

Her sister.

"Oh," she said, on an inhale. Everything ran through her head at once: her hair was in childish pigtails to keep it out of her face while she was reading, she wasn't wearing the dress she'd set aside for meeting Rosie, she wasn't ready, she wasn't ready . . .

But it all evaporated within seconds, because Rosie's eyes were just like her own, and they too were full of tears.

"It's you," Charlie choked out.

"You're Charlie Jones?" Rosie breathed.

"Who isn't?" Charlie said, grinning through her tears as she swung her legs off the bed and met Rosie halfway.

They stopped abruptly, face-to-face and just as breathless as each other. Charlie was ten years older than Rosie, and looking at her younger sister was dizzying—she had never seen herself in somebody else in this way, never known her own features on another face. Rosie's curls were tighter than hers, and mousier; they were held back from her face with a yellow silk scarf, and her earrings were little wooden cherries. Charlie couldn't get enough of the details: the slightly wonky eyeliner, the Charlie-like dip in the center of her chin, the tremble in her bottom lip. Everything about her was perfect.

"You know," Rosie said, reaching a tentative hand to cup her sister's cheek, "you might choose to call yourself Charlie Jones, but to me, you're Charlie Nicole."

They sat together on the back step, underneath a blanket Rosie said their mother had knitted, and they talked. Their hands met often—Rosie was affectionate, but tentative, a little afraid—*Is it OK for me to say that?* she'd say, stumbling over herself. There was just so much to tell.

Berty was there, a quiet, solid, reassuring presence in the corner of Charlie's vision, as he had been for so much of her life—her nurturer of a husband, a sweetheart in a frat boy's disguise. She knew he'd followed her out here to the island because he was worried about her, and she was fiercely proud that he had no need to be: she was seventy days sober. But she also knew that he was here because after two months of constant messaging, he was nudging her to take the step back to him. Charlie had always struggled with the final leap—Berty was the one who helped her jump.

Today, though, Berty hung back. This afternoon was about Charlie and Rosie.

Eventually the autumn chill drove the sisters back inside. On her way through, Charlie paused in the doorway of the farmhouse living room, looking at the back wall, which was painted in an extraordinary work of art. It was clearly about the island, though it was abstract enough that Charlie couldn't pinpoint precisely why she knew that—it was the colors, the feeling. And through the golds and greens of its scenery were tiny scenes: figures conjured in a few brushstrokes, some meeting, some hand in hand, some walking away.

"It's the story of our family," Rosie said, moving past her to lift her hand to the wall. "Toby painted it for me. He's an amazing local artist—he'll be famous one day. Here." She pressed her finger to a scene in the center. "This is you."

"What?" Charlie said, her voice catching. She stepped forward.

"I didn't tell Toby the specifics—Doc Laurry was the only one on the island who knew about you, and of course he wouldn't tell a soul, because of patient confidentiality. Mum and Grandma moved to the mainland when they found out Mum was pregnant at sixteen, and the family kept the pregnancy a secret—Mum and Dad were so young, I suppose. I wanted to honor their choice to keep that part of their story back from the islanders. And I wanted to honor you, too. I wanted it to be your decision to make yourself known to your wider Ormer family once you were ready. But I did ask Toby to add in a baby."

The tiny figure was wrapped in a cream brushstroke of blanket and caught in a swirl of sea spray, or cloud, perhaps.

"You were a secret, but you were always at the heart of the story. That's how I see it." She swallowed, tracing the baby's tiny cheek. "I like to think they would have told me about you, one day, if they'd lived. I have to believe they would have."

"Do you know . . . why . . ." The sentence died in Charlie's throat.

Rosie shook her head, her eyes filling with tears again. "I'm sorry. I know so little. I felt so angry about that, after they died—the way they kept you from me. But if you'd like to, I'd love to try to find out more together. Lots of people here on the island knew Mum when she was a teenager, for instance. I've never started those conversations, because it didn't feel right to without you, but . . ."

Charlie nodded, unable to speak. Rosie's smile was soft. She looked back at the painting, pointing.

"And this is me," she said.

There was a young woman—a teenage girl, maybe, wild haired in loose, bright clothes. She was shading her eyes with her hand, searching for something in the swirls of color around her.

"Looking for you," Rosie said.

Charlie's throat tightened. She pressed her fingertip to the baby at the center of the painting. Baby Charlie. *I love you*, she thought, as she looked at that helpless child, and it seemed so obvious that the tiny lost baby deserved nothing *but* love—a revelation to Charlie, who had always believed she was intrinsically, fundamentally unworthy of it.

When Charlie breathed in again and wiped her eyes, Rosie was there, smiling, waiting for her.

"There's something else I'd like to show you. If you think you're ready to see more?"

She led Charlie through to the kitchen and bent to pull a small keepsake box from the bottom of the large dresser behind the well-worn dog bed. Charlie thought for an instant of the box under the sink in her flat, packed with vodka, whisky and gin, and another warm wave of pride moved through her. So many parts of Charlie had been hidden away, waiting for her to be brave enough to show them. And now she had nothing left to face. Charlie had owned her drinking problem. She had come here to meet her sister, and Rosie had welcomed her with warmth and love. She had lost Berty, and then she had lost Fearne, and through the awful days of grief she had discovered the priceless truth that she could exist without the two of them to bolster her.

"I'm ready," she said.

The box held many details of Rosie's search for Charlie, but it also contained everything Rosie had found when their parents had died. A tiny gray knitted hat. A photograph of a baby, fingered so many times the little bundle was almost unrecognizable as a baby at all. And a note.

I want you to know, it read, *that I will always love you. I can't be your mama. But you will always be my baby.*

"I think she wanted it to go with you, to your new family," Rosie said. "But for whatever reason—oh, sweetheart."

Charlie could hold it in no longer. She had begun to sob.

Rosie held her. She smelled of roses and Parma Violets, and she hugged Charlie the way Charlie longed to be hugged—like she would never let her go.

The rest of the afternoon was an extraordinary, glorious blur. New faces, a new *home*, as she was assured it was—a whole farm that she had imagined a million times but that turned out to be both more beautiful and considerably muddier than she had ever anticipated.

And Aspen. Aspen was a surprise.

Charlie had been given a very brief rundown of the whole situation after meeting Rosie, and had absorbed approximately ten percent of it, registering only the important fact that Berty seemed as displeased by Aspen's presence on Ormer as she was. It was only later, when she caught sight of Aspen talking quietly with Berty in the living room, that she dedicated any time and energy to the woman who had, apparently, decided to steal her dream life.

She folded her arms as she entered the room, leveling her gaze at Aspen. As adults, they'd only spoken properly once, at Brianna and Stuart's wedding; Charlie had liked her, then. She was beautiful, just like Brianna—the resemblance was uncanny, despite Aspen having dyed that amazing ginger hair brown. Charlie marveled to feel none of the usual envy pass through her. Siblings used to fill her with longing, but now, she had her own.

She scanned Aspen, trying to compile everything she knew about her. She was a midwife; she'd always done well in school, the good-girl counterpoint to Brianna's rebelliousness. She was perpetually dating, never with much success. And, judging by Oliver's recent emails, she was pregnant.

With a dizzying shot of fear, Charlie considered the possibility that it could be Berty's baby. But no, he'd broken up with Aspen in July, and it was October now. Surely Aspen would be showing, and her stomach was conspicuously flat in her low-rise jeans and tank top. She didn't look pregnant at all, in fact.

"So. You stole my job," Charlie said to Aspen. "It was Brianna who came up with the whole plan, presumably?"

It was hardly surprising—Bri had been the one who'd planted the idea in Charlie's head, too. *That's it? You just turn up with this letter and say "Hi, I'm Charlie Jones"?* she'd said, and when Charlie had looked across the kitchen table at Oliver, her kind, sad, broken friend, those words had come back to her.

"I'm so sorry," Aspen said. Her eyes were wet; she was holding back tears. "If I'd had any idea that this place meant so much to you . . ."

"It's fraud, you know, what you did," Charlie said.

"And what I did," Oliver said from behind her.

She turned to look at him. Berty-lite, as she'd thought of him—but with Berty actually here, the contrast was more apparent. Berty was taller, more assertively muscular; Oliver had the compact build of a mountain biker, just as Fearne had had, and his energy was milder, more subtle. He paled beside Berty's clear-cut edges. Charlie immediately scolded herself for the comparison—Oliver was her friend, and she loved him dearly.

"You could have told me, you know," Oliver said gently. "I would still have come, and told you everything you wanted to know."

"Nobody knew about Rosie but Fearne and Berty," she said.

She locked eyes with Berty. There was a fierce pleasure in his face that made her shiver with delight. They had always been like this—all fire and strength and unity. Even now, with Oliver and Aspen in the room, she felt and resented every centimeter of the space between them.

"I see," Oliver said.

And he probably did. Charlie had never met anybody as *understanding* as Oliver. Could she have stopped drinking without that? She wasn't sure, but for a brief moment in their lives, Berty had not been able to reach her, and Oliver had. Charlie returned her attention to Aspen. Had she been that for Berty? Had she given him something Charlie couldn't? She loathed the very thought, but Berty did seem a little different, somehow. Less inclined to step in and save her, perhaps—and that would be good for them, now that Charlie had learned she could save herself.

"I'm so glad you decided to come here," Aspen said, "and I'm so happy for you and Rosie."

"All's well that ends well, is that what you're trying to say?" Charlie said, but she didn't like the sharpness in her own voice, and felt her shoulders sag.

She did not actually feel particularly angry with Aspen for stealing her job and her name. It was the kind of joyfully chaotic, ballsy thing Charlie herself might dream of doing. She just hated her because she'd had some small piece of Berty, and Charlie would never be able to abide that.

But it seemed that Aspen had found a home here. She had her own shit to deal with, if she really was pregnant—Charlie found herself feeling a little sorry for her. Plus everyone else seemed to like her, interestingly, even Marly, Rosie's delightfully take-no-shit wife, and that woman everyone called Galoshes, who Charlie had thus far only heard complaining about things.

And Oliver. Oliver definitely liked her, which Charlie begrudgingly had to admit was a point in her favor—Oliver was an excellent judge of character. After all, he'd chosen her, and Fearne.

"Tell me if there is something I can do to make up for what I've done," Aspen said, "and I'll do it."

That was an interesting offer.

Sunday October 5th 2025

Am just going to copy out Charlie's little list in here. It's fairly self-explanatory. Though might add some notes of my own.

Things Aspen Denby can do today (October 5th 2025) to make up for identity theft, job theft, rental property theft and theft of hairstyle

Did not steal her hairstyle. Cutting in a fringe during a midlife crisis is a classic move, and she doesn't own being brunette.

Did do the other stuff, though. So . . . should probably just let her have the hair thing.

1. Immediately give up stolen job as comanager of the farm shop

Knew this was coming. Obviously cannot object. And actually, as much as I love the farm shop, I miss midwifery, and this island is failing its women, IMO. Red belongs here, she wants to be here, and what, she has to leave because she's pregnant? That's crap.

This is the push I need to speak to Doc Laurry and make a case for bringing a midwife onto the medical team, which is currently made up of 1) Doc Laurry, 2) Rog (occasional tractor-ambulance driver), 3) Baptiste (resourceful vet, "can do humans at a push").

Problem is, am no longer sure he or the island will ever want me. In fact, am fairly confident the Ormer gossip mill will be working overtime right now, spreading the word that I'm a lying fraudster.

A huge part of me wants to flee. Head back to the mainland, give up on the dream I've found here, hide from the shame of it all. That's what I would have done, once.

But Ormer is my home now. And I don't want to go.

How can I stay, though? When everyone hates me? Don't know how I'll survive the barn dance tonight, let alone try to build a life here after what I've done.

But I want to do it. I'm <u>going</u> to do it.

I've screwed up, I've done everything wrong, but am a tiny bit proud of myself nonetheless.

2. Lend Charlie Jones (original, one and only) a pair of hiking boots

Somewhat surprised by this one. As tense as things are between me and Charlie, I actually quite <u>like</u> her, you know—she's quirky in a way that reminds me (no surprise here) of Rosie. She also has the wounded life-has-been-hard-on-me energy that always makes me interested in someone. All the best people are a bit screwed up, right? The happy untraumatized tell terrible anecdotes, in my experience.

But didn't think we were yet at sharing-clothes status. Am fairly sure she strongly dislikes me. When I looked surprised at the shoe request, she just said: "You've been wearing <u>my</u> shoes for two months. Metaphorically. And you look like a size five."

Was expecting her to come to the barn dance, but Rosie shook her head when Marly suggested it. We were gathered around the fire in the farmhouse living room, everyone on their fifth or sixth cup of tea (though Marly has me on decaf, for obvious reasons. Sigh).

"There's plenty of time for meeting everyone, but not today, right?" Rosie said to Charlie.

Charlie's eyes were swollen from crying and her cat-eye eyeliner was all smudged.

"Not today. I came here for you," Charlie said to Rosie, "but he—"

"Came here for you," Berty and Rosie said together.

"We have a lot to talk about," Charlie said. "We'd like to explore the island a bit—all the places we would talk about when we used to dream of the day we'd move here. Berty's determined to get to Pouque Rock today."

Oliver and I exchanged a quick glance, like, *Are you telling her about high tide, or am I?*

"Shh," Marly whispered, catching our shared look. On our confused expressions, she jerked her head toward the kitchen. "More biscuits needed! You two?" she barked at us.

We dutifully followed her. We shared another tentative glance—by this point in the day we'd been doing a lot of glancing, not a lot of talking. Back to how we'd begun. But where else were we meant to start? I was just about surviving the fact that everyone on this island hates me right now, but when I thought that *Oliver* might hate me . . .

"Don't you dare mention about high tide at the Rock," Marly said, clattering around in search of biscuits. "Sunset, stranded on Pouque together . . . it's perfect."

"Perfect for what?" Oliver asked her.

Marly rolled her eyes, exasperated. "Berty's going to re-propose, isn't he? Come *on*."

Oliver looked at me, testing how I felt about that, maybe. Was a little surprised to discover that I was genuinely happy for them.

With a bit of space and distance, it was easier to see that Berty wasn't a bad guy. He just wasn't my guy.

"Wouldn't they be better off at the viewpoint?" Oliver said to Marly. "Being stranded together in the sea sounds romantic but is actually just quite inconvenient, surely?"

"Do not interfere. Don't you think you've got in the way of those two enough?" Marly said.

At some point midafternoon, Marly's anger had melted into a sort of mock irritation—I'd guess she was approximately ten percent mad at us, ninety percent over it, but still planned to make us suffer.

"I resent that," Oliver said.

"The way I understand it, they're star-crossed childhood sweethearts and you're . . . the fling?"

Oliver just looked amused by this. Smiling without smiling, that way he does, all crinkling eyes. I had to look away, staring blindly at the Aga stove.

"You know me, Marly. You must know I would be a terrible fling," he said.

"True. Way too intense. But you!" Marly turned on me. She was enjoying herself now. "You were definitely the fling."

"I was not!" I said. "What is it about me that says fling, exactly?"

"You're too hot to be anything else," Marly said, almost kindly.

"You don't say fling to me," Oliver said.

Think it was the first sentence he'd uttered directly my way since we were in the trailer. It made me want to cry again. I longed to step into his arms for a hug, and just breathe him in, the man I knew, not the stranger called Oliver. His eyes were soft and full of meaning, but I didn't know what the meaning was.

We needed to talk, but every time either of us made a move to leave the farmhouse—either alone or together—Marly would say, "Ah-ah, nope, no sneaking off." Couldn't tell if she was just enjoying torturing us or wanted to make sure we didn't flee the island before the barn dance we were supposed to be running this evening.

"Well, you two are the exes, anyway," Marly said. "The baddies. The villains."

"What is it people say?" Oliver said. "Everyone is the villain in someone else's story."

"Oh no," I said, horrified. When most of your life has been dedicated to impressing everyone you've ever met, this is a pretty foundation-shifting thought.

Marly patted us both on the arms. "Better make sure you're the hero in your own, eh?"

3. Save a dance for Oliver

The final and most surprising task of all. Can't decide if Charlie attempting to matchmake me and Oliver is patronizing ("Here, have my ex!") or incredibly big of her.

Either way, I didn't need telling to save a dance for Oliver. I owe him an explanation, and not just about my name.

All the truth-telling today has been excruciating, but it's felt freeing, too. When I arrived here, I committed to singlehood because I knew if I dated, I'd relinquish control of my journey to motherhood to yet another guy. Losing my dad should have been the moment when I realized how short life can be, that I shouldn't waste another minute, but it wasn't. Too painful to teach me anything, maybe—too overwhelming, what with learning about his addiction, his life in LA, the parts of him I'd never been allowed to see. It took falling out with my mum, and the shock of realizing Berty didn't want a child, for me to realize how much of my life had been about other people's approval.

I had to do this by myself, for myself.

But if I'm really ready to become a mother alone, then I should be able to tell Oliver the truth as simple fact, not a question or expectation, as it's always been with men before. Should be able to say, I want to get pregnant within the next year, without any part of me waiting for him to allow it, withhold it or judge me for it. And I think I can—I think I'm ready. Standing there on the harbor telling the truth about my name made me realize I'm so much stronger than I used to be. And clocking that Oliver probably doesn't want a kid has kind of made it easier, too. I need to let him go—properly.

I know what I want. I want to be a mother, and nobody's judgments or opinions are going to stop me following that path on the timeline I've chosen.

I suspect everyone, Oliver included, thinks the two of us need to talk about our real names, but honestly, I'm not sure I even care what he calls himself. Throughout the day today it's become so obvious that he's still him. He's no different now that he's Oliver to me instead of Jones. He's still the first man ever to challenge me to be myself—to want me to be. Still the first man ever to hear that I'm afraid and rename that a kind of bravery.

Still the first man to make me wild enough to kiss him in the pouring rain when every logical part of me said I shouldn't.

I know he hoped there was a future for us, once. Maybe knowing I'm called Aspen changes that for him, but for me, there is only one reason I can't give Oliver my heart, no matter how much I want to.

Off to the barn dance now. Here's to telling the truth, the whole truth and nothing but.

And also . . . mastering line dancing.

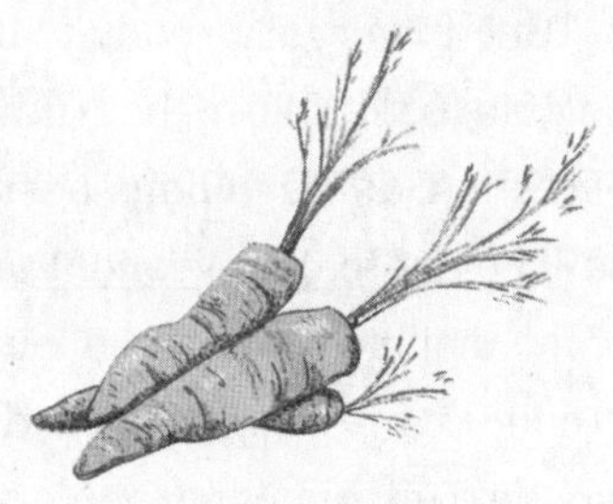

DRAFT

FROM: **Charlie Jones**

TO:

SUBJECT: **Barn dance debrief**

I'm not sure I'll send this one. Emailing feels strange now that we've seen each other again—I think I almost forgot that the person I was emailing was *you*, if that makes any sense. But I want to write this all down anyway. For me.

Marly just told me where you and Berty have gone, and I'm so pleased for you, Charlie. I think I knew, even when we were in love, that you would never stop loving him. When Fearne died, and the two of us were such a fucking mess, I remember thinking that you talked about Berty in the same way you talked about Fearne. Like he was gone.

It still hurts so much that neither of us can have Fearne back. But it makes me really happy that you *have* got Berty back. I hope you're having the most amazing time eloping, or vow renewing, whatever you two are calling it, and I'm looking forward to you coming back home to the island.

Because I think that's just what it is now—home.

Yesterday on the harbor, I was totally floored to discover who Aspen really was. I felt a little betrayed, too—which is *so* hypocritical, of course, but Aspen and I have talked a lot about being real with each other, and it hurt to know that even when she dropped the facade, she was still playing a role with me.

But then Marly locked us in that farmhouse with you all . . . and it was so obvious how hard Aspen was finding the day. Watching her make tea with shaking hands, watching her squaring her shoulders to face you, all I could think was, *I know how she's feeling. I know who she is.* She has so much going on right now—she's *pregnant*, and dealing with that, and her anxiety must be in overdrive with everyone talking about her. All I wanted to do was pull her into my arms and tell her she was being so brave.

And ask her about Aspen. Who she is—no, not that, I know who she is, but who she *was*. I can't believe I ever thought I could leave Oliver behind and be this new, sober, healed man, as though it was possible to sever myself from the mistakes I'd made and start again. I *am* the mistakes I made. Without them, I wouldn't be me. And I want Aspen to know *me*.

So this was my mindset when I pulled on my cowboy boots (borrowed from Rog) and headed to the sheep barn.

My eyes found Aspen the second I stepped inside the ramshackle old structure, despite the whole place being total chaos. She was in one of the dresses she wore when she first arrived here—a paisley peach-colored one, paired with a cowboy hat, plaits and boots. Dressing up again, but this time, there was no disguising her.

I don't know what a barn dance is supposed to be like, and as the preparations went on, it gradually became clear that nobody else did, either. Galoshes was watching YouTube videos of line dances at full volume on Toby's phone (nobody dared ask her to use headphones), Kim kept telling everyone that it was nothing to do with cowboys and we were all wearing the wrong things, and even the band seemed a bit confused: Jerry and the Milkmen were briefly under the impression they needed to perform a cappella.

"Gingham!" Aspen kept saying. "We need more gingham!"

"What's your name again?" Rog would shout back. Genuinely—he just couldn't get the hang of it.

"You know what, Rog," Aspen said eventually, in exasperation, after shamefacedly reintroducing herself to about a hundred Ormer residents who had popped into the old sheep barn to "help" throughout the hour before the dance. "You can just call me Charlie if you want."

Rog seemed greatly relieved and finally focused on fixing a tarp across the giant hole in the sheep barn roof. (That building was barely a building, really. I'm astonished we all survived the night unscathed and unsued.)

"She's doing well," Marly said approvingly, as we set up the bar at the back. "I thought she'd turn tail."

I pointed out that Marly had not really allowed this option. She'd practically barred the door at the farmhouse all afternoon.

"Look, you two had to face the music right away or nobody would ever forgive you," Marly said.

She was completely right, of course. "Thank you," I said. "For bringing us to the farmhouse this afternoon, and . . . for everything, really. For being my friend. I'm so sorry I lied to you."

"Hey, we're all putting on a front in one way or another. You two just went a little too far." She paused. "Maybe more than a little."

"I know. And Rosie . . ."

"Yeah. She was so invested. I was, too, in the end. I thought it was you, for what it's worth. I was genuinely looking forward to having you as a brother-in-law, mate."

I could only apologize, but Marly waved me off.

"I've simmered down now, I know you couldn't have had any idea that whole situation was going on. And Galoshes is right—you and Aspen have transformed the shop and we're making more money than we ever have before. It's not like we *actually* tried to hire someone good for that job. We literally chose them based on their name, didn't we? But you've both been great. Let's just call it a happy accident. Even this . . ." She spread her hands to take in the absolute carnage in the sheep barn. "You've brought new energy to the farm—to the island, actually."

I told her how incredibly grateful I was that she hadn't kicked us both out.

"Oh, you are fired," she said. "Was that not obvious?"

"Oh. Right. Well, fair enough."

"I'll leave it to the real farm shop manager to decide if she wants to hire you back sometime," Marly said to me with a wink. (So . . . maybe when you get back from eloping, you could give me a job? Please?)

I figured Aspen and I would finally be able to talk when the event got going, but I should have watched some YouTube videos, because it turns out country dancing is not conducive to conversation.

Galoshes really took to the role of caller.

"Get into groups of six!" she yelled at the crowd, half tourists, half locals. Someone had managed to persuade her to wear an autumn-themed crown, and she had to blow orange plastic maple leaves out of her eyes every few breaths. "Then split into two! No, split into two! Two threes! Split into threes! Come on, keep up, split the six into two threes! That's it! Now! Join hands! In a six! Now . . . music!"

Jerry and the Milkmen dutifully began. The tempo was a lot faster than I expected. Aspen was in my group (thanks to some machinations by Marly, I couldn't help thinking) but had ended up holding hands with Red and Toby, while I'd landed Kim and Karyn.

Within half an hour we were all significantly more advanced. I was whirling Kim around on my arm and then doing three jumps on one leg and then . . . I forget now, but it was pretty technical. I was out of breath, sweaty, and the longest I'd managed to spend with Aspen was about two seconds of hand-holding and an uncomfortable instance of stepping on her toe.

"Pairs for this next one!" yelled Galoshes, her autumn crown now lopsidedly dangling over one ear.

Aspen and I locked eyes. Her chest was heaving and she had flushed cheeks. I thought instantly of that night on the sofa at the stables, and it was as if the chaos of the barn dance faded to gray around her.

"Please," she said, approaching me, "save me from another dance with someone who wants to interrogate me about my immoral decision-making."

"You don't know what I want to talk to you about yet," I said, then saw the way her eyes flickered fearfully at that, and immediately took her hand. "Aspen, it's OK. I get it. I did exactly the same thing."

Aspen's plaits were unraveling, and her pupils were dilated; there was a kind of wildness about her tonight. I didn't know if it was the dancing or the honesty, but I liked it. She looked like herself.

"No, you took an opportunity that was gifted to you by a friend," Aspen said, as Galoshes commanded us all to join hands and "start spinning." "I stole something."

She slipped her hand into mine. I thought, *That belongs there.*

"You stole something you thought was going spare," I told her as we began to dance.

"I thought about what I wanted and didn't consider the consequences for other people."

"Actually, you did. You just backed yourself to do a good job for Marly and Rosie, even if you didn't have the relevant experience—and you did. Do you see me feeling bad for taking the job? I feel bad for the lying and the mess we've caused, but I know I was good enough for that job."

"Yeah, but you're a man," Aspen said miserably. The two of us began to spin in a rapid circle. "You think you're good enough for any job."

"Correct. Honestly, it's great. You should try it."

"Being a man?"

"Overinflated ego, overconfidence—seriously, it's brilliant."

She was beginning to laugh now. I love that I know how to get her smiling again when she's feeling afraid or overwhelmed. With my parents, I always longed to be able to shake them out of their dark spells, but you know better than anyone that depression doesn't work that way. I don't know much about anxiety—yet—but I'm learning that distraction actually does work when Aspen's anxious, and I love it. I love knowing I can *do* something when she's struggling.

"What is it you told me? Come back to your intentions," I told her. "You never intended to hurt Rosie."

"My intention was to do something for me," Aspen said, her voice small.

Galoshes yelled a lot of instructions at this point, and then some tips for Doc Laurry, who was carting Baptiste from the floor after an unfortunate interaction with Rog's sharp elbow.

"And is doing something for you such a crime?" I said, when everyone was back to dancing again.

"It literally is, actually, when it's fraud."

We parted at that, pairing up with different people, under Galoshes's instruction. I let Aspen's hand go reluctantly, then took Red's, and did a double take, frowning. She was crying again.

I asked her if she was all right as we linked arms, trying to avoid Rog's elbows.

"Happy tears," she said. "I talked to Toby."

It suddenly felt very appropriate to be skipping. I've been rooting for that kid from the start. The nice boys never win, especially when they've made bad hairstyling decisions, but Toby deserved to get the girl.

"I'm really glad," I told her. "Well done, Red."

"Tell Aspen thank you," Red said with a tearful smile, as we disentangled. "She'll know what for."

"Red says thank you," I told Aspen, as our hands connected again. "She talked to Toby."

"Oh!" Aspen's face lit up. "That is the best news! And Rog says he wants to know if you're actually sober or if that was 'part of the act.'"

"Rog is having the hardest time getting his head around all this, isn't he?"

"I'm still not convinced he understands who Berty is."

Aspen was out of breath now. I wondered fleetingly if she should be jumping around this much when pregnant, and then remembered that she's a midwife, so she probably knew what she was doing. By this point I was longing to talk to her about the pregnancy—I mean, I've been longing to for days—but if she wasn't ready to discuss it, I *had* to wait. This was her story to share.

"Are you jealous of Berty?" she asked.

The question surprised me. I thought for a moment. *Am* I? I mean, kind of, yeah.

"For having a whole year of you? Absolutely," I told her.

She dug her teeth into her bottom lip to try to keep the smile from growing, and I knew I was right to feel hopeful.

"So you're not . . . you know . . . still deeply in love with Charlie and pretending you're over it? For instance?" she asked.

"Am I Berty Jones, you mean?"

She blushed, but didn't correct me.

"No. I'm not, I promise, Aspen. Charlie and I are just good friends—we never made sense as a couple. After my friend Fearne died, the two of us just kind of . . . looked after each other. I'm not sure how healthy it was—we weren't together, but we weren't apart, either. But it got us through."

"I'm so sorry about your friend. I wish you'd . . ."

"Told you?"

"Well. Yeah. But I get it—if anyone does, I do. You figured it would help, right? Starting over and leaving all the pain behind . . ."

We ducked under an archway of arms.

"There she goes," I heard someone say. "That's the one who lied to everyone."

I glanced across at Aspen. Her jaw had tightened, and I could see she was fighting to hold back tears. It hadn't escaped me that everyone was being a lot harder on Aspen than they were on me—just like the committee had been when we arrived.

"I'm sorry they're—" I started saying, but she had begun to speak.

"What was it you said about overconfidence?"

"I . . . think I said it's great?"

"Right. I'm going to give it a go, I think," Aspen said, dropping my hands, lifting her chin and marching through the dancers toward Galoshes and her microphone.

"There she goes! Brazen as anything!" someone said.

"Will you shut up?" I snapped at them.

"Jones!" Red said in surprise behind me. "I mean—Oliver."

"Everyone's treating Char—Aspen like crap. Hardly anyone's talking about what *I* did."

"Oh, well, yes, it's sexism, through and through," Red said, coming to stand beside me as Aspen scaled the stage. "Is this a good idea?" she asked speculatively.

"I have a good feeling about it," I said.

"Excuse me, everybody?" Aspen said, taking the microphone from Galoshes's hands. "If I could just interrupt."

"Really?" Red said beside me. "I have a kind of ominous feeling."

"I want to introduce myself. Properly. Hi, I'm Aspen."

The mutterings around us were not positive.

"A lot of you are upset with me, which is totally understandable. I came here under false pretenses, and I took a job that wasn't rightfully mine. I'm so sorry for deceiving you, and I know lots of you will feel like you don't know me now. So I want to just take a quick moment to tell you my story.

"I'm thirty-seven years old. For the last ten years, I've wanted to have a baby."

Everyone was absolutely silent now.

"I dated. I fell in love, a lot, and kind of . . . wishfully, you know? Maybe this guy is good enough. Maybe this guy. Maybe this one. I got so good at reshaping myself for different people, and being the woman they wanted, because that was my best shot, right?

If I could just get a man to stick, I could have the life I ached for. Because when I say I wanted a baby . . . I mean, the wanting consumed me. I hid it, of course, because nobody likes a crazy lady who's desperate to pin you down and have your babies, do they? *That's* definitely not sexy. So I played it cool, and I lied, and I trained myself to be the perfect girlfriend.

"In the end, there was nothing special about the guy who broke me. I think that was *why* it broke me. As soon as he told me he didn't want to have a kid, I realized, I don't even like you that much. I like the idea of you, and I like what you might be able to give me, but what the hell am I doing trying to tie my life to somebody I don't even love?"

"Oh, poor soul," someone murmured behind me. "There's nothing quite like that baby fever."

"I needed to change something. Something *big*. And then the opportunity to work at the farm shop here on Ormer, and be somebody else, just landed in my lap, and I . . . took it. It's not like me. I promise. But it was such a unique chance, and I needed something drastic.

"I know this sounds strange, but almost as soon as I got here, I *stopped* pretending. As Charlie Jones, I started to ask myself who I actually am when I'm not trying to fit what someone else thinks I should be. I started to learn about myself and what I really want. I committed . . ."

Her voice faltered, and then she forged on.

"I committed to pursuing motherhood solo."

"Good for you, sweetheart!" someone shouted.

Aspen's eyes filled with tears. "Thank you," she said, with fervor. "But you don't need to say that. You actually don't. Two months ago, I knew I couldn't tell anyone my plans, because if they judged or questioned me, I'd lose sight of what I wanted. But

I've come a really long way, and I don't think there's anything any of you could say that would change my mind. I know what I want. And I'm not going to let anyone hold me back any longer."

Her eyes drifted to me, just for a moment. I thought of what she'd said that night we kissed on the sofa—she'd told me she *couldn't*, not now, that she wasn't looking for a relationship. I'd figured she was still heartbroken over an ex, or grieving a lost love. I'd never imagined that the reason she was determined to keep me at a distance was because she was afraid I'd ruin her plans to have a child.

"Anyway, thanks for your time," she said. "And nice to meet you all again properly."

I pushed my way through to her as she handed the microphone back to Galoshes.

"Aspen, that was amazing," I said, reaching for her hand.

I thought she'd be exhilarated, proud of herself. But her eyes were filled with anxiety when she looked at me.

"So, hey, turns out, you? Different category from everyone else!" she said, pulling her hand from mine and backing toward the barn doors, which were thrown open to the autumn sunset.

"What? Aspen . . ."

She was heading for the exit, for the open fields with their perfectly picturesque donkeys providing photographs for the tourists watching the dancing from outside. The farm shop was just visible across the other side of the field, its freshly painted windows catching the setting sun. I chased Aspen down, calling to her.

"Aspen, please, talk to me."

"Please, don't. If you say a single word right now there is a major risk I'm going to crumble, and I'm doing *so* well."

"What do you think I'm going to say to you?"

"Oh, I don't know, that you're never going to look at me the way you used to look at me now that you know? That you're not interested in me anymore? It's not so much about what exactly you say, it's how much I fucking care, that's why you can't say it. I'm scared you're going to change my mind."

I shouted at her to slow down. She was heading for Windward Ridge. We were on the western edge of the farm, and it was only a few minutes' walk away; we were almost there at Aspen's pace, half running through the sunset. The ridge was shadowed in the low sunlight, its path looking narrower than ever.

"Why don't you just wait and see what I actually say, and how it makes you feel?" I called.

"Nope! No thank you!" she yelled, powering on. "I like you way too much. And I can't give you that power over me, not now, so we're just going to have to . . . never have a conversation again, and just . . . avoid each other forever . . ."

She was slowing a little now as she approached the ridge path, reaching a hand out to steady herself on the balustrade.

"I know Charlie didn't want kids." Aspen still had her back to me. The wind picked up her plaits as we left the shelter of the cliffs, opening up to the sea breeze. "So I guess you probably don't, either. But can you just . . . not say it?" Her voice broke. "I don't want to hear you say it."

"Aspen . . . I *know*," I said. "And I love you. And I'm still here, chasing you down cliff edges to talk to you. I *know*. What does that tell you?"

She went still. Then she turned, very slowly, her eyes wide and wet with tears.

"Did you just say you love me?" she asked in a whisper.

I nodded, my heart suddenly pounding. I hadn't meant to say it. It had just come out, because it was so obvious to me, I think—as though I'd almost forgotten she could possibly not know.

"Wait," she said, eyes still wide. "What do you mean, you know? What do you know?"

"I know you're pregnant."

I was whispering, too, and for a moment I wondered if she'd not heard what I'd said. She was staring completely blankly at me, framed against the cliffs of Little Ormer. And then—

"Sorry, what?" she said, full volume.

So, yes. That was the barn dance. After that . . . we figured we should probably go home and talk.

Sunday October 5th 2025

We lit the fire and made peppermint tea. Have given up on chamomile—in the interests of being fully open and honest with each other at last, we both admitted it tastes like dust.

As we moved around each other in the stables, dark falling outside, I kept thinking of him standing there on Windward Ridge, his hair all scruffy in the wind, his gingham shirt billowing, as he said <u>I know. And I love you</u>. It was warm and cozy in the stables, but I was still shivering.

Once he was settled on the sofa, I showed him the catalog of donors.

"I've had the first couple of meetings and tests. Tentatively chosen a donor. But that's it." My voice sounded all trembly. Was so scared to say it out loud to him, even now, even when he'd told me he loved me.

Stared down into my peppermint tea as Oliver looked at the catalog.

"I can't believe you're not pregnant," he said hoarsely.

His reaction had been hard to figure out back on the ridge—he'd seemed completely floored by it as we walked home side by side, the sun sinking over the island. We'd talked about the logistics of how he "found out"—Caloshes, who I'm sure had delighted in letting that one slip—but we'd not gotten past the details to how he actually <u>felt</u>.

"I'm so sorry," Oliver said instantly, reaching forward to touch my knee. "What a thoughtless thing for me to say to you."

His hand on my leg made me think of the night we kissed, and my tears threatened to spill over. Had to turn my eyes up to the ceiling, which hardly ever works as well as you think it will, then I was just crying in earnest, wet and exhausted and relieved, in a way, because at least now it was all out there at last.

"It's OK," I said through the tears. "I mean, I do want to be pregnant—I will be, in the next year. And there's just... there's nothing you can say, I mean, I can't let you hold me back from this, I just..."

Oliver shuffled closer, legs tangling with mine. "You do get what this all means, don't you? What I said on Windward Ridge? I love you."

There was something about the way those words sounded in Oliver's soft, low, bedtime voice, with his gaze holding mine. I've had men tell me they loved me before, but nobody else has ever said it so I felt it right in the very center of my soul, as though they were speaking to something deep within me.

"Aspen..." Oliver reached for my hand. "I thought you were pregnant the day after we kissed. I was a little thrown at first, sure, and I wondered... well, I obviously wondered who the father was, given that you've been here for a couple of months now, so it was probably... someone on the island..."

"Oh, wow, you must've... Who...?"

"Believe me," Oliver said, voice warm with amusement, "I was really struggling to put that one together."

I started to laugh. "Oh my God, did you think I was, like, having Rog's baby?"

"I mean, I assumed a tourist fling, actually, but I did wonder when you'd found the time."

I wiped my eyes. The laugh had loosened something in my chest. I looked down at the freckles on the backs of his hands, the ones I'd traced that night I'd told him I couldn't be with him.

"Do you want to know how I feel about having children, Aspen?"

"No," I said instantly, letting go of him and covering my face with my hands. "Oh, God. Yes? I don't know. I mean, even if you say you're OK with me pursuing motherhood on my own, then I don't know that I could ever quite believe you."

"Really?" His voice was light. "Don't you get what I'm saying to you? I told you I love you. And I thought you were pregnant."

"Yes, I know that, I—"

"I was already ready to love you and your baby."

I almost couldn't absorb his words. I just blinked at him, my heart beating so hard.

"What are you . . . what are you saying?"

"I'm saying, if this is really the reason you've decided you don't want to be with me, you're going to have to come up with something else."

I threw myself across the sofa and wept as he closed his arms around me, that huge, kind heart pressed hard against mine.

"I've always wanted a family," Oliver said. "In answer to the question you have spent the last two months not asking me."

"Don't, don't," I sobbed into his shoulder. "It's too much."

"It's the truth. Charlie never actually told me she didn't want kids until we broke up. But I do want children, as it happens. And I'm not going to ruin your plans, or ask you to slow down for me. I just want to love you."

So I let it in. I let myself say it—the other big secret I've been carrying far longer than I'd like to admit.

"I love you," I told him, and kissed him, my tears on our lips.

It was my first time ever saying it with my whole self, not a single thing held back. It felt so new—richer, lovelier, deeper than any "I love you" I'd said before.

"Are you sure?" Oliver said, pulling back from me for a moment. "You know I can be . . . hard work. I want to say I won't ever go through a dark patch again, but I can't promise it, and . . ."

"I love you," I said again, leaning my forehead to his. "I love you now, and I'll love you then."

He closed his eyes and breathed out slowly.

"I didn't know I could feel like this."

"Feel like what?"

"Like the future is the brightest place."

I smiled. That made me <u>so</u> happy to hear.

"What happens now?" I whispered, settling my body fully over his on the sofa.

He shuffled down a little, bringing his arm around my waist. "Well," he said, in that soft, shiver-inducing voice of his, "accommodation's sorted. I'm suddenly very open-minded about sharing this place with you. Job, though . . ." He chuckled—I felt the rumble of it through his chest against mine. "I've been fired. I'm pretty sure you have, too."

"Oh, Charlie'll hire you back again," I said. "And I'm going to put together a case for an island midwife. Put it to the medical board, to Doc Laurry. If they say no, I'll find some work I can do remotely, but it'll have to be something to do with midwifery, whatever it is. It's what I was born to do."

"Why did you leave midwifery? If you don't mind me asking?"

"You can ask me anything." I chose my words carefully. "I realized my personal life was affecting my ability to do the job. I wanted a baby very badly, and I was pretending I didn't, so that was . . . difficult. I think I needed to work through processing that, and being honest with myself. I'm ready to go back now."

His hand tightened on my waist. "There's so much I want to talk about. Especially when it comes to you becoming a mother."

Didn't think I reacted, but I must've stiffened or something, because he lifted a hand to my hair, nudging my face up to look at him.

"Hey," he said gently. "I don't mean I need to talk about whether, or when. I don't want to hold anything up. But I'd like to know where you see me."

He glanced toward the catalog of donors, which had slid to the floor beside the sofa.

"Well . . . Where do you see you?"

His hand stroked my back. "You don't know much of my story yet," he said, "but you should know I've always been a dreamer. Very ambitious. Always overreaching. I was a downhill racer, you know? Mountain biking, fast, downhill. Very competitive."

I was fascinated. "No way! I thought you worked in a pub?"

"Oh, I did—I temped in all kinds of jobs, because you can't make much money in downhill racing, even if you're at the top of the game."

I bit back a smile. "And you were?"

"I was." His face was serious. "Until Fearne died."

"It was . . . a biking accident?"

He nodded. "It should have been me," he whispered. "I'd had some wine the night before—just dinner out with Charlie, but it had been enough. I was hungover. If I hadn't been, I'd have taken the lead. It would have been me that hit that root first."

"Oliver"—I brushed his hair back, kissed his forehead, then his cheeks, then his sad, soft eyes—"it wasn't your fault."

"You helped me believe that, actually. Now, whenever I start to feel guilty about Fearne's death, I think about my intentions, instead of blaming myself. It helps me see that I couldn't control what happened to Fearne. You can only do what you can do, and the fact is, I couldn't save her. If I could have, I would have, a hundred times over, but I couldn't."

I pressed my forehead to his chest for a moment, thinking of my dad. I hadn't even known about his struggles with addiction over in LA, let alone tried to help him with them. I'd idolized my dad, but he'd always kept me at a distance no matter what I did. It had been a shock to learn that the drugs were probably the reason for that distance. That maybe he had been protecting me by keeping me away. I wish he hadn't. If I could have helped him, I would have—a hundred times over, as Oliver put it—but I've had to let go of that guilt. You can only do what you can do.

I wish Dad and I had gotten a chance to truly know each other—his full self and mine. But the money he left me is allowing me to become a mother, and I knew him enough to be sure he'd have found joy in that.

I know I need to call my mum soon. I owe her an apology for the way I behaved after Dad's death, but I'd just wanted some time to grieve without always thinking about what she needed from me. *Is doing something for you such a crime?* Oliver had said at the dance, and I'd thought, *Well, yeah*. Until I came here, pretty much everything I did was in service to other people, and not in a good, selfless, I'm-a-great-midwife way—I mean everything I did was either to impress someone else or make them happy. I'd completely lost touch with myself, so much so that I couldn't even acknowledge the one thing I wanted more than anything.

But still—should call Mum. Bridget Denby is needy, chaotic, codependent and all the things I don't want to be as a mother, but she's still my mum, and I love her.

"The racing was a good outlet for the competitive spirit," Oliver said, bringing me back to him. "I stopped riding after Fearne died."

"And channeled your competitive spirit into trying to see me off the island?"

"I was never . . ."

He trailed off as I laughed, then slid his hand down to my hip. My skirt was ruched up, and I shivered. He was tantalizingly close to bare skin. But I didn't want to stop talking—it felt so good to be uncovering all his layers at last.

"You know I don't get on with the woo-woo stuff," Oliver went on wryly, "but I don't drive, and I ended up on an island where people can pretty much only get about on a bike, so . . . I got back in the saddle again. It's been so good for me."

I resettled on top of him, delighting in every inch of us that was touching. It seemed slightly miraculous—all those weeks obsessing over moments when his shoulder touched mine, and here he was, mine to touch.

"So you were saying . . . I asked you where you see yourself." I forced myself to say it instead of sliding around the topic, the way I always would have in the past. "In terms of me having a baby. You were saying that you're very ambitious . . ."

"Right. I may not think I deserve much in life, but I <u>want</u> a lot."

"Oh yes?"

"So when I told you the future looked bright to me . . ." He pressed his lips to my hair, thumb circling on my hip. "I meant, I've already imagined it. I want it all. I want to live here, with you, and turn that walk-in wardrobe into a nursery. I want to build a cot from scratch. I want to ask you to marry me when we're here, in front of the fire, on a night as perfect as this one, and I want to love your child like they're mine. I want them to be mine. However they come into the world."

He pulled me even closer, arms wrapping around me tightly.

"But we only started dating about"—he lifted his head slightly to check his watch behind my shoulder—"twenty minutes ago. So it's probably a little soon for all that. I told you: chronically overambitious."

I was crying again. "Do you know how fucking rare you are?" I said, pressing a tearful kiss to his lips.

"Are you kidding? There are three Charlie Joneses on this island," he said, seeking my mouth again as I pulled away. "We're common as stoats."

He laughed as he kissed me, and I felt so lucky. Luckier than I thought possible, even when I was at my most willfully hopeful, back when I first arrived here. I've made so many mistakes, but if they led me here, maybe they weren't mistakes after all.

And it's OK if not everyone sees it like that. I know I'm not perfect. I'm Aspen, in a way I've never let myself be before—I'm messy and complex and oh, to be loved like this, as I am instead of as I think I ought to be . . .

It feels like the perfect way to start.

Isle of Ormer, five years later

Oliver no longer raced because it made him feel alive. The heart-pounding thrill he'd craved as a younger man eluded him now, anyway. It didn't excite him to take risks—he had so very much to lose.

But he still raced to win.

"You're going down, bike boy."

Aspen's cycling helmet was jammed over the enormous ginger bun at the nape of her neck. She was poised at the starting line Rog had drawn with a stick in the dirt, which had already been disputed several times because tourists kept scuffing it. Tradition was tradition, however, particularly on the Isle of Ormer. At the first Harvest Festival Bramblebay Race, the starting line had been drawn with a stick, and so it always would be.

"Save it for the bedroom, Aspen. What *will* the committee say?" Oliver shot back, biting down on a small smile as her cheeks went pink.

He could still make Aspen blush just by looking at her. Sometimes he'd do it at council meetings—she was the Deputy for Health and Emergency Services, now that Doc was scaling back his duties, and Oliver had somehow got roped into being Speaker, because (he suspected) he was the only one who could get anyone to shut up. While everyone argued about the Ormer constitution, Oliver would hold Aspen's gaze across the table and watch her slowly lose focus on anything but him.

"Ready?" Rog yelled, adjusting his orange bucket hat. A permanent feature ever since his hair had gone from thinning to altogether absent, this hat was now as iconic an element of Ormer life as Toby's famous harbor mural.

"Ready," Oliver and Aspen confirmed in unison.

"Set?" Rog shouted.

There was a pause.

"Are you expecting us to—"

"GO!" Rog yelled.

Aspen pulled ahead initially. Her technique was shoddy, but it was that grit of hers—it was as if she could simply will herself into the lead. Tourists and locals cheered from the sidelines as Aspen, Oliver and the rest of the entrants raced down the Rue, ducked low, wholly focused on the finish line, which was just visible between the ears of Oliver's trusty steed.

"Come on, Maple, old girl," Oliver muttered, digging in his heels.

The Bramblebay donkey race was now one of the island's major tourist attractions. It was widely regarded to be Aspen's idea, but really, it was Galoshes who was responsible. She had told Aspen that the donkeys were untrainable, and so Aspen had decided she would train them all. In her long-running quest to find out who she was beneath her anxiety, Aspen had been delighted to discover that she was actually an extremely stubborn person, something she had announced to Oliver a few years ago, as though he hadn't known it all along.

"And Toby and Stardust win the prize!" Rog yelled.

"What!" Aspen shouted, straightening up on her donkey as she and Oliver crossed the finish line at what was, essentially, a slow trot.

The donkeys were trained, but they weren't *fast.*

"Sorry," Toby said, pulling off his helmet and ruffling up his hair. He wore it in a ponytail these days, or loose around his shoulders, but never hiding his face. Fatherhood had stripped away many of Toby's insecurities. *When you're this happy, and this tired*, he'd told Oliver once, *it's really hard to care about forehead acne.*

Aspen's phone rang before she could contest the result, which was probably for the best, since Toby had won by at least two donkey lengths.

"Brianna," she said to Oliver's unasked question, answering on speaker as they offered their donkeys carrots from the barrels waiting at the finish line.

"Hey, so, are you still riding a donkey like the island nutter you have become?" Brianna said.

She sounded out of breath, or a little strained, perhaps, as though she'd just climbed a hill.

"No, why?" Aspen said, glancing at Oliver.

Tourists milled around them, clutching cinnamon-spiced coffees and pumpkin-shaped buns, squinting at the sky as the inevitable autumn drizzle began.

"Just that I'm having some . . . contraction-like sensations," said Brianna, "and I wonder if you could drop by the B&B for— *Whooo . . .*"

Aspen's eyes widened as she listened. She scanned the crowd, then waved a frantic hand at Kim, gesturing for her to take their donkeys.

"You're in labor, you wally," she said into the phone.

"Not possible," Brianna said, once her contraction-like sensation was over. "My babies are always late."

"Well, this baby's an early bird, just like her auntie," Aspen said, already heading down the Rue at a jog. "Can Galoshes hold the fort for another few hours?" she asked Oliver, who was reaching for his phone to check. "I need you, too, Eliza's on holiday. Rog, where's the ambulance?"

"Parked up behind the pub. We used it to tow up the last batch of wines for the— Why, do you need it for an actual ambulance-type thing?" he said, jerking to attention.

"My sister's birth plan says, *Get me to a hospital and give me all the drugs*," Aspen said grimly. "So if we don't have time for part one . . . she's going to really want the gas and air cannister."

Aspen's new nephew arrived screaming and belligerent in Rosie and Marly's living room three hours later. Brianna had invented several new swear words during labor; when Rosie had innocently asked if she'd had acetaminophen yet, Bri had roared at her so loudly that Charlie had called from up at the farm shop to ask whether one of the cows was trapped in the fence again.

Now Brianna lay with her third child in her arms, sweaty and queenly and convinced that this situation was everybody else's fault.

"We did *tell* you it was risky to visit at thirty-eight weeks," Aspen called from the utility room, where she was tugging warm towels out of the dryer.

"Do you *want* her to kill you?" Oliver muttered under his breath.

"She would never kill me," Aspen said. "I brought the pain relief."

Aspen had been magnificent, in fact. It had been a long time since Oliver had seen her at work—he'd attended one inadvertent home birth before, when she'd called him to bring her bag from the medical center at short notice, and had fallen more in love with her with every second she'd spent coaxing a stranger to do the hardest thing she'd ever done. Today he'd been banished by Brianna—"I still have some dignity left," she'd yelled at him—but had heard everything from where he and Marly sat in the kitchen, Stuart on speakerphone between them. Aspen had a gift. Within ten minutes of her arrival, Brianna's blood pressure dropped to safe levels again, as though her sister's voice had magical properties.

"Darling!" came a loud voice from the hallway. One with *different* properties.

"Oh, now you turn up, Mum!" Brianna yelled over her new son's head.

"You know I don't do the blood and guts part," Bridget Denby said, as she swanned in with two large paper bags. "But I brought pastries, made by that handsome doctor. What a silver fox! And Berty wants to know if there's anything you need? He said witnessing one birth with Aspen was enough—he's hovering outside in that fancy new tractor of his."

Bridget and Brianna were visiting together for Aspen's birthday—they'd come a month early, because of Brianna's due date, and were insisting on throwing Aspen a large party, which she had largely ended up organizing herself.

"Coward," Brianna said, taking an enormous bite from a cherry Danish. "You can tell him Aspen's finished sewing up my—"

"Brianna!" Bridget squealed, covering her mouth.

"Oh, just tell him to come in, half the bloody island's here anyway—and his wife's in the kitchen making me some sort of broth that'll heal my womb, or whatever hippy shit Charlie's into these days. God knows who's running that shop. None of you ever seem to do any work here. Every time I visit it's all seasonal festivities and endless biscuit-fueled committee meetings, which I'm starting to think are just excuses to— *Mum*, back off, will you, I'm like twenty minutes postpartum, I do not need mascara on!"

"For the photos!" Bridget protested. "For Stuart!"

"He'll be here in an hour," Marly said from the doorway. "He chartered a boat from Portsmouth, apparently."

"Oh, how sweet," Bridget cooed.

"That'll have cost a fortune," Brianna said, but Oliver knew her well enough to see how pleased she was.

"Have you checked in with Galoshes? Everything OK?" Aspen asked him, preparing her weighing scales for the baby.

She was flicking through paperwork with her other hand; the frown between her eyebrows was so obvious to Oliver, a sentence that didn't need saying.

"Aspen needs space to check these two out properly," he announced to the room. "I'll go relieve Galoshes," he told her, kissing the top of her head. "You're amazing."

"Thank you," she said, tilting her head up to look at him upside down. Perhaps it was the new angle, but he saw her afresh for a moment, his beautiful, brave, extraordinary girlfriend, and a wave of wonder passed over him. He felt the kind of lucky a person can only truly feel when they've been low enough to know how bad life can be.

She was everything. He could need nothing more.

Extraordinary, then, to head home to the stables and be greeted by two pajama-clad little whirlwinds racing from the front door in their slipper socks. To have everything he needed and so much more.

"Dad!" Effie yelled. "Is it true we've got a new cousin?"

He lifted her up. She wrapped her legs around his waist as her sister toddled determinedly up the track to join them, comforter in one hand, china teapot in the other.

"It's true," Oliver said, raising a hand to Galoshes as she smiled at him from the doorway. "All OK?" he asked, as he put Effie down and reached for Hunter's outstretched arms, gently extricating the teapot from her fingers before picking her up for a cuddle. He breathed her in and felt himself instantly settle.

"They're terrors," Galoshes said. "Nobody ate any vegetables. I've been recruited to join the Paw Patrol. I think I'm getting a glitter-induced migraine."

Oliver laughed. "Thank you," he said.

"Anytime," Galoshes said, ruffling Effie's hair as she headed off. "Oh, and before you get cross with me about the pen on the new bedroom wall, just remember who convinced everyone to give you a second chance when Charlie and Berty first showed up here!"

"Oh, please—everyone gets a second chance on the Isle of Ormer," Oliver said as he took Effie's hand and hefted Hunter onto his other hip.

"We all need to stop advertising that fact," Galoshes called over her shoulder. "This place is overflowing with troublemakers these days."

Oliver snorted. It was true that the island population had grown over the last couple of years, and yes, there were more backstories to go around than you'd find in the average crowd, but there was nobody on this island who embodied its spirit better than Sally "Galoshes" Lowe.

The girls were too excited to sleep until their mum got home with news of their baby cousin's name, so Oliver eventually conceded defeat, made hot milks and let them join him in front of the log burner. Aspen returned around eight, hands on hips, smile on her face.

"Excuse me," she said. "Where's *my* hot milk?"

They got the kids down within half an hour after that, milky and sleepy, loose-limbed. As Aspen and Oliver collapsed together on the sofa, nonalcoholic beers in hand, Oliver reached for Aspen's ankles, pulling her feet into his lap.

"Tons of gossip from the B&B," she said, yawning. "Rosie and Charlie have got a new lead about Charlie's adoption at last—some guy over in Jersey who claims to know something. And the little boy who Marly and Rosie took in last year, the one with the dinosaur obsession? Returning in the morning. Social services rang Marly while I was finishing up with Bri's stats. He's back in foster care."

Marly and Rosie had begun fostering soon after Charlie's arrival on Ormer, and they'd not looked back since.

"Berty's picking him up off the first ferry tomorrow. Any excuse to drive that new tractor," Aspen said, but her tone was fond now, softened by years of sharing a small island with her ex-boyfriend, a man whom she had come to love in a way she never could have if they'd stayed together.

"It never stops around here, does it?" Oliver said, with mock seriousness, shifting his hands across the arches of Aspen's feet.

She gave a little moan and he smiled the slow smile of a man who knows it's not going anywhere, they're both too exhausted, but he *likes* that sound.

"It never stops," she agreed. "And it all goes too fast."

"You OK?" he asked, hand stilling on her ankle.

"Mm." She shifted around so she could curl into him, her face against his chest. "Just . . . feeling big-sky feelings. It's been a hell of a day. I keep thinking that I've lived so many of the beautiful moments I used to imagine with you, and it makes me feel panicky, because it's flying by and I can't . . . catch it all. I know it's an incredibly lucky problem to have. Loving your life so much you don't want it to go by. But it's getting to me all the same."

She turned her face up to his, a silent invitation for a kiss. He pressed his lips to hers, cool and hops-sweet.

"You don't need to catch it, Aspen," he whispered. "You just need to let it fly."

She nodded, leaning against his chest again. They watched the fire die down, breathing together as the birds quieted outside the stables. Oliver knew what people meant when they called their partner their *other half*. It was not that he had not been whole before her, but rather that he wouldn't be whole after her, now. He had grown and changed around the woman curled at his chest, and then again, and again, until he was a man of four parts: Oliver, Aspen, Effie, Hunter. Strange, really, that he had come here as Jones, determined to remake himself, and had ended up rewritten by the woman who had once shared his name.

The woman he hoped might accept the ring in his shirt pocket, and perhaps even choose to share his name again.

Author's Note

The Isle of Ormer doesn't exist, but it was inspired by the Isle of Sark, which has five hundred recorded inhabitants, no streetlights and no cars. Sark was feudal until 2008, and the ambulance there is tractor-drawn. Lots of the geography of Ormer is based on that of Sark—check out La Coupée if you'd like to see the inspiration for Windward Ridge, and for the Rue, try looking up the Avenue. (All the people, events and businesses are sadly fictitious, though—I *wish* I could get a cinnamon latte at the Bramblebay Farm Shop, or some pumpkin-spice truffles from Karyn the chocolatier . . .)

Like my characters, I was introduced to this island by a job ad. My husband saw that Sark was advertising for a doctor, and we found ourselves briefly fascinated by the idea of trying out a different sort of life, just as my Charlies do. The more we read, the more we realized it wasn't for us, though—so I invented two people for whom it would be perfect and sent them there instead.

Acknowledgments

First of all, I'd like to thank Tanera, my agent, who understands my brain in a way nobody else does ("Yes, I see," she said immediately when I said "I want this story to be shaped like an X"). I feel so lucky that *The Flatshare* found its way to you, and that you somehow steered us all the way from there to here. Thank you also to Laura, who has had the near-impossible task of filling Tanera's shoes while she's on maternity leave but has somehow pulled it off—I'm so grateful to you for all your guidance and support.

Next, I'd like to thank the editors who have worked on this book with me, particularly Cassie Browne, an extraordinarily talented editor (and wonderful human) who has helped shape my books from *The Switch* onward, and who I'll miss enormously now that she's leaving Quercus. To Kat Burdon and Cindy Hwang, thank you so much for the insights you've brought to this novel, too—as always, you've made it infinitely stronger.

Thank you to the wider team at Quercus and Berkley for all their incredible work reaching readers: Ella Patel, Emily Patience, Ella Horne, Katy Blott, Elizabeth Vinson, Kalie Barnes-Young, Chelsea Pascoe, Charlotte Webb and so many more. Thank you to Mary Darby and Sheila David, too, for spreading this story even further around the world.

Thank you to Hels of @thehelsproject, @jtayauthor, @amanda blair4 and others who shared their home birth stories or midwifery experiences with me. You might like to know that you ended up educating me on the idea so brilliantly that you changed my perception entirely and contributed to me having my second baby at home!

I'm forever grateful to the incredible author friends I've found along this journey—Gilly McAllister, Lia Louis, Lucy Clarke, Caroline Hulse, thank you for the voice notes, the writerly sympathy and the beautiful books you write, too. To the bloggers, journalists and booksellers who share their love for my stories—thank you *so* much for helping my books to find new readers. And to the readers who have given this book a chance: thank you. I'll never stop feeling lucky that I get to write you stories, and I hope this one has brought you joy.

Finally, to my little family. This is your novel, Lils—it began when you were a dream and a hope, was written with you sleeping on my chest and will publish with you as a joyful, determined two-year-old trying to steal your brother's bike. (I'm guessing, as these acknowledgments are written months before publication, but I'm confident of my prediction.) Both you and Bug have filled my life with a kind of love I couldn't have imagined before I knew you—and I spend a lot of time imagining love. Thank you. And, Sam, thank you for every quiet, beautiful thing you've done to enable me to write and promote this book, all while achieving extraordinary goals of your own. You are amazing, and I love you, I love you, I love you.

Photo © Holly Bobbins

BETH O'LEARY is an internationally bestselling author whose novels have been translated into more than thirty languages. Her debut, *The Flatshare*, sold over a million copies and changed her life completely. All five of her subsequent novels—*The Switch*, *The Road Trip*, *The No-Show*, *The Wake-Up Call*, and *Swept Away*—have been instant *Sunday Times* bestsellers. Beth writes her books in the English countryside with a very badly behaved golden retriever for company. If she's not in her writing shed, you'll probably find her chasing a toddler, with a strong coffee in hand.

VISIT BETH O'LEARY ONLINE

BethOLearyAuthor.com

BethOLearyAuthor

BethOLearyAuthor

BethOLearyAuthor